*Praise for Jonathan Kellerman
and his previous novel,*

A COLD HEART

"Artfully done . . . [A] classic whodunit sprinkled with hard-boiled lines and more twists than a plate of fusilli. Kellerman has an unusual knack for making his heroes and their personal lives as detailed and engaging as the crime solving."
—*People*

"Often, mystery writers can either plot like devils or create believable characters. Kellerman stands out because he can do both. Masterfully."
—*USA Today*

"No one does psychological suspense as well as Jonathan Kellerman."
—*Detroit Free Press*

"[A] highly successful series . . . Kellerman provides a meaty layer of interpersonal relationships beneath the surface of his plot."
—*Publishers Weekly*

"Detective fiction's best-loved shrink, handsome, intrepid, immeasurably sensitive, is in top form."
—*Kirkus Reviews*

BOOKS BY JONATHAN KELLERMAN

THE CONSPIRACY CLUB

JONATHAN KELLERMAN

BALLANTINE BOOKS • NEW YORK

A Ballantine Book
Published by The Random House Publishing Group

Copyright © 2003 by Jonathan Kellerman
Excerpt from *Therapy* copyright © 2004 by Jonathan Kellerman

Ballantine and colophon are registered trademarks of Random House, Inc.

www.ballantinebooks.com

This book contains an excerpt from the forthcoming book *Therapy* by Jonathan Kellerman. This excerpt has been set for this edition only and may not reflect the final content of the forthcoming edition.

ISBN 0-345-47162-8

Manufactured in the United States of America

First Hardcover Edition: December 2003
First Mass Market International Edition: May 2004

OPM   10   9   8   7   6   5   4   3   2   1

To the memory of my father, David Kellerman.
1918–2003

1

RAGING EMOTIONS, DEAD TISSUE.

Polar opposites was the way Jeremy Carrier had always seen it.

In a hospital setting, no two disciplines were less connected than psychology and pathology. As a practitioner of the former, Jeremy prided himself on an open mind; a good psychotherapist worked hard at avoiding stereotypes.

But during all his years of training and clinical work at City Central Hospital, Jeremy had met few pathologists who didn't fit a mold: withdrawn, mumbly types, more comfortable with gobbets of necrosed flesh, the abstract expressionism of cell smears, and the cold-storage ambience of the basement morgue, than with living, breathing patients.

And his fellow psychologists, psychiatrists, and all the other soldiers of the mental health army, were, more often than not, overly delicate souls repelled by the sight of blood.

Not that Jeremy had actually *known* any pathologists, even after a decade of passing them in the hallways. The social structure of the hospital had regressed to high school sensibilities: Us-Them as religion, a lusty proliferation of castes, cliques, and cabals, endless jockeying for power and turf. Adding to that was the end-means inversion that captures every bureaucracy: the hospital had devolved from a healing place needing funds to treat patients to a large-scale municipal employer requiring patient fees to meet its staff payroll.

All that created a certain asocial flavor.

A confederacy of isolates.

At City Central, like was attracted to like, and only the last-ditch necessities of patient care led to cross-pollination: internists finally admitting defeat and calling in surgeons, generalists taking deep breaths before plunging into the morass of consultation.

What reason could there be for a pathologist to contact a psychologist?

Because of all that—and because life's hellish wrist-flick had turned Jeremy Carrier into a tormented, distracted young man—he was caught off-balance by Arthur Chess's overture.

Perhaps Jeremy's distractibility formed the basis for all that followed.

For nearly a year, Jeremy had seen Arthur once a week, but the two men had never exchanged a word. Yet here was Arthur, settling down opposite Jeremy in the doctors' dining room and asking if Jeremy cared for company.

It was just before 3 P.M., an off-hour for lunch, and the room was nearly empty.

Jeremy said, "Sure," then realized he was anything but.

Arthur nodded and settled his big frame into a small chair. His tray bore two helpings of fried chicken, a hillock of mashed potatoes glazed with gravy, a perfect square of corn bread, a small bowl of succotash, and a sweating can of Coca-Cola.

Staring at the food, Jeremy wondered: Southern roots? He tried to recall if Arthur's voice had ever betrayed Southern inflections, didn't think so. If anything, the old man's baritone was flavored by New England.

Arthur Chess showed no immediate interest in conversation. Spreading a napkin on his lap, he began shearing through the first piece of chicken. He cut quickly and gracefully, using long fingers tipped by broad nails stubbed short. His long white lab coat was snowy-clean but for a disturbing spatter of pinkish stains on the right sleeve. The shirt beneath the coat was a blue pinpoint Oxford spread-collar. Arthur's magenta bow tie hung askew in a way that suggested intention.

Jeremy figured the pathologist for at least sixty-five, maybe older, but Arthur's pink skin glowed with health. A neat, white, mustachless beard, which gave insight into what Lincoln's would've looked like had Honest Abe been allowed to grow old, fringed Arthur's long face. His bald head was lunar and imposing under cruel hospital lighting.

Jeremy knew of Arthur's reputation the way one is aware of a stranger's biography. Once Head of Pathology, Professor Chess had stepped down from administrative duties a few years ago to concentrate on scholarship. Something to do with soft-tissue sarcomas, the minutiae of cell-wall permeability, or whatnot.

Arthur also had a reputation as a world traveler and an amateur lepidopterist. His treatise on the carrion-eating butterflies of Australia had been featured in the hospital gift shop, alongside the usual paperback diversions. Jeremy had noticed the single stack of dry-looking, dirt brown volumes because they drabbed in comparison with the jackets of lurid best-sellers. The brown stack never seemed to reduce; why would a patient want to read about bugs that ate corpses?

Arthur ate three bites of chicken and put down his fork. "I really do hope this isn't an intrusion, Dr. Carrier."

"Not at all, Dr. Chess. Is there something you need?"

"Need?" Arthur was amused. "No, just seeking a bit of social discourse. I've noticed that you tend to dine alone."

"My schedule," lied Jeremy. "Unpredictable." Since his life had gone to hell, he'd been avoiding social discourse with anyone but patients. He'd gotten to the point where he could fake friendly. But sometimes, on the darkest of days, any human contact was painful.

Life's little wrist-flick . . .

"Of course," said Chess. "Given the nature of your work, that would have to be the case."

"Sir?" said Jeremy.

"The unpredictability of human emotions."

"That's true."

Arthur nodded gravely, as if the two of them had

reached a momentous agreement. A moment later, he said, "Jeremy—may I call you Jeremy?—Jeremy, I noticed you weren't at our little Tuesday get-together this week."

"A situation came up," said Jeremy, feeling like a child caught playing hookey. He forced a smile. "Unpredictable emotions."

"Something that resolved well, I hope?"

Jeremy nodded. "Anything new come up at T.B.?"

"Two new diagnoses, an adenosarcoma, and a CML. Typical presentations, the usual spirited discussion. To be honest, you didn't miss a thing."

Our little Tuesday get-together was Tumor Board. A weekly ritual, 8 to 9 A.M., in the larger conference room, Arthur Chess presiding over a confab of oncologists, radiotherapists, surgeons, nurse specialists. Commanding the slide projector, wielding a light wand, and his voluminous memory.

For nearly a year, Jeremy had been the mental health army's representative. In all that time, he'd spoken up once.

He'd attended his first Tumor Board years before, as an intern, finding the experience an ironic grotesquerie: slides of tumor-ravaged cells *click-clicked* on a giant screen, the images obscured by nicotine haze.

At least a third of the cancer doctors and nurses were puffing away.

Jeremy's supervisor at the time, an astonishingly pompous psychoanalyst, had wielded a Meerschaum pipe of Freudian proportions and blown Latakia fumes in Jeremy's face.

Arthur had been running things back then, too,

and he'd looked much the same, Jeremy realized.
The chief pathologist hadn't smoked, but neither had
he objected. A few months later, a wealthy benefactor touring the hospital poked her head in and
gasped. Soon after, the hospital passed a no-smoking
rule, and the mood at subsequent Tumor Boards
grew testy.

Arthur sectioned a tiny square of corn bread
from the host slab and chewed thoughtfully. "No
loss for you, Jeremy, but I do believe that your presence contributes."

"Really."

"Even if you don't say much, the fact that you're
there keeps the rest of us on our toes. Sensitivity-
wise."

"Well," said Jeremy, wondering why the old man
was bullshitting him so shamelessly, "anything that
helps sensitivity."

"The time you did speak up," said Arthur,
"taught us all a lesson."

Jeremy felt his face go hot. "I felt it was relevant."

"Oh, it was, Jeremy. Not everyone saw it that
way, but it was."

The time he spoke up had been six weeks ago.
Arthur flashing slides of a metastasized stomach
carcinoma on the big screen, defining the tumors in
the precise Latin poetry of histology. The patient, a
fifty-eight-year-old woman named Anna Duran,
had been referred to Jeremy because of "unrespon-
sive demeanor."

Jeremy found her initially sullen. Rather than try

to draw her out, he refilled her empty cup with tea, got himself coffee, plumped her pillows, then sat down by her bedside and waited.

Not caring much if she responded, or not. It had been that way since Jocelyn. He didn't even try anymore.

And the funny thing was, patients reacted to his apathy by opening up more quickly.

Grief had made him a more effective therapist.

Jeremy, flabbergasted, gave the matter some thought and decided patients probably perceived his blank face and statue posture as some sort of immutable, Zen-like calm.

If only they knew . . .

By the time she finished her tea, Anna Duran was ready to talk.

Which is why Jeremy was forced to speak up, twenty minutes into a contentious exchange between Mrs. Duran's attending oncologist and the treating radiotherapist. Both specialists were voluble men, well-intentioned, dedicated to their craft, but overly focused, baby-bathwater-tossers. Complicating matters further, neither cared for the other. That morning they'd slipped into an increasingly heated debate on treatment sequence that left the rest of the attendees peeking at their watches.

Jeremy had resolved to stay out of it. Tuesday mornings were an annoyance, his turn the result of a mandatory rotation that placed him in too-close proximity to death.

But that morning, something propelled him to his feet.

The sudden motion fixed fifty pairs of eyes upon him.

The oncologist had just completed a pronouncement.

The radiotherapist, about to embark on a response, was deterred by the look on Jeremy's face.

Arthur Chess rolled the light wand between his hands. "Yes, Dr. Carrier?"

Jeremy faced the sparring physicians. "Gentlemen, your debate may be justified on medical grounds, but you're wasting your time. Mrs. Duran won't agree to any form of treatment."

Silence metastasized.

The oncologist said, "And why is that, Doctor?"

"She doesn't trust anyone here," said Jeremy. "She was operated on six years ago—emergency appendectomy with postop sepsis. She's convinced that's what gave her stomach cancer. Her plan is to discharge herself and to seek out a local faith healer—a *curandero*."

The oncologist's eyes hardened. "Is that so, Doctor?"

"I'm afraid so, Doctor."

"Quaint and charmingly idiotic. Why wasn't I informed of this?"

"You just were," said Jeremy. "She told me yesterday. I left a message at your office."

The oncologist's shoulders dropped. "Well, then . . . I suggest you return to her bedside and convince her of the error of her ways."

"Not my job," said Jeremy. "She needs guidance from you. But frankly, I don't think there's anything anyone can say."

"Oh, really?" The oncologist's smile was acrid. "She's ready to see her witch doctor, then curl up and die?"

"She believes treatment made her sick and that more will kill her. It's a stomach carcinoma. What are we really offering her?"

No answer. Everyone in the room knew the stats. Stomach cancer so advanced was no grounds for optimism.

"Calming her down's not your job, Dr. Carrier?" said the oncologist. "What exactly *is* your job, vis à vis Tumor Board?"

"Good question," said Jeremy. And he left the room.

He'd expected a summons to the Chief Psychiatrist's office for a reprimand and a transfer off the board. None came, and when he showed up next Tuesday, he was met with what seemed to be respectful looks and nods.

Drop your interest in patients and patients talk to you more readily.

Mouth off at the honchos and gain collegial esteem.

Irony stank. From that point on, Jeremy found excuses for missing the meeting.

"The thing is," said Arthur, "we cellular types get so immersed in details that we forget there's a person involved."

In your case, there's no longer a person involved.
Jeremy said, "Dr. Chess, I just did my job. I'm

really not comfortable being thought of as an arbiter of anything. Now, if you'll excuse me."

"Of course," said Arthur, unperturbed, as Jeremy bussed his tray and left the dining room. Mumbling something Jeremy couldn't make out.

Later, much later, Jeremy was fairly certain he'd decoded Arthur's parting words:

"Until the next time."

2

THE WAY JOCELYN HAD DIED—THE IMAGE OF HER suffering—was plaque on Jeremy's brain.

He was never allowed to read the police report. But he'd seen the look in the detectives' eyes, overheard their hallway conferences.

Sexual psychopath. Sadistic. One for the record book, Bob.

Their eyes. To do that to a detective's eyes . . .

Jocelyn Banks had been twenty-seven, tiny, curvy, bubbly, talkative, blond, a blue-eyed pixie, a source of great comfort for the senescent patients she chose to care for.

Ward 3E. All ye who enter here, abandon all reason.

Advanced Alzheimer's, arthrosclerotic senility, a host of dementias, undiagnosed rot of the soul.

The vegetable garden, the neurologists called it. Sensitive bunch, the neurologists.

Jocelyn worked the 3 to 11 P.M. shift, tending to vacant eyes, slack mouths, and drool-coated chins. Cheerful, always cheerful. Calling her patients

"Honey" and "Sweetie," and "Handsome." Talking to those who never answered.

Jeremy met her when he was called up to 3E for a consult on a new Alzheimer's patient and couldn't find the chart. The ward clerk was surly and intent on not helping. Jocelyn stepped in, and he realized this was the cute little blonde he'd noticed in the cafeteria. *Thatfacethoselegsthatrear.*

When he completed the consult, he went looking for her, found her in the nurses' lounge, and asked her out. That night her mouth was open for his kisses, breath sweet, though they'd eaten garlicky Italian food. Later, Jeremy was to know that sweetness as an internal perfume.

They dated for nine weeks before Jocelyn moved into Jeremy's lonely little house. Three months after that, on a moonless Monday just after Jocelyn ended her shift, someone carjacked her Toyota in or near the too-dark auxiliary nurses' parking lot half a block from the hospital. Taking Jocelyn with him.

Her body was found four days later, under a bridge in The Shallows, a borderline district within walking distance of the city's cruelest streets. A place of thriving businesses during the day, but deserted at night. On the periphery were derelict buildings and ragged fencing, stray cats and long shadows, and that was where the killer had dumped Jocelyn's body. She'd been strangled and slashed and wedged behind an empty oil drum. That much the detectives revealed to Jeremy. By that time, the papers had reported those bare facts.

A pair of detectives had worked the case. Doresh

and Hoker, both beefy men in their forties, with drab wardrobes and drinkers' complexions. Bob and Steve. Doresh had dark, wavy hair and a chin cleft deep enough to harbor a cigarette butt. Hoker was fairer, with a pig snout for a nose and a mouth so stingy Jeremy wondered how he ate.

Big and lumbering, both of them. But sharp-eyed.

From the outset, they treated Jeremy like a suspect. The night Jocelyn disappeared, he'd left the hospital at six-thirty, gone home, read and listened to music, and fixed dinner and waited for her. The hedges that sided his tiny front lawn prevented his neighbors from knowing what time he'd arrived or left. The block was mostly renters, anyway, people who came and went, barely furnishing the uninviting bungalows, never taking the time to be neighborly.

The late supper he'd prepared for two proved scant reassurance to Detectives Bob Doresh and Steve Hoker, and, in fact, fed their suspicions. For at 3 A.M., well after verifying that Jocelyn hadn't taken on an emergency double shift, and shortly after phoning a missing persons report to the police, Jeremy had placed the uneaten pasta and salad in the refrigerator, cleared the place settings, washed the dishes.

Keeping busy to quell his anxiety, but to the detectives, such fastidiousness was out of character for a worried lover whose girl hadn't come home. Unless, of course, said lover knew all along . . .

It went on that way for a while, the two buffaloes alternating between patronizing and browbeating

Jeremy. Whatever background check they did on him revealed nothing nasty and a DNA swab of his cheek failed to match whatever they were trying to match.

His questions were answered by knowing looks. They spoke to him several times. In his office at the hospital, at his house, in an interrogation room that reeked of gym locker.

"Was there tissue under her nails?" he said, more to himself than to the detectives.

Bob Doresh said, "Why would you ask that, Doctor?"

"Jocelyn would resist. If she had a chance."

"Would she?" said Hoker, leaning across the green metal table.

"She was extremely gentle—as I've told you. But she'd fight to defend herself."

"A fighter, huh . . . would she go easily with a stranger? Just go off with someone?"

Anger seared Jeremy's chest muscles. His eyes clenched and he gripped the table.

Hoker sat back. "Doctor?"

"You're saying that's what happened?"

Hoker smiled.

Jeremy said, "You're *blaming* her?"

Hoker looked over at his partner. His snout twitched, and he looked satisfied. "You can go now, Doctor."

Eventually, they left him alone. But the damage was done; Jocelyn's family had flown in—both her parents and a sister. They shunned him. He was never informed of the funeral.

He tried to keep up with the investigation, but his calls to the detective squad were intercepted by a desk officer: *Not in. I'll give 'em yer message.*

A month passed. Three, six. Jocelyn's killer was never found.

Jeremy walked and talked, wounded. His life shriveled to something sere and brittle. He ate without tasting, voided without relief, breathed city air and coughed, drove out to the flatlands or the water's edge, and was still unable to nourish his lungs.

People—the sudden appearance of strangers—alarmed him. Human contact repulsed him. The division between sleep and awareness became arbitrary, deceitful. When he talked, he heard his own voice bounce back to him, hollow, echoing, tremulous. Acne, the pustulant plague forgotten since adolescence, broke out on his back and shoulders. His eyelids ticced, and sometimes he was convinced that a bitter reek was oozing from his pores. No one seemed repulsed, though. Too bad; he could've used the solitude.

Throughout it all, he kept seeing patients, smiling, comforting, holding hands, conferring with physicians, charting, as he always did, in a hurried scrawl that made the nurses giggle.

One time, he overheard a patient, a woman he'd helped get through a bilateral mastectomy, talking to her daughter in the hallway:

"That's Dr. Carrier. He's the sweetest man, the most *wonderful* man."

He made it to the nearest men's room, threw

up, cleaned himself off, and went to see his next appointment.

Six months later, he felt above it all, below it all. Inhabiting a stranger's skin.

Wondering what it would be like to degenerate.

3

AFTER THE CHAT IN THE DINING ROOM, JEREMY braced himself for some sign of familiarity from Arthur Chess at the next Tumor Board. But the pathologist favored him with a passing glance, nothing more.

When the meeting ended, Arthur made no further attempt to socialize, and Jeremy wrote off the encounter as a bit of impulse on the older man's part.

On a frigid autumn day, he left the hospital at lunchtime and walked to a used bookstore two blocks away. The shop was a dim, narrow place on a grimy block filled with liquor stores, thrift outlets, and vacancies. A strange block; sometimes Jeremy's nose picked up the sweetness of fresh bread, but no bakeries were in sight. Other times, he'd smell sulfurous ash and industrial waste and find no source of those odors, either. He was beginning to doubt his own senses.

The bookstore was filled with raw pine cases and smelled of old newsprint. Jeremy had frequented its corners and shadows in the past, searching out the vintage psychology books he collected. Bargains abounded; few people seemed interested in first edition Skinners, Maslows, Jungs.

Since Jocelyn's death he hadn't been back to the store. Perhaps now was the time to return to routine, such as it was.

The shop's windows were black, and no signage identified the business inside. Once you entered, the world was gone, and you were free to concentrate. An effective ruse, but it also had the effect of discouraging venture; rarely had Jeremy seen other customers. Maybe that was the way the proprietor wanted it.

He was a fat man who rang up purchases with a scowl, never spoke, seemed pointedly misanthropic. Jeremy wasn't certain if his mutism was elective or the result of some defect, but he was certain the man wasn't deaf. On the contrary, the slightest noise perked the fat man's ears. Customer inquiries, however, elicited an impatient finger point at the printed guide posted near the shop's entrance: a barely decipherable improvisation upon the Dewey Decimal System. Those who couldn't figure it out were out of luck.

This afternoon, the bearish mute sat behind his cash register reading a tattered copy of Sir Edward Lytton's *Eugene Aram*. Jeremy's entrance merited a shift of haunches and the merest quiver of eyebrow.

Jeremy proceeded to the *Psychology* section and searched book spines for treasures. Nothing. The sagging shelves bore the same volumes he'd seen months ago. Every book, it appeared, remained in place. As if the section had been reserved for Jeremy.

As usual, the shop was empty but for Jeremy. How did the mute make a living? Perhaps he didn't. As Jeremy continued browsing, he found himself fantasizing about sources of independent income for the fat man. A range of possibilities, from the loftiest inheritance to the monthly disability check.

Or, perhaps the store was a front for drug-dealing, money-laundering, white slavery, international intrigue.

Perhaps piracy on the high seas was hatched here, among the dusty bindings.

Jeremy indulged himself with thoughts of unimaginable felonies. That led him to a bad place, and he cursed his idiocy.

A throat clear stopped him short. He stepped out of *Psychology* and sighted down the next aisle.

Another customer stood there. A man, his back to Jeremy, unmindful of Jeremy.

A tall, bald man in a well-cut, out-of-fashion tweed suit. White fringes of beard floated into view as a pink skull turned to inspect a shelf. The man's profile was revealed as he made a selection and extricated a tome.

Arthur Chess.

Was this the *Lepidoptery* section? Jeremy had never studied the fat man's guide, had never been interested in expanding.

Funnel vision. Sometimes it helped keep life manageable.

He watched Arthur open the book, lick his thumb, turn a page.

Arthur kept his head down. Began walking up the aisle as he read.

Reversing direction, head still down, coming straight at Jeremy.

To greet the pathologist would open the worm-can of obligatory conversation. If Jeremy left now, quickly, stealthily, perhaps the old man wouldn't notice.

But if he did notice, Jeremy would earn the worst of both worlds: forced to socialize and robbed of browsing time.

He decided to greet Arthur, hoping that the pathologist would be so engrossed in his butterfly book that the ensuing chat would be brief.

Arthur gazed up before Jeremy reached him. The book in his arms was huge, bound in cracked, camel leather. No winged creatures graced the densely printed pages. Jeremy read the title.

Crimean Battle Strategy: A Compendium.

The tag on the nearest shelf said, MILITARY HISTORY.

Arthur smiled. "Jeremy."

"Afternoon, Arthur. No lunch today?"

"Large breakfast," said the pathologist, patting his vest. "Busy afternoon, a bit of diversion seemed in order."

With what you do all day, it's a wonder you ever have an appetite.

"Lovely place, this," said the old man.

"Do you come here often?"

"From time to time. Mr. Renfrew's quite the crosspatch, but he leaves one alone, and his prices are more than fair."

For all his purchases, Jeremy had never learned the proprietor's name. Had never cared. Arthur had obtained the information because, like most gregarious people, he was excessively curious.

Yet, for all his sociability, the old man had chosen to work among the dead.

Jeremy said, "Very fair prices. Nice seeing you, Arthur. Happy hunting." He turned to leave.

"Would you have time for a drink?" said Arthur. "Alcoholic or otherwise?"

"Sorry," said Jeremy, tapping the coat cuff that concealed his wristwatch. "Busy afternoon, as well." His next patient was in an hour and a half.

"Ah, of course. Sorry, then. Another time."

"Absolutely," said Jeremy.

Later, that evening, walking to his car, he noticed Arthur in the doctors' parking lot.

This is too much. I'm being stalked.

But, as with the bookstore encounter, Arthur had arrived first, so that was ridiculous. Jeremy chided himself for self-importance—paranoia's first cousin. Had he slipped that far?

He ducked behind a pylon and watched Arthur unlock his car, a black Lincoln, at least fifteen years old. Glossy paint, shiny chrome, kept up nicely. Like Arthur's suit: well used, but quality. Jeremy envisioned Arthur's home, guessed the pathologist would inhabit one of the gracious old homes in Queen's Arms, on the North Side, a shabby-elegant stretch with harbor views.

Yes, Q.A. was definitely Arthur. The house would be a Victorian or a neo-Georgian, fusty and comfortable, chocked with overstuffed sofas in faded fabrics, stolid, centenarian mahogany furniture, layers of antimacassars, doilies, gimcracks, a nice wet bar stocked with premium liquors.

Pinned butterflies in ornate frames.

Was the pathologist married? Had to be. All that cheer bespoke a comfortable, comforting routine.

Definitely married, Jeremy decided. Happily, for decades. He conjured a soft-busted, bird-voiced, blue-haired wife to dote on Dear Arthur.

He watched as the old man lowered his long frame into the Lincoln. When the big sedan started up with a sonorous rumble, Jeremy hurried to his own dusty Nova.

He sat behind the wheel, thinking of the comforts that awaited Arthur. Home-cooked food, simple but filling. A stiff drink to dilate the blood vessels and warm the imagination.

Feet up, warm smiles nurtured by routine.

Jeremy's gut knotted as the black car glided away.

4

TWO WEEKS TO THE DAY AFTER THE BOOKSTORE encounter, a second-year medical resident, an adorable brunette named Angela Rios, came on to Jeremy. He was rotating through the acute children's ward, accompanying the attending physician and house staff on pediatric rounds. Dr. Rios, with whom he'd exchanged pleasantries in the past, hovered by his side, and he smelled the shampoo in her long, dark hair. She had eyes the color of bittersweet chocolate, a swan neck, a delicate, pointy chin under a soft, wide mouth.

Four cases were scheduled for discussion that morning: an eight-year-old girl with dermatomyositis, a brittle adolescent diabetic, a failure to thrive infant—that one was probably child abuse—and a precocious, angry twelve-year-old boy with a miniscule body shriveled by osteogenesis imperfecta.

The attending, a soft-spoken man named Miller, summarized the basics on the crippled boy, then arched an eyebrow toward Jeremy. Jeremy talked to a sea of young baffled faces, trying to humanize the boy—his intellectual reach, his rage, the pain that would only intensify. Trying to get these new physicians to see the child as something other than a diagnosis. But keeping it low-key, careful to avoid the holier-than-thou virus that too often afflicted the mental health army.

Despite his best efforts, half the residents seemed bored. The rest were feverishly attentive, including Angela Rios, who hadn't taken her eyes off Jeremy. When rounds ended she hung around and asked questions about the crippled boy. Simple things that Jeremy was certain didn't puzzle her at all.

He answered her patiently. Her long, dark hair was wavy and silky, her complexion creamy, those gorgeous eyes as warm as eyes could get. Only her voice detracted: a bit chirpy, too generous with final syllables. Maybe it was anxiety. Jeremy was in no mood for the mating game. He complimented her questions, flashed a professorial smile, and walked away.

Three hours later, Arthur Chess showed up in his office.

"I hope I'm not disturbing you."

Oh you are, you are. Jeremy had been working on the draft of a book chapter. Three years before, he'd been the behavioral researcher on a study of "bubble children": kids with advanced cancers treated in germ-free, plastic rooms to see if their weakened immune systems could be protected against infection. The isolation posed a threat to young psyches, and Jeremy's job had been to prevent and treat emotional breakdown.

At that he'd been successful, and several of the children had survived and thrived. The principal researcher, now the head of oncology, had been after him to publish the data in book form, and a medical publisher had expressed enthusiasm.

Jeremy worked on the outline for seventeen months, then sat down to draft an introduction. Over a year's time, he produced two pages.

Now he pushed that pathetic output aside, cleared charts and journals onto the chair that abutted his desk, and said, "Not at all, Arthur. Make yourself comfortable."

Arthur's color was high, and his white coat was buttoned up, revealing an inch of pink shirt and a brown bow tie specked with tiny pink bumblebees. "So this is your lair."

"Such as it is." Jeremy's designated space was a corner cutout at the end of a long, dark corridor on a floor that housed nonclinicians—biochemists, biophysicists. Bio-everything, except him. The rest of Psychiatry was a story above.

A single window looked out to an ash-colored air shaft. This was an older part of the hospital, and the walls were thick and clammy. The bio-folk kept to themselves. Footsteps in the hallways were infrequent.

His lair.

He'd ended up there four months ago, after a group of surgeons came by to measure Psychiatry's space on the penthouse floor of the main hospital building. Less glamorous than it sounded, the upper floor looked out to a heliport, where emergency

landings sometimes rendered therapy impossible.
Any view of the city was blocked by massive heating
and air-conditioning units, and pigeons enjoyed crap-
ping on the windows. From time to time, Jeremy
had seen rats scampering along the roof gutters.

The day the surgeons came, he'd been trying to
write and was rescued by their laughter. He opened
his door to find five dapper men and a matching
woman, wielding tape measures and *hmm*ing. A
month later, Psychiatry was ordered to relocate to a
smaller suite. No suite existed to accommodate the
entire department. A crisis of space was solved when
an eighty-year emeritus analyst died, and Jeremy
volunteered to go elsewhere. This was shortly *After
Jocelyn*, and isolation had been welcome.

Jeremy never came to regret the decision. He
could come and go as he pleased, and Psychiatry
was faithful about forwarding his daily mail. The
chemistry lab stink that permeated the building was
all right.

"Nice," said Arthur. "Very nice."

"What is?"

"The solitude." The old man blushed. "Which I
have violated."

"What's up, Arthur?"

"I was thinking about that drink. The one we discussed at Renfrew's shop."

"Yes," said Jeremy. "Of course."

Arthur reached under a coat flap and drew out a
bulbous, white-gold pocket watch. "It's approach-
ing six. Would now be a good time?"

To refuse the old man now would be downright
rude. And simply postpone the inevitable.

On the bright side: Jeremy could use a drink.
He said, "Sure, Arthur. Name the place."

The place was the bar of the Excelsior, a downtown hotel. Jeremy had passed the building many
times—a massive, gray heap of gargoyled granite
with too many rooms to ever fill—but had never
been inside. He parked in the humid subterranean
lot, rode the elevator to street level, and crossed a
cavernous Beaux Arts lobby. The space was well
past its prime, as was most of downtown. Discon-
solate men working on commission sat in frayed,
plush chairs and smoked and waited for something
to happen. A few women with overdeveloped calves
walked the room; maybe hookers, maybe just women
traveling alone.

The bar was a windowless, burnished mahogany
fistula that relied upon weak bulbs and tall mirrors
for life. Jeremy and Arthur had taken separate cars
because each planned to head home after the tête à
tête. Jeremy had driven quickly, but Arthur had gotten there first. The pathologist looked tweedy and
relaxed in a corner booth.

The waiter who approached them was portly
and militaristic and older than Arthur, and Jeremy
sensed that he knew the pathologist. He had nothing upon which to base the assumption—the man
had uttered nothing of a familiar nature, hadn't offered even a telling glance—but Jeremy couldn't
shake the feeling that this was a favorite haunt of
Arthur's.

Yet when Arthur put in his order, there was no

"The usual, Hans." On the contrary, the pathologist enunciated clearly, careful to specify: a Boodles martini, straight up, two pearl onions.

The waiter turned to Jeremy. "Sir?"

"Single malt, ice on the side."

"Any particular brand, sir?"

"Macallan."

"Very good, sir."

As he left, Arthur said, "*Very* good."

The drinks came with stunning speed, obviating painful small talk. Arthur savored his martini, showing no inclination to do anything but drink.

"So," said Jeremy.

Arthur slid a pearl onion from a toothpick to his lips, left the mucoid sphere there for several moments. Chewed. Swallowed. "I was wondering if you could clarify something for me, Jeremy."

"What's that, Arthur?"

"Your views—psychology's views on violence. Specifically, the genesis of very, very bad behavior."

"Psychology's not monolithic," said Jeremy.

"Yes, yes, of course. But surely there must be a body of data—I'll retrench. What's *your* take on the issue?"

Jeremy sipped scotch, let the subtle fire linger on his tongue. "You're asking me this because . . ."

"The question intrigues me," said Arthur. "For years I've dealt with the aftermath of death on a daily basis. Have spent most of my adult life with what remains when the soul flies. The challenge, for me, is no longer to reduce the bodies I dissect to their biochemical components. Nor to ascertain cause of death. If one excavates long enough, one produces. No, the challenge is to comprehend the larger issues."

The old man finished his martini and motioned for another. Motioned at an empty bar; no sign of the portly waiter. But the man materialized moments later with another frosted shaker.

He glanced at the nearly empty tumbler of scotch. "Sir?"

Jeremy shook his head, and the waiter vanished.

"Humanity," said Arthur, sipping. "The challenge is to maintain my humanity—have I ever mentioned that I served a spell in the Coroner's Office?"

As if the two of them chatted regularly.

"No," said Jeremy.

"Oh, yes. Sometime after my discharge from the military."

"Where did you serve?"

"The Panama Canal," said Arthur. "Medical officer at the locks. I witnessed some gruesome accidents, learned quite a bit about postmortem identification. After that . . . I did some other things, but eventually, the Coroner's seemed a fitting place." He took several thoughtful swallows, and the second martini was reduced by half.

"But you switched to academia," said Jeremy.

"Oh, yes . . . it seemed the right thing to do." The old man smiled. "Now about my question: What's your take on it?"

"Very bad behavior."

"The very worst."

Jeremy's stomach lurched. "On a purely academic level?"

"Oh, no," said Arthur. "Academia is the refuge of those seeking to escape the big questions."

"If it's hard data you're after—"

"I'm after whatever you choose to offer. Because you speak your mind." Arthur finished his drink. "Of course, if I'm being offensive or intrusive—"

"Violence," said Jeremy. He'd spent hours—endless hours, all those sleepless nights—thinking about it. "From what I've gathered, very, very bad behavior is a combination of genes and environment. Like most everything else of consequence in human behavior."

"A cocktail of nature and nurture."

Jeremy nodded.

"What are your thoughts about the concept of the bad seed?" said Arthur.

"The stuff of fiction," said Jeremy. "Which isn't to say that serious violence doesn't manifest young. Show me a cruel, bullying, callous six-year-old, and I'll show you someone worth watching. But even given nasty tendencies it takes a bad environment—a rotten family to bring it out."

"Callous . . . you've treated children like that?"

"A few."

"Six-year-old potential felons?"

Jeremy considered his answer. "Six-year-olds who gave me pause. Psychologists are notoriously bad at predicting violence. Or anything else."

"But you have seen youngsters who alarm you."

"Yes."

"What do you tell their parents?"

"The parents are almost always part of the problem. I've seen fathers who took great joy when their sons brutalized other children. Preaching restraint in the presence of strangers—saying the right things, but their smiles give them away. Eventually. It takes time to understand a family. For all intents and purposes, families still exist in caves. You have to be inside to read the writing on the wall."

Arthur waved for a third drink. No sign of intoxication in the old man's speech or demeanor. Just a slight increase in his high, pink color.

At least, Jeremy mused, a slip of *his* scalpel wouldn't kill anyone.

This time, when the waiter said, "For you, sir?" he ordered a second Macallan.

Finger food came, unbeckoned, with the drinks. Boiled shrimp with cocktail sauce, fried zucchini, spicy little sausages skewered by black plastic toothpicks, thick potato chips that appeared homemade. Arthur hadn't ordered the hors d'oeuvres, but he was unsurprised.

The two men nibbled and drank, and Jeremy felt warmth—a lacquer of relaxation—flow from his toes to his scalp. When Arthur said, "Their smiles give them away," Jeremy was momentarily confused. Then he reminded himself: those obnoxious, pathogenic dads he'd been talking about.

He said, "Do as I say, not as I do. It never works."

"Interesting," said Arthur. "Not counterintuitive, but interesting. So, it's all about families."

"That's what I've seen."

"Interesting," Arthur repeated. Then he changed the subject.

* * *

To butterflies.

Specimens he'd come across while serving in Panama. Off-duty forays into the jungles of Costa Rica. Weather that "had one drenched in sweat even as one showered."

The old man drank and fooled with his bumble-bee bow tie and ate skewered sausages, and a dreamy look came into his eyes as he embarked upon a story. A patient he'd seen back in Panama. A young officer in the Corps of Engineers who'd returned from a jungle hike, felt an itch under his left shoulder blade, reached back and fingered a slight swelling and believed himself bitten.

He'd thought nothing of it until a day later when the swelling had tripled in size.

"But still," said Arthur, "he didn't come in for examination. No fever, no other discomfort—the old machismo, you know. On the second day, the pain arrived. Wonderful messenger, pain. Teaches us all sorts of lessons about our bodies. This pain was electric—or so the fellow described it. A high-voltage electric shock running continuously through his torso. As if he'd been hooked up to a live circuit. By the time I saw him he was deathly pallid and shaking and in quite a bit of agony. And the swelling had trebled, yet again. Furthermore," Arthur leaned forward, "the lad was certain there was something moving within."

He selected a potato chip, slid it between his lips, chewed deliberately, dusted crumbs from his beard and continued.

"My assumption upon hearing that—motion— was crepitus. Fluid buildup secondary to infection, nothing alarming on the face of it. But the poor lad removed his shirt and as I observed the mass I became intrigued." Arthur licked salt from his lips. In the dim light of the bar, his eyes were the color of fine jade.

"The swelling was huge, Jeremy. Highly discolored, the beginnings of necrosis had set in. Black flesh, somewhat bubal, so one had to consider plague. But there was no serious probability of plague, the corps had cleaned the Canal Zone quite thoroughly. Still, medicine is predicated on surprise, that's the fun of it, and I knew I had to culture the mass. In preparation, I palpated—the wretch could barely contain himself from screaming—and as I did I noticed that there did, indeed, seem to be some sort of independent movement beneath the skin. Unlike any crepitus I'd ever seen."

Another potato chip. A slow sip of martini.

Arthur sat back again.

Jeremy had moved forward on his seat. He relaxed, consciously. Waited for the punch line.

Arthur ate and drank, looked quite content. The old bastard hadn't finished. Too drunk to continue?

Jeremy fought the urge to say, "What happened then?"

Finally, Arthur drained his martini glass and gave a low sigh of contentment. "At that point, rather than commence with the examination, I sent the fellow for an X ray and the results were quite fascinating, if inconclusive."

Munch. Sip.

"What did it show?" said Jeremy.

"A gelatinous mass of indeterminate origin," said Arthur. "A mass unlike any neoplasm or cystic formation I'd ever seen. My reference books were of no help. Neither was the radiologist—not the brightest fellow in the first place. In any event, I decided to cut the lad open, but gingerly. Which was fortunate because I was able to preserve it, intact."

Arthur stared at the empty martini glass and smiled in reminiscence. Jeremy busied himself with the last drops of single malt.

Unbuttoning his vest, the pathologist shook his head, in wonder. "Infestation. *Larval* infestation. The poor lad had been selected by a little known jungle beetle as the nutritional host for its new family—an unusually petite ectoparasitoid of the Adephaga family. The insect is equipped with a set of biochemical tools that prove extremely useful to its survival. It's brown and unassuming and, hence, hard to spot, and, to the uninformed, appears minimally threatening. Furthermore, it exudes a chemical that repels predators, and its excrement possesses anesthetic properties. Its modus is to deposit its feces on the victim's skin, which accomplishes the dual goal of relieving itself and numbing the host epidermis. That allows for a swift, clean incision large enough to accommodate an extravagantly curved ovipositor—a beak, if you will, connected to the creature's reproductive tract that allows for rapid injection of eggs. Of even further interest is the fact that it's the *father* beetle who accomplishes this. I was reminded of all this by your mention of violence-enabling fathers."

Smile. A rueful glance at the empty glass. Arthur

went on, "Once his mate's eggs have been fertilized, the male takes it upon himself to assume full responsibility for the family's future. He reenters the female, extracts the eggs, injects them into his own thorax and feeds the brood with his body tissue until a suitable host is found."

"Liberated man," muttered Jeremy.

"Quite." Arthur twirled his martini glass, ate the pearl onion, placed his large hands flat on the table.

"What happened to the patient?"

"I scooped out the entire mass, taking pains to do it cleanly. Thousands of larvae, all quite alive, thriving quite nicely, thank you, because of the high protein content of young, American military musculature. No lasting damage to the poor lieutenant other than a scar and some tenderness for several weeks. And several months of rather disturbing dreams. He applied for and received a discharge. Moved to Cleveland, or some such place. The larvae didn't survive. I tried to come up with substitute nutrition for the little devils. Agar, gelatin, beef broth, bonemeal, ground insect parts—nothing worked. The fascinating aspect of the case was that the very existence of this particular beetle had been under speculation for some time. Many entomologists believed it extinct. A rather interesting case. At least I thought so."

"The male beetle," said Jeremy. "Sins of the fathers."

Arthur studied him. Gave a long, slow nod. "Yes. You might say that."

5

JEREMY AND ARTHUR LEFT THE BAR TOGETHER and parted at the hotel's revolving brass doors.

Jeremy was drunk, needed to walk it off, and he headed out to the street. A light rain had fallen. The sidewalks smelled of burnt copper; the city glowed. He walked to the fringes of downtown, entered dark, murderous avenues, unmindful of his own safety.

Feeling curiously uplifted—fearless—after drinking with the pathologist. The gruesome story of the soldier with the larval hump cheered him. When he finally drove home, his head was clear and when he reached his small house he thought, *What a pathetic little place. More than enough for someone like me.*

Jocelyn's belongings had been packed up and shipped to the police. Four cartons, she'd brought so little.

Doresh and Hoker had stood around during the packing, and Doresh said, "Mind if we Luminol the bathroom? It's a chemical we spray and then we turn down the lights and if it glows—"

"—there's blood," finished Jeremy. "Go ahead." Not bothering to ask, Why the bathroom?

He knew the answer. The bathroom was the place, if you were going to . . .

They sprayed and found nothing. Uniformed officers carried the four cartons away. It was only when they'd left that Jeremy realized they'd taken something of his.

A framed snapshot that had sat on his bedroom dresser. He and Jocelyn, walking along the harbor, eating shrimp from a takeout stand, a warm day, but windy, her head barely high enough to reach Jeremy's shoulder. Her blond hair all over the place, masking half of Jeremy's face.

He phoned Doresh, asked for the picture back, never received a reply.

He stripped naked, dropped into bed, figuring he'd be up half the night. Instead, he fell asleep readily but woke up in the early-morning hours, head pounding, muscles aching, brain clawed by images of voracious, cannibal bugs.

Stay out of my life, old man.

Arthur did.

Shortly after drinks at the Excelsior, as Jeremy tagged along during psych rounds, he heard the page operator drone his name. He straggled away from the mental health army, phoned in, picked up a page from Dr. Angela Rios.

Over the past few weeks, the beautiful young resident had tried to catch his eye during at least four chance walk-bys in hospital corridors. Angela had a fine, quick mind and a soft heart, and she was as pretty as they came. Exactly the type of woman Jeremy would go for, if he was interested in a woman.

Careful not to be hurtful, he'd smiled and walked on.

Now this.

He answered the page, and Angela said, "I'm glad you're on service. I've got a problem patient— thirty-six-year-old woman with lupus in apparent remission but now her blood work's looking scary, and we need a bone marrow aspiration."

"Leukemia?"

"Hopefully not. But her counts are off in an ominous way, and I'd be derelict not to pursue it. The problem is, she has real difficulty with procedures—scared out of her wits. I offered to sedate her, but she says no, with the lupus receding she's worried about taking any drugs and messing up her system. Could you help me? Hypnotize her, talk to her, whatever calms her down? I heard you do that."

"Sure," said Jeremy.

The first patient he'd "helped" with a procedure had been a twelve-year-old girl with a resected brain tumor—a malignant glioma—about to undergo a spinal tap. The Chief Psychiatrist had given Jeremy's name to the neurosurgeon who'd put in the consult, and there was no turning back.

He showed up at the procedure room wondering, *What am I supposed to do?* Found the girl in restraints, kicking and screaming and foaming at the mouth. It had been six months since the tumor had been shelled out of her skull, and her hair had grown back as three inches of fuzz. Ink lines across her face and a yellowish tan said she'd been radiated recently.

Twelve years old and they were tying her up like a felon.

A frustrated second-year resident had just ordered a gag. He greeted Jeremy with a furrow-browed grunt.

Jeremy said, "Let's hold off on that," and took the girl's hand. Felt the shock of pain as her nails cut into his palm and drew blood, looked into her panic-poisoned eyes, tried not to wince as she shrieked, "*Nonononononononono!*"

Sweat poured from his armpits, his bowels shuddered, and his equilibrium started to go.

He stood by the gurney, frozen, as the girl's nails cut deeper. She howled, he swayed. His left foot began to slide out from under—

Blacking out—oh, shit!

The resident, staring at him. *Everyone* staring at him.

He braced himself. Breathed deeply and, he hoped, inconspicuously.

The girl stopped screaming.

His colon felt ready to explode and his back had

gone clammy but he smiled down at her, called her "Honey" because he'd forgotten her name though they'd just been introduced, and on top of that he'd just read the damn chart.

She stared up at him.

Oh, Lord, *trust.*

The room fish-eyed and shimmered, and he felt his knees give way again. Drawing himself up, he began talking to the now-silent girl. Smiling and talking, intoning, droning, uttering Godknewwhat-jibberish.

The girl commenced screaming again.

The resident said, "Shit, let's just *do* it."

"Hold on," ordered Jeremy. The violence in his voice silenced the room.

The girl, too.

He concentrated. Suppressed the shakes that threatened to betray him.

Talked her through it.

Within moments, the girl's eyes had shut and she was breathing slowly and able to nod when Jeremy asked if she was ready. The resident, now looking off-balance himself, did his thing with merciful skill, extracted the lumbar puncture needle, filled a vial full of golden spinal fluid, and left the procedure room shaking his head.

The girl cried, and that was okay, that was good, she had every right, poor thing, poor poor thing, just a child.

Jeremy stayed with her, endured her whimpers, stuck with her until she was ready to smile and he got her to do so. His full-body sweat was foul-smelling, but no one seemed to notice.

Later, out in the hall, one of the nurses cornered him, and said, "That was amazing, Dr. Carrier."

Angela's lupus patient was no screamer. A wan, pretty woman named Marian Boehmer, she expressed her terror by going rigid and silent. Dead eyes. Lips folded inward. In the wrong setting, some nincompoop shrink might've slapped her with a catatonia label.

Angela moved away from her and gave Jeremy room to work. Angela's silky hair was tied back and rubber-banded, her makeup had been eaten up by stress, and her skin bore a library pallor. She looked as if she hadn't slept in a very long time.

Here she is at her worst, thought Jeremy. *The way she looks on a bad morning. And still, pretty good.*

The bone marrow aspiration kit lay unwrapped on a bedside tray. Chrome and glass and dagger points, that horrible grinding thing used to puncture the sternum so that blood-forming cells could be sucked out. In order to gain leverage, the doctor loomed from above and leaned in hard, put some muscle into it. Patients willing to talk about the procedure said it felt like being stabbed to death.

Marian Boehmer's cheeks were clear of the wolf-mask rash that signaled her immune system had gone awry. If you got past the fear, she really did look okay. Fair-skinned and fair-haired, a bit underweight, nice features. Wedding band and a diamond chip on her ring finger. Where was the husband? Did that mean something, his not being here?

Everything means something. At the moment, so what? This woman was going to have her breastbone punctured.

Jeremy introduced himself. Smiled and talked and smiled and talked and held her hand and felt the familiar pangs of his own anxiety—the tight chest, the empathy sweat, the twinges of vertigo.

No danger of embarrassing himself—the horror of the first time had been his hazing.

By now he expected the fear. Welcomed it.

When he helped, he suffered. The key was to hide it.

The key to *life* was hiding it.

He stroked the woman's hand, chanced a gentle swipe of her brow and, when she didn't recoil, told her how well she was doing as he lapsed into the singsong seduction of hypnosis.

Not a formal induction, nothing that theatrically vulgar. Just a subtle, gradual reach for the parasympathetic reaction that combined relaxation and concentration and slowed down mind and body.

Transport yourself to a good place, Ms. Boehmer—may I call you Marian, thank you, Marian, that's good, Marian, excellent, Marian.

What a great job, Marian—and here's Dr. Rios and yes, yes, just hold on, good great—terrific, Marian and . . . there you go, you did a great job, it's over and you did great.

During the procedure, Marian Boehmer had wet herself, and he pretended not to notice as the nurse wiped her thighs.

When he took hold of her hand again, she said, "Oh, look at me. I'm such a baby."

Jeremy patted her hair gently. "You're a trouper. If I was in trouble, I'd want you on my team."

Marian Boehmer burst into tears. "I have two children," she said. "I'm a very good *mother*!"

Jeremy stayed with her until the orderly came to wheel her back to her room. As he opened the door, he braced himself for a hallway conference with Angela Rios. Clinical chitchat that would inevitably wind its way toward social overture. Rios was lovely but . . .

He stepped out to the echoes of distant voices, phones, clinical footfalls, page announcements, rattling gurneys. A single nurse sat charting at the nearest station, ten yards away.

Empty hallway. No sign of Angela.

6

On a rainy Thursday evening, just before seven, on his way out of the hospital, Jeremy encountered the raincoated bulk of Detective Bob Doresh.

Doresh was hanging by the main elevators, near the candy machines, rubbing his heavy jaw and munching on something. When he saw Jeremy, he pocketed a colorful wrapper and trotted over. "Got a minute, Doc?"

Jeremy kept walking and motioned for Doresh to accompany him.

"How've you been doing, Doc?"

"All right. And you?"

"Me?" Doresh seemed offended by the common courtesy. As if his job gave him the right of total privacy. *I'll ask the questions . . .*

"I'm fine, Doc." He wiped a speck of chocolate from his lips and blinked several times. "Well balanced and nourished. So everything's copacetic with you."

"I'm surviving."

"Well, that's good," said Doresh. "Especially considering the alternative."

They passed the marble wall engraved with the names of hospital benefactors, pushed through the glass doors, walked through the covered breezeway that led to the doctors' parking lot. The convenient lot. After Jocelyn, there'd been talk about moving the nurses closer, but nothing had materialized.

Doresh said, "Nice to keep dry."

Jeremy said, "What's up, Detective?"

"I'll get right to the point, Doc. This is going to sound like one of those movie cliches, but where were you last night, let's say between ten and midnight?"

"At home."

"Anyone with you?"

"No. Why?"

"Just routine," said Doresh.

For a moment, Jeremy thought he'd go along with the script. Then something snapped, and he barked, "Bullshit," and moved well ahead of Doresh.

The detective caught up. Chuckled loudly, but there was no humor to the sound he emitted. The warning growl of a big, watchful dog.

Those eyes. Regarding Jeremy with what seemed like new respect. Or maybe it was contempt.

Doresh said, "You're right, it's total bullshit. I'm not going to waste my time driving over here and making small talk. So tell me this: Is there any way you can verify being home by yourself last night? It would help both of us if you could."

Jeremy suppressed the reflexive *why-the-hell-should-I*? "Not for an entire two hours there isn't. I got home late—around eight-thirty, took a walk in my neighborhood for an hour or so. Someone may have seen me, but if they did, I didn't notice. After that, I returned home, showered, had a drink—scotch. Johnnie Walker, if you care—and called out for some dinner. Twenty-four-hour pizza place. I ordered a medium, half-cheese, half-mushrooms. It was delivered around ten-fifteen. I gave the boy a five-dollar tip, so he'll probably remember. I ate three slices of pizza—the rest is in my refrigerator. The scotch made my mouth dry, and the pizza didn't help, so I drank water. Three eight-ounce glasses. I read the papers, watched TV—if you'd like I can name the shows."

"Sure," said Doresh.

"You're kidding."

"Anything but, Doc."

Jeremy rattled off the list.

"That's a lot of TV, Doc."

"Normally I'd be reading by candlelight," said Jeremy, "but I just finished the entire Great Books Compendium and Chaucer and Shakespeare, thought I'd give myself some downtime."

Doresh studied him. "You've got a sense of humor. I didn't see that before."

The situation didn't exactly warrant it, idiot.

The doctors' lot came into view, and Jeremy walked faster. Rain pebbled down on the roof of the breezeway, poured down the sides, like glycerine drapery.

Doresh said, "What's the name of the pizza place?"

Jeremy told him. "Who got killed?"

"Who said—"

"Spare me," said Jeremy. "I went through hell, and you didn't make it any easier. Now you're still bugging me instead of finding out who killed Jocelyn."

Doresh's eyes narrowed, and he moved in front of Jeremy, blocked Jeremy's progress. "Making people feel good isn't my job."

"Fine. So let's cut to the chase. You're here because something happened. Something similar enough to Jocelyn to want to take another look at me."

Doresh's eyes dropped to the ground. As if the truth disgraced him. As if crime was a personal failure.

He said, "Why not, you'll read about it in tomorrow's paper. Yeah, something very much like Ms. Banks happened." He drew the lapels of his raincoat tight across his chest but left the coat unbuttoned. "What happened was a woman, a prostitute, over in Iron Mount. A girl known to the department for a while, drugs, soliciting, the usual. In that sense, not like Ms. Banks, at all. But the wounds . . ."

Jeremy said, "Dear God."

Doresh moved out of his way.

Jeremy said, "Iron Mount. That's not far from The Shallows."

"Not far at all, Doc."

"A prostitute . . . you really think—"

"From time to time, I do think," said Doresh. He smiled at his own wit. "That's all, Doc, have a nice day."

"I left several messages for you, Detective. A photo your guys took from my house—"

"Yeah, yeah. Evidence."

"When will I get it back?"

"Hard to say. Maybe never." Doresh's shrug was so casual Jeremy fought not to hit him. "Better get going, Doc. Have my work cut out for me."

7

THAT NIGHT, DORESH SAT IN JEREMY'S DREAMS, A raincoated Buddha, and the taste of slightly off, greasy harbor shrimp bit his tongue. In the morning, he got up early and retrieved the newspaper. The headlines were soaked with economic woe and the felonies of politics, the *Clarion*'s histrionic journalists exulting about wars-to-be, injustice and indignity.

He found what he was looking for on page 18.

The woman's name was Tyrene Mazursky. Polish surname notwithstanding, she'd been black, forty-five, a drug-addicted streetwalker with the extensive police record Doresh had cited.

Also a mother of five.

Iron Mount was a scrofulous warren of misshapen streets and afterthought alleys as narrow as they'd been since the city's horse-and-carriage, slag-and-smelt origins. Jeremy had been there exactly once: a very long time ago, as an intern, doing a home visit on a kid everyone was sure was being abused.

Drunken mother, junkie father, the five-year-old boy barely in the first percentile of height and weight, speech and vocabulary testing out as that of a two-year-old. One happy family plus some unnamed addict pals, living in a railroad flat above an auto body shop, far from the waterfront but close enough to where the Kauwagaheel River cut inland from the lake and swamp stench permeated the rotting plaster walls.

Jeremy did his thing, wrote it up. So did a terrified social work intern, but it turned out that despite their character flaws and bad habits, the boy's parents were doing a pretty good job of tending for the kid, who had picked up a viral liver infection with ensuing bowel blockage that choked off his nutrients and retarded his growth.

Surgery and IV antibiotics worked wonders. Counseling for the parents proved a good deal less miraculous, and three weeks after the kid's last surgical follow-up, the family cut town.

Iron Mount. Due east from The Shallows, a place that made The Shallows look like horse country.

He put down the paper, forced coffee down his throat, and thought about Tyrene Mazursky, savaged.

The wounds.

Five orphans.

He wondered how a black woman ended up with a Polish name, felt an inexorable sadness at the mysteries of Tyrene Mazursky's life.

All the mysteries of Jocelyn he'd never unravel. The thought of her—the gone-ness. The day had barely broken, but he had.

When he walked to his car, the neighbor two doors down—the Romanian woman with the victimized eyes, the one who rarely left her own place

and couldn't see Jeremy's house for the hedges—
was standing by her front window watching.

Had Doresh been by, asking questions?

Mrs. Bekanescu was one of the few on the block
who owned and didn't rent. He waved at her, and
her curtains snapped shut.

His ability to unsettle someone this early felt per-
versely gratifying, and he drove faster than usual,
switched on bright music. When he got to his desk,
he threw off his coat, organized some papers, booted
up his computer, and spent the morning punching
buttons and rechecking data tables and construct-
ing pretty charts for his book. He gave a try at
the introduction but his mind impacted and the
words crumbled. He switched topics, began an outline for the chapter he'd have to write: *Time/Space
Disorientation Secondary to Pediatric Gnotobiotic
Isolation.*

The only analogues in the literature were studies
of scientists stranded in the Antarctic or some such
hellhole.

Jeremy's mind wandered from bottomless glacial
rifts to blue ice that could kill you if you kissed it, to
the hackneyed horror of falling endlessly, a million
ice violins scratching out a tundra symphony. A
hard, confident knock on his door shook him upright, and Arthur Chess stepped in, beaming.

8

THE PATHOLOGIST MADE HIMSELF COMFORTABLE IN an uncomfortable chair. "Have you given any more thought to the question I posed?"

"The origin of evil," said Jeremy.

Arthur turned one hand palm-side up. "Evil is a . . . weighty word. Theologically burdened. I believe we'd settled upon 'very bad behavior.' "

We. "No, I haven't thought about it. As I mentioned, there's a database—sparse but suggestive. If you're really interested."

"I am, Jeremy."

"I'll get you some references. But the conclusions might be uncomfortable."

"For whom?"

"An optimist," said Jeremy. "A humanist." He waited to see if Arthur would place himself in either category.

The pathologist smoothed his beard and said nothing. Jeremy's desk clock ticked the hour.

"The bottom line, Arthur, is that certain people seem to be born with a hard-wired propensity for impulsiveness. Of those, a few turn to violence. Males, mostly, so testosterone may be part of it. But there's more than hormones at work. The significant variable seems to be low arousability. Slower than normal resting heart rates. A cool nervous system."

"Preternatural calm," said Arthur, as if he'd heard it before.

"You know the research?"

Arthur shook his head. "However, what you're saying makes perfect sense. A stranger to fear is a stranger to conscience."

"That's one theory," said Jeremy. "Fear's a terrific teacher, and those who don't learn from it miss out on valuable social lessons. But there's another way to look at it: adrenaline addiction. A congenitally understimulated central nervous system leads to a need for progressively stronger thrills. The everyday term is 'excitement junkies.' "

"I've seen that in Army snipers," Arthur agreed. "Fellows who lived for the thrill, registering heartbeats so slow one thought one's stethoscope was malfunctioning. Had one fellow could sit for hours at a time, a veritable statue. Would you say, then, that military service is a form of sublimated criminality?"

Jeremy recalled Arthur's own military history. The old man had enjoyed the service. "Thrill-seeking by itself isn't the issue. Mountain climbers and sky divers are all hooked on the adrenaline high, but most of them don't commit crimes. It's the combination of recklessness and cruelty that leads to your very, very bad behavior. And that's where environment comes in: Take a child with the biological markers, expose him to abuse and neglect, and you're likely to create a . . . problem."

Arthur smiled again. "A monster? Is that what you were going to say?"

"Monsters," said Jeremy, "come in all forms." He stood. "I'll pull those references for you, send them over by tomorrow."

A rude gesture, but Arthur was unfazed. Plinking a vest button, he sprang to his feet with the vigor of a much younger man. Those same pale pink stains speckled the left cuff of his lab coat. Identical color, different stains. "One more question, if you don't mind?"

"What's that?"

"Abuse, neglect—your assumption that those factors are environmental. Could it be that what you term family dysfunction is inherited as well? Violent parents passing on their proclivities toward their children?"

"Back to the bad seed," said Jeremy.

"Another theologically loaded concept. And, as you said, discouraging. But are the data inconsistent with that notion?"

"The data are too muddy to prove anything, Arthur. They merely suggest."

"I see," said Arthur. "So you find it inconceivable that the totality of violence—or even the majority— is passed along in the nucleic acid."

"Sins of the fathers," said Jeremy. "Your jungle beetle injecting his parasitical spawn."

Nothing's accidental with you, is it, Dr. Chess?

Arthur chuckled and crossed to the door. "Well, this has been illuminating. Thank you for your patience, and anytime I can reciprocate, please feel free."

He left, and Jeremy remained standing. Wondering if the old man's parting words were simple courtesy, or did he really expect Jeremy to drop in with a question.

What would he ever want from a pathologist?

His mind camera-shuttered to Jocelyn's face. What lay below her face. Wounds he'd never seen but had imagined. A rending of flesh that haunted him with its terrible ambiguity.

Now, Tyrene Mazursky.

There was nothing in common between a middle-aged hooker and sweet Jocelyn *but* the wounds.

Enough in common to put Doresh back on his trail.

His heart hammered as he punished himself with imagined horror. Arthur would be at home with all that, would reduce it to cell biology and organ weight and chemical compounds.

Arthur would deal with the stuff of screaming nightmares the way he waxed eloquent about carcinomas and sarcomas every Tuesday morning: avuncular manner, easy smile—perpetual coolness—what was *his* resting pulse?

The questions he wanted to ask the old man stuck in his craw.

Are we talking about this because you know what I've been through? Is this just morbid curiosity, or do you have a point?

Why hadn't he spoken up?

What do you want from me?

9

WHEN HIS HEART SLOWED, JEREMY WENT ON THE wards and comforted his patients. He must have functioned adequately because eyes brightened, a few smiles broke, hands clutched his fingers, and one teenage girl flirted with him, harmlessly. When he was alone, charting, the imprint—the feel—of every single patient remained with him. As if he carried them around, a mama kangaroo.

The flesh of the afflicted felt no different than anyone else's. Not until the terminal stages. Dying patients reacted in different ways. Some were gripped with last-minute bravura, became garrulous, told inappropriate jokes. Some reminisced endlessly or offered noble blessings to the acolytes who ringed their beds. Others simply faded. But they had something in common—something Jeremy had yet to identify. A person working the wards long enough could tell when death was imminent.

Jeremy had never felt anything but a terrible fatigue when a patient left him.

He tried to imagine someone getting a thrill out of another's death. Simply considering that possibility made his shoulders sag.

Taking a break in the doctors' dining room for coffee, he spotted Angela Rios eating yogurt by herself, walked up to her, made small talk, and asked her to dinner that night.

Amazed at the calm voice that issued from his mouth. Feeling a smile curl around his lips, as if his mouth was being manipulated by a ventriloquist, as he made his *play*.

No good reason to ask her, other than her beauty, intelligence, charm, and the fact that she was obviously interested.

She said, "I'm sorry, I'm on call."

"Too bad," said Jeremy. Could he have misread her that badly?

As he turned to leave, she said, "I'm off tomorrow. If that's convenient for you."

"Let me check my calendar." Jeremy pantomimed page-flipping. The old self-deprecating wit. Angela laughed easily.

Lovely girl. If I was interested . . .

"Tomorrow, then," he said. "Meet you here?"

"If you don't mind," said Angela, "I could use some time to go home and freshen up. I'm off at seven, how about eightish?" She pulled out her resident's spiral notebook, scrawled, ripped out the page, and handed it to Jeremy.

West Broadhurst Drive, in Mercy Heights.

Probably one of the old clapboard colonials converted to flats. Jeremy's sad little bungalow was in the Lady Jane district, a short walk from Mercy Heights Boulevard.

"We're neighbors." He told her his address.

"Oh," she said. "I'm not home much, the schedule, you know." Her beeper went off. She smiled apologetically.

Jeremy said, "As if on cue."

"As if." She hung her stethoscope around her neck, gathered her resident's manual and her notebook, and stood.

"See you tomorrow," she said.

"Eightish."

"I'll be ready."

Her apartment was on the second floor of a gloomy-looking, three-story structure that shouted boardinghouse. Medicinal smells bittered the creaky hallway—perhaps other interns and residents lived here and brought samples home—the carpeting was tamped down, brown, and stale, and two bicycles were chained to the oft-painted railing.

Angela came to the door within seconds of Jeremy's ring. She'd tied back all that glorious, dark hair and fashioned a tight braid that trailed down her back. A soft white sweater caused Jeremy to notice her breasts. The sweater ended just above her waist and was bottomed by black, cinch-waist slacks and black high-heeled sandals. She wore pearl earrings and a tiny ruby on a filament-thin gold chain. Unobtrusive makeup.

The tight hair accentuated the olive oval of her face. Her brown eyes were alive with interest, her lips parted in a smile. She smelled great.

"Ready, as promised!" She shot out her hand and gave his a firm, hard shake.

Almost a military maneuver, and Jeremy suppressed a smile.

Perhaps she sensed his amusement, because she blushed. Eyed his topcoat. "Is it really cold?"

"Nippy."

"I'm a sunshine baby, always cold. Let me grab a wrap, and we're off."

He took her to a midpriced, family-run Italian place on the better side of Lady Jane. The gentrified side: storefronts converted to softly lit pubs and bookstores and florists and five-table restaurants. Vestiges of the old days were represented by the painted-over windows of vacuum cleaner repair shops, immigrant tailors, Chinese laundries, cut-rate pharmacies. The rain—the clammy, acid spatter that had hectored the city for four days running— had ceased and the air was sweet and the streetlights beamed as if in gratitude.

Jeremy rushed to open Angela's door—old habits; the academy had pounded etiquette into him. When she got out of the car, she took his arm.

The feel—the faint clawing—of feminine fingers on his sleeve . . .

The hostess was the chef's wife. She had bosoms you could rest a dictionary on and a commodious smile. She seated them in a rear booth, brought breadsticks and menus and a small dish of garlic-scented olives. Perfect dating fare.

This was, indeed, a date.

What then, genius?

Angela ordered casually, as if food wasn't the issue.

They talked easily.

For some reason—perhaps it was her eagerness, or the simplicity with which she conducted herself—Jeremy had guessed Angela to be a high achiever of working-class origins, possibly the first of her family to go to college.

He was wrong on all accounts. She'd grown up sunny and comfortable on the West Coast, and both of her parents were physicians—rheumatologist father, dermatologist mother, each a clinical professor at a first-rate med school. Her only sibling, a younger brother, was studying for a Ph.D. in particle physics.

"Scholarly bunch," he said.

"It wasn't really like that," she said. "No pressure, I mean. Actually I never wanted to be a doctor. My freshman major was dance."

"You've covered a bit of territory."

"A bit." Her face grew old for half a moment. As if to cover, she ate a garlic-olive. "What about you? Where are you from?"

Jeremy weighed his options. There was the short answer: the last city he'd lived in, the school from which he'd graduated, the artful digression to work-talk.

The long answer was: an only child, he'd been five years old when Mom and Dad were killed in a twenty-car, New Year's Eve auto pileup on a sleet-slicked turnpike. At the moment of fatal impact, he'd been sleeping at his maternal grandmother's house, dreaming of the board game Candy Land. He knew that because someone had told him, and he'd preserved it like a specimen. But the rest of the preorphan years were a greasy blur. Nana had failed soon after and been sent to a home, and he was raised by his father's mother, a bitterly altruistic woman who never recovered from the crushing responsibility. After her fade to senility, the boy, then eight, was taken in by a series of distant relatives, followed by a sequence of foster homes, none abusive or attentive. Then, the Basalt Preparatory Academy agreed to accept him as a charity case because members of its new board decided something *Socially Conscious Finally Needed to Be Done.*

His formative years—the period psychoanalysts so absurdly term "latency"—were filled with bunk beds, drills, a full menu of humiliation, uncertainty for dessert. Jeremy turned inward, bested the rich kids at the academic game despite the tutors that flocked to them like remora. He graduated third in his class, turned down the chance to go to West Point, entered college, took five years to earn his baccalaureate because of having to work minimum-wage night jobs. Another year tending bar and delivering groceries and tutoring dull, rich children helped him save up some money, after which he attended graduate school on full fellowship.

Earning his Ph.D. hadn't been tough. He'd written his dissertation in three weeks. Back then, writing had come easily.

Then: starving intern, postdoc fellow, the position at City Central. Seven years on the wards. Jocelyn.

What he said was: "I grew up in the Midwest—ah, here comes the food."

During dinner, one of them, Jeremy wasn't sure who, steered the conversation to hospital politics, and he and Angela talked shop. When they returned to the car, she took his arm. Back at her door, she looked into his eyes, rose on tiptoes, kissed his cheek hard, and retracted her head. "I had a great time."

Drawing the boundary: this far, no farther.

Fine with him, he had no stomach for passion.

"I did, too," he said. "Have a good night."

Angela flashed perfect, white teeth. Clacked her purse open, found her key, and gave a tiny wave and was on the other side of the door before either of them was pressed to say more.

Jeremy stood in the grubby hallway and waited until her footsteps faded before turning heel.

10

OVER THE NEXT THREE WEEKS, ANGELA AND Jeremy went out four times. Scheduling was a challenge: twice, Angela had to cancel because of patient emergencies and a surprise request by the chief of medicine for Jeremy to deliver a grand rounds on procedural anxiety caused him to offer apologies—he needed the evening to prepare.

"No problem," she said, and when Jeremy delivered his talk, she was sitting in the fifth row of the hospital auditorium. Afterward, she winked at him and squeezed his hand and hurried off to join the other residents on morning rounds.

The next night, they had their fifth date.

Basic, unimaginative stuff, their time together. No couples-bungee-jumping, no edgy concerts or performance art exhibits, no long rides out of the city, past the harbor and the western suburbs to the flat plains, where the moon was huge and you could find a quiet place to park and consider infinity. Jeremy knew the plains well. He'd spent most of his life in the Midwest, but sometimes it still shocked him.

Long ago—before Jocelyn, when he'd been simply lonely—he'd driven out to the plains often, speeding alone on a soporific highway, wondering how many flat miles you'd have to travel before the earth shrugged itself a hillock.

Their relationship grew in mundane soil: a quintet of quiet dinners at five separate, quiet, serviceable restaurants: two Italian, one Spanish, a quasi-French place that termed itself "Continental." After Angela let loose her affection for Hunan cuisine, Jeremy found a blue-lit Chinese café that had gotten good reviews in the *Clarion*. More money than he was used to spending, but the smile on her face made it worth it.

Decent food, earnest conversation, a brushing of fingertips now and then, very little in the way of flirtation or sexual suggestion.

So different from the way it had been with Jocelyn. Jeremy knew comparisons were destructive, but he didn't care. Comparison was what came naturally, and he wasn't even sure he wanted a clear shot at something new.

Jocelyn had been sex and perfume, the perfume of sex. The serpentine duet of tongues, moist panties on their first date, hips lifted, a musky delta the gift proffered.

His first date with Jocelyn had ended before dessert. The frantic drive to her place, ripping each other's clothes off. Someone so petite, but so strong. Her small, hard body had slammed against Jeremy's with a force that thrilled him and left his bones bruised.

Jocelyn had always left him breathless.

Angela was polite.

On the second date, she said, "I hope this doesn't sound rude, but can I ask how old you are?"

"Thirty-two."

"You look a lot younger."

Not flattery, the truth, and offered as such.

Jeremy had looked twelve at sixteen, didn't need to shave until he entered college. He'd hated the reticence of his hormones, all those girls he desired regarding him a kid.

By his thirties, he'd ended up with one of those smooth, angular faces that resists aging. His hair was fine and straight, an unremarkable light brown, and no bald spots or gray strands had intruded. He wore it parted on the right, and unless he used some kind of hair product, it flopped over his forehead. He believed his complexion to be sallow, but women had told him he had great skin. One, a poet, had taken to calling him "Byron," and insisted that his unremarkable brown eyes were well beyond intense.

He was medium-sized, medium weight, not muscular, wore 10D shoes and a 40 regular suit.

To his mind, about as average as you could be.

Angela said, "I mean it. You look really young. I figured you had to be about that because you told me you've been on staff at Central seven years. But you could easily pass for my age, or even younger."

"Which is?"

"Guess."

"Two years post M.D. means twenty-eight."

"Twenty-seven. I skipped third grade."

Same age as Jocelyn. He said, "I'm not surprised."

Angela said, "I was just a precocious brat," and began talking about the rigors of residency.

Jeremy listened. You never knew when professional training would come in handy.

The good-bye pattern begun on the first date continued: walking Angela to her door, the silence, the smile, the outstretched hand.

Then: a hard, defensive peck on the cheek and her claim, a bit too emphatic, of having had a wonderful time.

Jeremy began wondering what she wanted.

After the fifth date, both of them filled with Chinese food, she invited him into her compulsively neat but shabbily turned-out apartment, showed him to a secondhand sofa that still smelled of disinfectant, poured wine for both of them, excused herself, and slipped into the bathroom.

Jeremy looked around. Angela had a good eye. Each component was cheap, scarred, and conspicuously temporary. A sorry houseplant struggled for life on a chipped windowsill. Yet the composite was pleasing.

Still, he wondered: two physician parents. Surely, she could have afforded better.

She emerged from the bathroom wearing a long, green robe—silk or something like it—sat next to him, drank wine, sidled closer, dimmed the lights. They began kissing deeply. Moments later, her robe fell open, and Jeremy was inside her.

Being there brought him no tremor of triumph. On the contrary, he felt a cold wave of letdown course through him: She wasn't moving much, didn't seem *there*. He pumped away, hard, steady, detached, thinking irreverent thoughts.

Maybe it's the Chinese food.

Maybe after five dates she feels obligated . . .

Jocelyn had been . . .

Opening his eyes, he looked down at her face. What he could make out in the ashy darkness was serene. Lying back, accepting him passively, as he thrust himself into her. Her eyes were clamped shut. Would they flutter open, sense his *objectivity*?

He decided, *To hell with it, pleasure myself, and forget about her.* The next time he looked down her face had changed. As if an internal switch had been flicked. Or she'd decided to come alive. Was she just one of those women who needed time— who the hell ever really knew about women? Now, she flipped her head to the side, grimaced, began grinding back at him. Gripped him with heels and hands and bit his ear and quickened her breathing to a hoarse pant as she tightened her pelvic vise and held him fast.

Jeremy's objective, disinterested hard-on became something else completely as she cupped his balls and kissed him and cried out.

A shout—a bellow of pleasure—escaped from his mouth, and he collapsed, they both did, lying on the stinking couch, entwined.

Later, when thoughts of Jocelyn crept into his head, he shooed them away.

He drove home tingling below the waist. It was only later, hours later, lying fetally in his own bed, alone, aware of every detail in the room, that he allowed the twinges of guilt to temper his pleasure.

11

THE DAY AFTER MAKING LOVE TO ANGELA, JEREMY paged her and drew her away from the wards and took her to his office. After locking the door, he reached under her skirt and placed her hand upon him. She whimpered, and said, "Really?" He rolled down her panty hose and her panties in one smooth swoop, and they connected standing against the door, intermittently aware of passing footsteps out in the corridor.

As she clung to him, she said, "This is terrible."

"Should I stop?"

"Stop and I'll kill you."

They finished on the cold, linoleum floor. Angela dusted off her white coat and straightened herself, fluffed her hair and kissed him, and said, "I've got patients." Her face grew sad. "Guess what, I'm on call for the next twenty-four."

"Poor thing," said Jeremy, stroking her hair.

"Will you miss me?"

"Sure."

She placed her hand on her skirt, directly above the soft spot where he'd just filled her. "Will you do this to me again when I'm off call?"

"*To you?*"

She grinned. "Men do it to women, that's what it is."

Jeremy said, "Again, as in here?"

"Here, anywhere. God, I needed that."

"Put that way," said Jeremy, twining her hair around his fingers, "you leave me no choice. Easing the schedule and all that."

She laughed, touched his face. Was off.

Alone, Jeremy tried to work on his sensory deprivation book chapter but got little done. He went over to the doctors' dining room for coffee. White coats got it for free, one of the few perks left, and he took advantage of it often. He knew he was swallowing way too much caffeine, but why not? What was there to be slow about?

The room was sparsely occupied, just a few attendings taking time off between patients.

And one whose patients didn't talk back. Arthur Chess sat alone, at a corner table, with a cup of tea and an unfurled newspaper.

Jeremy's pathway to the coffee urn took him right into Arthur's sights, but the pathologist gave no sign of recognition. Ignoring Jeremy—if he saw Jeremy at all.

Jeremy found a table at the opposite end of the dining room, where he drank and found himself studying Arthur.

Now he saw why Arthur hadn't noticed him. The old man was busy observing.

The object of his fascination was a group of three physicians hunched over pie and coffee, two tables over. A trio of men, engaged in what looked to be spirited academic discussion.

Jeremy recognized one of them, a cardiologist named Mandel. A good man, if a bit distracted. He'd thrown a few consults Jeremy's way, some ill-conceived, all well-intentioned. His back was to Jeremy, and he hunched forward, paying close attention.

The other two men wore surgical greens. One was tan, maybe Latino, with dark, well-groomed hair and a barbered black mustache. The other was white. Literally. His long, drawn face bore an indoor pallor Jeremy had only seen in long-term patients. Clipped yellowish hair topped a domed cranium. His nose was a beak, and his cheeks were sunken.

He was doing all the talking, moving his lips and gesturing with spidery hands that served a surgeon well. Mandel remained rapt. The dark-mustached man's attention seemed to flag, as if he was put-upon, being there.

The pale man pulled a pen out of his pocket, drew something on a napkin, and gesticulated some more with those long-fingered hands. Mandel nodded. The pale man made a sawing motion and smiled. Mandel said something, and the yellow-haired surgeon sketched some more. Words were exchanged all around. Arthur kept staring.

Obviously some sort of technical demonstration. Why would Arthur, a delver into death, a wielder of bone saws and carpentry tools, find it fascinating? The old curiosity kicking in?

That was probably it. Arthur was mentally voracious, a true intellectual. Jeremy, who read magazines in his spare time and rarely opened the classic psychology texts he collected, felt shallow by comparison.

He wondered why the pathologist didn't get up and join the group. An intrusion to be sure, but Arthur was an important man at Central, and his stature would have guaranteed a welcome.

Then Arthur's interest seemed to wane and he turned a page of his newspaper, and Jeremy wondered if he'd been wrong. Perhaps Arthur wasn't noticing the three men any more than he'd noticed Jeremy. Maybe the old man was caught up in some internal rapture—butterflies, predatory beetles, the minutiae of body fluids, whatever—and the cant of his big, bald head toward the discussion had been a coincidence of angulation.

Now, the old man's eyes were glued to the paper. All the better. Jeremy could drink his coffee in peace, return to his office unmolested, put his feet up on his desk, and recall the wonders of making love to Angela.

He allowed himself to wonder what the next time would be like.

Men do it to women.

The pale man stopped waving his pen. Seemed to draw himself away from his demonstration. Stared across the room at Jeremy.

Intense stare.

Or perhaps, Jeremy had imagined it because now the man was back to his lecture.

Arthur stood, folded his paper, fixed the tilt of his bow tie. Headed straight for Jeremy's table. Big smile on the pink face. "How fortuitous," he said. "I was just about to call you."

12

He took a seat at Jeremy's table, unbuttoned his white coat, stuffed the paper in his pocket. His shirt was snowy-white piqué, heavily starched, with a high, stiff collar. The bow tie of the day was mint green, a luxuriant silk specked with tiny gold *fleur-de-lis*.

"I wondered," he said, "and please don't think me forward—I wondered if you'd care to join me for supper this Friday evening. There are some people, interesting people, whom I'd like you to meet. Who, I'm allowing myself to presume, you might enjoy meeting."

"Friends of yours?"

"A group . . . so to speak." The old man's speech, usually fluid, had grown choppy. Arthur Chess, embarrassed?

Perhaps to cover, he smiled. "We meet from time to time to discuss matters of mutual interest."

"Medical matters?" said Jeremy. Then he remembered Arthur's persistent curiosity about "very bad behavior." Had all that been a prelude to this?

"A wide range of issues," said Arthur. "We aim

for erudition, but nothing ponderous, Jeremy. The company's amiable, the food is well prepared—quite tasty, really—and we pour some fine spirits. We sup late. Though I don't imagine that will be a problem for you."

How could Arthur know of his insomnia? "Why's that?"

"You're an energetic young man." One of the pathologist's big hands slapped the table. "So. Are we set?"

Jeremy said, "Sorry, Friday's tough." He didn't have to lie. Angela's on-call ended Thursday night. No date had been set for Friday, but there was no reason for her to turn him down.

"I see. Well, another time, then." Arthur got to his feet. "No harm trying. I didn't mean to put you on the spot. If you change your mind, feel free to let me know." He placed a palm on Jeremy's shoulder. Weighty; Jeremy became aware of the pathologist's bulk and strength.

"Will do. Thanks for thinking of me, Arthur."

"I thought *precisely* of you." Arthur's hand remained on Jeremy's shoulder. Jeremy whiffed bay rum and strong tea and something acrid, possibly formaldehyde.

"I'm flattered," said Jeremy.

Arthur said, "Do consider this: During times of abject disorder, a good, late-night supper can be most fortifying."

"Disorder?" said Jeremy.

But the old man had already turned and left.

*   *   *

Back in his office, he failed to conjure anything to do with Angela, past or future.

The word caromed around his head: *Disorder*.

Not mine; the city's. The world's.

Mine.

The old bastard was right. What better description of a time when women were stalked and hunted and brought down like prey simply because they were women. Where men with low resting heart rates chose their victims with all the gravitas of grocery shoppers squeezing melons.

Men who craved blood gas and terror-struck eyes, the confiscation of body juice, the ultimate power.

Monster-men who *needed* all that to get their *own* blood rushing.

Disorder was the perfect description of a world where Jocelyn's death enlisted her in the same sorority as Tyrene Mazursky.

He hadn't been able to conjure Angela, but now Jocelyn's face flew into his head. Her laughter, even at his lamest jokes, the way she cared for her hopeless patients. Her pixie face when it flushed and compressed in the throes of pleasure.

When it had been really good for her, the flush that rose from her pelvis to her chin.

Then, another kind of face. Also compressed. No pleasure.

Nausea coiled around Jeremy's gut. He felt the urge to vomit, grabbed his wastebasket, and plunged his face into it. All that came were dry heaves. He sat low, dangling the basket, his head between his hands, sweating, panting.

Monster-men, creating human dross. Then other men—coarse civil servants like Hoker and Doresh—fashioned careers from the waste.

He managed to expunge a plug of mucus from his throat and throp it into the trash. Removing the plastic bag from the basket, he took it to the men's room, tossed it, returned to his office, locked the door, and thumbed through his address book.

He found the number and punched it.

Detective Doresh answered, "Homicide," and Jeremy said, "I was wondering why a black woman would have a name like Mazursky."

"Who's—Dr. Carrier? What's going on?"

"It just struck me as odd," said Jeremy. *It struck me as profoundly disordered.* "Then I thought: Maybe she used an alias. Because prostitutes do that. I've seen it—we treat them here at the hospital, they come in for their STDs—sexually transmitted diseases—and their nonspecific urinary tract infections, malnutrition, dental problems, hepatitis C. One woman will have five different charts. We don't expect much in the way of reimbursement, but we do try to bill the state because the administrators order us to. But with prostitutes it's mostly futile, because of how rapidly they switch names. They do it to fool the courts—to conceal evidence of prior arrests. So maybe that's what she did. Tyrene Mazursky. Maybe there's more to her than one identity."

"An alias," said Doresh, enunciating slowly. "You don't think we thought of that."

"I—I'm sure you did. It just occurred to me."

"Anything else occur to you, Doc?"

"Just that."

Silence. "Anything else you want to tell me, Doc?"

"No, that's it."

"Because I'm listening," said the detective.

"Sorry if I bothered you," said Jeremy.

"Tyrene Mazursky," said Doresh. "It's funny you should mention her because I just got back her final autopsy report and have it here in front of me. Not pretty, Doc. *Another* extremely not-pretty. Kind of a Humpty-Dumpty situation."

The detective let the message sink in. No way to put her back together again . . . *another* . . . the same had happened to Jocelyn.

It was the closest, since the murder, that he'd come to being informed.

He nearly screamed out loud. Took a breath, said, "That's horrible."

"Tyrene Mazursky," said Doresh. "Turns out, she was married to a Polish guy, years ago. Commercial fisherman, one of those guys who goes out on the lakes and seines and hauls in whatever comes up. Also, he was part of those crews that go looking for submerged logs—hundred-year-old logs that fell off the barges. Fancy maple wood, they use 'em for violins. Anyway, this guy was a big drunk. He died in a capsize a few winters ago, left her with nothing. Even before that, she was whoring a little, what with him being gone all the time, drinking away his wages. After he died, she got serious. About her profession, that is."

Hearing Tyrene Mazursky's life reduced like that froze Jeremy's heart and his mouth. His hands began to tremble.

He said, "Poor woman."

"Sad story," Doresh agreed. "Guess we both know about that, huh? Have a nice day, Doc."

Jeremy placed the phone in its cradle. Imagined Tyrene Mazursky working the docks. Waiting for her ship to come in.

Jocelyn. Working the wards, waiting to see Jeremy that night.

Men do it to women. That's what it is.

He sat there bathed in sweat, sour-mouthed, watching as evening darkened the air shaft outside his window.

Finally, he picked up the phone again and punched an extension.

"Chess," boomed a familiar voice.

"It's me, Arthur. Turns out Friday's fine."

13

LATE THURSDAY, JEREMY FOUND A HANDWRITTEN message in his box, forward-slanted script, black ink on substantial blue rag paper, the liquid elegance of a fountain pen.

> *Dr. C:*
>
> *Friday, 9:30 P.M. I'll call with details.*
>
> *AC*

On Friday, serious rain arrived, frigid, unannounced, relentless as a military assault. Overtaxed storm drains backed up, and some regions of the city were assailed by filth. Auto collisions played a drumbeat on tight urban skin. The air smelled like mercurochrome. The docks at the harbor grew slick with accumulated slaps of oily lake water, boats rocked and sank, and unshaven men in knit caps and waders retired to dark bars to drink themselves senseless.

Jeremy's car fishtailed all the way to the hospital. Angela phoned him at shift's end, sounded exhausted.

"Rough day?"

"A bit rougher than usual," she said. "But I'll try to be sociable. If I fall asleep, you can prop me up."

"I'm sorry," Jeremy told her. "Something came up. An evening with Dr. Chess."

"Dr. Chess? Well, then go, of course. He's brilliant. What's the topic?"

Jeremy had hoped for disappointment. "Something erudite. He wasn't clear about the details."

"Have fun."

"I'll give it a shot."

"Why don't you call me when it's over?"

"It could be late," said Jeremy. "Dinner doesn't begin until half past nine."

"I see . . . how about Saturday, then? I'm not back on until Sunday morning."

"Okay," said Jeremy. "I'll call you."

"Great."

Jeremy saw his patients and filled the rest of the day with futile attempts at writing. Two hours were wasted in the hospital library, running searches of behavioral and medical databases, as he looked for backup articles he knew didn't exist. Rationalizing his folly by telling himself that scientific research moved at a quirky pace, you could wake up one day and find out everything you'd believed in was wrong. But the facts hadn't altered in six months: If he wanted to produce a book—even a chapter—he'd have to go it alone.

When he returned to his office it was 8:40 P.M., and his box was stuffed with mail. He sifted through it, found a handwritten note in the middle of the stack: the same black cursive on blue paper.

Dr. C:

It's best if I drive tonight.

A.C.

He phoned Arthur's office, got no answer, tramped over to the main building and down to the basement, where the path lab was housed, found the entire department locked up, halls dim and silent, but for the mechanical whine of arthritic elevators.

A few doors down, the morgue was closed as well. Arthur had left. Had the old man forgotten?

Jeremy climbed the stairs to the ground floor, entered the cafeteria, and poured the day's eighth free cup of coffee. He sat, drinking slowly, in the company of worried families, sleepy interns, jaded orderlies.

When he returned to his office, Arthur was waiting outside his door, dressed in a black, hooded slicker so long it nearly reached galosh-encased shoes. Puddles spread beneath rubber soles. The slicker was beaded with rain, and Arthur's nose was moist. The old man had left the hospital and returned.

The hood covered Arthur's face from eyebrow to lower lip. A few white beard hairs straggled above the latex seam, but the end result was near-total concealment.

How fitting for a man of his profession, thought Jeremy. *The Grim Reaper.*

"Cheers," Arthur said. "We've got ourselves a torrential situation. I do hope you've come protected."

Jeremy collected his briefcase and his trench coat. Arthur regarded the wrinkled, khaki garment with what might have passed for parental concern.

"Hmm," he said.

"It'll do," said Jeremy.

"I suppose it will have to. You don't object to my driving, do you? Under the best of circumstances our destination's a bit out of the way. Tonight . . ." Arthur shrugged, the plastic hood rattled, rain sprayed.

The Reaper goes fishing, thought Jeremy.

Then: *What would he use for bait?*

The interior of Arthur's Lincoln was warm and sweet-smelling, upholstered in a dove gray felt that Jeremy had only seen in much older cars. The engine started up with a purr, and Arthur backed out smoothly. Once they were out of the lot, Arthur sat up straight, big hands resting lightly on the wheel, eyes shifting from windshield to rearview, glancing at both side mirrors, then back on the road.

Alert, but that gave Jeremy meager comfort. The storm had reduced visibility to a few yards. As far as he could tell, Arthur was driving blind.

The old man aimed the Lincoln downtown but turned left just short of the high, distant twinkles that meant skyscrapers. Jeremy tried to follow Arthur's route but quickly lost it.

East, north, east again. Then a series of brief turns that addled Jeremy completely.

Arthur hummed as he drove.

When taillights flickered up ahead, the old man seemed to use them as navigational aids. When darkness dominated, and the windshield was a matte black rectangle, he seemed equally at ease.

Raindrops pelted the Lincoln's roof, a frantic steel drum concert. Arthur seemed unmindful, kept humming. Relaxed—more than that, *enjoying* the impossible conditions. As if the Lincoln was set on a track and the drive was no more daunting than a bumper-car circuit.

Jeremy looked around. From what he could tell in the darkness, the Lincoln was spotless. Nothing on the backseat. Before they'd set out, Arthur had unlocked the trunk, revealing freshly vacuumed gray carpeting, an emergency kit, and two umbrellas bracketed to the firewall. He'd deposited Jeremy's briefcase next to the kit, closed the trunk gingerly.

Hum, hum, hum.

Jeremy felt himself nodding off. When he jolted awake, he checked his watch. He'd slept for just over a quarter hour.

"Good evening," said Arthur, jovially.

The rain was coming harder. Jeremy said, "What part of town are we in?"

"Seagate."

"The docks?"

"My favorite part of town," said Arthur. "The vitality, the sensory stimulation. The working people."

"The working people."

"The spine of any civilization." A moment later: "I come from a long line of working people—mostly farmers. Where did you grow up, Jeremy?"

"The Midwest. Not this city but not far." Jeremy named the town.

"A mercantile community," said Arthur. "Any farming in your background?"

"Not for generations," said Jeremy.

"A farm can be an educational place. One learns about cycles. Life, death, everything that falls in between. And, of course, the transitory nature of it all—one of my fondest memories is helping to birth a calf. A rather sanguinary process. I was seven and terrified. Petrified of being swept away in some great flood of bovine issue. My father insisted."

"Did that inspire you to become a doctor?"

"Oh, no," said Arthur. "If anything, quite the opposite."

"How so?"

Arthur half turned, smiling. "The cow did it all by herself, son. I was made to feel quite redundant."

"But you became a physician anyway."

Arthur nodded. "Just a few more blocks."

14

SMELLS OF FISH, FUEL, RUST, AND CREOSOTE TOLD Jeremy the docks weren't far. But no water in sight, just rows of stout windowless buildings, stripped of architectural fancy.

Arthur Chess had driven to an oppressively narrow street lined with what appeared to be warehouses. The rain turned the pavement to gelatin; the Lincoln's headlights were pathetic amber smears that died before they hit the asphalt. No stars, no moon, nothing to use as a navigational tool; the force of the storm induced myopia.

The Lincoln turned onto another unlit strip and reduced its speed. Jeremy saw no blocks, no sidewalks, just one plain-faced building after another.

A sanguinary process.

Predatory bugs. What did he really know about the old man? What had he gotten himself into?

Arthur continued a while longer, glided to a gentle stop, and brought the Lincoln to a rest in front of an unmarked, two-story cube. All Jeremy could make out were slab walls and a narrow door topped by a roll-out awning. Under the awning a bulb in a frosted glass case cast a fan of light. The illumina-

tion was of a hue Jeremy had never seen before—
pale blue, purple-tinged, clinical.

The moment Arthur switched off the engine, the
door opened, and a small man stepped under the
awning. The blue light reached his waistline; below
that, he was dark, nearly invisible. The illusion was
that of truncation.

The half man's arm extended, an umbrella
snapped open, and he hurried to the rear of the Lincoln. Arthur pushed a button, the trunk popped,
and when the small man circled back to the driver's
door he held a pair of umbrellas.

He held the door open for Arthur, stood on tiptoes to shield the much taller pathologist, and got
wet doing so. After handing Arthur an umbrella, he
came around and opened Jeremy's door.

Up close Jeremy saw that the man was closer to
Arthur's age than his own, and no taller than five-
five. Thin dark hair, parted and slicked, topped a
round, puckered capuchin face of a type seen on
some types of dwarfs. Bright black eyes picked up
light from somewhere and sparked back at Jeremy.

Under the eyes, a lipless smile.

The man wore a dark suit, white shirt, dark tie.
Once again, he stepped out into the downpour so
that Jeremy could benefit from his umbrella. Jeremy
moved closer, wanting to share, but the little man
stayed out of reach as they ran for the door.

When Jeremy stepped into the pale blue light, his
eyes were assaulted by pupil-popping fluorescence.

A tall figure filled the doorway. Arthur was already inside.

The monkey-faced little man waited until he'd

passed. Soaked, but still smiling. The three of them stood in a small, white anteroom backed by a white door. The ceiling was acoustical tile. The bright light spewed from an industrial fixture that resembled an elongated waffle. No furniture, no odors, no chill. But for specks, splotches, and pools of gritty water dispersed on the black linoleum floor, a thoroughly inorganic place.

"Laurent," said Arthur. "Thank you for providing shelter."

"Of course, Doctor." The little man took both umbrellas and placed them in a corner. He took Arthur's coat, then turned to Jeremy.

"This is Dr. Carrier, Laurent."

"Pleased to meet you, Doctor." Laurent extended his hand, and Jeremy shook what felt like a knob of knurled oak.

"The others are here," Laurent told Arthur. His suit, like Arthur's, was beautifully cut but of another era. Blue-black gabardine, over a white-on-white shirt. The shirt's collar was fastened by a gold pin. His tie was true black satin. Tiny, narrow feet were encased in cap-tipped black bluchers so highly polished the rainwater beaded on the leather and rolled to the floor.

"Lovely," said Arthur.

"Everything looks wonderful, sir." Laurent turned back to Jeremy. His cheeks were flushed. "You're a lucky young man."

Arthur pushed open the white door and held it as Laurent scooted forward. The panel closed behind

Jeremy with a swoosh, and his eyes adjusted, yet again. Dimmer light. Soft, amber, caressing light.

Before him was a long hallway paneled in a golden, bird's-eyed wood. Linenfold paneling, hand-carved, was topped by notched edging. Beneath his feet was carpeting of a deeper gold, plush as the seats of Arthur's Lincoln. The ceiling was high, domed plaster, veneered with pale gold leaf.

Jeremy thought: *A bird in a gilded cage.*

Laurent led them up the muffled corridor. The air was warm, sweet with rosewater. The passageway terminated at massive double doors. Carved into the capstone were three letters in flowery script.

CCC

The year three hundred?

Something bygone and Soviet—was Arthur an unregenerate communist?

The thought amused Jeremy, but before he could speculate further, Laurent had thrown both doors open. He and Arthur flanked the doorway. Arthur's long arm swooped theatrically. "After you, my friend."

Jeremy stared out at a beautiful space. Four faces stared back at him.

A quartet of smiles.

A different silence—the sudden, percussive hush of conversation brought to a sharp halt. His nose filled with the aroma of roasted meat. His eyes accommodated to yet another quality of light: scores of chandelier bulbs dimmed low. Monumental chandelier, a riot of crystal swags and pendants and orbs.

The fleshy smell was delicious.

Jeremy stepped inside.

The room was over twenty feet high, wide as a chateau ballroom, long as a yacht. Like the corridor, the walls were wood—burled walnut the color of hot cocoa, incandesced by layers of polish, sectioned into octagonal panels and embroidered with boiserie. Where the massive chandelier wasn't crystal it was sterling silver. The ceiling plaster was vaulted and embellished by swirls and medallions. A dozen paintings—pastoral scenes—were suspended from wires hooked over stout crown moldings.

Twin swinging doors backed the room, and Laurent disappeared through one of them. Between the doors, a baronial sideboard fitted with brass mounts hosted a centerpiece teeming with white orchids.

Under the chandelier was a mirror-polished, Chippendale mahogany dining table trimmed in vanilla satinwood. Long enough to accommodate twenty, but set for six.

Half a dozen mirrored place settings. One chair on each side of the table was empty.

Arthur motioned Jeremy to the left and took the facing chair on the right. "My friends, our guest, Dr. Carrier."

A quartet of polite mumblings.

Three men, one woman. One of the men was black. He, like the other males, was dressed in a good suit and an eloquent necktie. The woman wore a white knit dress and a string of spectacular, purplish black pearls the size of concord grapes.

All four were elderly. By his very presence, Jeremy was lowering the median age significantly.

Where's the children's table?

He tried to take in as many details as possible without seeming rude. The paintings appeared French. All were housed in intricately carved frames and biased toward the saccharine: lush forests, honeyed sunlight, gamboling fauns, tender-breasted, vacant-eyed women captured in stunned repose.

Extra chairs, upholstered in raspberry silk, were positioned along the walls, as were a quartet of smaller sideboards. White marble columns supported exquisitely painted Chinese vases. Decorative tables expertly situated were festooned with marquetry; a glass étagère held jade carvings. Jeremy knew something about antiques; his long-suffering paternal grandmother spent much of her pension on a few quality Georgian pieces. These looked better than anything Gram had collected. What had happened to Gram's pieces . . . ?

No one spoke. The old people kept smiling at him. He half expected a pat on the head. Smiling back, he continued to take in details. A bower of three dozen red roses adorned the table. The mirrored place settings were glass hectagons, bordered in platinum. Each hosted pure white bone china of a simple, graceful design, an assortment of heavy, sterling utensils, ruby-colored linen napkins slipped into gilded rings, cut-crystal glasses for water, red and white wines, and much taller, long-stemmed repoussé silver goblets with glass insets.

Six settings, five goblets.

To the right of Jeremy's plate was a simple champagne flute—clunky, cheap, it could have come from a discount chain.

Membership had its privileges . . .

Arthur had begun to speak, was gesticulating for emphasis. ". . . indeed nice to infuse some new blood into our grayed gathering."

Appreciative chuckles.

"Jeremy, let me introduce this band of miscreants." Arthur indicated the farthest of the two people sitting on Jeremy's side of the table. A white-bearded man with eyes so blue that even at a distance they sparked like gas jets. "Professor Norbert Levy." Arthur named a prominent Eastern university.

Levy was ruddy, heavy in the jowls, with a full head of unruly, wavy hair. He wore a wide-lapeled, charcoal tweed suit, a tattersall button-down shirt, a butterscotch cravat tied in a beefy Windsor knot.

"Professor," said Jeremy.

Levy saluted and grinned. "Professor emeritus. In plain talk, I've been put out to pasture."

Arthur said, "Norbert built their engineering department from scratch."

"More like I scratched a few backs," said Levy.

The woman sitting between the engineer and Jeremy placed a hand on her breast. The black pearls clinked. "A sudden paradigm shift to modesty, Norbert? I don't know if my heart can take the shock."

"Anything to keep you awake, Tina," said Norbert Levy.

Arthur said, "Her eminence, Judge Tina Balleron, formerly of the superior court."

"And now *of* the golf course," said the woman in a smoky voice. She had the paper-bag complexion and dangerously freckled hands to back up the assertion of eighteen holes a day, was lean and strong-boned, with short wavy hair dyed champagne blond. She wore no jewelry other than the pearls, but they were enough. She'd probably been a stunner a few decades ago. Even now, sagging, wattled skin failed to obscure the determined line of her jaw. She murmured rather than spoke, and Jeremy found that surprisingly seductive. Her eyes were clear, dark, amused.

"Superior court," said Professor Emeritus Norbert Levy. "The question is, superior to what? Is there an inferior court, dear?"

Judge Tina Balleron made a low, throaty sound. "Given the quality of attorneys nowadays, I'd say there are plenty."

Arthur shifted his glance to his side of the table, eyed the man farthest down. "Edgar Marquis."

No professional designation; as if the name said it all.

Marquis appeared to be the oldest of the group— well into his eighties. Shrunken and hairless with blue-veined, papery skin, he seemed nearly devoured by his clothing. His face sat low on his shoulders, pitched forward, as if deprived of the support provided by a neck. His upper lip protruded like that of a turtle's beak. The suit was a black silk shadow stripe. Satin-covered buttons trimmed the sleeves. Jeremy had only seen those on tuxedos.

Marquis's shirt was pearl gray, his skinny tie the cheerful red of oxygenated blood. An old dandy, Edgar Marquis.

He also appeared to be asleep, and Jeremy began to glance away. Then Marquis crooked a crescent of skin where his eyebrows should've been and winked.

"Edgar," said Tina Balleron, "was a rare example of coherence and judgment at the aptly named Foggy Bottom."

"The State Department," said Arthur, as if explaining to a schoolchild.

Everyone smiled again, including Marquis. Not amusement—*let's-get-comfortable* smiles. All of them working at amiable.

They're treating me, thought Jeremy, *with the edgy reverence reserved for a bright but unpredictable offspring.*

As if I'm some kind of prize.

Edgar Marquis shifted in his chair. "Dr. Carrier," he said in a shockingly resonant voice, "I'm no longer bound to be diplomatic, so forgive me if I occasionally lapse into reality."

"As long as it's occasional," said Jeremy, aiming for banter. Wanting Marquis—wanting all of them—to feel at ease.

Marquis said, "Definitely, sir. Anything more than occasional reality would be oppressive."

"Words to live by," said Tina Balleron, tapping her silver goblet with long, curving nails.

The man next to her—the black man—said, "The occasional brush with reality would be a step upward for Mr. Average Citizen." He faced Jeremy:

"Harry Maynard. Obviously, I'm slated for last. Back of the table, too. *Hmmph*. Apparently, some things never change."

"Tsk, tsk," said Norbert Levy, beard splitting in a grin.

Edgar Marquis said, "A matter of social import has intruded upon our little conclave. Shall we establish a committee of inquiry?"

"What else?" said Harry Maynard. "I appoint myself de facto chairman. You're all guilty as charged. Feel thoroughly chastened."

"Guilty of what?" said Levy.

"Take your pick."

Edgar Marquis said, "All in favor, say aye."

Laughter, all around.

"There you go," said Judge Balleron. "Participatory democracy at its finest. Now, behave yourself, Harry, and we'll get to you in good time."

Maynard wagged a finger. "Life's too short for good behavior." He turned back to Jeremy, "Your training will do you well, here. Pleased to meet you, kid."

Large and bulky in a navy suit, baby blue shirt and teal blue tie, he was probably the youngest—midsixties or so. His complexion was a couple of shades lighter than the walnut paneling. Iron-filing hair was cropped short, and his toothbrush mustache was precisely as wide as his mouth.

Arthur said, "Last and never least is the inestimable Harrison Maynard. He lives in a world of his own."

Tina Balleron said, "Harry writes books."

"Used to," said Maynard. To Jeremy: "Trashy

stuff. Pseudononymous trashy stuff. Great fun. I've mined the mother lode of estrogen."

Tina Balleron said, "Harrison is a past practitioner of what used to be termed The Romance Novel. Countless women know him as Amanda Fontaine or Chatelaine DuMont or Barbara Kingsman or some other such vanillish alias. He's a master of the crushed bodice. God only knows how you did your research, Harry."

"Looking and listening," said Maynard.

"So you say," said the judge. "I think you've been a fly on too many walls."

Harrison Maynard smiled. "One does what one needs to do." His eyes shifted to the rear of the dining room. The right door had swung open, and Laurent emerged pushing a cart on wheels. The monkey-faced man had changed to a starched white serving jacket. On the cart were six silver domes. Behind him marched a woman his size and age, wearing a black shirtwaist dress and toting a magnum of wine. Her dark hair was drawn back in a bun. Her skin was the color of clotted cream, and her eyes were toasted almonds—tilted by the faintest trace of epicanthus.

Eurasian, Jeremy decided. As she drew near, their eyes met across the table. She smiled shyly and stopped at Edgar Marquis's seat.

"At last, food," said the ancient diplomat. "I'm wasting away."

Jeremy looked at Marquis's shriveled frame and wondered how much of that was jest. Laurent let the cart come to rest at Tina Balleron's right.

"Smells delish," said Marquis. "Alas, ladies first."

"Ladies deserve to be first," said the judge.

Marquis groaned. "It's times like these, dear, that one understands those poor wretches who opt for sex-change surgery."

"Wine, sir?" said the Eurasian servingwoman.

Marquis looked up at her. "Genevieve, fill my cup to the brim."

15

GENEVIEVE POURED A WHITE WINE, AND LAURENT served a first course of fish mousse quenelles in a peppery reduction with citrus overtones.

Edgar Marquis tasted, licked his lips, pronounced, "Pike."

"Pike and turbot," said Arthur Chess.

"Scallops and lobster roe in the sauce," added Norbert Levy.

Tina Balleron said, "Enough speculation," and pressed a buzzer at her feet. Moments later, Laurent emerged.

"Madame?"

"Composition, sir?"

"Whitefish, turbot, and gar."

"Gar," said Edgar Marquis, "is basically pike."

"I," said Harrison Maynard, "am basically *Homo sapiens*."

Tina Balleron said, "The sauce, Laurent?"

"King crab, crawfish, lemon grass, a splash of anisette, ground pepper, just a touch of grapefruit zest."

"Delicious. Thank you." As Laurent left, the judge raised her wineglass and the others followed suit.

No toast; a moment of silence, then crystal rims touched lips.

Edgar Marquis sipped faster than the others, and Genevieve was there, as if by magic, to refill his glass. The wine was pale and crisp, with a lemony nuance that harmonized with the delicate mousse.

The quenelle was so light it dissolved on Jeremy's tongue. He found himself eating too quickly, made a conscious effort to slow down.

Take discreet bites. Chew inconspicuously but energetically. A young gentleman doesn't gulp.

A young gentleman doesn't tell anyone when upperclassmen creep into his bunk at night . . .

Jeremy drained his wineglass. Almost immediately, his head began to swim. He'd had breakfast but no lunch, and the fish mousse was substantial as crepe. The wine had gone to his head.

Laurent emerged again with a basket of flatbreads and slices of softer baked goods. Jeremy selected olive bread and something studded with sesame seeds. A few seeds rolled onto his tie. He flicked them off, unreasonably embarrassed.

No one had noticed. No one was paying attention to him, period.

Everyone concentrating on eating.

He'd seen that before in old people. Knowing time was short and every pleasure needed to be savored?

Jeremy's forkful of buttery fish paused midair as he observed his companions. Listened to the clink of tines against china, the barely audible samba of determined mastication.

So single-minded. As if this could be their last meal.

Will I be that way, he wondered, *when the passage of time hits me hard?*

Arthur Chess had labeled the group "our grayed little assemblage," but as Jeremy looked around the table, he saw alertness, self-satisfaction, self-sustainment. Were these people looking back on lives well lived?

A blessing . . . then he thought of Jocelyn, never afforded the luxury of a gradual fade.

Tyrene Mazursky.

He tried to salve the resultant flood of images with a greedy swallow of cool wine. The moment it emptied, his glass was refilled. In the next chair over, Tina Balleron glanced at him—was he being indiscreet? Had he betrayed his feelings?

No, she'd returned to the food. He'd probably imagined it.

He drank too much and ate more bread, cleaned his plate. Conversation resumed—floated around him. The old people talked steadily but at a leisurely pace. No conflict, nothing ponderous, just several light glosses over the day's headlines. Then Norbert Levy said something about a hydroelectric dam project slated for the next state over, quoted facts and figures, talked about the Aswan disaster in Egypt, the futility of trying to conquer nature.

Tina Balleron cited a book she'd read about the inevitability of Mississippi floods.

Harrison Maynard pronounced the Army Corps of Engineers "Frankenstein monsters in khaki," and quoted Jonathan Swift to the effect that if one learned to plant two ears of corn where one had grown previously, he had serviced mankind better than 'the entire race of politicians.' "

Arthur Chess said, "Swift was one of the greatest thinkers of all time—his take on immortality is near biblical in its acuity." The pathologist went on to describe a visit to Swift's grave in Dublin, then segued to the pleasures of the reading rooms at the libraries of Trinity College.

Edgar Marquis said the Irish were finally getting it right: giving up on potatoes and embracing technology. "Unlike . . . other nationalities, they know how to cook, too."

Norbert Levy spoke of a fabulous meal at a family-run restaurant in Dublin Harbor. Perfectly grilled black sole—the Irish would never deign to call it Dover sole because they hate the English. The husband the chef, the wife the sommelier.

Harrison Maynard said, "What do the kids do, bake?"

"Doctors and lawyers," said Levy.

"Pity."

Tina Balleron turned to Jeremy. "How's your fish, dear?"

"Wonderful."

"I'm so glad."

The second course was a warm salad of pigeon breast and porcini mushrooms over field greens lubricated by a pancetta-laced dressing. Another white wine was poured—deeper in color, woody and dry and fine, and Jeremy swallowed it with joy and worried giddily if he'd pass out.

But he remained alert; his system seemed to be absorbing the alcohol better. The beautiful room was clearer, brighter, his taste buds were electric in anticipation of each new mouthful, and his companions' voices were as soothing as poultice.

Arthur spoke of butterflies in Australia.

Edgar Marquis opined that Australia was the States in the fifties and New Zealand was England in the forties. "Three million people, sixty million sheep. And they don't let reptiles in."

Harrison Maynard described a spot in New Zealand where one could peer down on the Tasman Sea and the South Pacific simultaneously. "It's the ultimate contrast. The Tasman roils constantly, the South Pacific's glass. I found a crag where the gannet birds mate. Golden-headed, gull-like creatures. They're monogamous. The mate dies, they go into seclusion. The crag reeked of frustration."

Jeremy said, "Not too adaptive."

Five pairs of eyes aimed at him.

"Reproduction-wise," he said. "Is there a population control issue?"

"Good question," said Maynard. "I just assumed they were moral little buggers."

"It is a good question," said Arthur.

Tina Balleron said, "It should be looked into."

The third course was a pale pink sorbet of a flavor Jeremy couldn't identify, accompanied by ice water.

As if sensing his curiosity, Norbert Levy informed him, "Blood orange and pomelo. The latter's a cousin to the grapefruit. We seem to be in a citrus thing, here."

"Larger than a grapefruit, no?" said Edgar Marquis. "I believe in Mexico they sell them at village markets."

"Huge, misshapen things," Levy agreed. To Jeremy: "Sweeter than grapefruit but unsuitable for commercial production because of a very low pulp-to-rind ratio."

Harrison Maynard said, "Expediency trumps virtue."

"Yet, again," said Tina Balleron.

Arthur said, "How true." He touched his bow tie.

Everyone stared at their food.

Silence.

As if all the energy had been sucked from the room. Jeremy turned to Arthur for clarification. The pathologist offered a long, searching glance in response. A sad glance.

"Well, then," said Jeremy, "perhaps one should concentrate on virtue."

The silence stretched. Crushing silence.

Arthur lowered his head, plunged his spoon into his sorbet.

16

JEREMY WASN'T SURE WHEN IT HAPPENED—
sometime during the meat course.

Three meats, arranged like corporeal jewelry,
along with braised root vegetables and *haricots
verte* and toasted spinach, complemented by a vel-
vety Burgundy.

Jeremy, once a hearty eater, but of late poorly in-
clined toward pleasure, had his plate filled with a
medallion of rare beef, slices of goose breast, veal
loin wrapped around a *foie gras* nugget. Laurent
distributed the flesh while Genevieve doled out the
greens.

All of which fit handily on his plate. Jeremy
noticed for the first time that the dinnerware was
oversize—closer to platters than chargers.

Soft violin music streamed down from the ceiling. Had it been playing all along? Jeremy searched
for the speakers and spotted eight of them, positioned around the room, nearly camouflaged by
plasterwork.

A room put together with care. And big money.

The old people ate with continued alacrity. Edgar

Marquis said, "Genevieve, be a dear and bring me the goose leg."

The woman left the room and returned shortly with a daunting cudgel of meat. Marquis lifted the leg with both hands, attacked at the top, and proceeded to gnaw his way down the limb. Jeremy tried not to stare—no one else seemed to consider the behavior unusual. Marquis made slow but steady progress, seemed no less shrunken for the accomplishment.

Jeremy recalled something he'd never really been conscious of knowing: a joke some distant relative had tossed his way during a family gathering. Back when he'd been part of a family. Somewhat. How old had he been? Not much more than a toddler.

Where do you put it, kid? Got a hollow leg?

Who'd said it? An uncle? A cousin? Had he really been a ravenous child? What had happened to his appetites? Where had his life gone?

Next to him, Tina Balleron fanned her napkin and dabbed daintily at her lips. Across the table, Arthur Chess chewed away like a stud horse.

Norbert Levy said, "Yum."

Jeremy faced the food. Dug in.

It wasn't Arthur who brought it up, of that Jeremy was nearly certain. *Nearly,* because red wine and protein overload had pushed him to the brink of stupor.

Who had it been . . . Maynard? Or possibly Levy.

Someone had raised the topic of criminal violence.

Ah, thought Jeremy. *The punch line, this is why they've brought me here.*

But no one consulted him. Not in the least. They talked among themselves, as if he weren't there.

Might as well seat me at the kids' table.

He decided to withdraw into his own mental space. But the old people's voices were hard to ignore.

Harrison Maynard was saying, "Punditry is nothing but fatuous prigs reciting the same nonsense so many times they come to believe it. Poverty causes crime. Hah." He placed his knife down. "I won't bore you with yet another sad reminiscence of my wretched, racism-blighted, brutally segregated youth, but suffice it to say that no matter where you grow up it becomes apparent, early, who the bad guys are, and that's a color-blind phenomenon. Villains stand out like boils on a supermodel."

Tina Balleron made an index-finger gun and pointed it at no one in particular.

"Pardon, dear?" said Maynard.

"Bad guys and good guys, Harry. Very macho, it's rather . . . Louis L'Amour."

"Great writer," said Maynard. "Great human being. Do you quibble with the concept?"

"I was a judge, darling. Bad guys were my stock-in-trade. It's the alleged good guys I'm not sure of."

Edgar Marquis said, "I encountered a good deal of evil in the corridors of foreign service. Lying for fun and profit, if you will—at times venality seemed to be the department's primary product. The profession *attracts* rapscallions."

Maynard said, "Ah, the things they don't tell you in diplomat school."

"Oh, yes," said Marquis. Mournfully, as if it really troubled him.

"Don't fret, Edgar, the same goes for academia," said Norbert Levy. "I coped by ignoring the fools and concentrating on my work. I suppose your work didn't afford you that privilege, Eddie. The collaborative nature and all that. How did you stand it?"

"For years I didn't, lad. My Washington days were a torment. I finally figured out the key was to avoid what passed for civilization. I was offered a position in England—the Court of Saint James, as it were. Assistant to the harlot who'd been appointed ambassador. I couldn't imagine anything more repugnant than that particular amalgam of double talk and peerage. I turned the job down, doomed my future, sought out remote outposts where I could be useful without succumbing to the culture of cravenness."

"Micronesia," Arthur explained to Jeremy. The first indication, in a while, that anyone was aware of his presence.

"The smaller, more obscure islands of Micronesia and Indonesia," said Marquis. "Places where antibiotics and common sense could make a difference."

"Why, Eddie," said Judge Balleron, "you're a social worker at heart."

The old man sighed. "There was a time when good deeds went unpunished."

Another silence engulfed the room and, once again, Jeremy thought they all looked sad.

There's some back story I'm not privy to. Something they share—something they're not going to explain because I'm temporary.

Why am I here?

Another attempt to catch Arthur's eye was unsuccessful. The pathologist's eyes were back on his plate as he dissected his veal.

Norbert Levy said, "I think your point is well-taken, Harry. There will always be bad guys among us and they're not that hard to spot. On the contrary, they're banal."

"Banal and cruel," said Harrison Maynard. "Entitlement, callousness, the inability to control one's drives."

Jeremy heard himself speak up: "That's exactly what the data show, Mr. Maynard. Habitually violent criminals are impulsive and callous."

Five sets of eyes upon him.

Tina Balleron said, "Doctor, are we talking about actual psychological data, or mere supposition?"

"Data."

"Case histories or group studies?"

"Both."

"Conclusive or preliminary?" The woman's murmur did nothing to blunt the force of her questions. Judges start out as lawyers. Jeremy imagined Balleron cross-examining strong men and reducing them to whimpering sots.

"Preliminary but highly suggestive." Jeremy filled in details. No one responded. He went on, elaborating, quoting sources, getting specific.

Now they were interested.

He continued. Delivered a little speech. Found himself heating up, having trouble separating the cold facts from the images that danced in his head.

Humpty-Dumpty situation.

Science was woefully inadequate.

He felt a sob rising in his throat. Stopped. Said, "That's all."

Arthur Chess said, "Fascinating, absolutely fascinating."

Harrison Maynard nodded. The others followed suit.

Even Tina Balleron looked subdued. "I suppose I've learned something," she said. "And for that, I thank you, Dr. Jeremy Carrier."

An awkward moment. Jeremy didn't know what to say.

Edgar Marquis said, "Will anyone be offended if I call for the goose wing?"

"Knock yourself out, Eddie," said Harrison Maynard. "I'm calling for champagne."

This time, a toast.

Clean, dry Möet & Chandon bubbled in the repoussé goblets, the chill seeping through the glass insets, frosting the silver.

The wine fizzed in Jeremy's cheap flute. He took hold of the glass and raised it as Arthur toasted.

"To our articulate guest."

The others repeated it.

Five smiles. Real smiles, pure welcome.

The evening had gone well.

Jeremy had *done* well. He was sure of it.

He sipped his champagne, thought he'd never tasted anything quite so wonderful.

Never before had he felt so *accepted*.

17

MORE SMALL TALK AND SACHER TORTE AND CO-gnac finished him off.

Arthur Chess said, "My friends, we'd best be going." He got up from the table, and Jeremy staggered as he did the same.

Tina Balleron touched his elbow.

He mumbled, "I'm okay."

She said, "I'm sure you are," but she kept her fingers on his sleeve until he stood. It was well into the morning, but the others remained in their seats. Jeremy circulated the table, shaking hands, offering thanks. Arthur came up to him, escorted him out. As though Jeremy had lingered too long on the pleasantries.

Genevieve was just outside the door with their coats, and, as Jeremy passed under the capstone, he glanced back at the triplet of C's carved into the wood.

The black Lincoln was waiting at the curb, engine running, and Genevieve stayed with them, sticking especially close to Jeremy.

Once again, he felt like a child. Cosseted. Not an unpleasant feeling. He allowed Genevieve to open his door. She waited until he'd latched his seat belt, waved, closed the door, and stepped back into darkness.

The rain had let up, replaced by a soupy fog that smelled of old wool. Jeremy was in no condition to drive, wondered about Arthur. Arthur sat upright, both hands on the wheel. Looked fine.

The Lincoln pulled away from the curb and glided.

"Arthur, what does CCC stand for?"

Arthur's hesitation lasted long enough to make an impression. "Just a little joke. Are you comfortable?"

"Very."

"Good."

"Fine cuisine, no?"

"Excellent."

Arthur smiled.

He drove without comment as Jeremy alternated between nodding off and springing awake. Cracking the window a couple of inches helped a bit, and by the time they approached the hospital, Jeremy's brain had settled, and his breathing was slow and easy.

Arthur reached the doctors' parking lot and drove through the nearly empty tier to Jeremy's car.

"I do hope you had a good time," said Arthur.

"It was great, thanks. Your friends are interesting."

Arthur didn't answer.

"They seem," said Jeremy, "to have lived full lives."

Pause. "They have."

"How often do you meet?"

Another pause, longer. "Irregularly." Arthur touched his bow tie, flicked a button, and unlocked Jeremy's door. Avoiding eye contact, he pulled out his pocket watch and consulted the dial.

Curt dismissal.

Jeremy said, "An interesting bunch."

Arthur clicked the watch shut and stared straight ahead.

What had become of Arthur's amiability? Jeremy had found the old man's gregariousness off-putting, but now—maddeningly—he missed it.

He wondered if he'd given his little performance undue credit. Had his discourse been too long-winded? Boring? Offensive, in some way?

Did I screw up, somehow?

Why should I care?

Unable to summon up apathy; he hoped he hadn't blundered. The Lincoln idled, and Arthur stared out the windshield.

Jeremy opened his door, gave Arthur one more chance.

The warmth of being part of something lingered in his belly. Suddenly—inexplicably—he wanted to be *popular*.

Arthur kept staring straight ahead.

"Well," said Jeremy.

"Good night," said Arthur.

"Thanks again."

"You're welcome," said Arthur. And nothing more.

18

BY THE TIME HE REACHED HOME, JEREMY HAD PUT Arthur's strange, sudden coolness aside. There were worse things in life than social error. When he crawled into bed, his mind was empty, and he slept like a corpse.

The cold light of morning—and a hangover— killed further introspection. He popped aspirin, hazarded a run in the icy air, took a scalding shower, called Angela at home but got no answer. It was Saturday morning, but patients depended on him, and he suddenly felt like working. He was at his desk by nine, trying to ignore the grit in his eyelids and the throbbing in his temples.

His pathetic stab at the book chapter glared at him reproachfully. He decided to do personal rounds earlier than usual, see all his patients before lunch, spend more time with each one of them.

He'd dressed as he always did but felt rumpled and uncouth. Grabbing his white coat off the door hook, he threw it on. The coat was something he generally avoided, wanting to separate himself from the physicians.

I'm the doctor who doesn't hurt you.

That helped with kids. Not that he saw many kids anymore. Too much pain. Some things he just couldn't handle.

Adult patients didn't seem to care how you dressed as long as you avoided extremes of grooming and demeanor. Some were even comforted by the image the lab coat imparted.

Clinical rites, priestly vestments. Here's an *expert.* If they only knew.

A few minor crises kept him working past noon, and he stretched the day farther by extending his bedside contacts, taking time to sit down with the nursing staff, charting carefully, with atypical legibility.

A page-message from Angela said, "Sorry about today, got called in."

A major crisis arose just before three: man with a gun near the Ob-Gyn Clinic, and the page operator was adamant that Dr. *Carrier* was needed.

The threat turned out to be the husband of a hysterectomy patient who'd been spotted by a nurse with a telltale bulge under his sweater and now sat alone and smoldering in a vacated waiting room.

Security had been called, the charge nurse informed Jeremy. The husband was an angry man, he'd always made her nervous. Hospital regulations said someone from Mental Health needed to be there, and the department said he was next up.

The affair turned out to be sad rather than frightening. Against everyone's advice, Jeremy entered the room before the guards arrived. The man was unshaven, red-eyed, and under the influence of depression. Jeremy sat down and talked to him and listened and when the man said, "Why's everyone so nervous?" Jeremy pointed to the bulge.

The man laughed and lifted his sweater and shirt. Underneath was a colostomy bag. The man said, "They can frisk me if they want. At their own fucking risk."

He laughed harder, and Jeremy joined in. The two of them talked some more, and the poor fellow got into topics he'd never opened up about to anyone. Raged about his illness, his wife's, the prospect of childlessness; there was plenty to be angry about. After an hour, he seemed calm, but Jeremy wouldn't have been surprised if next time he did show up armed.

When the two of them exited the room, three members of the useless security detail the hospital employed were standing by, trying to look competent.

Jeremy said, "Everything's under control. You can go."

The biggest guard said, "Now, Doc—"

"Go."

The time he spent with the poor man cheered him. Someone else's problems. He'd snapped to attention like the faithful member of the mental health army he was. Any good soldier knew the key to efficient battle: death of the individual in service of the greater good.

Feeling noble and depersonalized, he returned to his office.

Angela had called thirty minutes earlier. He paged her, was transferred to Thoracic Medicine, where a ward clerk told him Dr. Rios had just been called to an emergency lung surgery.

That puzzled him. Angela was a medical resident, not a cutter. No doubt, there'd be an explanation.

He glanced at the sheaf of scolding papers, left to collect his mail. A hefty stack, today; he sorted through the usual memos, solicitations, announcements of conferences and symposia, came to a large, brown interoffice envelope at the bottom.

This one had been sent from the Department of Otolaryngology. No name in the recipient blank. He'd last consulted on an ENT case several months ago—an inner ear tumor that had proved fatal—wondered what they wanted, now.

Inside the envelope were photocopied pages that had nothing to do with ears, noses, or throats.

A seventeen-year-old article reproduced from an ophthalmology journal.

Ablation of corneal tissue using the CO2 Vari-Pulsar 4532 2nd Generation Laser Scalpel . . .

The authors were a surgical team headquartered at the Royal Medical College of Oslo. An international team—Norwegian names, Russian names, English names. None of them meant a thing to Jeremy.

Obviously a mistake; he'd gotten someone else's

mail, not a rare occurrence for the parcels that zipped through the mail tubes veining the hospital's moldy walls. Perhaps some secretary had confused psychology with speech pathology.

He phoned Otolaryngology and spoke to a male secretary who hadn't the faintest idea what he was talking about. Tossing the article in the trash, he put aside the envelope for further use. Fiscal responsibility and all that. Financial Affairs had issued yet another order to tighten up.

As he folded it, something rattled inside. Something had wedged at the bottom, and he pulled it out. A small, white index card, a typed message.

For your interest.

He took another look at the envelope. No name in the recipient blank; this had to be a mistake. He rarely saw eye patients, couldn't recall one in ages—the last, he was fairly certain, had been five years ago, a blind woman who'd decided to curl up and die. After two months of psychotherapy, Jeremy believed he'd helped her, and no one had told him different. No, there could be no connection to this. Why in the world would he have an interest in lasers?

He retrieved the article from the wastebasket, read it, found it to be typical medical jargondygook, stuffed with numbers and tables, barely comprehensible. He cut to the summary. The main point was that seventeen years ago laser scalpels had been judged to be a good, clean way to cut.

Cutting techniques . . . *Humpty-Dumpty* . . . no, that was silly. If his mind hadn't been addled by the last night's booze and confusion and pontification about criminality, he'd never have stretched that far.

What a strange night. In retrospect, comic and surreal. He smiled painfully, remembering his acute bout of neediness. Why had he ever cared what a group of elderly eccentrics thought of him? Even if they asked him back, he wouldn't accept.

Tomorrow was Tumor Board. He was curious how Arthur would treat him.

Then a thought occurred to him: Perhaps *Arthur* had sent the article.

No, the pathologist handwrote with a fountain pen, used that heavy, blue rag paper. A traditional man—an antiquarian, as witnessed by the vintage suits, the old car, the quaint vocabulary.

A typed message on anything so mundane as an index card would be out of character.

Unless Arthur was being coy.

The obliqueness fit—that would be just like the pathologist. Gregarious one day, frosty the next.

A game player, everything a puzzle. Was this a challenge to Jeremy to figure out?

Ablation of corneal tissue? Laser eye surgery? Had Arthur assumed Jeremy would share his eclectic interests? The old man hopped around from butterflies to carcinomas to Grand Discussions of Issues That Matter, so why not lasers?

Still, his approach to Jeremy hadn't been scatter-shot. On the contrary, Arthur had sought to find common ground between the two of them. Pathology and psychology converging. Sharing the cold, black space where twisted minds brought about bloody deaths.

The roots of very, very bad behavior.

Arthur had had a very clear focus, and Jeremy had been right about his invitation to supper having something to do with that.

He recalled the pall that had set upon the room after someone—the writer, Maynard, he was pretty sure—had said, "Expediency trumps virtue."

"Yet again," the woman judge, Balleron, had added.

Then, the silence. Nothing weighty was being discussed—something about fruit, grapefruit—those other things—pomelos. Sweet taste, but they shipped poorly.

Yet, for just a few moments, the mood in the room had changed.

Expediency trumps virtue.

What a strange bunch, no point wasting any more time on them.

Same for this—laser scalpels . . . just a postal snafu; he was making too much of it.

Filling his head with a flotsam of random thoughts because he was avoiding his chapter.

Still, his thoughts shifted back to Arthur. Treating him coolly for no apparent reason—rudely, really.

A puzzle. But not an important one.

Jeremy folded the card into an airplane, sailed it into the wastebasket. Followed up with a toss of article. The envelope, too, fiscal responsibility be damned.

Two paragraphs of chapter outline stared up at him from his desk.

Time to put aside silly stuff. Confront his creative inadequacies.

19

IT WAS 10 P.M. AND THEY WERE IN ANGELA'S BED, naked in the dark, wide-awake.

They'd been together nearly three hours. Angela had phoned just as Jeremy was preparing to leave the hospital. She said, "Good, I got you." Her voice was faint.

"Everything okay?" he said.

"Sure," she said. "No, I'm lying. Can we get together, maybe a quick dinner, then just hang out at my place?"

"Sounds like a plan. Any dinner in particular?"

"How about that Italian place over on Hampshire—Sarno's? It's close and I need to move my legs."

"Sarno's it is. On me."

"No, it's my turn to pay."

"You get no turn. You're a starving resident, deserve a free meal."

She laughed. Nicest sound he'd heard all day.

They met at the hospital entrance and walked, arm in arm, to the restaurant. Angela wore a long, navy blue coat. Her dark hair streamed over the faux-fur collar. She looked waifish, young, worn, and stared at her feet, as if needing to orient herself. The rain was light, dissipating from their clothes almost instantly.

Jeremy put his arm around her shoulder, and her head dropped. He kissed her hair. If she'd put on makeup, it had faded long ago. The shampoo she'd used that morning was tinctured with operating room antisepsis.

Within seconds, she was leaning against him. Heavy, for a woman so thin. They moved slowly and awkwardly through the three dark blocks to the restaurant.

When Sarno's neon sign—the tricolor boot of Italy—came into view, Angela said, "Jeremy, I'm *so* tired."

She got down a third of a plate of pasta carbonara and half a glass of iced tea. Jeremy was back to his feeble appetite; last night's gluttony seemed distant, an aberration. He picked at his ravioli, managed to finish a glass of coarse Chianti.

They bickered playfully over the check and Angela finally allowed him to pay. Her beeper went off, and she phoned in. She returned to the table smiling. "That was Marty Bluestone—another R-II. Tomorrow night's his anniversary, and he wants to take his wife out. So he offered to finish my shift tonight. I'm free till tomorrow."

Beneath her blue coat, she wore resident's casuals—sweater and jeans and tennis shoes. Relieved of the garment and her stethoscope, she looked like a college kid.

"On the phone you said everything wasn't okay."

"I was just being a baby," she said. "It was right after I got off shift."

"Tough day, huh?"

"One of *those*. Couple of problem bleeds, a few other bad surprises." She gave her pasta another go, gave up.

"This morning, I watched Dr. MacIntyre crack the chest of a woman who'd never smoked. Her right lung was black as coal. It looked like barbecue ash. The left one's not much better. I didn't have to be there, but I'd done the intake and liked her. And I wanted to see what really happens to my patients. Jeremy, she's a really sweet, kind woman, used to be a nun, served the poor. Now she's got nothing but agony to look forward to."

"Poor thing."

"She came in thinking she had bronchitis, or maybe a cold gone chronic. I did the old blow-the-ball test, and her lung capacity was the lowest I've ever seen, it's amazing she could stand on her feet. I sent her straight to X-ray. I started with her, so I ended up with her. It was the attending's job to give her the diagnosis, but he punted to me—too busy. I sat down with her, told her she needed to be opened up and why. She didn't even blink. Just said, 'Thank you, Doctor, for letting me know so kindly.' "

"You must've done a good job."

Angela's eyes watered. She wiped them, reached for Jeremy's Chianti. "May I?"

"I'll order you a glass."

"No, let's share." She sipped, held the glass out. They linked arms and Jeremy drank. He'd seen that at a wedding—an ethnic affair—maybe a Jewish wedding. Bride and groom entwined. Heady symbolism.

He said, "Not a smoker. Any secondhand smoke?"

"Her father," said Angela. "He's old, sick with diabetes, she's been taking care of him for twenty years in a two-room apartment. He chain-smokes and it circulates and she breathes it in. He had a chest scan last year. His sugar's 320 and his circulation's shot, but his lungs are as clear as bells."

"Sins of the fathers," said Jeremy, without thinking.

"Guess so." Her voice was low and defeated. She played with her fork.

Jeremy wondered if he'd come across glib. He said, "You've earned some relaxation. I'd be happy to provide aid and comfort."

"Sounds good—let's go."

She'd taken the bus to the hospital, so Jeremy drove her home. During the ride, she kept her hand on his thigh. Once, at a red light, she leaned over and kissed him deeply, and he heard her purr.

When they got to her place, the routine commenced: She seated him on the ratty couch and disappeared into the bathroom to change into her green robe. The struggling houseplant on her windowsill was gone. The apartment was no less shabby for its absence.

The bathroom door opened, and Angela glided over, the robe firmly cinched. She sidled onto the couch, lay with her head in his lap. He touched her chin, stroked her hair.

She said, "Let's get into bed."

Her bedroom was chilly. When they drew the covers up around their necks, she said, "Don't take this the wrong way, but I don't want to do it, tonight. I just want to be held."

"The wrong way?"

"As if I've been leading you on."

"You haven't."

"Okay."

They lay on their backs, holding hands.

Angela said, "You're sure?"

"I'm positive."

"It's not that I don't want you. I do. Physically, I do. I just—mentally, it wouldn't work. Okay?"

"No need to explain." Jeremy brought her hand to his lips.

She snuggled close and slid down so that her head rested in his lap. Jeremy heard her let out a low, contented breath. For some crazy reason, the sound evoked Judge Tina Balleron's murmuring voice.

An old woman but still . . . alluring. No, not her, specifically. Women. The sounds they made. The wonderful things they did. Jeremy preferred women to men. Always had. A certain type of woman especially: smart, bookish, tending toward reticence. Vulnerable.

Jocelyn had been none of that, and yet . . .

He bent low, cradled Angela's head, kissed her brow.

She shifted position, reached down. "*You're* interested."

"Physically, only."

"Bull."

"I'm offended that you would think me so crass."

She laughed and moved back to eye level. They began kissing, stayed with it for a long time. No groping, no tongue duels, just whispery grazes of lip upon lip.

Angela said, "Oh, boy."

"What?"

"Just oh, boy. You make me happy."

"I'm glad."

"Do I make you happy?"

"Sure."

"Are you?"

"What do you mean?"

"Are you happy? It's hard to tell; you don't say much," she said. "In general, I like that. My dad and my brother are talky guys. Great guys but overpoweringly verbal. Whenever my brother was home from college, I was relegated to bystander."

"What about your mother?"

"She just leaves the room. Being a doctor, she can be as busy as she'd like."

"The convenient patient call," said Jeremy.

"You know of such things, huh? So tell me, why are you reluctant to talk about yourself?"

"It's a boring story."

"Let me be the judge of that."

Jeremy didn't answer. Angela's windows were covered by cheap shades. Moonlight transformed them to oversize sheets of parchment. Somewhere out on the street, a radio was playing. Scratchy rock music. A too-strong bass.

Angela said, "I've upset you."

"Not at all."

"I don't want to be nosy, but we have been . . . intimate."

"You're right," said Jeremy. "What do you want to know?"

"Where you were born, what your family's like—"

"I don't have a family."

"None at all?"

"Not really." He told her why. Kept talking. Starting with the accident, being shunted from place to place. The feelings of being alone—feelings he'd never put into words, not during his training analysis, not during clinical supervision, or pillow-talk ventures with other women.

Not with Jocelyn. He realized, with a shock, how little he and Jocelyn had talked.

He finished breathless, convinced opening up had been a grave mistake. A nice, wholesome girl from a well-to-do, intact family—a clan of confident professionals—would be put off by his rootlessness, the sadness of it all.

People talk about sharing, but you can't share the past. Or anything else of consequence.

He was reflecting upon what that implied for his chosen profession when Angela sat up and cradled him and stroked his hair and played with his ears.

"That's the whole sordid tale," he said.

She placed one of his hands on her breast. "Don't take this the wrong way, but I changed my mind."

"About what?"

"Not doing it."

Later, when she began to yawn, Jeremy said, "I'll let you sleep."

"Sorry. I'm so *bushed*." She squeezed him hard. "Do you want to stay the night?"

"I'd better not," he said.

"You haven't yet. I suppose there's a reason."

"I'm a restless sleeper, don't want to disturb you. You've got a long day ahead of you, what with taking that guy's shift."

"Yes," she said. "Guess so."

Simultaneously they said, "The schedule."

When she walked him to the door, she said, "So how was that dinner with Dr. Chess?"

"Not much of anything."

"Was it a medical thing?"

"No," he said. "More of a general thing. Believe me, it's not worth getting into."

He left her rooming house, got into his Nova and started up the engine. When his headlights went on, so did those of another car, behind him, mid-way down the block. When he pulled from the curb, the other car followed suit, driving in the same direction.

What the hell is this?

Jeremy sped up. The other car behind him didn't.

A big SUV from the height of the headlights. When
he turned left on Saint Francis Avenue, it continued
straight.

So much for high intrigue.

"I've got to get hold of myself," he said, aloud.

*No matter what those old fools think about
reality, I need some.*

20

ARTHUR WASN'T AT TUMOR BOARD. ANOTHER PA-
thologist presided, an associate professor named
Barnard Singh, bright and turbaned and dressed in
a perfect gray suit. He got right to business, flashing
slides of a synovial sarcoma. Gentian violet stain
turned the specimens beautiful.

Jeremy asked the radiotherapist next to him,
"Where's Dr. Chess?" and received a shrug.

He sat through the hour, restless, and, despite
himself, curious.

He called Arthur's office extension, heard the
phone ring. Went up to see his patients and tried three
hours later. Not knowing what he'd say if Arthur
picked up.

*Just saying hi, old chap. Harumph pshaw.
How're the old CCC chumskys?*

No answer.

Then he thought: What if something's happened
to him? Despite his outward robustness, Arthur
was an old man. And the way he packed away alcohol and cholesterol . . .

Perhaps he'd had a heart attack and lay untended on the floor of his lab. Or worse.

Jeremy pictured the pathologist's long frame stretched out, surrounded by jars of floating viscera, skeletal specimens, bodies in various states of dissection. Sterile tools laid out in preparation for human carpentry . . . *laser scalpel?* . . . an expensive gizmo. Would there be any reason for a pathologist to invest in one?

He hurried to the main wing, took the stairs down to the basement. Once again, Arthur's office door was closed, and no one responded to Jeremy's knock.

The morgue sat at the far end of the hall, and its door was open. The sleepy-looking attendant at the front desk was doing paperwork. No, he hadn't seen Dr. Chess today, had no idea where he was.

"Was he here yesterday?"

"Uh, no, I don't think so."

Jeremy backtracked to the Pathology Office, on the opposite end and around a bend.

A chubby woman in her forties sat sentry.

"Hi," she said. "Can I help you, Doctor?"

"I'm looking for Dr. Chess."

"He's out."

"Is he okay?"

"Why wouldn't he be?"

"I just wondered," said Jeremy. "He wasn't at Tumor Board, and I've never known him to miss one."

"Well," she said, "he's as fine as he could possibly be. I believe he's taken some time off."

"Vacation?"

"It's not like that," said the receptionist.

Jeremy's puzzled look made her smile. She said, "You don't know him well, do you? How long have you been attending T.B.?"

"A year."

"Ah," she said. "Well, Dr. Chess isn't really on staff, anymore. Not officially, anyway." She cupped her hand around her mouth, and whispered, "He doesn't get paid."

"He's volunteering his time?" said Jeremy.

"You could call it that, but that really doesn't describe it." She lowered her voice even further, forcing Jeremy to lean in close. "He doesn't do autopsies anymore, or analyze specimens. Doesn't do much at all, except Tumor Board. But he's such a brilliant man, has given so much to this hospital, that they allow him to keep his office, do any research he wants to do. It's not a secret, but we don't publicize it either. For Dr. Chess's sake. It's not like he's deadweight or anything. He's a major asset to this department because of his reputation. In fact, I'll have you know, he turned this department into what it is."

Her voice had risen. Indignant. Protective.

"He's brilliant," Jeremy agreed, and that seemed to mollify her.

"That's why we don't talk about his . . . employment status. As far as everyone's concerned, he's a full-fledged member, welcome here whenever he wants. And his running T.B. is a big help. Everyone says he's got an encyclopedic memory. And, of course, he's available when the younger pathologists have questions for him. Which they frequently do. They have tremendous respect for him, everyone does. He's a beacon in his field."

"Yes, he is," said Jeremy. "So . . . you're saying he just decided not to come in."

"It's happened before. Why all the questions, Dr. . . . Carrier?"

"Dr. Chess and I had dinner a couple of nights ago. He seemed . . . a little shaky."

The receptionist's hand flew to her mouth. "Oh, my. I certainly hope he's all right."

"I probably overstated. He just seemed a little tired. Less energetic than what we've come to expect from him. That's why, when he didn't show up this morning for T.B., I got a little concerned."

"Who ran Board this morning?"

"Dr. Singh."

"Let me call him." She punched her phone. "Dr. Singh? It's Emily, sorry to disturb you, but I've got Dr. Carrier here asking about Dr. Chess . . . Carrier. From . . ." She inspected Jeremy's badge. "Psychiatry. He had dinner with Dr. Chess last night, thought Dr. Chess looked a wee bit tired. He wants to make sure Dr. Chess is okay . . . what's that? All right, I'll tell him. Thanks, Dr. Singh."

She placed the phone in its cradle. "Dr. Singh says Dr. Chess called him last night to inform him he'd be taking additional time off and wouldn't be making Board. Dr. Singh said he sounded fine."

"Great, that's good to know. Thanks." Jeremy turned to leave.

"It's so nice," she said. "The way he does that."

"Does what?"

"Dr. Chess. The way he gets people to care about him. The dear."

Her phone rang and she picked it up and got involved in a conversation with someone named Janine who'd just had a baby and wasn't that great, and she was sure he was cute, just the cutest, when could she stop by with the baby gift she'd bought thecutestlittlebootieandjammy set.

21

THE PSYCHIATRY SECRETARY PHONED JEREMY, AND said, "You're requested on Six West."

It was Wednesday, well past his late-night supper with the old eccentrics and but for occasional surreal remembrances, the experience had been expunged from his head. Arthur Chess was out of his head, as well. He couldn't believe he'd actually cared about the old man's well-being.

Over the past few days, he'd seen Angela once—half an hour for coffee and hand-holding before she rushed off. During that time she talked more about her lung cancer patient, who was not doing well, and said, "For the rest of my chest rotation, I'll be shifting from lung to heart. That should be good."

"Absence makes the lungs grow fonder?"

"Ouch," she said.

"Sorry."

"No, I like it. Another side of you."

"What side is that?"

"Regular. Not so . . . composed."

"Happens all the time," he said.

"Well, I haven't seen it before. I like it."

She squeezed his hand, left to talk to dying people.

He said, "Who requested me?"

The psych secretary said, "Dr. Dirgrove."

"Don't know him."

"Well, that's what it says, here. 'Dirgrove.' He's a surgeon." A redundancy; Six was a surgical ward. "He wants you to evaluate a preop patient."

"For what?"

"That's all I've got, Dr. Carrier."

"He asked for me personally?"

"Sure did. Guess you're famous."

He found Dirgrove in scrubs, charting in the Six West physicians' room.

The pale, blond man he'd seen demonstrating some sort of technique in the dining room to Mandel the cardiologist and the dark, mustachioed surgeon.

The trio Jeremy had believed Arthur to be observing, only to have Arthur shift his attention to the daily paper. And ask Jeremy to supper.

Seated, Dirgrove had appeared tall. On his feet, he was of medium height, no larger than Jeremy and ten pounds lighter. One of those rangy men who seems to be moving even while standing still. He greeted Jeremy with a warm smile and a hearty handshake. "Dr. Carrier. Great to meet you. Thanks so much for coming, I'm Ted."

The photo on his badge was a good likeness—a

rarity. A thumbnail shot of Dirgrove smiling just as he was now.

T.M. DIRGROVE, M.D. ATTENDING, CARDIAC SURGERY.

"Jeremy. What can I do for you?"

Dirgrove put the chart aside, leaned against the desk, rubbed one paper slipper against the other. His eyes were deep blue, thatched with laugh lines, clear, earnest, tired. Faint yellow-gray stubble dotted his angular face. Hands pinkened by frequent washing fluttered restlessly. His surgical scrubs were wine red. Jeremy found himself thinking: *The better to hide the blood.*

"I'm slated to operate on a young woman with a ventricular septal defect. On the face of it, routine." Dirgrove smiled. "You know what they say: Routine is when it's happening to someone else. Anyway, this girl worries me. She's highly anxious. We cutters generally don't pay much attention to that kind of thing, but I've learned to be a bit more careful."

"Careful about anxiety?" said Jeremy.

"About the whole mind-body connection." Dirgrove tented his spidery fingers. He'd indulged in a beautiful manicure, but the rest of him seemed put together casually: short, spiky, uneven haircut, and the scrubs were wrinkled. Careless shaving had left a grid of longer, pale hairs at the juncture of his jaw and neck. "A guy like me can do all the right things technically, but if the mind's not cooperating, it can be a problem."

"You're concerned about an anxiety attack during surgery?"

"About any significant sympathetic nervous system reaction. Even with the premedication, I've seen it happen. Patients who are ostensibly out and you cut them open and for some reason their adrenaline kicks in and their S.N.S. spikes and their blood pressure goes through the roof. When the anesthesiologist has his hands full, I can't do my job optimally. That's why I play mellow music in my O.R., and everyone shuts up. My instinct on this girl is she needs calming down. I've heard you're the man for that, so if you don't mind, could you see her? The family's got good insurance."

"What can you tell me about her?"

Dirgrove rummaged in a pile of charts, found one, flipped it open, passed it to Jeremy, and crossed to the door. "Everything you need to know is in here. Thanks. And I'd appreciate if you'd do it ASAP. We're scheduled for tomorrow, first thing, in the A.M., so if you think we need a delay, try to let me know by 5 P.M."

A brief wink, and he was off.

Merilee Saunders. The chart had lots to say about her congenital heart defect and her family's ability to pay (excellent private insurance, indeed) but nothing about her psyche. None of the nurses had recorded any untoward anxiety, and Dirgrove's only assertion to that effect was a neatly printed addendum to yesterday's notes: *Poss hi anx. Call psych.*

Jeremy went to see her.

*   *   *

Dirgrove hadn't told her about the consult.

She was a chubby young woman with grainy skin and unruly dark hair tied up in a knot. Her hospital gown had bunched around her shoulders, and she lay propped uncomfortably. Coal-nugget eyes aimed at Jeremy the moment he entered the room, and she glared but said nothing. Cheap silver rings banded eight of her fingers. Three pierces in one ear, four in the other. A tiny rosy dot above her left nostril said she'd changed her mind about the nose stud.

The chart said she was twenty years old, but the reading material on her bed table was all teen zines.

Jeremy introduced himself, and she frowned.

"A shrink? You're kidding. What, someone thinks I'm crazy?"

"Not at all. Dr. Dirgrove would like you to be as calm as possible before the surgery, and he thought I might be able to help you with that."

"If he wants me to be calm, he shouldn't cut me up."

Jeremy pulled a chair up to her bed. "May I?"

"Do I have a choice?"

"Sure."

Merilee Saunders rolled her eyes. "What the hay. Park."

"So," he said, "surgery wasn't in your game plan."

She turned sharply, regarded him as if his skull had split open and his brain had tumbled out. "Sure," she said. "It's a fun thing for me, I can't wait to be sliced. What a rush."

"Has the reason for the surgery been explained to—"

"Blah-*blah*, blah-*blah*, blah-*blah*, blah-*blah*. Yeah, Freaky Dirgrove told me the facts."

"Freaky," said Jeremy.

"He's a stiff. Roboticon. Except when he wants to turn on the charm. My mom loves him."

The chart said the Saunders family was intact.

"What about your dad?" said Jeremy.

"What about him?"

"Does he like Dr. Dirgrove?"

"Sure, why not." Merilee Saunders looked over at the TV suspended from the wall. "The channels here suck. Home shopping and Spanish crap and other crap."

"True," said Jeremy. "We're a bit behind the times."

The young woman shifted position under her covers. "Dirgrove tell you I'm nuts?"

"Not in the least. He just wants to make sure you're in peak shape for—"

"Maybe I am," she said. "Nuts. So what? And what does that have to do with getting my heart sliced open? And why now? All these years I've been fine and all of a sudden . . . I'm twenty, I don't have to do something I don't want to do."

"If you have doubts about the—"

"Look, I've had *this*"—she patted her left breast—"since I was born. They tell me it's a hole in my heart, but I don't feel any different from anyone else. Not until some docko slips me the old steth and he hears it and everyone starts freaking *out*."

"You feel fine, so why should you—"

"It just doesn't feel right, know what I *mean*? I come into this shithole all okay and they poke me and jam crap in me and give me X-rays and CAT scans and all kinds of crap and now tomorrow I'm gonna wake up feeling like I got run over by a truck. It doesn't make sense, but try telling *Mom* that. She's only out for my best *interests*."

"Your mother—"

"My mother *loves* doctors," said Merilee. "Especially the cute ones. She thinks Dirgrove's cute. I don't. I think he's a stiff. And since you're obviously going to ask about my dad, let's just say he works like eight hundred hours a week, pays the bills, goes with the flow."

"You're right," said Jeremy. "You're an adult, and it's your body we're talking about. So if you have serious reservations—"

"Nah. I'll go with the flow, too. Why not? What's the worst that can happen, I die?" She laughed.

Jeremy started to speak, but she waved him off. "Don't think I'm gonna talk shrinky, to hell with that. Even if I *am* nuts, so what? It's not my brain we're talking about, it's my heart."

"Sometimes there are things we can do to make the experience easier," he said. "Relaxation exercises."

"I hate exercise."

"This is more like meditation—hypnosis."

She regarded Jeremy through slitted eyes. "What, you want to put me asleep and tell me my heart's okay and the hole closed up by itself? If you can pull that off, sure, let's party."

"Sorry," said Jeremy. "That's a bit beyond my abilities."

"Then who the hell needs you?" said Merilee

Saunders, shaking her fingers as if discarding flecks of filth. "Leave me alone, I'm tired."

Pt. More angry than anx. Understands need for surgery intellec. but not emot. More discussion of procedure from Dr. Dirgrove recommended. Pt. Refuses relax.trng.

J. Carrier, Ph.D.

Not one of his triumphs.

But later that day, he picked up his voice-mail messages and the third of a dozen said: "Jeremy, this is Ted Dirgrove. You were a great help. Thanks."

22

ANOTHER ENVELOPE ARRIVED IN THE INTEROFFICE mail. Same source: *Otolaryngology*. Once again, an unnamed recipient, but it had ended up in Jeremy's stack.

This one was copied from a five-year-old gynecology journal. Laser hysterectomy technique in the treatment of uterine lieomyomata, endometriosis, and pelvic adhesive inflammation.

Optimally, the patient should be positioned in the dorsal lithotomy posture with low stirrups, prepped and draped . . .

Another team of authors, physicians, and biomedical engineers. Americans, working at a West Coast university hospital.

Construction of a bladder flap . . . endoscopic kittner . . . dissection of the broad ligaments.

Jeremy slipped the article back in the envelope, walked over to the Psychiatry Department, and asked Laura, the secretary who disbursed the mail, if she had any idea who had delivered the envelope.

"It all comes in a batch from the mail room, Dr. Carrier." Laura was barely twenty, just out of junior college. Still sufficiently green to hold the professional staff in awe.

"This wasn't addressed to me." He showed her. "So it had to be dropped off in person. Any idea how it got in my pile?"

"Uh-uh. Sorry."

"When the batch gets here, where's it stored?"

"Right here." She pointed to a bin on the counter, just to her left. "I go through it, divide it by staff member, and tie up each stack with a rubber band and a Post-it with your name on it. Then someone—me or a clerk or a volunteer—brings it around to each office. Yours we do last because you're on a different floor."

"So once the batch is divided, anyone could insert another envelope into any pile."

"I guess so—is something wrong, Dr. Carrier?"

"No, just curious."

"Oh," she said, looking frightened. "Have a nice day."

He barged in on the ENT receptionist. A young man, beautifully dressed and groomed, whose fingers flew over a computer keyboard.

"May I help you?" he said, without looking up. Same voice Jeremy had spoken to when he'd inquired about the first envelope.

Jeremy said, "I have a question about this."

The young man stopped typing, and Jeremy handed him the envelope.

"Didn't you call me about this before?"

"That was the first, this is the second. So I don't

think it's an accident. I've obviously been confused with someone else."

The young man inspected the photocopied article. "Hmm . . . well, I didn't send it. These envelopes get reused all the time."

"I guess someone's stockpiling ENT envelopes."

The young man grinned. "That's because we're so charming." He tried to hand the article back.

"All yours," said Jeremy.

The young man touched his hair. "First time anyone's *given* me anything in a long, long time, but no thanks."

He placed the article on the counter. Jeremy took it.

Now he wondered.
Dissection of the broad ligaments.

Jeremy returned to his office and called Detective Bob Doresh. This time he introduced himself. He heard Doresh sigh.

"Yes, Doc?"

"Last time we spoke you called Tyrene Mazursky a Humpty-Dumpty situation and implied Jocelyn had been the same—"

"I never implied, Doc, I was—"

"Fine, Detective, let's not quibble. I've got a question for you. Did the murders bear any signs of surgical skill? Was there any dissection?"

Doresh didn't answer.

"Detective—"

"I heard you, Doc. Now, why would you be asking that?"

"An egg," Jeremy lied. "It breaks in clean pieces. Straight edges, there's a certain precision to the destruction. Is that what you meant when you used the term 'Humpty-Dumpty,' or were you speaking in general terms?"

"Doc, I don't think I'm going to get into what I meant." Doresh's voice had grown soft and threatening.

Nervous, Jeremy had definitely made him nervous. As far as he was concerned, that was answer enough. "All right, then. Sorry for bothering you."

"No bother," said Doresh. "We always like to hear from concerned citizens. Which is how you see yourself, right?"

"No, Detective. I'm more than that. I loved Jocelyn."

"So you told me when we first met."

"Did I?" Jeremy harbored only fuzzy memories of the initial encounter at the station. Small room, big men, bright lights, everything moving at a methedrine pace.

"Sure," said Doresh. "In fact it was the first thing you said. 'I love her.'"

"Okay," said Jeremy.

"I thought that was interesting. That that's the first thing you'd say."

"Why's that?"

"It's just not something I've heard before. In that situation."

"There you go," said Jeremy. "New experiences every day."

"Like a person with Alzheimer's," said Doresh.

"That's the good part of the disease, right—you get to meet new people every day."

Several moments passed.

Doresh said, "You're not laughing."

"Tell me something funny, and I will."

"Yeah, you're right, Doc. Tasteless. We tend to get that way—dealing with the so-called dark side of life. To alleviate the stress, I'm sure you understand."

"I do," said Jeremy. "Thanks for your—"

"Ms. Banks," said Doresh. "She worked with Alzheimer's patients. All kinds of patients with . . . whadyacallit—cognitive problems?"

"That's right."

"I hear some folks at the hospital make jokes about that. Call it 'the vegetable garden.' Sounds like you guys aren't that different than us. People need to cope."

"They do—"

"How're you coping, Doc? You doing okay, otherwise?"

"Otherwise?"

"Other than wondering about the evidence."

"Oh, sure," said Jeremy. "Life's a blast."

He hung up, sat there trembling, was still unsteady when he walked to the box down the hall and collected his mail.

Totally irrational, calling Doresh. What could he have hoped to accomplish?

The second article had spooked him. Made it impossible for him to brush it off as a mail screwup. But what if he was wrong, and some fool had simply made the same mistake twice?

Dissection . . . even if someone *was* playing with his head, there couldn't be any real connection to Jocelyn.

Could it be Arthur?

Jeremy entertained visions of the old man stockpiling interoffice envelopes and other hospital supplies in his musty old Victorian house.

Retired, but hanging on.

Hoarding was consistent with Arthur's clothing, his car, his excessive reminiscences. Holding on to old things.

Living in the past. An inability to let go.

Jeremy vowed to forget about him and the envelopes, once and for all. Time to keep going on his book chapter, which miraculously seemed to be falling into place. Since receiving the first laser article and realizing how poorly written it was—how clunky and pompous most medical writing was—he'd decided he could do better.

He'd written twenty good pages, done a redraft, felt satisfied he was on his way.

Onward: the book and Angela.

They'd seen each other only twice during the last eight days, made love on both occasions, drunk wine, talked for hours, seemed to be moving toward that comfort two people experience when the chemistry quiets but doesn't vanish.

Shoptalk with Angela had cleared one thing up: It was she who'd given his name to Dr. Ted Dirgrove.

"I was rotating through cardiothoracic, and he gave us a terrific lecture on transmyocardial revascularization. Then he brought up the topic of anxiety as a surgical risk factor, and I thought that was admirable, for a cutter."

"Being concerned about anxiety?"

"Most of those guys, you can't get them to see beyond their scalpels. Dirgrove actually seems to realize there's a human being at the other end. I mentioned the work you did—the strides you'd made relaxing anxious patients. I gave the example of Marian Boehmer—my lupus patient. Who, incidentally, is doing fine. Whatever that blood dysgrasia was, it self-limited. Anyway, Dirgrove seemed very interested. I hope you don't mind."

"Not at all," said Jeremy. "Unfortunately, I didn't help his patient much."

"Really?" said Angela. "He said you did."

"I think he's being kind."

"Maybe you had more of an effect than you figured."

Jeremy thought about the brief encounter with the hostile Merilee Saunders and doubted he'd accomplished anything other than to convert her anxiety to anger.

On the other hand, that could sometimes be therapeutic—if anger made the patient feel in charge, reduced the panic that came from crushing vulnerability.

Still, it was hard to see the Saunders girl as anything more than failed rapport. How long had he been with her? Five, ten minutes?

Angela said, "Dirgrove sounded pretty pleased."

He supposed she could be right. There'd been instances when patients got in touch years after treatment, to thank him. Some were specific about what had helped.

Things he'd said. Or hadn't. Word choices and phraseologies that had proved crucial in tipping them over the therapeutic brink.

In every case, the "cure" had been unintentional. He'd had no idea he'd shot the magic bullet.

Then there were the cases where he'd drawn upon every technique in his shrink's arsenal and fallen flat on his face.

What did that say? That he was a pawn, not a king?

What a strange way to make a living.

"I think," said Angela, "that you sometimes sell yourself short."

"Do you?" He kissed her nose.

"I do." She ran her fingers through his hair.

"You're a nice woman."

"Sometimes."

"I haven't seen otherwise."

"Ha," she said.

"Are you trying to scare me?"

"No," she said, suddenly serious. She pressed her cheek close to his. Her breath was warm, light, alcoholically sweet. "I'd never do that. I'd never do anything to put space between us."

23

TUMOR BOARD WAS CANCELED FOR THE WEEK. THE following session, Arthur was back at the lectern, running the show.

Jeremy arrived late and had to sit at the rear. The room was dark—slides, always slides—and it stayed that way for most of the hour. The old man's sonorous baritone rhapsodizing about mediastinal teratomas.

But when the lights went on, Arthur was gone, and Dr. Singh had taken his place, explaining, "Dr. Chess had to leave early for a prior engagement. Let us proceed."

The final ten minutes were taken up by a spirited debate about cell permeability. Jeremy had trouble staying awake, managed to do so by scolding himself:

At least this is science, not some randomized process where the so-called expert doesn't have a clue.

The next day, the third envelope arrived. Jeremy had nearly finished a rough draft of his chapter and

was feeling pretty flush. The sight of "Otolaryngology" in the sender slot froze his fingers on the
keyboard.

He thought about throwing it out unopened.
Couldn't resist temptation and tore the flap so hard
the little metal clasp flew off.

No medical reprint inside. Instead, Jeremy extracted a newspaper clipping, crumbling at the edges
and browned with age. No identifying marks—
the article had been trimmed well below the upper
margin—but the tone and the locale suggested a
British tabloid.

Vanished Bridget's Chum Found Murdered

Two years ago pretty Bridget Sapsted left a
pub in Broadstairs, Kent, after a night of serving pints only to vanish. Despite extensive police inquiries, the fate of the lovely lass was
never discovered. Now a close friend of the
pretty brunette has been murdered brutally,
and efforts are being made to learn if the fate
of one girl is connected to that of the other.

The case took a grisly twist when, early this
morning, the body of 23 yr old Suzie Clevington was found by a man walking to work on
the outskirts of Broadstairs. Suzie and the viva-
cious Bridget had been classmates at Bel-
vington School, Branchwillow, Kent, and the
two girls had remained fast friends. With as-
pirations as a dancer, Suzie had spent some
time in London and on the Continent, but had

returned home recently to seek employment opportunities.

"At this point," said the principal investigator, Det Insp Nigel Langdon, "we are treating these as independent incidents. However, should the facts warrant, we will pursue them as related."

In response to rumours that the body had undergone horrible mutilation, Det Insp Langdon would say only that the police could not reveal all the details of the case in the interest of an "efficient investigation."

Suzie Clevington was described by friends and family as an out-going, friendly—

And there the article ended, cut off in midsentence.

Laser scalpels, female surgery, a dead girl. Mutilation.

A Humpty-Dumpty situation.

This was not a postal screwup.

Someone in the hospital, wanting Jeremy to *know*.

Who could it be, other than Arthur?

He called Arthur's office. No answer. Was the old man still caught up in yesterday's "prior engagement"? The exigent circumstance that had caused the pathologist to flee Tumor Board before the meeting had ended?

Jeremy realized something: All three envelopes had arrived during periods when Arthur had been impossible to reach. What was that, an *alibi*?

For what?

Slipping on his white coat, he walked to the faculty office and lied to the secretary—an exceptionally cheerful woman named Anna Colon with whom he'd always gotten along—about having bought a gift for Dr. Chess and needing a home address.

"I didn't know you two were friends," Anna said, as she handed over the black-bound *Medical Staff* binder. Not thinking to ask: *If so, why don't you know his address?* Some people were blessed with a trusting nature. Jeremy often woke up in the middle of the night, mistrusting his own existence.

He said, "We're more like teacher and student. Dr. Chess has taught me a lot, and I wanted to repay the favor."

"Well, that's nice. Here you go."

24

NOT THE VICTORIAN HOUSE IN QUEEN'S ARMS THAT Jeremy had conjured. An apartment in Ash View—the southern suburbs, far from the water, a good twenty miles out of the city.

Wrong, yet again. Everything about Arthur seemed to be taking him by surprise.

Or perhaps Arthur had given him hints. Ash View had once been farmland and Arthur had spoken, fondly, of agrarian roots.

Birthing calves . . . a sanguinary process. The old man had grisly sensibilities.

Did he sense that Jeremy shared them?

Because of Jocelyn?

Lately, he'd been thinking more about Jocelyn.

He could talk to Angela, make love to Angela. But Jocelyn.

So *gone*.

He needed to *see* the old man.

He hurried to the wards early, saw his patients, hoped he'd shortchanged none of them because his mind was elsewhere.

People smiled at him—familiar smiles, grateful smiles. A wife thanked him, a daughter squeezed his hand and told him her mother looked forward to his visits, he was the one doctor who didn't hurt her.

He couldn't be screwing up too badly, fraud that he was.

Tomorrow, he'd do better.

He drove his Nova out of the doctors' lot just after noon. A rare dry day, but a mournful one, flying-saucer rain clouds looming over the skyline, blackening the roiling waters of the wind-whipped lake. The promised installment of another storm seemed to be bewitching motorists. From the time Jeremy got on the Asa Brander Bridge until he exited onto an industrial road that fed to the southern turnpike, he witnessed multiple driving aberrations, near collisions, and, finally, one accident that bred detours and congestion and foul tempers. Finally, he squeezed onto the toll road, battled traffic for miles before the midday commuter clog dropped off and he was sailing.

Zipping through the flatlands. He'd consulted a map before setting out but nearly missed the obscure left-hand exit that took him past a cemetery big as a town, middle-class shopping, and several retirement communities, each of them touting *independent living*.

Had Arthur opted for that? Canasta and bingo and accordion concerts, he and the doting wife blending in?

A cheerfully colored sign said *Two miles to Ash*

View. The terrain stepped down a notch: working-class shopping, gas stations, tire dealers, shacks whose scratchy lawns accommodated rusting autos.

A far cry from the splendor of *CCC*. Whatever that stood for.

Jeremy passed a Dairy Queen and a Denny's and three hamburger chains. Far cry from *foie gras*, too.

Independent living by day, gourmandizing by night. Arthur Chess was a man to be reckoned with.

Ash View was empty land and stray dogs and scattered multiple dwellings. Arthur's address matched a large, flat-roofed, frame house overlooking what had once been a wheatfield and was now just endless acres of grass. The nearest landmark was a quarter mile north, a dormant drive-in theater with a chipped marquee.

The rain clouds turned the flatlands to shadowy moonscape.

Jeremy parked and studied the building. Once elegant, now shabby and subdivided. Not all that different from Angela's place.

The old man lived in a rooming house. Had chosen to distance himself from the pleasures of the city and who knew what else.

A detached carriage house to the right of the main building had been converted to a four-car garage. Four closed doors, but no locks in sight. Jeremy got out, lifted the left-hand door, and found a Nissan. The next stall contained a Ford Falcon, the third was empty, and the last harbored Arthur's black Lincoln Town Car.

Prior engagement. The old man had cut out from Tumor Board early and simply gone home.

Jeremy climbed the big house's cement steps, read the names on the weathered brass mailbox.

A. Chess—no degree listed—lived in Unit Four.

The front door was etched glass—a remnant of bygone glory. Jeremy opened it.

Up the stairs and to the right. The house smelled of corn and curdled milk and laundry detergent. The stairway was steep, guided by a spotless white wooden rail. The walls were textured plaster, the same white, just as clean. Below Jeremy's feet were weathered pine boards under a well-trod blue carpet. Old wood, but not a single squeak. The building was maintained lovingly.

Arthur's door was unidentified as such. *Okay, here we go.*

Jeremy's knock was met with silence.

"Arthur?" he called. No response. Louder rapping caused the door of the unit across the landing to crack. As he repeated Arthur's name and appended his own, the crack widened and Jeremy made eye contact with a single, dark iris.

"Hi," he said. "I'm Dr. Carrier, and I'm looking for Dr. Chess."

The door opened on a short, round sweet-looking woman in a pale yellow housedress. She had white hair and dramatic, russet brown eyebrows. Someone else of Arthur's generation. She held a flowered teacup in one hand and smiled at him. Her eyes were a darker brown, as deep as brown can be without veering into black. Large, hoop earrings tugged at her lobes.

Like an old fortune-teller.

"Was the professor expecting you, dear?"

"Not exactly," said Jeremy. "I work at Central Hospital, and there's a treatment issue to discuss."

"An emergency?"

"Not quite, ma'am. But an important issue."

"Oh . . . and you came all the way out here. How dedicated—it's such a fine hospital. All my children were born there. Professor Chess was a young man back then. Tall and handsome. He had an excellent bedside manner." She giggled. "Of course, I was young, too. He did a masterful job."

"Professor Chess delivered your babies?"

"Oh, yes. I know he's a pathologist, now, but back in those days he did all kinds of medicine. What a wonderful man. I was so pleased to find out we'd be neighbors. I'm afraid he's not in, dear."

"Any idea where he went?"

"Oh, he travels all the time," said the woman. "Shall I tell him you were by, Doctor . . ."

"Carrier. So he's definitely traveling?"

"Oh, yes. When Professor Chess travels, I pick up his mail, see to his messages." She smiled, shifted her teacup to her left hand, and extended her right. "Ramona Purveyance."

Jeremy crossed the landing. Her palm was soft, slightly moist. Chubby fingers exerted no pressure.

He said, "He does like to travel."

Ramona Purveyance nodded with enthusiasm.

Jeremy said, "I wonder how long he'll be gone this time."

"Hard to say. Sometimes it's a day, sometimes it's a week. He sends me postcards."

"Where from?"

"Everywhere. Come, I'll show them to you."

Jeremy followed her into a compact apartment brightened by rear windows that afforded a view of the infinite grass. A meadow, really, with just the faintest rise as it swooped toward the horizon. A dozen or so ravens circled, blending with the sooty sky only to dart out into the fissures of light that separated the storm clouds. The effect was startling— airborne static.

Ramona Purveyance said, "They're always out there. Beautiful things, despite their reputation."

"What reputation is that?"

"You know, like in the Bible? Noah sent the raven out to seek peace, but the raven failed. It was the dove that brought back the olive branch. Nevertheless, *I* consider them beautiful creatures. Not peaceful, though. Sometimes we get cardinals, lovely red things that they are. The ravens scare them off."

She placed her teacup on a low, glass coffee table, waddled to a maple bureau, opened a top drawer, and said, "I'm pretty sure I put them in here."

Jeremy looked around the flat. The walls were painted green—a hospital green—and the furniture was newish and blond and inexpensive. A couple of prints—framed seascapes clipped from calendars— were the sole art pieces. No bric-a-brac, no mementos. None of the family history you'd expect for an old woman.

But that was a foolish assumption, a romanticized version of family life. Things fell apart. Or never took off.

What would *he* have to show when he was old?

Ramona Purveyance opened drawers, closed them, repeated the process, said, "Hmm." The living room opened to a small, spotless kitchen. If the woman cooked, her cuisine left no scent.

"Ah, here we go," she said. In her hand was a sheaf of postcards bound by a wide red rubber band. Without hesitation, she handed them to Jeremy.

The first dozen or so were from overseas. London, Paris, Constantinople, Stockholm, Munich. The Canal Zone—Arthur revisiting his old military haunts?—Brazil, Argentina. The next batch were all American: Oregon's Crater Lake, New York City, St. Louis, Los Angeles, Bryce Canyon, Santa Fe, New Mexico.

Beautiful pictures of familiar landmarks on one side, the same message on the other, in a familiar hand:

Dear Mrs. P—

Traveling and learning.

A.C.

Ramona Purveyance said, "He's a dear to remember."

"Since I've known him, he's lived here," Jeremy lied. "Must be . . ."

"Ten years," she said. "Five years after I arrived.

It's a quiet place, for some city people the adjustment is hard. Not for the professor. He sold his big house and its contents and fit in quite beautifully."

"The house in Queen's Arms."

"Oh, yes," said Ramona. "He showed me pictures. A big old thing—Victorian."

Something right! Finally!

"Must've been a lovely place to live in," she went on. "Fine old furniture, those pretty leaded glass windows. But far too spacious for one person. The professor told me he'd knocked around there far too long. Well after . . . he should have." She flinched. "Are you a pathologist, as well, Dr. Carrier?"

"Psychologist. After he should have, Mrs. Purveyance?"

The chocolate eyes remained steady. "After he realized how ill suited such a big place was for a person living alone."

"Being alone can be an adjustment."

"Have you ever lived alone, Doctor?"

"Always."

Ramona Purveyance knitted her fingers and studied him. "A psychologist. That must be quite interesting."

Smiling, but something in her tone told Jeremy she couldn't have cared less. He said, "Professor Chess and I discuss interesting clinical issues from time to time. He's deeply interested in psychosocial topics."

"Of course he is," she said. "The man's as curious as a child. Sometimes I see him out there." She motioned out the window to the endless grass. Ravens had congregated near the horizon, small and black as flyspecks. "He walks and explores, kneels and peels back the grass, looks for insects and whatnot. Sometimes he brings his metal detector and just goes clicking around. Sometimes he brings a garden spade and digs around."

"Has he ever found anything?"

"Oh, absolutely. Arrowheads, old coins, bottles. Once he found a pearl necklace that he gave to me. Small baroque pearls, some were pitted, but overall still lovely. I gave the necklace to my granddaughter Lucy—she's just old enough to appreciate things of beauty. The world's a treasure trove if you know where to look." She eyed the door. "Would you like some tea?"

"No, thanks. I'd better be going."

"Dr. Carrier," she said, "that term you used— 'psychosocial.' What exactly does that mean?" She canted her head to one side, a parody of coyness. "I do like to work on my vocabulary."

"The interaction between psychology and social issues. Issues that confront society. Poverty, crime, violence. Professor Chess is especially interested in criminal violence."

Ramona Purveyance looked down at her hands. "I see . . . well, I've got laundry to do. Shall I tell him you were by?"

"Sure, thanks," said Jeremy. "I guess we have no idea when he's coming back—did he pack a large suitcase?"

"I wouldn't know, sir," said Ramona, retrieving her teacup. The contents must've been cold, but she sipped slowly. Over the rim of the cup, the dark eyes studied him.

"No idea?" said Jeremy.

"He slipped a note under my door asking me to look after his mail last night. He must've done it late because I was up until eleven. When I woke up at six, he was gone."

The teacup lowered. Ramona Purveyance's expression was bland, but her eyes were guarded. Jeremy smiled. "That's Professor Chess. Driving off on another adventure in that beautiful Lincoln."

"It is a lovely car, isn't it? He maintains it like a clock—washing, polishing, vacuuming every week, but, no, I wouldn't think he'd take it. When he travels he generally has a cab pick him up. Or he drives his other car and leaves it at the airport."

"His other car?"

"His van," she said. "He's got a Ford van, an old one, but in perfect shape. He told me he bought it at a city auction. Used to belong to the Coroner's Office, isn't *that* a bit delicious?" The old woman hugged herself. "Professor Chess assured me it had been cleaned out thoroughly. They always are."

"They?" said Jeremy.

"Morgue things." Another giggle. "Death things."

25

HALFWAY BACK TO THE CITY, THE STORM HIT. JEREMY fishtailed for miles, drove with a misted windshield, felt his brakes lose confidence, was nearly part of a seven-car pileup. Toward the end, he gave himself over to the Fates. Miraculously, he arrived home in one piece and had a dinner of canned soup and toast and black coffee.

The following night, he and Angela finally stole away from the hospital, and he took her to a higher grade of restaurant than ever before; off Hale Boulevard, on the North End. Because of the weather, they rode in a taxi, and Jeremy supplied umbrellas for both of them.

A lesson from Arthur.

The place was green suede walls, granite banquettes, starched linens the color of fresh butter. On the way to their rear booth, Jeremy and Angela passed an iced case of fish so fresh the creatures' eyes stared back reproachfully, another containing fat-marbled prime cuts of beef and pork. Pugnacious lobsters, their pincers bound, clawed the spotless sides of a ten-foot aquarium.

The savagery of good living.

Jeremy had made a reservation two days before and gotten another resident to cover for Angela. A guy who'd rotated through Psych as an intern and sat in on a couple of Jeremy's lectures.

The ambience, the food, all that was great. The planning was what impressed Angela to the point of moist eyes.

She sat right up against him, their thighs laminating.

"After this, how am I going to go back to resident's fare?"

"Ease into it," said Jeremy. "Avoid undue sensory shock."

"This is pretty shocking," she said. "Being treated like this."

"I'll bet you're no stranger to that."

"Why do you say that?"

"Only daughter in a professional family. Something tells me you've experienced the finer things in life."

"You're right," she said. "They raised me with love, gave me what I wanted, always told me I could achieve anything I put my mind to. By all accounts, I should never lose confidence, right? But I do. Nearly every day. This job, all those people, depending on me. What if I misplace a decimal place on an order? Or fail to catch it when someone else does—that actually happened to me when I was an intern. Some puffed-up attending more concerned about billing than taking care of his patients dashed off an insulin scrip for a diabetic. A hundred times too much. We would've had a sudden death, and everyone would've been puzzled."

"You caught it?" said Jeremy.

She nodded. A China Doll waitress brought complimentary melon liqueur in tiny green glasses and a lacquered tray of various fried things. Angela massaged her glass. Picked up a baby octopus, muttered, "Too cruel," and placed it back on the plate.

"So you saved a life. Good for you."

"I almost *didn't* catch it, Jer. The syringe was already loaded—prepared by a nurse—and I was supposed to give the shot, and I just happened to glance down and read the order. I'll never forget the look on the patient's face. An old guy, an old sturdy guy who'd operated heavy machinery in his heyday and still liked to flirt. He must've seen my face, realized how thrown I was. He said, 'Everything okay, girlie?' 'Sure,' I said and I made a big show of inspecting the syringe. Then I lied, told him something was wrong with the needle, too many air bubbles, we needed to get a fresh one. I left him there, tossed that damn syringe in the nearest biohazard bin, called the head nurse over, and showed her the order. This was a smart woman, an experienced woman, she knew as much about dosages as most physicians. She said, 'Oh, my,' then she recovered, and it was, 'Of course, we're not going to tell anyone, are we?' And I said, 'Of course not.' She suggested I alter the original order to where it should've been, and I did. Then I loaded up a new syringe, went back in, gave the poor patient his shot. He smiled at me. 'There you are, I been missin' you. Maybe you and I can go out some day, honeybunch, cut a rug.' I smiled back—too shaken up to be offended and besides, he's an old guy, another generation, how can you take offense? I said, 'Well, Mr. So and So, you just never know.' And when I left, I give my rear a little shake. To cheer him up—I know it was tacky, but this guy almost died, and I was almost the one who killed him. He deserved a little joy, no? A little atonement from me, too."

Her lips shook. Lifting the tiny green glass, she tossed back her drink.

Jeremy said, "Nothing to atone for. You're the hero of the story."

"Pure luck. So close. Since then, I've been paranoid about dosages, double- and triple-check everything. Maybe it'll make me a better doctor. You know the worst part of it? The attending—the idiot who couldn't keep his decimal places straight—he never knew. We protected him, never told him. So what does that make me? A coconspirator?"

"If you'd told him, he'd have denied it. And you'd have come out the worst for it."

"I know, I know," Angela said, miserable. "This is some romantic evening—I'm sorry, Jer."

Jeremy nuzzled the warm, sweet place behind her ear. So smooth, women. So finely wrought.

She said, "You're a wonderful guy. Please, let's keep this going."

A week later, he received a postcard from Oslo.

Stunning photography, some place called the Vigeland Sculpture Gardens. Monumental carvings of hypermuscular figures displayed in a verdant park-like setting. To Jeremy's eye, the images were aggressively proletarian—*Wagnerian*.

On the back of the card was fore-slanted writing in black fountain pen ink:

Dear Dr. C—

Traveling and learning.

A.C.

The old guy picks up and leaves just like that. And why not? Arthur was retired, lived alone, had no work obligations.

Had downsized.

Jeremy was certain the Victorian had been abandoned for some reason other than Arthur's sudden insight that the house was too large.

Ramona Purveyance knew the reason, she'd almost let it slip—*he'd knocked around there too long after . . .*

But when Jeremy had pressed, she'd finessed.

Had there been some tragedy in Arthur's life? Some life-changing event? Perhaps the old man had simply confronted one of life's routine tragedies: widowerhood.

Loss of the doting wife Jeremy had imagined. That would've been more than enough to insult Arthur's gregariousness. Leading him to seek his pleasures elsewhere.

Late suppers with like-minded eccentrics.

Jeremy placed the postcard in a desk drawer. The next time he saw Anna, the faculty office secretary, he thanked her for providing Arthur's address, told her Arthur loved the gift, was now traveling.

"Yes, he does that," she said. "Sends me the prettiest postcards. So considerate."

"A good way to occupy oneself," said Jeremy.

"What is?"

"Travel. What with his living alone and all that."

"I'm sure you're right."

"How long has he been single?"

Anna said, "Ever since I've known him—I believe he's always been single, Dr. Carrier. Confirmed bachelor and all that. A pity, wouldn't you say? Such a nice man?"

Living single meant you could hop to the airport, charm the ticket agent, board, loosen your shoelaces, nibble salted nuts, down a martini with two pearl onions, and settle back for the long flight.

If Arthur was behind the interoffice envelopes, he'd sent Jeremy two articles on laser surgery and left the country shortly after posting an old clipping about a missing English girl and her murdered chum.

At least, Jeremy had assumed the story was old because of the dry, brown paper. What was the point? A crime-history lesson? Wanting Jeremy to ponder yet another example of very bad behavior?

Wanting to lead Jeremy somewhere . . .

If so, the old man was being maddeningly oblique. Where was the clipping . . . Jeremy searched his desk, remembered he'd thrown it out. What was the murdered girl's name ... Suzie something, a surname beginning with C ... he struggled to retrieve the memory, felt it evade him maddeningly, a sour aftertaste, lodged in the soft, spongy tissue behind his tongue ...

But the other name came to him, unbidden.

The girl who had vanished—an unusual name—*Sapsted—Bridget Sapsted*.

He turned on his antiquated computer, endured the squawks of his temperamental modem (the hospital had converted to word processing years after every other health facility, still refused to install an integrated system), sat back, and counted the dots in his acoustical tile ceiling until he finally connected to the Internet.

He entered the missing girl's name into a search engine, heard the computer hum and snore and flatulate—indatagestion.

Three hits, all from British tabloids.

The case wasn't ancient at all; the acid-laced pulp paper had deteriorated quickly.

Six years ago: As the clipping had stated, Bridget Sapsted had gone missing.

Two years later, Bridget Sapsted had been found, dead.

The young woman's skeletonized remains had been buried shallowly, in a densely wooded area, less than a quarter mile from those of her "chum" Suzie *Clevington*. Found three weeks after Suzie. Nothing left but bones; the coroner estimated that Bridget Sapsted had been interred for the full two years before being sniffed out by dogs.

"Finding Suzie helped narrow the search,"
said Det Insp Nigel Langdon. "We are now
considering both young ladies the victims of
the same killer. For evidentiary reasons we are
unable to divulge an explanation for that as-
sumption at the present time."

Jeremy plugged the policeman into several data
banks. Only one hit for any *Nigel Langdon*, and it
had nothing to do with police work: Last year, a
man by that name had delivered a lecture on the
cultivation of peonies to the Millicent Haverford
Memorial Garden Club. Kent.

Same district, had to be the same guy. Perhaps the
Det Insp had also retired, chosen quieter pursuits.

Jeremy phoned overseas information, was stalled
by several false starts, finally connected to the right
English operator and obtained a listed number for a
Nigel Langdon in Broadstairs.

Where the murdered girls had gone to school.

The time difference made it evening in England,
but still early enough for a polite call.

He punched in the number, listened to the overseas squawk, was momentarily stunned when a
cheerful woman's voice chirped, "Hallo, who is it
then?"

"Is Mr. Langdon there, please?"

"Watching the telly. Who shall I say is calling?"

"Dr. Carrier, from the United States."

"The States—you're joking."

"Not at all. Is this Mrs. Langdon?"

"Last I checked. No joke? What, then? What
kind of an American doctor are you?"

"A psychologist," said Jeremy. "I'm a friend of Dr. Arthur Chess."

"Are you now?" said the woman. "I'm sure that's good for *him*, whoever *he* is. So you think Nige needs a head-shrink?"

"Nothing like that, Mrs. Langdon. Dr. Arthur Chess—Professor Chess is a renowned pathologist, with an interest in one of Mr. Langdon's cases—we are talking about Detective Inspector Nigel Langdon?"

"*Re*tired inspector . . . Nigey's well past all that ugly business—it's the murdered girls, right? Has to be that."

"As a matter of fact, yes—"

"Aha! So who's the detective in this family!" The woman laughed.

"How did you know?" said Jeremy.

"Because it's the only case Nige's been involved with any psychologist would be interested in. Had to be a crazy man, it did—but I shouldn't say more. Indiscreet, and all that. What do *you* and your professor friend want with Nigey?"

"I'd just like to ask him a few questions."

"You and everyone else."

"There's been recent curiosity about the case?"

"Not recent. But after it happened—when they found the second one, Bridget—you couldn't keep this phone cold." Silence on the line. The woman said, "Thank goodness, all that's passed. So you want to talk to him, eh?"

"I would appreciate it. Just for a—"

"I suppose it wouldn't hurt. Lately he's been complaining about boredom. *Nige!*"

*   *   *

The man's voice was clogged—as if he'd stuffed his mouth full of eggs.

"What's this?" he demanded. "Something about Suzie and Bridget? Who *are* you? What's this *about*?"

Jeremy spun a web about Arthur's forensic skills, erudite discussions between the two of them concerning important cases, the old man asking Jeremy to do psychosocial follow-up on cases he believed were yet unresolved.

"Well, this is certainly bugger-all unresolved," grumbled Nigel Langdon. "Never closed it. Surprised me at every turn. What with two bodies, I thought there'd be more. One of those serial things, you know? But that was it, two. Bastard ravaged those poor girls and just stopped. One of them had a boyfriend, a bad lot, served some time in Broadmoor for assault, I was certain he'd be the one. But he had an alibi. Locked up in Broadmoor—that's about as good as it gets, wouldn't you say? Other than him, nothing. Now, good night—"

"Ravaged," said Jeremy. "Was there sexual assault?"

"I was speaking . . . dramatically, sir. Why should I tell *you*? It's a bit impertinent—"

"One more question, Inspector Langdon. Please. Was there evidence of surgical precision to the murders?"

Silence.

"What," said Langdon, "are you really asking?"

"Just that. Were the bodies dissected with . . .

notable skill? Something that implied medical expertise?"

"Where'd you say you were from, lad?"

"City Central Hospital." Jeremy rattled off the address, told Langdon he'd be happy to give his number and Langdon could call to verify.

Langdon broke in: "Why all this curiosity from City Central Hospital, sir?"

"Just what I said, Inspector. Intellectual curiosity. And a deep concern on Professor Chess's part—and mine—about psychosocial issues. The origins of violence."

"Have a case like it over there, do you?"

Jeremy hesitated.

Langdon said, "I give all the answers, and you go dumb?"

"It's possible, Inspector. Nothing decisive. Professor Chess is a pathologist, worked at the Coroner's Office, here. He and I review cases—you've never heard of Professor Chess?"

"Chess . . . as in the game?"

"Exactly."

"No, can't say as I have."

"He's world-renowned," said Jeremy. "Currently, he's traveling in Oslo."

"Too bad for him," said Langdon. "As an overgrown fishing village it's not half-bad. But *those* blokes. Sardines and oil is all *they're* about. Which makes sense, har. Used to eating their fishies oily and got themselves bloody rich on oil, the Norsers. Worse than the Arabs. All that money, and they can't bring themselves to install indoor plumbing in their summer homes, still walk around with rucksacks. Does that make sense to you—rich men eschewing indoor plumbing?"

A long speech. Langdon's voice had risen—anxiety—and Jeremy wondered if he'd prattled to hide something.

"You've been to Oslo, Inspector."

"Been all kinds of places," said Langdon. "Anyway, I am going to cut you off, now, because you're bringing nasty stuff back into my life. Give me flowers, I like flowers. Flowers don't rip each other apart for no good reason, then disappear and never show their ugly, psychopath faces again."

Snorting once, he cut the connection.

Langdon had been to Oslo and didn't want to talk about it.

Jeremy thought about that, decided there was nowhere else to take it. That was that.

But it wasn't. Two days later, he received an e-mail from *NigelLfleur@uklink.net*.

Ever the detective, Langdon had remembered Jeremy's name and that of the hospital, traced his faculty account, obtained his address.

Dear Dr. Jeremy Carrier,

I fear I may have been unnecessarily curt with you during our recent phone chat. Perhaps I can be forgiven that curtness due to the unannounced nature of your call and the unpleasant subject matter foisted upon me by you during an otherwise restful evening.

*However, I do feel it incumbent upon me to
pass along the following truths:*

*With regard to your inquiry about various
aspects of cases we discussed that have passed
from under my responsibility, I'm afraid I'm
not able to divulge details. Especially as said
cases remain open. The new man in charge
of the Clevington/Sapsted file is Det Insp
Michael B. Shreve, however to my knowledge
he is not actively investigating these cases as
they have been deemed inactive, pending new
evidence, none of which, to my knowledge, has
surfaced. Therefore, they are likely to remain
closed. However, I have now passed along Det
Insp Shreve's name to you and feel that with
that action I have acquitted my responsibilities
in this matter.*

*Furthermore, I doubt that Det Insp Shreve
would fancy discussing said case with non-
police personnel. However, here is his phone
number, should you decide to persist.*

Best wishes,
Nigel A. Langdon (very definitely Ret.)

Jeremy phoned Michael B. Shreve's office and
was informed by an officious male officer that the
detective inspector was on holiday.

"Until when?"

"Until he returns, sir."

"When might that be?"

"I'm not at liberty to divulge personal details,
sir."

Jeremy left his name and number and the fact that he was inquiring about Suzie Clevington and Bridget Sapsted.

If that rang a bell with Mr. Officious, he gave no indication.

"Is he in Norway?"

"Thank you, sir. Good day, sir."

26

SOMETHING THAT HAD NEVER HAPPENED BEFORE:

Jeremy forgot to turn off his pager, and it went off during a therapy session.

The patient was a thirty-year-old man named Josh Hammett, an electrician, undergoing a final set of skin grafts for deep-tissue burns suffered last year when a storm-snapped power line had scythed across his chest and severed his left arm.

Months after the amputation, phantom pain had set in, and when nothing else seemed to work, the plastic surgeon put in a psych consult.

This was the sixth time Jeremy had seen the young man. Josh had proved an excellent hypnotic subject, responding readily, even eagerly, to Jeremy's suggestion that his arm had found a peaceful resting place.

Now, he reclined on a couch in the treatment room with Jeremy hovering near his head. Breathing slowly, regularly, the innocent smile of a dreaming toddler spread across his lips.

The bleating at Jeremy's belt failed to rouse him. Deeply under. Jeremy switched off the beeper, let him stay wherever he was for a longer while than usual, finally brought him out gradually. When the young man thanked him and told him he felt great, really great, fantastic, actually, Jeremy turned it back on him: "You did all the work, Josh. You're excellent at this."

"Think so, Doc?"

"Definitely. You're as good as it gets."

Josh beamed. "I never thought it was something I could do, Doc. Tell the truth, when you first mentioned it I thought it was bogus-pocus. But that power-board idea ended being a great idea. The minute I visualize it, all the circuits in place, see all those lights blinking, everything working real smooth, I just go right under. Like that."

He snapped the fingers of his only hand.

"Today," he went on, "I really got into it. Pictured I was fishing, out off the sound. Hauling up pike and whitefish, so many it was almost too much for the boat. I tell you, I could smell those guys frying in the pan."

"Set aside some for me."

"You bet, Doc."

Jeremy left the treatment room content. Angela's number on the beeper brought a smile to his face.

"I've got half an hour," she said, when he reached her on the thoracic ward. "How about coffee and Danish in the DDR?"

"I'm on my way."

When he got to the doctors' dining room, she was sitting at a table with Ted Dirgrove, the heart surgeon. Coffee and a chocolate cruller sat in front of her. Nothing in front of Dirgrove. He was out of his crimson scrubs, wore his white coat buttoned. In the exposed V was the curve of a black T-shirt.

Very hip.

He got up as Jeremy approached. "Hey, Jeremy."

"Ted."

Dirgrove turned to Angela. "I'll be doing it on Thursday, so if you want to watch, no prob, just let my secretary know."

"Thanks, Dr. Dirgrove."

Dirgrove returned his attention to Jeremy. "I've been meaning to call you about the Saunders girl."

"Everything okay?"

"Not quite," said the surgeon. His spider fingers flexed, and his bony face turned rigid. "She died on the table."

"God. What happened?"

Dirgrove rubbed an eye. "Probably a reaction to anesthesia, one of those idiopathic things. Her vitals went haywire—a peak, just what I was worried about—then a really deep trough. Everything just tanked. At first I was sure it was a typical, anesthesia screwup. Tube down the esophagus instead of the airway, because all of a sudden her oxygenation just plummeted. It stinks, but it happens, you spot it, you fix it. The gas-passer checked, and everything was in place. He just couldn't stop her from losing function. I'd opened her, retracted the sternum, had just gotten to the heart."

Dirgrove related the incident in a hollow voice, as if projecting through a bamboo tube. His eyes were weary, but he'd shaved closely this morning and looked well put together. "Everything was rolling along fine, then she was gone. It just stinks."

Jeremy thought of the chubby young woman with the multipierced ears and the unruly hair. All that anger. Dirgrove picking her out as high-risk.

I come into this hellhole feeling fine and tomorrow I'm gonna wake up feeling like I got run over by a truck.

You're an adult and it's your body . . . so if you have serious . . . reservations . . .

Nah. I'll go with the flow . . . what's the worst that can happen, I die?

"Stinks bad," said Jeremy.

"Stinks to high hell." Dirgrove rolled his shoulders. "The autopsy results should come in shortly. No sense dwelling."

He walked off.

"Poor man," said Angela.

"Poor patient," said Jeremy.

His tone was harsh, and she blanched. "You're right, I'm sorry—"

"I'm sorry," said Jeremy. "I'm on edge." He sat down opposite her, reached for her hand. She offered her fingertips. Cold, dry. "It took me by surprise. When I didn't hear from him again, I assumed . . ."

"Terrible," she said. "Any other reason you're on edge?"

"Too much work, not enough play."

"Wish I could play with you, but they're exploiting me, too."

He looked at her cruller. She said, "Take it, I'm finished."

"You're sure."

"More than sure."

Breaking off a piece, he chewed, swallowed. "I didn't mean to snap at you."

"It's okay. He shouldn't have dropped it on you like that. I guess I felt sorry for him because I identified with him. Losing a patient. It's what we all dread, and sooner or later it's going to happen. I've lost a few, already, but I wasn't the attending, they weren't really *my* patients. That's one good thing about what you do, isn't it? Patients don't die. Not for the most part."

"There's always suicide," said Jeremy.

"Yes. Of course. What was I thinking?" She drew back her hand, ran it through her hair. Her eyelids were heavy. "I'm not doing very well, am I? Too much work, not enough play. I did love that dinner, though. That was a great escape. I like the things you do for me, Jeremy."

Her hand returned to his. The entire hand. Her skin had warmed.

"May I ask you something?" she said. "When it does happen—a suicide, or when a consult patient goes, like this one—how do you deal with it?"

"You convince yourself you did your best and move on."

"Basically, what Dirgrove said. No sense dwelling."

"Basically," said Jeremy. "You can't be a robot, but you can't bleed for everyone, either."

"So you learn to do that. Distance yourself."

"You have to," he said. "Or you wither."

"Guess so."

"Want coffee?"

"No, I'm fine."

Jeremy got up, poured himself a cup from the doctors' urn, and returned.

Angela said, "The girl who died. Do you think there could've been something to Dirgrove's worries?"

"What, she scared herself to death?"

"Nothing that pat . . . yes, I suppose that is what I mean. Could there be something unconscious going on? Is there a death force that grows in some people and takes them down—causes their autonomic system to go haywire, poisons their system with stress hormone? Isn't there some tribe in Vietnam that has a high rate of sudden death? Nothing's predictable, is it? You go through all that basic science in premed, think you've got a handle on it. Then you see things: Patients coming in looking hopeless, but they recover and walk out on their own two feet. Others who aren't that sick, end up on the wrong side of the M and M reports."

Morbidity and Mortality. The right-hand column reserved for deaths. The M and M's were the purview of Arthur's department. The old man again . . . let him stay in Scandinavia, consuming *lutefisk* and pornography and whatever else they produced there . . .

Angela was saying, "What if the difference isn't what *I* do? What if it comes down to psych factors? Or voodoo? For all we know, there's the equivalent of a psychic virus that colonizes our basic survival instincts and bends us to its will. Merilee Saunders could've felt it taking her over. That's why she was nervous."

She smiled. "Weird. I am *definitely* sleep-deprived."

Jeremy pictured Merilee's face. Angry, taut with . . . *knowing*? "What you're talking about," he said, "is an autoimmune disorder of the soul."

Angela stared at him.

"What is it?" he said.

"What you just said—autoimmune disorder of the soul. The way you phrase things. I wish you'd talk more. I love listening to you."

He said nothing.

She squeezed his hand hard. "I mean it. I could never put it that way."

" 'Psychic virus' is pretty good."

"No," she said, "words aren't my thing. All through school, I aced math and science but throw a three-paragraph essay at me, and I'm lost." Her eyes looked feverish. A faint sweat had broken out on her upper lip.

"You okay?" he said.

"Tired, that's all. I'll bet essays came easy for you."

He laughed. "You should only know."

He told her about his struggle to write the book.

"You'll do it," she said. "You've been distracted."

"By what?"

"You tell me."

He laughed again and ate the rest of the cruller.

"Jeremy, you master words, they don't master you."

"Words are all I've got, Ang. You've got science

backing you up. For me, it's what I say and when I say it. Period. At root, it's a primitive field—"

She placed a cool finger on his lips and he smelled Betadine and French soap.

"The next time we're together," she said, "tell me more about yourself."

27

THE NEXT TIME WAS TWO DAYS LATER, AT ANGELA'S apartment. She was off call, working mere fifteen-hour days. Had somehow found time to fix a beef-and-bean casserole and a salad of baby greens. They ate on the secondhand couch, listening to music. Her taste was rock about ten years too current for Jeremy.

For the first time, he spent the night.

He did talk. Not about himself, about Angela. Telling her she was beautiful, letting her know how she made him feel. She kept her eyes on him until pleasure forced her to close them. After they washed and dried the dishes, they returned to the couch and entwined. She clawed him, wrapped around him like a crab engulfing its dinner, and after it was over, they stumbled to her bed and slept until daybreak.

He drove her to the hospital and dropped her off at the elevators. After buying a newspaper in the gift shop, he grabbed vending machine coffee and brought caffeine and the day's tragedies to his office.

He flipped pages idly, same old stuff. Then an item at the rear of the Metro section stopped his breathing.

A woman had been murdered last night, just east of Iron Mount, not far from where Tyrene Mazursky had been savaged. An unnamed woman. Her body had been left out in the open, on a sand spit north of the harbor called Saugatuck Finger.

Jeremy knew the place, a boomerang-shaped quarter mile of gritty silica, surrounded on three sides by pines and spruce and dotted by the occasional rickety picnic table. Nothing to do there but kick sand and toe out into pebble-bottomed, lapping water that looked cleaner than it was. Sometimes a stink rose from the cove. Poor families could be seen picnicking on the spit during the friendly months.

When the sky turned to pig-iron, no one came. An abandoned spot. At night, it would be ghostly.

The article offered no further details and made no attempt to connect the killing to Tyrene Mazursky.

Humpty-Dumpty on the beach?

Jeremy fought the urge to call Doresh. He put the paper aside and tackled the nearly completed first draft of his chapter. Time to earn Angela's praise. He'd thought of a few more research suppositions he wanted to add.

In the end, the chapter had turned out nearly twice as long as he'd intended.

He'd known more than he thought he did.

Knew nothing about the woman on Saugatuck Finger.

He said, "Screw all that," and wrote all morning.

The next day, Detective Inspector Michael Shreve phoned him from England, just as he was about to leave for lunch.

What time was it there—9 P.M. Shreve sounded alert. Sounded younger than Nigel Langdon, and more levelheaded. Clear voice, educated enunciation. He returned Jeremy's greeting heartily.

"Good day, to you, too, Doctor."

"Thanks for calling back, Inspector."

"Not a chance I wouldn't, sir. A doctor from America calls me, my curiosity gets the best of me. Why don't you tell me what's on your mind?"

Jeremy spun him the same tale he'd offered Langdon.

Shreve said, "Professor Arthur Chess."

"You know him?"

"No, but perhaps I should—is he something on the order of your local Sherlock Holmes?"

"Not quite," said Jeremy. "Just a venerated doctor with a curious mind."

"You work with him."

"At City Central Hospital."

"I see. And Professor Chess spoke to you about our girls."

"He sent me an old clipping of the case. We'd been talking about the origin of criminal violence. I suppose it struck him as an example."

"Sent you?" said Shreve.

"He's traveling."

"Where to, sir?"

"Oslo."

"Ah," said Shreve. "Not the worst time of year

for the upper regions, but not happy, either. They'd be getting a bit of daylight, that's all."

Like Langdon, Shreve spoke about Norway as if he'd been there.

"You know Oslo, Inspector?"

"As a tourist . . . this Professor Chess, would you say his curiosity is focused on any specific aspect of our case?"

"As I said, he's interested in the genesis of violence," said Jeremy. He switched to a bald lie: "The question also came up about a surgical quality to the murders."

"Did it—Professor Chess had this question?"

"Yes."

"Why's that?"

"I couldn't say, Inspector. He brought it up. Notated it on the clipping—'Dear Jeremy, do you suppose this could be surgical.' "

Ah, what a tangled web we weave.

"Hmm," said Shreve. "A pathologist—do you suppose he was relating our poor girls to a case of his?"

"Not to my knowledge. He's no longer a forensic pathologist."

"But he was, at one time."

"Years ago. Inspector, we barely spoke before he left. Then I got the clipping. Inspector Langdon's name was in it, so I phoned him, out of curiosity. He referred me to you, and I did the same. I've probably overreacted—wasted your time. I'm sorry, sir."

"From Oslo," said Shreve, as if he hadn't heard. "That's where the card came from."

"Yes. It bore a picture of the Vigeland Sculpture Gardens."

"Aha . . . well, sir, as you know these cases remain open, so I'm afraid I can't divulge any details. However, feel free to pass along the following to your professor: We continue to seek a solution, we've eliminated no one."

"I'll tell him."

"As you wish, Doctor. Good talking to you."

Both detectives had been to Norway, and now Arthur was there. Norway had piqued Shreve's interest.

A northern link to killings in England? To killings, here?

Jeremy remembered the authorship of the first laser scalpel article. Eye doctors from Norway and Russia and England. Americans, in the second reprint.

He'd tossed both.

He logged onto the Ovid medical database, strained to recall the exact title of the Norwegian article, but couldn't. Coming up with the date—seventeen years ago—helped somewhat, and he ended up winnowing through three dozen citations until he found the right one.

Seven authors. Three ophthalmologists from the Royal Medical College of Oslo, an equal number of Moscow-based eye surgeons on sabbatical in the Norwegian capital, and a British physicist who worked for the manufacturer of the laser.

No names that meant anything to him. He wrote

them all on a card and filed it away. No real reason, except he was tired of retrieving lost information.

He spent the rest of the morning in Psychiatry Department meetings. Fatuous stuff, the usual suspects droning. He pretended to be awake, shrugged off the invitation by three other shrinks to have lunch, and returned to his office.

Detective Bob Doresh was waiting outside his door.

28

"**H**ELLO, DOCTOR."

"Hello, Detective."

"Can I come in?"

Jeremy shoved the door open and allowed Doresh's beefy body to pass. Doresh wore a gray-blue raincoat and gave off a seawater odor. His size made the office seem even smaller than it was. He stood, dangling thick arms until Jeremy invited him to sit.

"So, Doc, how've things been going?"

"You're here because of the woman at Saugatuck Finger," said Jeremy. "Another Humpty-Dumpty situation?"

Doresh eyed Jeremy's coffeemaker. The scorched swill Jeremy still brewed daily but rarely drank.

"It's stale, but you're welcome to some, Detective."

"Thanks." Doresh stretched for a mug, managed to fill it without getting up. He drank, grimaced, put the mug down. "As advertised, Doc. Ever been out to the Finger?"

"A few times," said Jeremy. "I drive out there occasionally, during the summer."

"Pretty place."

"Not really. If you look closely, the filth in the water becomes obvious. I grew up miles from water, so I'm easy to please. Who was she?"

"Another one," said Doresh.

"A streetwalker?"

The detective didn't answer. Jeremy said, "And you're here because . . ."

"Your last call to me—about the Mazursky woman—I could see you're really interested in all of this. Seeing as my partner and I haven't exactly racked up any big-time progress, I thought maybe I could tap into some of your insights."

"Bravo." Jeremy loosened his tie. "What a sterling line of bullshit."

Doresh crossed his legs and dangled a thick ankle and looked injured.

Jeremy said, "For some unfathomable reason, you consider me a suspect in all this. If you want me to account for my whereabouts last night, all I can tell you is I was home, watching TV and sleeping. Alone. This time I didn't have the foresight to call out for food, so there's no delivery boy to verify my presence."

"Doctor—"

"I know you follow protocol. Doctors do, too. Most of our cancer patients are treated by protocol. But we leave room for creativity, and so should you. Granted, those close to the victim always fall under scrutiny. So even though being put through the wringer on Jocelyn made a hellish experience even worse, I understand it. But by now—the other two killings? Prostitutes? That would make no sense, switching from a girlfriend to strangers. It doesn't happen that way, does it?"

Doresh picked up the mug, stared into it, transferred it to his other hand. "Like you say, Doctor, there's always room for creativity. Stick around long enough, and everything happens." He cupped a knee with his free palm and sat forward. "The question you asked me, about surgical precision, where did that really come from?"

"As I told you—"

"My Humpty-Dumpty remark. Right." Doresh smiled. Most of his teeth were white and even, but a single, corn yellow canine snaggled and caught on his upper lip. He curled the purplish tissue back, and the smile turned predatory. "*Now,* who's laying on the bullshit?"

"That's all it was," said Jeremy. "Humpty-Dumpty images. I wish you hadn't told me."

"Bothered you, did it?"

"I could've done with not knowing."

"Overactive imagination, Doc?"

Jeremy didn't answer.

Doresh said, "Must be helpful for all that hypnotizing you do. My wife tried that—being hypnotized. Wanted to lose weight, so her doctor sent her to some guy downtown."

"Did it help?"

"Not one damn bit," said Doresh. "No matter, I love her huge." He put the mug down and used both hands to shape a wide hourglass. "You know what that's like? Loving a woman so bad you don't care what she looks like or does?"

Jeremy's face went hot, then cold. He felt as if he were changing colors, chameleon-like—livid to pallid. Not blending in, just the opposite. Betraying his vulnerability.

Doresh was studying him. Serene.

Jeremy breathed slowly, deeply—keeping his rage in his belly, no way would he let this bastard in.

"You're a romantic, Mr. Doresh. Do you buy your wife flowers? Are you good about remembering anniversaries? Do the two of you trade pet names?"

Now it was the detective's turn to color.

"Anything else?" said Jeremy.

"As a matter of fact," said Doresh, "I was wondering about Dr. Chess. He's your pal, right? He have theories about the cases?"

So that was it. Detective Inspector Michael Shreve, ever the inquisitive detective—ever the suspicious sonofabitch—had gotten off the phone with him and worked feverishly at finding a colleague in this city on the trail of a psychopathic killer. Something Jeremy had said—or had failed to say—had revved the Englishman's suspicions, and he'd decided to check things out.

The surgical question, had to be the surgical question. Meaning he'd been right about the English murders. Or, rather, Arthur had.

He said, "Dr. Chess has a general interest in crime. He's a pathologist, used to work at the Coroner's Office."

"Did he? So, what does he think? Insight-wise."

"That I couldn't tell you," said Jeremy. "He's traveling, right now."

"Where?"

"Norway."

"Pretty place," said Doresh.

Him, too?

"Ever been there?" said Jeremy.

The detective snorted. "Except for the Army, I've been out of the country exactly once. Four days in Rome, and that was years ago. My wife likes to eat. She came back all excited about learning to cook Italian, but it's still pot roast and macaroni casserole."

Doresh's domesticity set Jeremy's teeth on edge. Lucky man . . .

"Where'd you serve in the Army, Detective?"

"Philippines. How 'bout you? Any service?"

"You don't know?"

"Why would I?"

"I figured you've checked me out thoroughly."

Doresh's smile said Jeremy had delusions of grandeur. "No service, huh?"

Jeremy shook his head.

"Too bad," said Doresh. "You missed out."

"No doubt."

The detective got to his feet. "I mean that in all seriousness, Doc. Service to your country—anything you do for others—is good for the soul. Then again, you probably get that by working. Your hypnosis work, whatever."

Mentioning hypnosis more than once to let Jeremy know he *had* checked him out.

Games, always games. Meanwhile, women died. This guy was useless.

Jeremy got up.

Doresh said, "Relax, don't bother seeing me out. And anytime you have an idea, Doc, feel free to call."

29

DORESH'S DROP-IN LEFT JEREMY RATTLED.

He barges in, and I feel like a suspect. What's the matter with me?

Maybe it was the woman on Saugatuck Finger, no name. Tyrene Mazursky had been named. What did that mean? Old hat? Throwaway victims? Now, they didn't even merit a *name*?

His breath quickened, and his eyes hurt. The walls of his office closed in on him. He paged Angela, but she didn't answer. Tried it again—thinking a second time meant dependence and was he ready for that?

Still, no answer.

So tired of going it alone.

The air shaft outside his window was black, and all at once the window was wet and oily. Rain, a hard, dirty downpour, spitting at the glass.

He threw on his coat, left the hospital, walked to the surly mute's bookstore.

By the time he got there, his coat was soaked through, his shoes sloshed, and his hair was plastered to his skull.

No one else was out on the street. No one stupid enough. A late-model station wagon was parked in front of the store. White, that made it easy to see. The blackened windows rendered the shop nearly invisible in the gloom. The door was open, and he walked in.

No fat man at the desk.

No desk.

No bookshelves, books. Nothing. The lights were on, but the space was empty, save for a coat folded over a chair, an unplugged cash register on the gray linoleum floor, and a strawberry blond woman sweeping up.

She said, "You poor thing—are you a customer?"

"I was."

"You don't know. I'm sorry. I wish I had a towel or something."

"Don't know what?"

"The shop's gone. My father died."

Jeremy groped for the fat man's name—Arthur had mentioned it . . . *Renfrew.* Finally, some neurons were firing correctly.

"Mr. Renfrew died?" he said.

The woman leaned her broom against the wall and came forward. She had a roundish, pleasant face, hips you could rest your hands on, maternal breasts, and curly, shoulder-length hair of the prettiest shade Jeremy had ever seen. Buttermilk complexion, light freckles, green eyes, forty or so. Little makeup because she knew she was aging well.

Her clothes were ill suited for janitorial work—a well-cut, mint green suit and matching shoes, discreet gold necklace, a diamond-studded wedding band. The raincoat on the chair was camel-colored, dry, folded neatly.

"I'm Shirley Renfrew DePaul, Mr. Renfrew's daughter." She gazed around the empty shop. "It's the end of an era, I'm afraid."

"Yes, it is." Jeremy introduced himself.

"From the hospital," she said. "Lots of doctors and nurses came here. Dad created an institution. Back when the neighborhood was better, you had all kinds of intellectuals dropping in—writers, poets, people of artistic stature. They weren't loyal. It was you hospital people who helped sustain Dad during the last few years. Did you know that he studied medicine when he was young?"

"Really."

"For two years, then he decided against it. Poetry was more to his liking. He was a soft man, raised me all by himself."

Shirley Renfrew DePaul shoved a weak smile past her grief, and Jeremy pushed aside memories of the old grump who'd never acknowledged him. "This was a great place, Mrs. DePaul, and your father made a big impact. When did he pass on?"

"Just over a month ago. He'd had throat cancer years before—he used to puff on a pipe, nonstop. They took out most of his palate and damaged his vocal cords, but he beat the disease. Then his heart started to go bad, and we knew it was only a matter of time. My husband and I wanted him to come live with us, but he refused, insisted he wanted to be close to the shop."

Palate surgery. Jeremy had attributed the fat man's mutism to general surliness.

With my track record, I've got to stop assuming.

Renfrew dying a month ago meant shortly after Jeremy's last visit.

The man had been terminal, gave no indication.

Shirley DePaul's smile failed, and tears misted her eyes. Green irises, deepened by the suit. Stunning, really. Not a beautiful woman—not by far—she was barely handsome. But Jeremy was certain she'd never lacked for male attention.

She said, "I hoped it would happen the way it did. Dad came into the shop on a Monday, sat down, brewed his Postum and drank it, put his head down on the desk and never woke up. He couldn't have scripted it better, dying among the books he loved."

The last time Jeremy had been here he'd encountered Arthur reading something on war strategy. A couple of weeks later, Arthur had shown up at his office and turned on the charm. As an old customer—someone who'd known Renfrew's name—he must've been aware of the bookseller's passing. Yet he'd never said anything.

He said, "He didn't suffer."

"A blessing. So was his life." Shirley DePaul's new smile flickered and faded. "For the most part."

She took a deep breath and eyed her broom. "Dad adored everything to do with bookselling. I'm an only child, but not really. This place was my sibling. There were times when I considered it a rather daunting rival."

A high heel tapped the linoleum. "The building's been sold. A development firm. They called a week after Dad passed. Vultures, I said, they probably check death notices. But my husband said, Why not deal with them, what use do we have for it? He's a dentist, very practical. We have six children, and I barely have time to breathe. We live far, out past the county line, it just wouldn't be practical. So we sold. They gave us a good price, even after taxes. No doubt, they'll tear it down and put up something monstrous, but it's not about bricks and mortar, is it? Dad put his soul into this place, and now he's resting somewhere else."

"Absolutely," said Jeremy. "What happened to the books?"

"All sold."

"Was there an auction? I would've tried to buy some."

"There was no public sale, Doctor. Everything went to one buyer."

"Who?"

She shook her head. "I can't say—one of those tax things. It's all for the best; I believe they'll be appreciated. At least I hope so." She wiped the corner of one eye. "Anyway, I'd best be finishing up. Though to tell you the truth, I don't know why I'm cleaning up, they're going to tear it down anyway."

She returned to the broom, stepped daintily to another corner, and began striking the floor, using broad, hard strokes.

Striking progressively harder. *Whoosh whoosh.* Flogging the linoleum floors.

Jeremy left her and stepped out into the punishing rain.

30

HE MADE IT BACK TO THE HOSPITAL LOOKING LIKE A half-drowned dog. Used a rear exit, never guarded, that brought him past a utility area and up the stairs to the main lobby.

Past the marble donor wall. Names etched in beveled capitals. He was in no mood to think about charity.

As he headed for the elevators, he spotted Angela and Ted Dirgrove, white-coated, smiling, walking down the corridor, engaged in spirited discussion.

Walking close to one another. For a second their flanks brushed.

Angela spotted him, stopped. Waved gaily, said something to Dirgrove, and came Jeremy's way.

She gave him a too-hard kiss on the cheek. Jeremy looked for Dirgrove, but the surgeon had disappeared around a corner.

Taking in his soaked clothes, she said, "Oh my God, what happened to you?"

"Didn't know enough to come in out of the rain."

She touched his wet hair, linked her arm in his, withdrew quickly from his sodden sleeve. "You really *are* soaked through." She touched the tip of his nose. "I'm a physician, so you need to listen to me. Though the research doesn't show any link between getting drenched and getting sick, I feel obligated to warn you about this kind of thing."

"Thank you, Doctor." Jeremy's voice sounded stale, and Angela looked at him curiously.

"Everything okay?"

"Yup."

"Do you have a dry change?"

"Once I get this off, I'll be fine." Jeremy peeled off the raincoat and held it at arm's length. Water dripped on the floor of the lobby. Angela appraised him again.

"I suppose you'll survive."

She slipped her arm back in his, and they continued toward the lifts. As they rode up in an otherwise empty car, Jeremy said, "I paged you a couple of times."

"I know," she said. "I was in Pulmonology Conference, Dr. Van Heusen was lecturing, and he doesn't brook interruption. I should've turned the darn thing off, luckily it was on vibrate." She grinned. "You know us girls and vibration. When I got out, I called you, but you weren't in your office. What's up?"

"I just wondered if you had any free time."

"Oh." She frowned. "No, I don't. I really don't. It's been a crazy day, Jer, and bound to get crazier. I've got over a dozen seriously sick patients, then walk-in clinic, and with this weather we'll be sure to fill up with bronchitis and asthma and little kids barking with croup. Then it's meetings, meetings, meetings, and after that I'm on call."

"The schedule."

"Sometimes I wonder," she said. "Sometimes baking cookies doesn't sound half-bad. Then again, maybe not. You've had my beef-and-bean casserole. That's a good indication of my culinary skills."

Jeremy knew a clever riposte was expected. He was too damn tired to meet the challenge, muttered, "Domestic life wouldn't sustain you."

She drew back and looked at him. "Is something wrong, honey?"

Honey.

"No," he said, forcing a smile. "Sometimes baking cookies *doesn't* sound half-bad."

She laughed and rubbed his shoulder. The elevator stopped at Angela's floor, and Jeremy got out with her.

"Soon as I have time, I'll call you."

"Great."

As she turned to leave, he said, "So Ted Dirgrove's a new friend?"

The ward was busy with foot traffic, wheelchairs guided by dead-eyed orderlies, doctors reading charts as they strolled, nurses darting between rooms. Angela stopped and swiveled quickly, stepped closer to Jeremy, drew him away from the bustle into a corner. Her dark eyes had narrowed.

"Something *is* bothering you."

"Nothing—forget it; that was out of line."

"Jeremy, I'm on Pulmonology service and Dirgrove's a chest surgeon. We've got cases in common and, yes, I have developed an interest in what he does. Not for myself, I'd never want to be a cutter. But I do want to be the best physician I can, and as I told you, that means really grasping what my patients go through—their innards, the total experience. It's not enough for me to dispense lung medication without having a feel for how a sick lung looks and reacts. Talking about a diseased heart is one thing. Watching it limp along, struggling to pump, is another."

She stopped, waited.

Giving off heat. Her color was high. She usually ran on high gear, but this was more.

Jeremy said, "Makes sense."

Angela took hold of his hands and kissed his lips. As they embraced, the stethoscope around her neck bit into his sternum. A few passersby stared. Most didn't. Jeremy tried to break the clinch, but Angela held fast, not caring about the public display. Whispered in his ear: "You're jealous. You have no reason to be, but it touches me. Turns me on—it's lovely to be cared about. I'm *going* to find time, you bet on it. One way or the other, you bet on it."

He didn't hear from her that day, or the next, worked on the introduction to his book that had proved so daunting and made no more progress.

He searched the *Clarion* for follow-up on the most recently murdered woman, found nothing.

Why should there be? She didn't even merit a name, no sense wasting ink.

At least, there'd been no more envelopes from ENT. No more postcards from Arthur, either.

Maybe whatever had possessed the old man had passed.

When Angela finally called on the third day, her voice was hoarse, enfeebled, barely audible.

"I'm sick," she said. "The flu, can you believe that? All through my rotation on pediatrics I didn't catch any kiddie bugs. And those little guys were *contagious.* Then they put me on lung service, where the patients are on antibiotics and the rooms are as clean as you get around here, and I come down with this *crud.*"

"You poor thing. Where are you?"

"Home. Van Heusen banished me from his service. Made a big, snide joke about it—no Typhoid Marys consorting with the ill and infirm. Made me feel like a pariah. I should be grateful for the time off, but I can't enjoy it. Too sick to read, and the few stations my dinky little TV picks up are all garbage."

"When did it start?"

"Yesterday."

"Why didn't you call me, then?"

"I was too wiped out even to talk, slept all day and woke up feeling even more exhausted. I'd love to see you now, but no way, I will *not* give you this—do *not* come over."

"I'll be over tonight."

"No," she said. "I mean it."

"I'm sure you do."

"Really, Jeremy." Then: "Okay."

31

HIS SECOND NIGHT SLEEPING AT ANGELA'S.

It took her a long time to come to the door. When Jeremy saw her, his heart melted.

She looked smaller. Stood hunched, reaching for the doorjamb for support.

He guided her back to bed. She was flushed, dry-skinned, hot with fever, a physician too foolish to keep up with fluids and analgesics. He fed her Tylenol, held her in his arms, pressed on her the hot-and-sour soup he'd picked up at a Chinese dive—assured by the proprietress that the seasoning would "kill germies"—and tea and silence. She drifted in and out of sleep, and he stripped down to his shorts and lay next to her, on her lumpy, narrow bed.

She kept him up most of the night, hacking and sneezing and snoring.

One time she woke up, and said, "You're going to get *sick*. You've *got* to go." He rubbed her back gently, and soon she was snuffling again, and he was staring into darkness.

An hour later, she reached for him, half-asleep. Found his arm, trailed her fingers lower, placed his hand upon her. He felt the bouncy thatch of hair under cotton panties. She pressed his hand down and he flattened his palm over her pubic bone.

"Mmm," she mumbled. "Kind of."

"Kind of what?"

Snore, snore, snore.

In the morning her fever broke, and she awoke clammy, teeth chattering, covered to the neck by two blankets.

Her long hair was mussed, her eyes bleary, and a trail of dried snot punctuated the space between her nose and her lip. Jeremy wiped her clean, pressed a cool towel to her brow, cradled her face in his hands, brushed his lips against her cheek. Her breath was sour as spoiled milk, her face mottled by tiny red dots.

Pinpoint petechiae—mementos of coughing spasms. She looked like a stoned, befuddled teenager, and Jeremy needed very badly to hold her.

By 9 A.M., she'd sponged off and tied her hair back and was clearly coming out of the virus. Jeremy fixed her mint tea, showered in her cracked, tiled stall, deodorized his pits with her roll-on, and got into yesterday's clothes. He had patients scheduled from ten through two and hoped he wouldn't ripen throughout the day.

When he stepped back into her bedroom, she said, "You look good. I look terrible."

"You are physically incapable of looking terrible."

She pouted. "Such a nice man, and now he's leaving me."

Jeremy sat down on the bed. "I can stay a little longer."

"Thanks," she said. "That's not really what I mean."

"What?"

"I want to make love with you. In here." She patted her left breast. "But I can't, down here. It's what you guys call what . . . cognitive dissonance?"

"No," he said, "just frustration. Heal up, sweetheart. There's plenty of time."

She sniffed, reached for a tissue, blew her nose. "So you say. Sometimes it doesn't feel like there is."

No, it doesn't.

Jeremy's head filled with Jocelyn. Her face, her voice, the way she held him.

"Did I say something wrong?" said Angela.

"Of course not."

"Your face changed—just for a second. As if something had scared you."

"Nothing scared me," he said. "Let me get you more tea before I go."

He fixed her another pot, heated up a can of tomato soup, kissed her forehead, now blessedly cool, and drove to work.

Feeling . . . domestic.

With Jocelyn, he'd never felt domestic.

The afternoon's interoffice mail brought lots of nonsense. And the fourth envelope from Otolaryngology.

And: Via the U.S. Mail, he received a postcard from Arthur.

The article was ten years old, taken from *The Journal of the American Medical Association.* Physician suicide. Risk factors, statistics, recommendations for prevention.

Sensible stuff, but nothing Jeremy hadn't heard before. But that didn't matter, did it? This had nothing to do with education.

What it *was* about eluded him.

The picture on Arthur's postcard was that of an eighteenth-century kitchen filled with pottery and iron appliances. The legend on the other side said, *Le Musée de l'Outil. The Museum of Tools. Wy-dit-Joli-Village, 95240 Val d'Oise.*

Familiar black ink cursive, no surprise to the message:

Dear Dr. C—

Traveling and learning

A.C.

Jeremy checked the postmark. *Wy-dit-Joli, France* three days ago. Arthur could've returned to the States since then.

He phoned the old man's office. No answer.

The Pathology secretary said, "No, he won't come in."

He called information and got a number for

Arthur's neighbor, Ramona Purveyance, of the nonstop good cheer and the yellow housecoat. She picked up on the first ring and sounded overjoyed to hear from him.

"How nice! . . . no, he's not back yet. I've got all his mail. Mostly solicitations but I'd never take it upon myself to throw anything out. If you see him before I do, say hello, Dr. Carrier. I'm so jealous."

"Of what?"

"France, he went to France. Sent me the loveliest postcard from there!"

"The Museum of Tools?"

"What's that?"

Jeremy repeated it.

"Oh, no. This is a beautiful picture of Giverny. Monet's flower gardens? Beautiful weeping willows and water and flowers too gorgeous to be real. He knows I love flowers. He's such a thoughtful man."

Flowers for her, tools for me.

Tailoring the message?

What *was* the message?

It was unclear if Arthur was in town when the first articles had arrived. He'd presided over Tumor Board the day before the clipping about the English girls had shown up. But this one—all indications were the old man was still abroad.

So who'd sent the suicide article?

Did Arthur have a surrogate?

Or had Jeremy been wrong, yet again, and Arthur had nothing to do with the ENT envelopes.

Could he be *that* wrong?

Then what of the postcards? Coincidental?

Arthur traveling, being thoughtful. Sending pretty postcards to everyone.

Flowers for Mrs. Purveyance, tools for me.

Laser surgery on eyes, laser surgery on women. Murdered women. Doctors killing themselves.

Sculpture in Norway—Norwegian authors of the first article. Russians, Americans . . .

Tools in France. No French authors.

When you looked at it coldly, there was no rationale tying the medical reprints to the cards.

No reason they couldn't be connected, either.

Arthur and his damned curiosity. Death and violence and haute cuisine and paternally obsessed insects that burrowed under your skin.

A late-night supper so weird in retrospect that Jeremy was beginning to doubt it had even occurred.

Any way you looked at it, the envelopes were a manipulation. Sending stuff to him but leaving his name off the envelopes. Someone taking the time to stash them in the rubber-bound stack that sat atop the counter in Psychiatry.

Open season on his mail.

He phoned Laura, the young receptionist, and asked her if she'd noticed anyone near his stack.

"Uh, no," she said. "Was I supposed to be looking or something?"

"Not really. Don't worry about it."

"It gets pretty busy around here, Dr. Carrier."

"Forget I asked."

She hung up, and Jeremy had visions of her reporting the exchange to family and friends. *Working with those shrinks is weird. Crazier than the patients. Like there's this one guy, obsessed with his mail* . . .

Which is what it had become. An obsession and, like any neurosis, time-wasting and energy-depleting.

Enough. He was a busy guy, patients to see, a book to write.

But someone was definitely *playing* him. If not Arthur, who?

Arthur setting up expectations, then dashing them, yet again?

The old man had even scrambled Jeremy's intuition. Before meeting Arthur, Jeremy had had faith in his ability to judge people, to sum up, predict, all those tricks you convinced yourself you knew so that you could go from room to room and comfort the ill and the scared and the dying.

Lately, he had nothing to show for his efforts but a slew of bad guesses. The doting wife, living well, haute cuisine. Turned out the old bastard roomed out in the flatlands, surrounded by fast-food joints.

That first time at the bookstore, assuming Arthur would be reading a book on butterflies, turned out he'd been studying war strategy.

Where's the war, old man?

At least he'd been right about the house in Queen's Arms. Decades off the mark, but technically right.

A feeble vindication. He was turning into Wrong Man. He *needed* his intuition. Without it, where would he be?

Arthur had definitely led him up a path.

Late-night supper, fine wine, haute cuisine, the old eccentrics filling their geriatric guts.

All that good cheer, then a curt dismissal.

Now, this. Postcards.

The old eccentrics . . .

Had Arthur appointed one of *them* to send the articles? Handed over a pile of ENT envelopes to one of his pals and left instructions about mailing them, in his absence?

Why not? The articles hadn't been posted from the outside, simply dropped down the intrahospital tubes. Anyone could gain access to the system. Just waltz through the lobby, find a mail drop, and *poof.*

How did the tube system actually work? He thumbed through his hospital directory and found the number for Postal Collection. Down on the sub-basement, a floor below Pathology.

A deep-voiced man answered his call. "Collection, this is Ernest Washington."

"Mr. Washington, this is Dr. Carrier. I was just wondering how mail got from the tubes to each department."

"Dr. who?"

"Carrier."

"Carrier," Washington repeated. "Yeah, I recognize the name. First time anyone's ever asked me that."

"There's always a first."

"Dr. Carrier, from . . ."

"Psychiatry."

"Yeah, that's it." Then: "This a prank?"

"Not at all. If you want to call me back, my extension is—"

"I know what it is, got it right here, hold on . . . Jeremy Carrier, Ph.D., Extension 2508."

"That's it."

"It's really you, huh?"

"Last time I checked."

Washington chuckled. "Okay, okay, sorry. It's just that no one ever asked me . . . is this some kind of *psychiatry* experiment?"

"No, sir, just curiosity. I was walking past a chute and realized I've worked here for years, had no idea how my mail gets to me. It must be quite a challenge."

"For sure. You don't have no idea," said Ernest Washington. "We're down here all day, and no one ever sees us. Like invisible folk."

"Know what you mean."

Washington harrumphed. "The system's divided up. The U.S. Mail don't go through the tubes, they bring it all in trucks, once a day, and it goes straight to our central clearing area—right where I am. We sort it and send it to you."

"And the intrahospital mail?"

"That goes through the tubes. The way it works is the tubes all lead to three collection bins, all down here in the Sub-B. One on the north end of the building, one on the south end, and one right here, in the middle. My staff checks each bin out— we do it regular, so you doctors can have your important mail ASAP. We sort it and send it on to your departments. Not once a day like the U.S. Postal Service. Twice. So you doctors can keep up with your important medical issues. That clear it up for you?"

"Crystal clear," said Jeremy. "Does it matter where the mail comes from?"

"What do you mean?"

"If it comes from Otolaryngology as opposed to let's say Surgery, is it handled differently?"

"Nope," said Washington. "To us, you're all the same."

Any port of entry. A sweet old person could slip an envelope down a chute and walk away, and no one would notice or care. A *bomb* could be dropped down the tubes . . .

Then he realized he'd been wasting his time and Ernest Washington's. The envelopes had found their way to him, *despite* being unmarked. That meant someone was getting to his mail between the time it arrived at Washington's dominion and ended up at his door.

Someone in Psychiatry? Or afterward?

He couldn't see anyone in the mental health army doing this. A pleasant, bland bunch, the lot of them. Caring people, nice. Vanilla nice. He was happy to be housed away from them.

Someone else knew he was an isolate, was taking advantage of that.

"Who? How?" he said out loud.

Obsessed.

So this was what curiosity was all about. It had been a long time since question marks had danced in his head. Then Arthur Chess, the most inquisitive man Jeremy had ever encountered, had come along, and now his own mind couldn't sit still.

Contagious, like a virus.

That made him think about poor Angela. He

phoned her apartment, got no answer. Probably sleeping. Good.

The suicide article and the postcard from the Museum of Tools stared up at him. He found the drawer where he'd tossed the card from Oslo, placed all of it in a folder that he labeled *Curiosity*.

Then he took pen in hand and composed a list. Alphabetizing, because it blessed him with a sense of pseudocontrol.

Tina Balleron
Arthur Chess
Norbert Levy
Edgar Marquis
Harrison Maynard

His first patient was scheduled soon—half an hour—and he had several more appointments after that. Meaning for the rest of the day he'd stuff his ego in the closet and concentrate on others. For thirty minutes, he'd indulge himself.

32

NONE OF THE CCC GOURMETS HAD LISTED PHONE numbers.

Twenty minutes before he had to run. Jeremy scrambled to remember personal details.

Harrison Maynard had written romance novels under female pseudonyms; no easy avenue of inquiry, there. The ancient Edgar Marquis was ex–State Department and had served on remote islands. That, too, offered little promise.

Norbert Levy. The engineer was emeritus at an Eastern university. A campus one thousand miles away and Levy living here implied an appointment in name only.

If Levy lived here.

No more assuming. Jeremy phoned the institution, connected to the Engineering Department, and asked for Professor Levy.

"Retired," said the secretary. "Quite a while back."

"Do you have a current address for him?"

"What's this about?"

Jeremy gave his name and the hospital's, spun a

tale about a biomechanical engineering convention, wanting to invite Levy.

"Okay," said the secretary. "Here it is."

Levy took his mail at a post office box south of downtown, not far from the Seagate district where Arthur had taken him for supper and confusion.

In a movie, Jeremy would rush over to stake out the mail drop. In real life, he had neither the time nor the ability—nor a sane reason to do so. Sitting day and night waiting in the rain? And what if, through some quirk, he encountered the white-bearded academic?

Professor Levy, what a coincidence! You wouldn't happen to be sending me weird stuff in hospital envelopes, would you?

He needed to *talk* to someone. Look into their eyes, read the nonverbal messages he'd supposedly been trained to decode.

That left Judge Tina Balleron, formerly of superior court.

Now *of* the golf course.

The woman's gigantic black pearls said she was fixed financially. Perhaps the good life included country club golf.

The city hosted three clubs. The Haverford, a relative upstart at sixty years old, accepted selected minorities. The Shropshire and the Fairview remained Protestant and lily-white.

Was Balleron a Latin name?

He called the Haverford first and asked for the

judge. The man who answered said, "I don't believe she's arrived yet."

"This is Dr. Carrier. When's she due?"

"Let's see . . . she's scheduled to tee off at 3 P.M. A doctor . . . is the judge all right?"

"She's dandy," said Jeremy, hanging up. The man had made no inquiries about a husband or other family member. Assuming any trouble would be the judge's.

Did that mean Tina Balleron lived alone? Just like Arthur.

Just like Jeremy?

So what?

No more assuming.

He saw his patients nonstop, eschewed coffee or lunch or breaks, hurried through his charts and kept his trench coat with him so he'd be able to leave the hospital without returning to his office.

At two-fifteen, he drove city streets to Hale Boulevard, continued on that sleek condominium-lined byway with its views of the lake, and continued out to the northern countryside.

The scenic route. Opposite direction from the journey to Arthur's rooming house in Ash View.

This trip was upper-level exurbia, then equestrian estates and gentleman's farms, the occasional riding academy, a couple of boarding schools surrounded by obstructive greenery. A mesh of finger lakes appeared, the land between them sodden as rice paddies. More empty meadows followed. Brightly painted signs advertised hundred-acre parcels. At

2:40 P.M., Jeremy was rolling up to the twenty-foot stone posts and iron gates of the Haverford Country Club.

Beyond the scrollwork was a sloping drive bordered by a low fieldstone ledge. Monumental trees sprouted on all sides. A white guardhouse sat in the distance. Jeremy parked at the side of the road.

The sun was recalcitrant, but that did little to ruin the scenery. He rolled down his window, and the air smelled sweet. Miles of barbered grass were too green, and rain-inked tree trunks glistened like obsidian columns. Stalwart rhododendrons and courageous roses defied the season and tossed off arrogant color. Ferns dripped with promise, and a few scarlet cardinals flitted in and out of the foliage.

No marauding ravens out here. A sky that had gloomed the city managed to be pretty: planes of polished silver striped with apricot deepening to crimson where the moisture refused to budge.

Jeremy thought of a poster in one of his colleague's offices. A psychologist named Selig, a kind, smart man who'd made a bundle in the stock market but continued to see patients because he enjoyed healing. He drove an old Honda to work, kept a new Bentley in the garage.

I've Been Poor and I've Been Rich. Rich Is Better.

Jeremy wondered what it would be like to be rich. He'd treated enough wealthy depressives to know that money didn't buy you happiness. Could it do anything to blunt the misery when things went really bad?

He sat in his car, eyes on the country club's gates. During a fourteen-minute period, five luxury cars arrived, punched in at the call box and, when the ironwork swung open, cruised through confidently.

The sixth car was Tina Balleron's white Cadillac and Jeremy was waiting, standing several feet in front of the gate, when she pulled up.

Not a new Caddy. Five, six years old, with dark-tinted windows and chromed, spoked wheels. A thin red pinstripe bisected the robust chassis, and a fresh wax job repelled moisture.

Like Arthur's Lincoln, beautifully maintained.

The dark windows were rolled up. When they lowered, Jeremy noticed they were much thicker than usual—a good half inch of convex glass.

He'd expected Tina Balleron to be startled by his presence, but her face was serene. "Dr. Carrier."

"Your Honor."

"Do you golf?"

Jeremy smiled. "Not quite. I was hoping to speak with you before you teed off."

She glanced at a diamond wristwatch. No black pearls today; a pink cameo on a gold chain. Diamond chip in the coral woman's eyes. One of Tina Balleron's silver-nailed hands curled on the Cadillac's padded steering wheel. The other rested on a cream-colored ostrich handbag. A long fur coat lay across the rear seat.

She said, "Let me pull over."

She parked behind Jeremy's car. He followed on foot, heard a click that meant she'd unlocked the doors, and headed for the passenger door.

The passenger window lowered. The same thick glass. "Come in out of the cold, Jeremy."

When he opened the door, he felt its extra weight.

The panel closed with the hiss of a bank vault. An armored car.

He slid onto the passenger seat. The car's interior was ruby red leather. A tiny gold plaque on the glove compartment was inscribed: *To Tina, With All My Love, Bob. Happy Birthday!*

An August date, just over five years ago.

So there had been a husband. Maybe there still was.

The ostrich purse rested in Tina Balleron's sleek lap. She wore a baby blue, knit pantsuit and navy patent shoes. Her champagne-tinted hair was freshly done. The fur across the backseat was dyed mink—a precise match to her coiffure. A crystal bud vase bracketed between the windows on the driver's side held a single white rose.

"So," she said. "What's on your mind?"

"Sorry to barge in like this, but I'm looking for Arthur. I haven't been able to reach him in nearly a week."

"He's traveling."

"I know that," said Jeremy. "He's been sending me postcards."

"Has he? Well, that's good."

"Why is that?"

Tina Balleron smiled. "Arthur's fond of you, Jeremy. It's good when people express their fondness, don't you think?"

"I suppose . . . does he travel much?"

"From time to time—Jeremy, my dear, you can't have driven all the way out here to discuss Arthur's travel habits. What's really on your mind?"

"I've been getting other things in the mail—the hospital mail."

"Things," she said. Her fingers played with the clasp of the ostrich-skin bag.

"Articles from medical journals—on laser surgery. Then an account of a six-year-old murder in England and a piece on physician suicide."

He waited for her reaction.

She didn't offer one.

"Judge, I assumed Arthur was sending them to me because I couldn't think who else might be behind it. But he's in Europe, so it's not him."

"And you're puzzled."

"Wouldn't you be?"

"And you drove all the way out here to indulge your puzzlement."

Indulge; same word he'd used when rationalizing.

"What's behind it," said Tina Balleron, stroking the bag. "That sounds as if you think it's a plot of some sort."

"I guess I do feel that way. The articles arrive unannounced, unexplained, and I can't find any reason why I'd be the recipient. It's a little unnerving, wouldn't you say?"

Tina Balleron turned contemplative.

When she didn't speak, Jeremy said, "I assumed Arthur was sending them because he's interested in violence—from what I heard at supper, you all are."

Balleron unclasped the purse, clicked it shut. "And you consider that an unusual interest."

"Violence?"

"Life-and-death issues," she said. "Wouldn't they

be core issues for any civilized person?" She waved
a hand around the car. "Pretty things are nice,
Jeremy, but in the end they're all diversions."

"From what?"

"Important issues. Arthur's a man of substance
and experience. One lives a certain amount of time,
one *experiences*."

"You're saying there's something in Arthur's past
that has given him—"

"Don't worry about Arthur, my dear." She
reached over and rested her fingers atop Jeremy's
sleeve. "Stay on target."

"What's the target?"

"That's up to you to find out."

"Really, Judge—"

She hushed him with a finger on his lip. Angela
had done the same thing.

Be quiet, little boy.

A Mercedes pulled up to the gates. Its window
rolled down, and a well-fed male face smiled at the
judge.

"Hank," she said. "Are you ready?"

"Ready as ever, Teen. See you on the green."

The Mercedes rolled to the gates, and the gates
swung open automatically. An unseen sentry—up
at the guardhouse—knowing who belonged and who
didn't.

Balleron smiled at Jeremy. "Nice to see you
again, but I'm afraid I'm going to have to cut our
little chat short. Tee time is sacred. Golf's less a
game than a religion. Miss one's start, and one in-
curs the wrath of one's cobelievers."

Her hand left his wrist and lowered the sun visor.

On the inner side was a mirror, and she checked her reflection. Opening the ostrich purse, she pulled out a compact and began dusting her face.

Fixing herself up for golf?

Leaving the ostrich bag wide open and allowing Jeremy to see what lay on top of the usual female stuff.

A shiny little automatic pistol.

Tina Balleron knew he'd seen it. She clicked open the door, and said, "Bye, now."

"Judge Balleron, something was said that night. 'Expediency trumps virtue.' It caused the room to go silent—"

"Silence can be a virtue in and of itself, dear. Till the next time, then." She smiled and leaned over and kissed his cheek. Jeremy got out of the Cadillac, and the white car rolled toward the gates of the country club.

She stopped. Down came the window.

"By the way," she said, "I inquired about those gannet birds—the little monogamous thingies Harrison told us about. You suggested a population issue. I can't find evidence of such."

She smiled up at Jeremy.

He said, "Okay."

"Maybe," she said, "they just do the right thing."

She raised the window, resumed driving. Jeremy stood there as the gates rolled open for her. Leaving him outside.

The outsider, always the outsider.

33

HE WAS BACK AT HIS DESK BY FOUR-THIRTY AND COL-
lected his messages—consult requests, announcements of meetings, some utter rubbish.

No postcards, no Otolaryngology envelopes.

But there wouldn't be. Too soon. Everything was
paced.

He got back on the computer.

The *Clarion* was your typical journalistic medi-
ocrity, but it did host an on-line archive that one
could access for a fee. Jeremy surrendered a credit
card number and logged in.

"Robert Balleron" pulled up five hits, all four to
five years old.

Industrialist Found Slain in Office
Some Theorize Balleron Murder Related to
    Real Estate Success
Balleron Murder Remains a Mystery
Balleron Spouse, a Judge, Questioned
Police Continue to Probe Balleron Murder

Robert A. Balleron, sixty-nine, had been murdered sixty miles away, in Greenwood, an affluent bedroom community. The paper hadn't covered the crime directly; each piece came over the wire service.

Jeremy pulled them up, one by one. The "developer and real estate magnate" had been found in the home office of his "palatial Tudor mansion," slumped at an "ornate desk" dead of multiple gunshot wounds. Robert Balleron had been politically active, highly competitive, confrontational when he felt his interests were being threatened. A tough man but beyond reproach ethically—somewhat of a prig, actually, with a history of leveling corruption charges at those he deemed deserving.

The crime scene details were thin: no forced entry, the house's alarm system had been switched off, and the killer had apparently entered through the office's French doors, after crossing "the multiacre estate."

"Unnamed sources" speculated that Balleron's sharp tongue and aggressive business tactics had alienated the wrong person, and suggestions of murder-for-hire were made. But no follow-up to that theory was offered.

The victim's wife, Superior Court Judge Tina Balleron, had been out the night of the murder—dining with friends—and had come home to discover the body. She'd been questioned, but a police spokesperson insisted she'd not been considered a suspect.

Jeremy plugged "Balleron Murder" into the

archives, got no more hits. Logging out of the news-paper file, he tried several Internet search engines and pulled up a solitary wire-service piece the ar-chive had missed: six months after the murder, the police had come up with no leads, and the case re-mained open.

He returned to the paper and scanned the next few years for anything on Tina Balleron. Zero.

A prominent woman like that, a notable crime. She'd made a point of keeping out of the public eye.

He searched for homicides of other Greenwood developers and found only an accidental death: Three years ago, a builder of shopping malls named Michael Srivac had perished in a single-car acci-dent. Srivac merited a four-line obituary. *In lieu of flowers, contributions should be sent to Planned Parenthood.*

Jeremy organized his thoughts. Robert Balleron had been slain five years ago. Tina Balleron's Cadil-lac wasn't much older than that. The developer had gifted his wife with an armored car shortly before his death.

Knowing she was in danger.

She'd survived. And thrived. Stepping down from the bench, moving to the city, joining the Haverford.

One good way to keep a low profile was to leave home.

Pearls and fur and a gun in the purse . . . the mer-riest of widows. A strong woman who took care of herself.

Jeremy thought of something the judge had said that afternoon: *One lives a certain amount of time, one experiences.*

Maybe they're just doing the right thing.

Was *tragic experience* what the CCC people had in common? Crime victims, all of them? Did that explain all the interest in the genesis of violence?

That fit with the pall that had followed Maynard's comment about expedience trumping virtue.

Finally, he sensed he was on to something. Heart pounding, he plugged "Chess homicide" into the archive.

Found nothing.

The same for "Marquis homicide." "Levy homicide" pulled up the case of a missing Washington intern, but Jeremy could find no connection to Professor Norbert.

Switching back to the general databases proved no more successful.

Wrong Man. Maybe he should just start feeling comfortable with that.

The third postcard arrived three days later. During that period, Jeremy had seen Angela once for coffee, and they'd shared a hurried dinner in the doctors' dining room before she rushed back to on-call. Both times, she'd looked tired and talked of being worn down.

Yet she'd found time to observe two of Dirgrove's surgeries.

"You're okay with that, right?"

"Why shouldn't I be?"

"He's all business, Jer . . . I guess I'm feeling guilty. Overloading my already crazy schedule, not having time for you—I promise to be better when things ease up."

"You're fine."

"That's nice of you to say—now you see that side of me."

"What side?"

"Driven, obsessive. My father always kidded me about it. 'Where's the race, Princess?'" She shot Jeremy a wan smile. "Intellectually, I know he's right, but the thing is I *do* feel there's a race. Against time—against the time when your mind and body slow down and grind to a halt and you end up six feet under. Morbid, huh?"

"Maybe it's too many hours on the wards," said Jeremy.

"No, I've always been this way. If the assignment was to write a five-page bio paper, I handed in seven. When the gym teacher said ten girl push-ups, I did boy push-ups and struggled for twenty. I'm sure part of it's OCD. When I was eight, I went through a ritual phase—checking my bedroom for an hour before I'd go to sleep. Lining up my shoes. No one knew. I'd let my mother put me to bed, sneak out, go through the entire rigamarole. If something interrupted me, I started from scratch."

"How'd you stop?"

"I told myself it was stupid and lay shaking under my covers until the urge passed. For months I got the urge, but I stuck to my guns. When I was twelve I developed an ulcer. The doctor—and my parents—insisted it was a bacterial infection. They treated me with antibiotics and I got better. But still . . . now you know my whole sordid past. Any analysis, Doctor?"

He shook his head.

"Really," she insisted. "What do you think?"

"Have you ever lost anyone close to you?"

"My grandma," she said. "I was six and she was old and ill, but we were close . . . it shocked me. The fact that I'd never see her again."

Jeremy nodded.

She said, "So what you're saying is that loss was so profound that it traumatized me about death? The essence—the permanence? And now I need to race through life like a headless chicken, piling up experiences?"

"I was thinking more of an untimely death. Someone struck down prematurely. But sure. If your grandmother's passing was a shock, it could influence you that way. Traumatic loss does that. The *gone*-ness of it all."

"The gone-ness." She shook her head, smiling. "You and words. How's your writing, by the way?"

"Torturous."

"It'll work out." Angela's eyes grew distant. "Maybe you're right. I don't know." She looked away, lowered her voice. "Premature death. You've been through that."

"What do you mean?" said Jeremy, louder than he'd intended.

"You know."

Jeremy stared at her. Knew he was glaring but couldn't stop.

He said, "Let's change the subject."

Her face drained of color. "Sure, I'm sorry, forget I mentioned it."

"Don't worry about it," he said, but his heart was pounding, and he needed to get out of there.

As close as we've become, there are places she can't go. Some things I will not share.

"Jeremy?"

"Yes."

"I'm sorry."

"Nothing to be sorry about."

"I've got to go," she said. "I'm not sure when I'm going to have free time."

"Are you on tonight?"

"No, but I need to hit the sack early. I'm still feeling kind of run-down—maybe the flu hasn't left my system."

"Want me to walk you up to the ward?"

"No, it's okay."

"Take care of yourself."

"You, too."

The following afternoon, she called to tell him she'd been tied up in surgery, planned to observe more.

Ted Dirgrove had "performed" a quintuple bypass. The verb made Jeremy think of a stage and a baton.

"Interesting," he said.

"Amazing. It's something to see."

"And the patient survived."

"What do you mean?"

"The only patient Dirgrove and I have in common didn't."

"Oh." She sounded deflated. "Yes, that was bad . . . I guess I'd better be going—did I ever thank you for babying me through my flu?"

"More than once."

"I wasn't sure if I did. Since I got back on service, things got so hectic so quickly, and I know we haven't—anyway, thanks again. For the soup and everything else. That was beyond the call of duty."

Her gratitude sounded formalized. Putting space between them.

Who was he kidding? *He'd* done that. The conversation-killing glower, when all she'd done was ask about . . .

"Still feeling run-down?" he said.

"A little, but better."

"So the bypass was amazing."

"Really, Jer. The human heart, this little thing, like a big plum—like a skinless tomato. What a *gorgeous* thing, the way the chambers and valves work in concert. It's . . . *philharmonic*. While the arteries are being spliced in, they keep the heart pumping artificially and . . . it's . . . I keep thinking in orchestral terms, that perfect balance, the tempo—uh-oh, I just got another page, have to go."

The third postcard was from Damascus, Syria. A picture of the ancient Casbah—a shiny shot of jumbled stalls and their proprietors. White-robed men peddling brassware and carpets and dried nuts.

Postmarked Berlin.

Aha!

Aha, *what*?

All Jeremy could come up with was that Arthur's wanderlust had its limits. The old man was unwilling to forgo the creature comforts of the Western World for a Levantine jaunt.

But he wanted *Jeremy* to think Levantine.

Damascus . . . Jeremy knew Syria was a brutal dictatorship, but, beyond that, the country and its ancient capital meant nothing to him.

Oslo, Paris, Damascus . . . Oslo, Paris, *Berlin*, Damascus? If this was a game, he wasn't even on the playing field.

He stuck the postcard in the *Curiosity* file. Had a second thought and pulled out the file and reviewed its contents and ended up with a crushing headache.

He popped aspirin, took the risk of drinking his own lousy coffee.

By the end of the day, alone, with no chance of seeing Angela, with the prospect of his dark, cold house in his immediate future, he found himself hoping for another Otolaryngology envelope. Anything to clear the haze. He stopped by the Psychiatry Office to make sure no new mail had come through.

The office was closed.

Nothing arrived in either of the next day's deliveries. Same for the day after that.

Suddenly, life was too quiet.

The weekend rolled around. Angela was back on call and Jeremy endured a solitary Saturday, doing crosswords, pretending to be interested in sports, smiling at Mrs. Bekanescu when she stuck her head out to sweep her front porch. Receiving an ugly look in return.

What had Doresh told her?

He read the entire Sunday paper, wondering if any details about the nameless woman on the Finger would surface. They didn't. By Sunday evening he was ready to climb the walls.

His beeper had been silent all weekend. He phoned the page operator and asked if any calls had come through.

"No, Doctor, you're all clear."

He drove to the hospital anyway, attacked his book introduction, was astonished to find the words flowing. He finished the damn thing by 10 P.M., reread it, made a few changes, and packaged it to send to the Head of Oncology for review.

Now what?

Not long ago he'd have cherished the solitude. Now, he felt incomplete.

He logged on to the computer, returned to the *Clarion* archive, activated his account and entered Norbert Levy's name as a search-word. Not limited, this time, by "homicide."

Zero.

The same went for "Edgar Marquis" and, not surprisingly, the·pseudonym-protected "Harrison Maynard."

Tina Balleron had mentioned a couple of Maynard's aliases. "Amanda . . . Fontaine," "Barbara Kingsman."

Nothing under either *nom de plume*.

He gave up, turned the computer off, drove to the Excelsior Hotel, made a beeline for the bar. Empty bar, he had his pick of booths and chose the same one where he and Arthur had drunk and talked and nibbled on hors d'oeuvres.

He ordered a double scotch.

The old waiter who'd served them wasn't on duty. The young man who brought his drink was bland-faced and cheerful and had a high-stepping, prancing walk that made Jeremy think of a race-horse straining at the bit.

"Any particular brand, sir?"

"Nope."

Same room, same booth, but nothing was the same.

Jeremy sat there for a long time, stretching out his refills in an attempt to simulate self-control.

The young waiter was bored and took to reading the paper. Insipid music played in the background. By the time Jeremy finished his third scotch, his body was buzzing.

No sadder place than Sunday in a big-city hotel. This city prided itself on Midwestern wholesome-ness, and Sunday was family day. Even the lobby was deserted, saurian salesmen departed to long-suffering wives, hotel hookers doing whatever working girls did on Sunday.

Sometimes they died.

Jeremy waved that away. Actually moved his hand to dispel the thought. No one was around to notice the ticlike gesture, and he repeated it. Amused, like a naughty kid who'd gotten away with something.

He called for still another drink, filled his blood with alcohol, drank himself rosy. On some level—a cutaneous level—it was a pleasant experience. But for the most part he felt detached.

Living in someone else's skin.

34

ON MONDAY HE WOKE UP MEAN AND LOGY AND stiff, and he wondered if he'd caught Angela's flu.

A brisk walk in the chilled air burned his chest and woke him up and by the time he drove to work, he felt semicivilized. Stopping for coffee in the dining room, he spotted Ted Dirgrove and another white-coat engaged in what looked like tense conversation. The same swarthy, mustachioed man who'd sat with the surgeon the first time Jeremy had noticed him. The two of them, and the cardiologist, Mandel.

No reason to notice them now, because the room was filled with white-coats, and Dirgrove and his companion were off in a far corner. But something about the heart surgeon . . . Angela's enthrallment with what Dirgrove did . . .

He *was* jealous.

He filled a cup, headed out of the room. Dirgrove and the other man hadn't budged. Their discussion looked tense—something academic? No, this seemed personal. Their body postures were those of two dogs facing off.

Then Dirgrove smiled, and so did the other man.

Two dogs with their teeth bared.

Even match. The other doctor was Dirgrove's height, had a similar, slender build, and, like Dirgrove, his hair was close-cropped. But this curly cap was as dark as his mustache.

The dark man talked with his hands. Offered a parting shot and exited the dining room. Dirgrove stood there alone, his hands clenched. That cheered Jeremy, and he decided he was hungry and went back for a sweet roll.

He decided to sit down to eat. Dirgrove left. A few moments later, Angela appeared, in a group of residents.

Chattering, happy, hyperactive. All of them, looking so young.

She'd talked about feeling worn-out, but now she was the essence of vitality.

All of them were. Kids.

Suddenly, the five years between Angela and Jeremy seemed a generation. Jocelyn had been Angela's age, but she'd seemed more . . . seasoned. Maybe it was the years she'd put in as a nurse. Or the grunt jobs she'd worked to put herself through nursing school.

Angela, anxious and driven despite a happy childhood, her father's princess, might never get past the guilt of being wellborn.

Jocelyn's family was trailer-park poor, and she'd been on her own since adolescence. She'd appreciated everything.

A working girl.

No. That sounded *so* wrong.

Tears filled Jeremy's eyes. He put his roll and his

coffee aside, hurried out, careful to escape Angela's notice.

The fourth envelope arrived. Finally.

Tuesday morning, stuck in the middle of a stack of ignorables. Jeremy had taken to cruising by the Psychiatry Office or sticking his head out of his door at random moments in hope of coming upon the anonymous mailer.

To no avail. And it really didn't matter, did it? The medium *was* the message.

Thin envelope—thinner than usual. Inside was a single slip of paper upon which was typed a single line:

Ethics of the Fathers, Sforno, 5:8e

Obviously some kind of reference. An ancient text? Something Buddhist? Italian?

He got on the computer and had his answer within moments.

Religious but not Buddhist. *Ethics of the Fathers* was a volume—a "tractate"—from the Jewish Talmud, the only one of sixty-three that didn't deal primarily with laws.

"The Bartlett's of Judaism," one authority called it.

"A compendium of morality," opined another.

"Sforno" was Ovadiah Sforno, an Italian rabbi and physician who'd lived during the Renaissance and was primarily known for his commentary on the Bible.

He'd also written a lesser-known companion to *Ethics of the Fathers*.

Where would you find something like that?

Maybe at Renfrew's, back when the mute man had been alive.

He called two city libraries. Neither carried the book in any edition. Pulling out the phone book, he looked up bookstores in the yellow pages.

He tried several sellers of new books and antiquarian tomes. None of the proprietors had any idea what he was talking about. A couple of stores advertised themselves as "religious booksellers," but "religious" turned out to be Catholic and Lutheran, respectively.

The owner of the Catholic bookstore said, "You might try Kaplan's."

"Where's that?"

"Fairfield Avenue."

"Fairfield, east of downtown?"

"That's it," said the man. "What used to be the Jewish neighborhood before they all moved out to the suburbs."

"Kaplan's still there?"

"Last I heard."

Fairfield Avenue was a brief, drizzly ride from the hospital, two lanes of sinuous, potholed asphalt crowded with soot-blackened, prewar buildings. Nearly all the storefronts had been bricked over, and the once-commercial avenue was mostly U-rent storage facilities. Faded signs painted on grimy walls hinted at a previous life:

SCHIMMEL'S PICKLES
SHAPIRO'S FISH MARKET
KOSHER BUTCHER

The bookstore was ten feet wide, with flaking gold lettering that read BOOKS, GIFTS AND JUDAICA above what Jeremy assumed was the same legend in Hebrew. The glass was dark—not blackened like Renfrew's but dimmed by what appeared to be unlit space.

Closed. The last holdout, folding.

But when Jeremy turned the brass doorknob, it relented, and he stepped into a tiny, dim room. No overhead lights; an amber-shaded, copper-based lamp cast a cone of illumination on a battered, oak desk. The room should've smelled musty but didn't.

Behind the desk sat a man, elderly, clean-shaven, wearing a black suede skullcap over a head of bluntly cut gray hair. An old man but a big man, undiminished by time. Wide-shouldered and heavy-boned, he sat with military posture, wore a white shirt and dark tie and braided leather braces. Gold-framed half glasses rested on a thin, slender nose. Behind him was a glass case filled with a mix of objects: silver cups and candelabras, record albums festooned with Stars of David (*Uncle Shimmy Sings the Zemiros*), children's games, what appeared to be plastic spinning tops, velvet bags embroidered with more six-pointed stars. Below all that, three shelves of books.

The man was tinkering with a black leather box attached to a series of matching straps and looked up. "Yes?"

"Do you have Rabbi Sforno's commentary on *Ethics of the Fathers*?"

The man studied him. "You can get it over the Internet."

"I'd rather have it, now."

"Eager to learn?" said the man. "It's a very good commentary."

"So I've heard."

"How did you find me?"

"The Catholic bookstore recommended you."

"Ah, Joe McDowell, he was always loyal." The man smiled and stood. At least six-three. His torso was huge, and Jeremy wondered how he'd adjusted to the closet-size premises. He extended a hand. "Bernard Kaplan."

"Jeremy Carrier."

"Carrier . . . is that French?"

"Way back," said Jeremy. Then he blurted, "I'm not Jewish."

Kaplan smiled. "Few people are . . . excuse my curiosity, but Sforno's commentary is a rather eso-teric request. For anyone."

"Someone recommended it to me. A doctor at Central Hospital, where I work."

"Good hospital," said Kaplan. "All my children were born there. None became doctors."

"Did Dr. Chess deliver them?"

"Chess? No, don't know him. We used Dr. Op-penheimer. Sigmund Oppenheimer. Back then he was one of the few Jewish doctors they allowed in."

"The hospital was segregated?"

"Not officially," said Kaplan. "But of course. Everything was. Some places still are."

"The country clubs."

"If it was only the country clubs. No, your hospital was not a citadel of tolerance. During the early fifties there was some agitation about expelling the few Jewish doctors on staff. Dr. Oppenheimer was the reason it didn't happen. The man delivered so many babies that losing him would've slashed revenues too severely. He delivered the mayor's children and just about anyone else's who wanted the best. Golden hands."

"It often comes down to dollars and cents," said Jeremy.

"Often it does. And that's the point of the *Ethics of the Fathers*. It shouldn't. There's more to life than dollars and cents. It's a wonderful book. My favorite quotation is, 'The more meat, the more worms.' Meaning, he who dies with the most toys, simply has the most toys. Also, 'Who is happy? He who is satisfied with what he's got.' If we could just realize that—and I include myself. Anyway, Dr. Carrier, I just happen to be *carrying* one copy of the Sforno edition because I ordered it for a man who changed his mind and stuck me with it when he bought it at discount over the Internet." Kaplan opened the glass case, pulled out a paperback with dusty-rose covers, and handed it over.

Jeremy read the title. "Pirk-eye . . ."

"*Peerk-ey,*" said Kaplan. "That means chapters in Hebrew. *Pirkei Avos*—literally the chapters of the Fathers."

"Who were the Fathers?"

"Not priests, that's for sure." Kaplan chuckled. His eyes were gray-blue, amused, slightly bloodshot. "It doesn't mean father literally, in Hebrew the term also applies to scholars. In our tradition, when someone teaches you something important, he becomes as valued as a parent. Feel free to inspect the book."

"No, I'll take it," said Jeremy. "How much?"

"Fifteen dollars. For you, twelve."

"That's not necessary."

"You're doing me a favor, young man. I'm not likely to sell it to anyone else. No one comes here anymore. I'm a relic and should be smart enough to engage in voluntary extinction. But retirement means death, and I like the old neighborhood, this street, the memories of the people I used to know. I own this building and a few others on Fairfield. When I die, my kids will sell everything and make out like bandits."

That caused Jeremy to think of something. "Did you know Mr. Renfrew—the used-book seller?"

"Shadley Renfrew," said Kaplan. "Certainly. A fine man—ah, you knew him because his shop was right near the hospital."

"Yes," said Jeremy.

"I heard he passed on. Too bad."

"He beat cancer, then his heart gave out."

"Throat cancer," said Kaplan. "That's why he never spoke. Before the cancer, he used to sing. Had a wonderful voice."

"Did he?"

"Oh, yes. An Irish tenor. Maybe he was lucky."

"In what way?"

"Enforced silence," said Kaplan. "Perhaps it made him wiser. That's something else you'll find in there."

He tapped the book. " 'Be cautious with your words, lest they learn to lie.' Here, let me wrap it for you." He reached into a drawer and drew out something shiny and orange. "And here's a hard candy to go with it. Elite, from Israel. They're very good. I used to give it out to the kids when they came in. You're the youngest person I've seen around here in ages, so today *you'll* be the lucky kid."

Jeremy thanked him and paid for the book. As he left the shop, Bernard Kaplan said, "That customer could wait for his ethics. I'm glad you couldn't."

35

ON THE WAY TO THE CAR, JEREMY POPPED THE orange candy in his mouth and ground it to sweet, citrus dust.

He opened the book while the Nova's engine idled. The right side was Hebrew, the left English translation. During the brief time he'd been in the shop, the temperature had dropped, and the car had turned frigid. Still a good ways from winter, but his windshield was coated with a gossamer layer of rime. It could get like that because of the lake. Winds whipping across the water, churning up the cold.

His first year at City Central, a storm from the north had plunged the mercury from forty above to forty below in two hours, and the hospital's auxiliary generators had threatened to shut down.

No deaths, the bottom-liners claimed, but Jeremy'd heard tales of respirators hesitating, operating lights switching off midincision.

He switched on the heater, reached to activate the wipers to clear the frost and thought better of it. Privacy was good.

Time to soak up some ethics from the Fathers.

From Bernard Kaplan's quotations and the Bartlett's analogy, he'd expected a collection of homilies, and the pages he flipped on the way to Chapter Five seemed consistent with that.

But Chapter Five, paragraph 8 was different.

A litany of punishments wreaked upon the world for a host of transgressions.

Famine for failure to tithe, a plague of wild beasts for vain oaths, exile for idolatry.

Section e read:

> **The sword of war comes to the world
> for the delay of justice.**

Rabbi Ovadiah Sforno's commentary backed that up with a citation from Leviticus: *A sword avenging the vengeance of the covenant.*

Someone out to set things in order.

A covenant—an agreement—to set things straight.

By clearing up unsolved murders?

Or committing new ones—a cleansing plague?

36

VIEWED THROUGH THE PRISM OF VENGEFUL JUSTICE, the articles took on a different cast.

Laser surgery on women. Newspaper accounts of two murdered women.

The laser, a cleansing weapon—a cleansing *tool*?

Had some madman used an ancient text as rationale for his personal brand of justice?

Or worse: a fiend, simply bragging?

Jeremy flipped through the pink book and gazed, uncomprehending, at the Hebrew letters. Could there be a Jewish link to all this? Someone wanting him to think there was?

That brought to mind something he'd read years ago, in college. About Jack the Ripper. An abnormal psych professor, straining for relevance, had placed a true-crime account of the Whitehall murders on his reading list, claiming it illustrated sadistic psychopathy better than any textbook.

Straining for relevance was generally a fool's game, and Jeremy had considered the work yet more gratuitous dumbing-down: lots of speculation, theories that could never be proved or disproved, pages of gory photos.

But one particular illustration came to mind, now. An etched reproduction of chalk graffiti scrawled on a black brick wall in London's East End. A message left at the scene of a prostitute killing—something about "the Juwes" not being blamed for nothing. The original writing had been sponged off, and some police constable had jotted from memory. The etcher had drawn upon his imagination.

The Ripper had done his thing in a heavily Jewish slum, and the accepted interpretation of the scrawl was an attempt to cast blame upon an already distrusted ethnic group.

According to Bernard Kaplan, Central Hospital had once been besmirched by anti-Semitism.

The murdered girls in the clipping had been English.

His head spinning, Jeremy closed the book and started the drive back to the hospital.

Oslo, Paris—Damascus by way of Berlin. The Syrian capital was sure to be a place hostile to Jews. And nowhere had Jew-hatred blossomed more fully than in Germany. Was Arthur guiding him in a certain direction?

Arthur and others? Tina Balleron hadn't been the least bit surprised to hear about the envelopes.

So maybe the articles weren't correspondence from a killer but precisely what he'd guessed initially: one of Arthur's surrogates doing the old man's bidding.

Leading him to an ancient Jewish book.

The only CCC member with a Jewish surname was Norbert Levy and during Jeremy's initial search nothing had come up linking the engineering professor to any homicides. Maybe he just needed to dig deeper.

He pressed down on the gas pedal, drove too quickly on streets slicked by oil and rain, found his way to the doctors' lot, parked quickly. Bounding out of the car, he hurried to his office.

A specific assignment. That felt good.

He'd barely hung his coat and booted up the computer when Angela phoned.

"I need to come over."

"Right now?"

"Yes—may I? Please?"

"Are you okay?"

"I don't want to talk about it over the phone. Are you free? Please say you are."

"I am," said Jeremy.

"I'm coming now."

She burst in wearing a black blouse tucked into khakis, and sneakers. No coat or stethoscope. Her hair was tied back carelessly and loose strands flew out wildly. Her eyes were raw, her cheeks tear-streaked.

"What is it?" said Jeremy.

She flashed a smile that sickened him. Pure defeat. When the words came out, her voice was strangled.

"I am so, so stupid."

*   *   *

Dirgrove had hit on her. Hard.

It had just happened—thirty minutes ago—in the surgeon's office. She'd been sitting shell-shocked in the female residents' locker room since then, had finally garnered the energy to call Jeremy.

Dirgrove had set it up carefully, inviting her over to discuss the aftereffects of coronary bypass surgery.

Something you should know, Dr. Rios, as a practicing physician.

When she showed up, he greeted her warmly but with formality, remained behind his desk and pointed to the journal articles he'd laid out for her in a neat, overlapping row. Bookmarks designated pages he deemed noteworthy.

When she sat down, he began lecturing her about patient care, then instructed her to have a look at one article in particular. His tie was tightly knotted, and he smelled freshly showered. When Angela began reading, he came around from behind his desk, made a show of smoothing the tailored white coats and freshly pressed scrubs that hung from a wooden rack next to a burbling saltwater aquarium.

Then he moved behind her. Stood there as she read.

She was halfway through the methodology section when a hand alit on her shoulder.

That was the way she thought of it. Alighting. Like a bird—no, an even flimsier creature—an insect. A mayfly.

Such a delicate touch, those spidery fingers.

Proximity added a new fragrance to the squeaky-clean aroma. A nice cologne, something herbaceous, masculine, applied sparingly.

She could hear her own breathing but not his.

He kept talking. His words blurred, and all she could feel was the touch of his fingers.

Drumming her shoulder, slowly. Moving to the nape of her neck, warm and dry.

Confident. It was that—his confidence, realizing how smug he felt—that froze her.

She shrugged him off—violently, she thought. But he didn't react except to lift the mayfly fingers.

She told herself to forget it, keep reading for an obligatory interval, then make some excuse and get out of there.

She heard him sigh. Regretful, she hoped. No harm, no foul.

Then the hand—both hands—returned. Got busy immediately. Before she realized what was happening, one had slid down the front of her blouse, wormed under her bra, cupped her breast, grabbed hold of a nipple, and pinched it gently to erection. The other stroked the nearly invisible down along her jawline. As if sketching the contour. As if drawing a preincision line.

She jumped up, faced him.

He stood there, hands at his side. Bent a knee because no gesture could be more casual than that.

"I can make you very happy," he said.

She'd prepared an outraged retort; her words died. He smirked.

She croaked out: "How . . . could you!"

He said, "Is that an objection? Or an inquiry about technique. If it's the latter, I'd be happy to show you how I *could*."

He touched his crotch. Massaged himself, showed off the obvious enthusiasm that tented his trousers.

She fled. Heard him laughing as she slammed his door.

"Report the bastard," said Jeremy, squeezing the words out between clenched jaws. Fighting to keep his voice even.

She flew into his arms, freed herself, began circling the office. Stopping at the window, she stared out at the air shaft, threw up her hands.

"Oh, shit," she moaned. "I left my coat there. And my scope. I'm going to have to go back there."

"No way. I'll get them for you."

"No—please. I don't want a scene. Let's just forget it. I'll figure something out."

Jeremy didn't answer.

Angela said, "What? Why are you so quiet?"

"Are you really able to forget it?"

"I don't know."

"He should be reported, Angela."

"What happens, then? His word against mine? An R-II against a tenured professor? It could never be proved. Copping a feel? I'll be drawn into a huge mess. Things will never be the same for me, here."

She pounded the windowsill with her fist. "Damn him! *Fuck* him!" A sickly smile spread across her lips. "Poor choice of words . . . God, Jeremy, how could I be so *dumb*!"

She hurried to his patient chair and slumped down heavily. "My coat and my scope. That's all I care about, I just want never to see him again. I'm off Thoracic in two days, anyway. There'll be no reason to see him. What was I thinking? I'm not going to be a cutter. What possessed me to want to waste my time with him?"

"This isn't about you being dumb. You wanted to be a better doctor. You believed he wanted to teach you."

"Yes. That's true." Her chest heaved. "But you knew better, didn't you?"

"No," he said. "I was just jealous."

She managed a half smile. "Oh, Jer, how could I have been so gullible? Would I have hung out with him if he looked like a troll? If he hadn't paid attention to me—singled me out from the other residents? I'd like to think I would've. I just wish I could be sure."

She doubled over in the chair. When she looked up her eyes were heavy with . . . guilt.

She'd been attracted to Dirgrove.

My jealousy wasn't baseless. Maybe my intuition's coming back.

He said, "It really doesn't matter what you thought or felt. He's the offender. He brought you in under false pretenses, touched you abusively, and when you let him know you weren't interested, he compounded the insult by grabbing his dick."

"Yes," she said. "That's what it was. Gross. And the way he smirked. 'I can make you happy.' What macho bravado b.s. The idiot's watched too many porno movies. He was letting me know I was nothing to him. That he was in charge . . . but jeez, how could I be so *stupid*!"

"You were caught off guard," said Jeremy. "It happens to all of us."

"Not to you, I'll bet. You're so . . . composed. You think everything out. Choose your words before you speak. Your training—all the people you've worked with—you probably never get caught off guard."

A knock sounded on the door, and Angela jumped. Jeremy opened it.

A young man in orderly's yellows stood there holding a white coat and a stethoscope.

"Is there a Dr. Rios, here?"

"I'll take those," said Jeremy.

"Sure, Doc. Dr. Dirgrove says you left them in his office. He says to tell you hi."

Jeremy closed the door.

Angela said, "He knew exactly where I'd go."

Jeremy said, "I guess it's no secret."

Thinking: *That's the point*. Dirgrove had gotten a kick out of letting the two of them know he had them pegged. This was all about power. Telling them who was in charge.

An errant memory flashed in his head. Last week, leaving Angela's house late at night, he'd believed someone had followed him in a car.

When the vehicle quickly went its own way, he'd dismissed it as paranoia. Now, he wondered.

Shortly after that, Dirgrove had asked for his help with Merilee Saunders.

Dr. Sensitive, worried about his patient's anxiety. Or something else?

Not bothering to inform the patient about the consult—setting Jeremy up for failure.

Then the patient dies. Just one of those things.

Informing Jeremy via Angela that he'd done a great job when he'd accomplished nothing.

Playing with him? One way or the other, he sensed he'd be dealing with Dr. Theodore Dirgrove.

37

HE WALKED A VERY SUBDUED ANGELA BACK TO THE wards and told her he'd stay late, they'd have dinner in the cafeteria.

"Not the doctors' dining room," she said.

"Not tonight, but eventually we'll go there, too. To hell with him."

"If I get phobic, will you do therapy with me?"

"Rapid therapy," he said. "You'll be fine."

She kissed him full on the lips. "Despite all you went through as a kid, you grew into a prince."

"C'mon up to my place, got a glass slipper for you."

"I mean it. I'm serious."

Jeremy returned to his office remembering boarding school bunks hard and flat as slate, the crispness of early-morning reveille, institutional food, the knowing smiles of those who fit in.

Back to the computer. There'd been nothing on Norbert Levy in the *Clarion* archive so it was time to expand to the Internet.

The first few citations Jeremy found for the retired professor had to do with his scientific work. Levy had been instrumental in the development of ultrahigh-reliability capacitors for use in spacecraft, ship gyroscopes, and weapons systems.

But the hit that held Jeremy's attention longest was something else completely: an account of an East Coast symposium on the Holocaust, convened by a survivors' group.

The rubric of the gathering was the complicity of non-German Europe: Swiss bankers hoarding stolen billions, Spanish and Italian and Scandinavian diplomats purchasing plundered artwork on the cheap, French politicians claiming to have resisted the Nazis when the facts revealed them to have been easy collaborators.

Levy, a holder of two doctorates—in physics and engineering—had become involved because of personal history. His father, Oscar Levy, a prominent German-born physicist, had left the Fatherland in 1937, when anti-Semitism at his university department led him to seek, and receive, a teaching post at Oxford. The following year, Levy, his mother, and two sisters were spirited to England and avoided the deportations that resulted in the deaths of their entire extended family. The family home in Berlin and its contents were confiscated by the Nazis. Gone were generations of personal effects as well as a collection of Egon Schieles, Gustav Klimts, and other expressionist masterpieces.

Those paintings, now valued in the tens of millions, had never been recovered, most probably hoarded by some private collector. Norbert Levy had chosen to address the symposium about morality.

The old professor hadn't been victimized by any single homicide. His focus was on the worst of crimes.

Jeremy found no full-text account of the remarks, but after considerable web-surfing, he managed to find a summary in a site called JewishWorldnet.com.

Noted Scientist Says Intelligence Has Nothing to Do with Morality

Renowned physicist Professor Norbert Levy delivered an address to the members of the Committee on Plundered Art (COPA) in which he criticized the continuing inertia of European governments and museums in owning up to complicity with Nazi war crimes. Despite continued evidence that a substantial number of current European art holdings consist of treasures confiscated by Hitler's SS, very little has been done to locate stolen art or to compensate the original owners.

Levy's speech drew from a wide range of sources as he illustrated how some of the brightest minds of the most civilized nations in the world had stooped to barbarity with relative ease. The award-winning scientist, in the past mentioned as a potential Nobel nominee, quoted the psychiatrist/ novelist Walker Percy to that effect: "You can get straight A's but still flunk life."

"Intelligence is like fire," Levy went on to say. "You can burn down the house, learn to cook, or forge beautiful works of art in a kiln. It comes down to personal morality, and that quality is sorely lacking in a good deal of what passes for intelligent society. The key to personal and national growth is combining moral training with intellectual rigor. The thirst for justice trumps everything else."

Though emphasizing that he was not a religious man, Levy stressed the influence Jewish humanistic values had played in his upbringing and he drew upon scriptural texts, citing calls for justice in the Bible and in the Talmudic tract, *Ethics of the Fathers*.

Jeremy searched for more on Levy's extracurricular activities but found nothing.

He plugged in "Edgar Marquis" minus the "homicide" limitation, and came up empty, again. Against all hope, he tried "Harrison Maynard." The writer had hidden behind a pen name, no reason to assume he'd go public about anything.

But Maynard's name appeared on the tribute committee of an East Coast dinner honoring the memory of Martin Luther King. Just a list with no links, one of those isolated cyberscraps floating around the cosmos, bereft of context.

"Martin Luther King memorial dinner" produced a single reference, a recent affair in California, and Maynard's name was nowhere to be found. Jeremy broadened the search to "Martin Luther King memorial" and came up with nearly three thousand hits. He downloaded for nearly two hours before finding what he was looking for.

Pages from a banquet journal. Photos of celebrated guests and benefactors. And there was Harrison Maynard, a trifle thinner, his hair and mustache a bit less gray, but otherwise the same man Jeremy had supped with.

Smiling and well fed and natty in a tuxedo. Next to him stood Norbert Levy, also in formal wear. The white-bearded physicist remained unidentified in the caption. Maynard was described as a former associate of Dr. King, among the first to rush to the slain civil rights leader's side as he lay dying in a motel parking lot. Harrison Maynard was now "a major benefactor of humanitarian causes." No mention was made of how he'd made his money.

From the civil rights struggle to bodice rippers. Maynard's philanthropy said he'd maintained a focus on morality, just like Norbert Levy.

Now Jeremy believed he was beginning to understand the old eccentrics.

Maynard had fought for equality and watched his idol die violently. Levy's extended family had been exterminated, and his inheritance plundered. Tina Balleron had lost her husband to violent crime.

Victims, all. What about Arthur? And Edgar Marquis? The ancient diplomat had alluded to witnessing too much duplicity in the foreign service—his reason for ending a career rise by requesting transfer to obscure posts in Micronesia and Indonesia.

Places he could do some good.

Idealists, all of them.

Good food and wine notwithstanding, they were all about justice—their vision of justice.

And now *he* was being courted.

Because of Jocelyn.

He wanted to think it out more, but evening had fallen, and he was due to meet Angela for a quick bite in the dining room in ten minutes.

Before he left, he looked up Theodore Dirgrove's office in the Attending Staff roster.

The penthouse floor of the Medical Office Building. The space occupied by Psychiatry until the cutters had deemed it theirs.

When Psychiatry had occupied the premises it was just an upper floor, dingily walled and floored. Now, the carpeting was fresh and clean, the walls, wainscoted. Polished mahogany doors replaced white slabs.

Dirgrove's door was closed. The surgeon's name was mounted in confident gold letters.

Jeremy stood in the hallway for several moments, finally approached, and knocked.

No answer.

He left to meet Angela and encountered Dirgrove as he got off the elevator.

Dirgrove wore a well-cut black suit over a black turtleneck. His nails were impeccable. His lips compressed when he saw Jeremy.

The two of them locked eyes. Dirgrove smiled but kept his distance. Jeremy smiled back and took a step forward. Putting so much intensity into the smile that his eyes burned.

Dirgrove held his ground, then he shrugged and laughed, as if to say, "This is trivial."

Jeremy said, "Lose any other patients, recently, Ted?"

Dirgrove's lips dropped suddenly, as if yanked down by fishhooks. His long, pale face turned deathly white. As he walked away, Jeremy stayed and watched. Dirgrove's hands kept clenching and unclenching, spidery fingers fluttering wildly, as if sparked by random synapses.

Jumpy. Not good for a surgeon.

38

ANGELA WORKED HARD AT FINISHING A THIRD OF her turkey sandwich. There wasn't much time till she went back on-call. Jeremy picked at his meat loaf, watched her push wilted lettuce around her plate.

She said, "I'm not very good company. Maybe I should just go."

"Stay a while." His beeper went off.

Angela laughed, and said, "There's an omen for you."

He took the call in the doctors' dining room, now empty. An oncologist named Bill Ramirez was phoning with an emergency. A patient they'd both seen seven years ago, a young man named Doug Vilardi, with Stage III Ewing's sarcoma of the knee, was back.

Jeremy had counseled Doug and the entire family shortly after diagnosis. Between the bad news, debilitating treatment, and losing a leg, there was plenty to cry about. But Jeremy finally figured out that what really bothered the seventeen-year-old was the prospect of sterility caused by radiotherapy.

Touching optimism, he'd thought, at the time.

The survival statistics for advanced Ewing's weren't encouraging. But he'd gone along with the fantasy, talked to Ramirez about sperm donation prior to treatment, learned it was feasible, and helped set things up.

Doug had lost his left leg but survived his cancer— one of those bright spots that energize you. No phantom pain, no tortured aftermath. He'd started with crutches, progressed to a cane, adjusted beautifully to his prosthesis. Jeremy had heard from him last, four years ago. The kid was playing basketball with his plastic leg and learning to lay brick.

What, now?

"Relapse?" he asked Ramirez.

"Worse, goddammit," said the oncologist. "Secondary cancer. AML or possibly a newly converted CML, I'm still waiting for Pathology to clear it up. Either way, it's leukemia, no doubt from the radiotherapy we gave him seven years ago."

"Oh, no."

"Oh, yes. 'The good news, kid, is we nuked your solid tumor to oblivion. The bad news is we nuked your hemopoietic system and gave you goddamn leukemia.' "

"Jesus."

"Him I could use," said Ramirez. "However, given the fact that Jesus didn't answer his page, I'll take you. Do me a favor, Jeremy. Make time to see him tonight. Soon as you can. They're all here— him, his parents, his sister. And get this: to make matters even more pitiful, a wife. Kid got married two years ago. Used the sperm we stored for him and now she's pregnant. Isn't life grand? He's up on Five West. When the hell can you make it over?"

"Soon as I finish dinner."

"Hope I didn't ruin your appetite."

He returned to the table. Angela hadn't taken a bite in his absence.

"Trouble?" she said.

"Not our trouble." He sat down heavily, ate a bit of meat loaf, washed it down with Coke, tightened his tie, and buttoned his white coat. Then he explained the situation to her.

She said, "That is *beyond* tragic. Helps put things in perspective. My petty little issues."

"Being petty's a constitutional right," he said. "I can't name the amendment, but believe me, it's definitely right there in the Bill of Rights. I see families falling apart after a traumatic diagnosis, everyone working hard at concentrating on the Big Issues. In a crisis that's fine, but you can't live like that indefinitely. Eventually I get around to telling them, 'When you start to be petty again, you'll know you're adjusting.'"

She placed her hand on his. "Where is he, on Five?"

"Five West. You still on Four?"

"Uh-huh."

"Let's ride up together."

He dropped her off and continued up to the cancer ward. Entertaining fantasies of bypassing the

ward and taking the passageway that connected to
the medical office wing. Then jogging the stairs up
to the penthouse level.

He had no idea what he'd say or do if he ran
into Dirgrove again, but he had a feeling he'd pull it
off well.

When the elevator door opened on Five West, he
walked out, looking to the most casual observer
like a man with a mission.

What the hell would he say to Doug Vilardi and
his family?

Most likely, he'd keep his mouth shut and listen.

The virtue of silence. *Ethics of the Fathers*.

At seventeen, Doug had been a tall, gawky, dark-
haired kid, not much of a student, his best class,
metal shop. Since then, he'd put on weight, lost
some of the hair that had grown back after chemo,
stuck a diamond chip in his left ear, grown a tea-
colored goatee, and gotten a tattoo on his right
forearm. *"Marika"* in blue script.

He looked like any regular guy who worked for a
living, except for the pallor—that certain pallor—
that sheathed his skin, and the jaundiced eyes that
lit up as Jeremy entered the room.

No family, just Doug in bed. The prosthetic leg
leaned in a corner. He wore a hospital gown, and
bedsheets covered him from his waist down. An IV
had already been hooked up, and every so often it
clicked.

"Doc! Long time, no see! Look what I did to
myself."

"Being creative, huh?"

"Yeah, life was getting too friggin' boring."
Doug laughed. Held out his hand for a soul shake.
Muscles flexed and *"Marika"* jumped as he held on
to Jeremy's fingers.

"It's good to see you, Doc."

"Good to see you, too."

Doug cried.

Jeremy sat down by the bed, took hold of Doug's
hand again, and held it. Blue-collar guy like this, try
it in any other situation and you'd be cruising for a
bruising.

Seven years ago, Jeremy had done a lot of hand-
holding.

Doug stopped sobbing, and said, "Fuck, that's
exactly what I didn't wanna do."

"I think," said Jeremy, "that you can be excused
a little emotion."

"Yeah . . . oh, shit, Doc, this reeks! I got a baby
coming; what the fuck am I gonna *do*?"

Jeremy stayed with him for two hours, mostly
listening, occasionally commiserating. The parents
stuck their heads in after the first hour, saw Jeremy,
smiled weakly, and left.

A nurse came in and asked Doug if he was experi-
encing pain.

"A little, in the bones, nothing heavy." He rubbed
his ribs and his jaw. The chart said his spleen was
already enlarged, maybe dangerously so.

"Dr. Ramirez says you can have Percocet if you want."

"What do you think, Doc?"

Jeremy said, "You know how you feel."

"It wouldn't be chickenshit?"

"Not hardly."

"Yeah, then. Shoot me up." Doug smiled up at the nurse. "Can I have some rum, too? Or a beer."

She was a young one, and she winked. "On your own time, stud."

"Cool," said Doug. "Maybe Doc here'll get me something refreshing."

"Aiding and abetting?" said the nurse.

Everyone chuckled. Filling the time. The nurse shot Percocet into the IV line. The drug had no clear effect for a while, then Doug said, "Yeah, it's taking the edge off—Doc, mind if I sleep?"

The parents and the wife were waiting right outside the door. Marika, short, pretty, with shaggy blond hair and stunned blue eyes. Her belly bore the swell of early pregnancy. She looked around sixteen.

She didn't talk and neither did Doug's father, Doug, Senior. Mrs. Vilardi talked for all of them, and Jeremy stayed with the family for another hour, filled his ears with weeping, stuffed his soul full of misery.

After that came the conference with Bill Ramirez, another twenty minutes answering the reasonable, caring questions of the night nurses, thinking out plans to be made for future psychological support, and, finally, charting.

When he finally stepped out into the hallway, it was early morning, and he could barely keep his eyes open.

He returned to his office to collect his raincoat and his briefcase, considered another go at the computer, thought better of it.

He drove home on autopilot, passing the now-dark façade of the Excelsior, gliding through empty, sepia streets, unaware of the moon, head blessedly free of thoughts and pictures.

Stumbling into his house, he managed to get out of his clothes before his feet gave way. He was deeply asleep before he hit the pillow.

39

HE OVERSLEPT, ATE NO BREAKFAST, DRESSED AS IF donning a costume.

His first appointment was Doug Vilardi at eleven. The young man would be starting chemotherapy that afternoon. If that and more radiation didn't bring about remission, the only option was a bone marrow transplant, and that meant transfer to another hospital, fifty miles away.

The decision to opt for treatment could have been agonizing. Treatment had saved Doug's life, but it had also poisoned his bone marrow.

Doug hadn't wavered. "What the fuck, Doc. What'm I supposed to do? Curl up and die? I got a baby coming."

Not a particularly smart kid, not sophisticated or articulate. The challenge for Jeremy had been helping him put his thoughts into words. But once he'd gotten there, Doug had sailed.

Jeremy's approach had been to ask about bricklaying.

"You should see, I built some walls, man. Some serious walls."

Me too.

"Know that cathedral—St. Urban's, over on the south end? The rectory on the side—the smaller building, it's all brick, not like the church, which is stone? We repaired that, my company and me. Had all these curves, you look at it, think how'd they do that."

Jeremy knew the cathedral, had never noticed the rectory. "And it came out good."

"Better than good, man, it was . . . beautiful. Everyone said so, the priests, all of 'em."

"Good for you."

"It wasn't only me, it was the whole crew. I learned from those guys. Now we got newer guys, and I'm teaching them. I gotta get back to work. If I don't work I feel . . ."

Doug threw up his hands.

Jeremy nodded.

"My mom's scared of them treating me. Says they caused my new problem. But what the fuck, Doc. What'm I supposed to do . . ."

Jeremy drove to the hospital thinking about the young man's optimism. Probably something constitutional; from what Jeremy had seen, a positive outlook had little to do with your actual life experiences. Some folks saw the donut, others the holes.

That late-night supper said the old eccentrics were donut people. Survivors believing themselves worthy of linen and china and silver, three meats, *foie gras,* petits fours, the driest of champagnes.

The late-night supper had been the first fabulous meal Jeremy had enjoyed in . . . years.

Where did he fit in the donut-hole continuum?

Observer, ever the diarist.

When he got to his office, a note from the Head of Oncology was in his box.

JC: Perused your chapter. Here are a few suggestions but all in all, fine. When can we look forward to a completed manuscript?

Also in the box was a cardboard box, stamped BOOK RATE, and postmarked locally.

Inside was a hardcover book bound in forest green cloth.

THE BLOOD RUNS COLD:
Serial Killers and Their Crimes
by
Colin Pugh

Twelve-year-old copyright, British publishing house, no jacket, no details on the author.

Inside the cover was a penciled price—$12.95— and black, rubber-stamped, Gothic lettering that read *Renfrew's Central Book Shop, Used & Antiquarian,* followed by the defunct store's address and phone number.

He'd never thought of the place as having a name, let alone a number—could never recall hearing a phone ring as he browsed. He dialed the seven digits, got a "disconnected" message, and felt comforted.

His name and hospital address were typed on the

carton. He checked inside for a card or message, found none, flipped the book's pages.

Nothing.

Turning to the first chapter, he began reading.

Fifteen chapters, fifteen killers. He'd heard of most of them—Vlad the Impaler, Bluebeard, the Boston Strangler, Ted Bundy, Son of Sam, Jack the Ripper (the chapter on the Whitehall fiend confirmed Jeremy's graffiti recollection; the exact wording of the chalked scrawl had been: *"The Juwes are the men That Will not be Blamed for nothing"*). A few he hadn't: Peter Kurten ("the Dusseldorf Monster"), Herman Mudge, Albert Fish, Carl Panzram.

He lapsed into skimming. Details of the outrages blurred and the perpetrators merged into one ghastly mass. For all their grisly work, murderous psychopaths were a boring bunch, creatures of morbid habit, forged from the same twisted mold.

The final chapter caught Jeremy's eye.

Gerd Dergraav: the Laser Butcher.

Dergraav was a Norwegian-born physician, the son of a German diplomat father stationed in Oslo and a dentist mother who abandoned the family and moved to Africa. A brilliant student, young Gerd studied medicine and qualified as both an otolaryngolist and an ophthalmologist. Shifting interests, yet again, he served as a chief resident in obstetrics-gynecology at the Oslo Institute for Female Medicine. The war years were spent doing research in

Norway. In 1946, he took an advanced fellowship in the treatment of obstetric tumors in Paris.

His father died in 1948. Fully certified in three subspecialties, Dergraav moved to his mother's home city, Berlin, where he built a highly successful practice delivering babies and attending to the disorders of women. His patients adored him because of his sensitivity and his willingness to listen. All were unaware of the six hidden cameras in Dergraav's examining room that allowed the doctor to amass a six-hundred-reel library of naked women.

Early details of Dergraav's childhood were lacking, and author Pugh supplanted fact with Freudian speculation. One fact had been verified: Shortly after arriving in Germany, the urbane young doctor began picking up prostitutes and torturing them. Ample payments to the street women procured their silence. So did the absence of scars; Dergraav had a brute's lust but a surgeon's touch. Later interviews with the early victims revealed Dergraav's penchant for humiliating his victims, and a secret cache of videotapes from the doctor's later years showed him whipping, punching, biting, and jabbing with hypodermic needles over two hundred women. He also enjoyed plunging their hands into icy water and compressing their limbs with blood-pressure cuffs, then measuring time latency till pain sensation. Frequently, Dergraav filmed himself, as well, in close-up. Smiling subtly.

A handsome man, Pugh claimed, though no photo confirmation was offered.

During the late fifties, Dergraav married an upper-class woman, the daughter of a fellow physician, and fathered a child.

Shortly after, bodies of prostitutes began showing up in the slums of Berlin, cut into pieces.

Street gossip eventually led to attention being focused on Dr. Dergraav. Questioned in his office, the gynecologist professed surprise that the police would suspect him of anything sinister, and he evinced no anxiety or guilt. The detectives had trouble imagining the charming, soft-spoken surgeon as the demon behind the horrific mutilations they were encountering more and more frequently. Dergraav was filed as a low-probability suspect.

The prostitute butcherings continued on and off for nearly a decade. The killer's disdain for his victims intensified, and he dehumanized them by mixing up body parts and combining them, so that limbs and organs from several different women came to be found bagged together in plastic sacks and left in trash bins. When forensic evidence from a victim in 1964 led the coroner to conclude that a laser had been used for dissection, the police reviewed their notes and discovered Dergraav traveled to Paris, yet again, to learn how to use the still-experimental instrument for eye surgery. This seemed curious, as Dergraav wasn't an ophthalmologist, and they questioned him again. Dergraav apprised them of his ophthalmologic training, proved it with certificates, and claimed he was thinking of switching back to his former subspecialty because of the promise offered by lasers for corneal ablation.

The police asked if they could search his office. The doctor's consent was needed; no grounds for a warrant existed. Charmingly, smilingly, Dergraav declined. During the interview, he laughed and told the investigators they couldn't be farther off the mark. *His* use of the laser was limited to academics, and the instrument was far too expensive for him to own. Furthermore, his gynecologic specialty was the surgical treatment of vulvodynia—vaginal pain. He was a physician, his mission in life was to alleviate agony, not cause it.

The police left. Three days later, Dergraav's office suite and his home were emptied and padlocked and wiped clean of fingerprints. The doctor and his family were gone.

Dergraav's wife surfaced a year later in England, then in New York, where she professed ignorance of her husband's behavior and his whereabouts. She sought, and was granted, a divorce from Dergraav, changed her name, and was never heard from again. Colin Pugh cited speculation that the doctor had been taken in by American officials as payback for wartime cooperation by Dergraav's father. The Oslo-based diplomat had deceived his Nazi masters and passed crucial information to the Allies. However, this remained rumor, and subsequent sightings of Gerd Dergraav placed him far from the States: in Switzerland, Portugal, Morocco, Bahrain, Beirut, Syria, and Brazil.

The last two locales were verified. Some time during the early '70s, Dergraav slipped into Rio de Janeiro using a Syrian passport issued in his own name and managed to obtain expedited Brazilian citizenship. Remarried, with a child, he lived openly in Rio, purchasing a villa above Ipanema Beach and volunteering his services to a human rights group that offered free medical service to the slum dwellers of the city's fetid *favillas*.

Dergraav swam, sunbathed, ate well (Argentinian beefsteak was his favorite) and worked tirelessly without pay. Among the human rights workers and the *favillitos*, he came to be known as the White Angel—a tribute to both his pale coloring and his pure soul.

During his known residence in Rio, that city's prostitutes began showing up dead and cut into pieces.

Dergraav's second reign of murder lasted another decade. In the end, he was snared by the most banal of circumstances. The screams of a prostitute he was attempting to asphyxiate attracted a gang of hoodlums from the neighboring slum, and Dergraav fled into the night. The thugs exploited the bound and gagged woman's helplessness by gang-raping her, but they left her alive. After some indecision, she reported the doctor to the police.

Dergraav's house was searched by Rio detectives, less concerned than their German counterparts with due process. The cache of videotapes was found, including one in which the doctor reduced a woman's body to forty chunks using a laser scalpel. In the film, Dergraav narrated as he mutilated, describing the procedure just as he would a bona fide surgery. Also retrieved was a suede box filled with women's jewelry and a cache carved of rosewood, rattling with vertebrae, teeth, and knucklebones.

Imprisoned in Salvador de Bahia prison, Dergraav awaited trial for two years, ever the charmer.

Jailers brought him international newspapers, literary magazines, and scientific journals. Catered food was delivered. Citing worries about his cholesterol, Dergraav ate less beef, more chicken.

Rumor had it that money would soon exchange hands, and the doctor would be deported under cover of night, back to the Middle East. Then German authorities learned of the arrest, requested and received permission to extradite. That process stretched on, and Dergraav could be seen sitting in the prison's courtyard, relaxed, dressed in tropical whites, nuzzling with his wife, playing with his child.

Finally, the German authorities got their way. The day after the extradition certificate was drawn, Dergraav blocked the peephole in his cell with chewing gum, ripped up his jail-issue clothing, knotted the strips into a rope, and hung himself. He was nearly sixty, but had the appearance of a forty-year-old. The jailer who discovered him remarked on the healthy, peaceful appearance of the White Angel's corpse.

Nearly seventeen years ago, to the day, Gerd Dergraav's ashes had been strewn at sea.

40

SEVENTEEN YEARS AGO JUMP-STARTED JEREMY'S memory.

The first laser article had been published that very year.

Norwegian authors. Russians, an Englishman. He rechecked the names. No Dergraav.

It was the *date* he was supposed to notice. Origins in Oslo.

Seventeen years ago, a murderous doctor had hung himself.

Laser surgery, physician suicide.

Oslo, Paris, Damascus by way of Berlin.

Gerd Dergraav had been born and trained in the Norwegian capital, learned female surgery in France, settled and tortured and murdered in Berlin.

Escaped to Damascus.

Arthur and surrogates had traced the Laser Butcher's bloody swath.

How long before a postcard of Rio arrived in the mail?

A pretty picture of Sugarloaf or the white sands of Ipanema or some other Brazilian panorama?

Dr. C,

Traveling and learning.

The cards had set up the pattern; the articles had filled in blanks. Laser surgery on the eyes, because Dergraav had begun as an ophthalmologist, before switching to ENT, the source of the envelopes.

Lasers for female surgery to match Dergraav's final career switch: women's doctor. Women's killer.

Where did the English girls fit in? Dergraav was long dead by the time of their murders.

Why all this attention paid to someone whose ashes had dissolved in a warm, welcoming ocean seventeen years ago?

Then he remembered his night drinking with Arthur. Collegial time in the Excelsior bar that old man had been so intent on sharing. Telling that apparently pointless story. Predatory insects that burrowed under their victims' skins in order to plant their parasitic spawn.

The moral he, himself, had drawn from the tale.

Sins of the fathers.

Arthur's pet topic: the origins of very, very bad behavior.

When Gerd Dergraav fled Germany, his wife escaped to the States, changed her name, disappeared into the great American freedom.

Along with her son.

Dergraav.

Dirgrove.

Arthur laying it out for him. Wanting Jeremy to *understand*.

The son was here.

Now Jeremy knew that his initial instinct had been right: That day in the dining room, Arthur *had* been studying Dirgrove.

And, for some time, Dirgrove had been studying Jeremy. Watching, following. Jeremy and Angela. Such a sensitive guy, always there to listen to a needy resident. No doubt his patients loved him— a nice case of genetic charm. Merilee Saunders's mother had been smitten, but Merilee hadn't been taken in.

Freaky Dirgrove. Roboticon.

Now Merilee was dead.

Did Sensitive Ted have a camera hidden in his office? Today's technology made that so much easier than in his father's day, everything miniaturized, computerized.

Getting rid of the daughter, taking the mother.

The take was the *core*—Dirgrove had targeted Angela because she was already seeing another man.

Just as apes raided colonies of other apes, murdered the males, made off with the females, some humans did the same thing under cover of war or religion or whatever dogma was at hand.

Some humans needed no excuse.

A sickening realization hit Jeremy.

Sensitive Ted and Jocelyn.

Putting a face on his lover's killer drove home

the horror, and suddenly Jeremy was as wrenched and raw and overcome by weeping as the day he'd found out. A red film blanketed his vision, and he lost balance, had to struggle to remain on his feet.

He walked to the window, threw it open on stale air shaft fumes. Stood there, hearing the rattle of a generator, snippets of human speech, the wind. Heart tripping, breath raspy. Swallowing the scream.

Jocelyn, taken from him. *Because* of him.

Now, Dirgrove had turned his sights on Angela.

He forced himself to stay calm. Reasoned it out, still staring out at the air shaft.

Killing and dissecting was late-night supper for a monster. A nice girl like Jocelyn as the main course, street girls tossed in as snacks.

Angela as . . . dessert?

No, the banquet would never end unless the diner choked.

He thought about Dirgrove's technique. Attracting Angela with his sensitivity. Being different than the other surgeons.

The same ploy his father had used. Charming Ted had been how old—late twenties—when his father hung himself. The barest progress from adolescence to manhood, an age of strong sexuality, strong impulses.

Well aware of his father's impulses.

The origin of very, very bad behavior.

A bright man, a careful man. He'd set up the move on Angela with surgical precision. Inviting her over for a medical lesson, all the journals, book-marked, laid out neatly on his desk.

Angela, ever the good student, begins reading, he steps behind her.

I can make you happy.

Had all that just been a setup—an appetizer—for his ultimate plan?

Had Dirgrove set Jocelyn up the same way? She'd never mentioned his name to Jeremy, but why would she? A surgeon conferring with a nurse was the essence of usual.

Would Dirgrove have had anything to do with Jocelyn's neurology patients? If one of them had developed heart problems, sure.

Was it possible that he'd hit on Jocelyn, and she'd chosen not to tell Jeremy?

People talked about sharing, but . . .

Jocelyn had cared deeply about her patients. A doctor pretending to do the same would have impressed her, mightily.

Angela was a highly intelligent woman, and she'd been fooled.

Jocelyn, for all her street smarts, had been an innocent.

Easy pickings.

A surgeon showing up, late at night, in the nurses' lot, waving, smiling, wouldn't have sparked any panic in Jocelyn. As always, she was overconfident, laughed off Jeremy's suggestions that she not walk to her car alone.

A weary, white-coated warrior dragging his way toward her after a tough day on the wards would have evoked sympathy from Jocelyn.

He approaches her, they chat.
He takes her.

The more he reasoned it out, the more convinced he became that Dirgrove had toyed with him, too. Asking him to see Merilee Saunders but not telling Merilee. Knowing Jeremy would encounter anger, resistance, walk away feeling like a failure.

Taunting him by telling him he'd been a big help.

Delivering the message through Angela.

The referral had been a sham.

Or something much worse? Was all Dirgrove's talk about the risk of an autonomic spike simply laying the groundwork for what he knew would happen in the O.R.?

Had Merilee been frightened about her surgery because she sensed something about the *surgeon*?

He's a stiff . . . except when he wants to turn on the charm. My mom loves him.

Dirgrove hadn't even bothered to inform Jeremy about the O.R. disaster. Had dropped the news in the cafeteria, after finishing a chat with Angela.

How had he managed it? The merest flick of his wrist after he'd flayed the chest, sawed through bone, exposed the pericardial sac, dipped lustily in to take hold of the pulsating plum—the skinless tomato—that nourished Merilee's soul?

What's the worst that can happen, I die?

Jeremy was due to see Doug Vilardi in five minutes. He took a detour to the ground floor of the office wing, entered the Attending Staff office, and asked the secretary for a look at his own *curriculum vitae* in the Academic Status File.

"Yours, Doctor?"

"I want to make sure you've got the most current version." He was dry-mouthed, felt shaky, hoped he was coming across credible. Hoped she wouldn't take the trouble to remove his CV from the loose-leaf binder, but rather hand over the entire book.

"Here you go, Doctor."

Yes!

He took the binder to a chair across the room, sat down, flipped to cardiothoracic surgery and when the secretary became involved in a personal phone call, tore out Theodore G. Dirgrove's most current résumé, folded it hastily, and stuffed it in his pocket.

He hurried to the nearest men's room and locked himself in a stall. The folded papers were burning a hole in his pocket, and he ripped them free.

Theodore *Gerd* Dirgrove. Born in Berlin, Germany, April 20, 1957.

A perfect match to Colin Pugh's chronology of the Laser Butcher's life: marriage to an upper-class woman, birth of a child, during the late fifties.

Dirgrove listed himself as growing up in Baltimore, attending college and medical school at an elite, Eastern university. Not the same ivy-covered citadel where Norbert Levy had taught engineering and physics, but one very much like it.

Science awards, graduation with high honors, the usual hurdle-jumps.

The bastard had published a fair number of academic papers in surgical journals. Angela had mentioned a lecture on revascularization of the heart and there it was: one of Dirgrove's specialties.

Endomyocardial laser channeling for revascularization.

Perhaps that's what he'd been demonstrating to Mandel and the dark, mustached man. Showing off his technique, proud of his virtuosity with the instrument his father had wielded so creatively.

A Humpty-Dumpty situation . . .

Jeremy scanned the résumé, and something else caught his eye.

For the past six years, Dirgrove had spent his summers in London, teaching bypass surgery at Kings College of Medicine.

Six summers ago, Bridget Sapsted had been abducted and murdered in Kent, a couple of hours' drive from the city, her skeleton retrieved two years later, after her chum Suzie had met the same fate.

Dirgrove had been in England during both killings.

That's why Jeremy's question about surgical precision had seized the attention of Detective Inspector Nigel Langdon (Ret.). Who'd undoubtedly called his successor, Det Insp Michael Shreve. And Shreve had taken the time to return Jeremy's call. Not to inform him, to *pump* him. Then Shreve tracked down and alerted his American counterpart, Bob Doresh.

Leading to Doresh's showing up at Jeremy's office.

Both Langdon and Shreve had been to Oslo. Random travel? Or were the British investigators familiar with the details of Gerd Dergraav's swath of horror and aware of similarities to the Kent murders?

And, now, a spate of American murders.

How much did Doresh understand? The man came across as cloddish, but Jeremy remembered his first impression—he and his partner, Hoker. Eyes that didn't miss a thing.

But they were missing plenty now.

Why do they still suspect *me*?

Because bureaucracy trumps creativity and expediency trumps justice.

There was no point dealing with Doresh or his ilk. Despite what Jeremy knew—the nightmare truths of which he was *certain*—sharing with the mulish detective would be useless. Worse—it would cast more suspicion on Jeremy.

Great theory, Doc. So . . . you're pretty interested in this gory stuff, huh?

Going through channels wasn't going to work.

He needed to be unfettered.

And that, he realized with staggering clarity, was the whole point. Of Arthur's correspondence, the messages the old man had sent directly and through his CCC pals.

The focus of the entire late-night supper.

Tina Balleron's suggestion that he stay on target.

Think about the gannet birds, simply doing the right thing.

Evil happened and, too often, expediency did trump justice. The law demanded evidence and due process, but provided little to make things right.

Husbands were murdered at their desks, their killers never brought to justice. Men of spirit and peace were gunned down in greasy parking lots, fortunes were plundered, entire families—entire races—wiped out, and no one paid the price.

A tiny, blond beauty born to smile, could be taken so easily . . .

You couldn't depend on others to fix things.

Arthur had been certain Jeremy would understand that because Jeremy had been *through* it.

Sitting in the toilet stall, a wave of peace washed over him.

Pathology and psychology were polar opposites, but none of that mattered. What counted was the *ordeal.*

The sword of war comes to the world for the delay of justice.

A two-thousand-year-old lesson from the Fathers, but it couldn't have been more timely.

A glance at his watch reproached him.

Twice-stricken Doug Vilardi was waiting for him. Another type of ordeal.

At least this pain was something Jeremy had been trained to deal with.

Words. Strategic pauses, kindness in the eyes. *Meaning* it.

Not enough, not nearly enough . . .

Here I come, victims of the world. God help all of us.

41

DOUG LOOKED LIKE A PATIENT.

Hooked up to his chemo drip, still in good spirits and voluble, but his facial muscles had slackened.

His prosthesis was covered in a vinyl case and lay on the floor.

Jeremy sat down, made small talk, tried to edge him toward masonry. Doug shook off the distraction.

"You know what bugs me, Doc? Two things. First of all, they let other guys get their chemo at home, but me they want to keep cooped up here."

"Did you ask Dr. Ramirez about that?"

"Yeah, my spleen's fucked up. They'll maybe have to take it out." He grinned. "No heavy lifting, I might explode, make a big fucking mess." The grin faded. "Also my liver's not primo. See?"

He tugged down an eyelid. The sclera was greenish beige.

Jeremy said, "No beer, today."

"Too bad about that . . . so, how've you been?"

"You said two things were bothering you."

"Oh, yeah. Number two: Everyone's being too damn nice to me. Creeps me out. Like they think I'm gonna die, or something."

"I can write an order, if you'd like," said Jeremy. " 'Everyone be obnoxious to Doug.' "

The young man laughed. "Yeah, do that . . . so, you've been okay, Doc?"

"Fine."

"You look a little, I dunno, wiped out. They working you too hard?"

"Same old same old."

"Yeah . . . no offense—that crack about looking tired. Maybe it's me, maybe I'm not seeing things right. Fact is, when I saw you yesterday, after all those years, I'm thinking, 'This guy doesn't change.' It was like, back then, when I first met you, I was a kid and you were a grown-up, and now I'm grown-up and you haven't really changed that much. It's like . . . what, life slows down when you get older? Is that what happens?"

"It can," said Jeremy.

"Guess it depends on how much fun you're having," said Doug.

"What do you mean?"

"You know—what they always say? Time goes fast when you're having fun. My life's been a blast, zip zip zip. One thing after the other, fucking adventures, one day I'm knocking up walls and then . . . and now I'm having a baby." He glanced at the butterfly needle embedded atop his hand. "I hope they hurry up with getting me better. Gotta get the fuck outta here. Got lots of things to do."

When he drifted off to sleep, Jeremy left the room and encountered Doug's parents and wife. That turned into another hour in the cafeteria, where Jeremy brought the three of them coffee and food. They protested weakly, thanked him profusely. Young Marika barely spoke. Still stunned, she avoided Jeremy's eyes when he tried to make contact.

Doug Vilardi, Sr. spent most of his time putting on the good cheer. That seemed to weary his wife, but she rolled with it. Most of the hour was filled with small talk.

When Jeremy got up to leave, so did Doug's mother. She walked him out of the cafeteria, said, "I've never met a doctor like you." Then she took Jeremy's face in both of her hands and kissed his forehead.

A maternal kiss. It reminded Jeremy of something that had happened to him a long time ago. But he couldn't be sure.

He saw his other patients, went to meet Angela up on the chest ward where she was finishing her last day. He found her in the company of three other residents, on the way to some kind of meeting. Got her away from the group with a raised eyebrow and herded her into an empty nurses' room.

"How are you doing?"

"Fine." She bit her lip. "I've been going over what happened. I think I overreacted."

"You didn't," said Jeremy. "It happened, and it was bad."

"Well, that's not very comforting."

"It happened, Angela."

"Of course it did. I never doubted it did, but—"

"I repeated it for emphasis," he said. "Because eventually, you may start to doubt that it happened. Denial's like that."

"I'm *denying*?" Her dark eyes flashed.

"It's not a put-down. Denial's not weakness— not neurotic. It's a fact of life, a natural defense. Your mind and body will naturally want to protect themselves. Go with that. You may surprise yourself by feeling happy. Don't fight that."

"I may surprise myself?" she said. "What's that, some sort of posthypnotic suggestion?"

"It's a reasonable prediction."

"I'm not *close* to happy."

"Sooner or later you will be. The feelings will pass. But it happened."

Angela stared at him. "All this advice."

"Here's more," said Jeremy. "Stay away from him. He's very bad news."

"What do you—"

"Just stay away."

"I wouldn't worry about that," she said. "This morning he was rounding, heading straight at me in the hall. I held my ground and when he saw me, he changed directions. Turned around and walked around to the other side. Took a circuitous route just to avoid me. So you see, *he's* worried about *me*."

If you knew. "Let's keep it that way."

"What are you saying, Jeremy? You don't think I can handle him?"

"I'm sure you can. Just avoid him. Listen to me. Please." He took hold of her shoulders, drew her close.

"This is scaring me a little."

Good.

"If you're careful, there's nothing to be scared of. Promise me you'll stay away from him. And look out for yourself."

She pulled away from him. "Jeremy, you're really freaking me out. What is going on?"

"He's a bad guy, I can't say more."

"What? That heart patient who died? Did you learn something about that?"

"That may be part of it."

"Part of it—God, what is going on?"

"Nothing," he said.

"You come in here with all these dire pronouncements, and now you're holding back? What's gotten into you?"

"You're off Thoracic, so it shouldn't be a problem. Just do your work and stay away from him." He smiled. "Don't take candy from strangers."

"Not funny," she snapped. "You can't just—"

"Do you think," he said, "that I want to upset you?"

"No—I don't know. I wish I knew what's come over you. Why won't you tell me what's going on?"

He thought about that.

"Because I'm not sure."

"About Dirgrove?"

"About everything he's done."

"Everything." Her eyes got hard. "This is about her—Jocelyn—isn't it—and don't close up the way you did when I hinted around about her the other day. I know you went through hell, know I can never really understand it. But don't you think, with what's happened to us—with how close we've gotten so quickly—that you could trust me enough to not throw up barriers?"

Jeremy's head pounded. He wanted to hold her, kiss her, drive her away. "It's not a matter of closing up," he said, softly. "There's just nothing to talk about. And this isn't the time."

"Nothing," she said. "You go through something like that and nothing?"

Jeremy didn't answer.

She said, "That's the way it has to be, huh?"

"For the time being."

"Okay," she said. "You're the expert on human emotions—I've got to go. You pulled me away just as we were going to conference with the chief. Tropical pulmonary disease. Maybe I'll take a rotation in some jungle clinic."

Jeremy's head filled with teeming, squirming insects.

"The jungle," he said, "is an interesting place."

She gaped at him as if he was mad, walked around him, avoided touching him, made it to the door, and turned the knob hard.

He said, "When will you be free?"

"Not for some time," she said, without looking back. "You know how it is. The schedule."

He finished his charts, talked to Ramirez about Doug Vilardi, and paged Angela from a phone on Five West. No reply. Returning to his office, he repeated the page. His beeper remained silent. He tried the nursing station on chest ward, the residents' locker room, the House Staff office. Zip.

Two hours had passed since he'd angered her, and he found himself missing her.

Being alone was different, now. No longer part of him, a phantom limb.

You couldn't miss someone after two hours. Silly.

And even if Angela shut him out for a while, it was all for the better. As long as she heeded him and stayed away from Dirgrove.

He thought she would, she was an extremely bright person, a well-adjusted person.

He thought of the obsessive-compulsive rituals to which she'd confessed.

A driven woman. All the better. In the end, good sense would prevail, and she'd stick with it.

Besides, *he* needed to be alone for a while.

Had work to do.

42

NIGHT WORK.

Jeremy avoided scrutiny by keeping odd hours and entering the hospital through another out-of-the-way rear door—one on the basement level that led to a loading bay. One of those forgotten places inevitable in a place as old and sprawling as City Central. Same level as Pathology and the morgue, but the opposite wing. Here, he passed laundry rooms, boiler housing, electrical entrails, storage space for defunct medical charts.

The guts. He liked that.

He kept to a schedule: saw Doug, and his other patients, at the assigned times, but left the wards by the stairs, rather than the elevators.

No coffee or meals in the DDR or the cafeteria. When he was hungry—which was infrequent—he grabbed something at a fast-food stand. His skin grew greasy, but that was the price you paid.

Once, as he stuffed french fries down his gullet without tasting, he thought: *a far cry from foie gras.*

Cheap food sat in his gut, just dandy, thank you. Perhaps, he'd never been destined for better.

He made sure to check his mail at day's end but received no more cards from Arthur, no surprises in interoffice envelopes.

They know: I've been educated sufficiently.

When he left the hospital, he put the place out of his mind. Concentrating on night work. Driving.

Cruising through the garbage-strewn alleys of Iron Mount, past the pawnbrokers and bail bondsmen and rescue missions and discount clothing stalls that filled the slum. A couple of times he headed out to Saugatuck Finger, where he removed his shoes despite the frozen air and walked barefoot in the hard, wet sand. No remnants of the crime scene remained, just beach and lake and gulls and ragged picnic tables. Behind the spit loomed the backdrop of big trees that would have served the killer so well.

Both times, he stayed for just a few moments, studying the rippling murk of the water, finding a dead crab here, a storm-buffeted rock, there. When the rain came, so cold it was a step away from sleet, he allowed it to pummel his bare head.

Sometimes he cruised the industrial stretch that separated the two kill spots and wondered where the next woman would be found. Driving openly, with the Nova's radio blasting oldies. Thinking about terrible things.

After dark, he took the scenic route, north. The same route that had led him to the gates of the Haverford Country Club and the brief, cool talk with Tina Balleron. This time, he stopped well before Hale gave way to estate acreage, at the far end of the boulevard, where he motored slowly up chic, elm-shaded streets edged with bistros and boutiques and custom jewelers and graystone town houses, until he found the kind of parking space he needed.

A spot that gave him a full, close view of a particular, cream-colored, limestone high-rise.

A postmodern thing, with gratuitous trim, a green-canopied awning, a cobbled circular drive, not one, but two maroon-liveried doormen. One of the best addresses on Hale, a premium condo.

The place Theodore G. Dirgrove, M.D. listed on his curriculum vitae under "Home Address."

Exactly the kind of sleek, stylish building in which you'd expect a successful surgeon to live with his wife and two children.

That had been a bit of a surprise, Dirgrove married, with kids, playing at domestic life. Then Jeremy thought: *No, it's not. Of course he'd play the game. Just as his father had done.*

> *Spouse: Patricia Jennings Dirgrove*
> *Children: Brandon, 9; Sonja, 7.*

Sweet.

Another surprise: Dirgrove drove a dull car—a five-year-old Buick. Jeremy had expected something pricier—something smooth and German, wouldn't that have been a nice tribute to Daddy?

Once again, Dirgrove's cleverness became apparent: Who'd notice the grayish blue sedan nosing its way out of a darkened alley in a low-rent neighborhood?

When you knew what you were dealing with, everything made sense.

Clarity was a heady drug. Jeremy worked all day, drove all night, lived on insight, convinced himself he rarely needed to eat or sleep.

The surgeon kept surgeon's hours, often leaving for work before 6 A.M. and not returning until well after dark.

On the third day of watching, Dirgrove took his family out to dinner, and Jeremy got a good look at the wife and kids as they piled into the Buick.

Patricia Jennings Dirgrove was short and pleasant-looking, a brunette with a curly, rather mannish hairdo. Good figure, high energy, nimble. From the flash of face Jeremy caught, a determined woman. She wore a black, fur-collared wrap and left it unbuttoned. Jeremy caught a glimpse of red knit pants and matching top. One step above sweats. Dressing for comfort. Dirgrove hadn't changed out of the day's suit and tie.

The children resembled Patty—as Jeremy came to call her—more than *Ted*. Brandon was stocky with a mop of dark hair, little Sonja slightly fairer but with none of Dirgrove's Nordic bone structure.

For their sake, Jeremy hoped the lack of resemblance to their father didn't end there.

Cute kids. He knew what was in store for them.

*   *   *

He followed them to dinner. Ted and Patty chose a midpriced Italian place ten blocks south, where they were seated up front, visible to the street behind a plate-glass window decorated by ornate gold leaf lettering. Inside were wooden booths, a brass-railed cappuccino bar, a copper espresso machine.

Jeremy parked around the corner and made his way past the restaurant on foot, drawing the lapels of his raincoat around his face, a newly purchased black fedora set low.

He strolled past the window, eyes concealed by the hat's brim. Bought a newspaper from a stand to look normal and repeated the pass. Back and forth. Three more times. Dirgrove never looked up from his lasagna.

The surgeon sat there, bored. All the smiling conversation, between Brandon and Sonja and Mom.

Patty was attentive to the kids, helped the little girl twirl spaghetti on her fork. During his final pass, Jeremy saw her glance at her husband. Ted didn't notice; he was staring off at the espresso machine.

Family time.

When would he leave the comforts of hearth and home and do what really turned him on?

It happened on the fourth night.

A day full of surprises; that morning, Jeremy received a postcard from Rio.

Beautiful bodies on a white sand Brazilian beach. He felt smart.

Dr. C:

Traveling and learning.

A.C.

So am I, my friend.

As if that wasn't enough, he received a call from Edgar Marquis at 6 P.M., just before he was ready to embark on the night's surveillance.

"Dr. Carrier," said the ancient diplomat. "I'm delivering a message from Arthur."

"Oh?"

"Yes, he'd like me to inform you that he's enjoying his vacation—finding it quite educational. He hopes you've been well."

"Thank you, sir," said Jeremy. "Well, and busy."

"Ah," said Marquis. "That's good."

"I imagine you'd think so, sir."

Marquis cleared his throat. "Well, then, that's all. Good evening."

"Where'd he call from, Mr. Marquis?"

"He didn't say."

Jeremy laughed. "You're not going to tell me a damn thing, are you? Not even now."

"Now?"

"I'm on the job, Mr. Marquis."

No answer.

Jeremy said, "Just indulge me on one small detail. 'CCC.' What does it stand for. How'd it get started—what drew you together?"

"Good food and wine, Dr. Carrier."

"Right," said Jeremy.

Silence.

"What was your ordeal, Mr. Marquis? What lit the fire in *your* belly?"

The merest hesitation. "Chili peppers."

Jeremy waited for more.

"The cuisine of Indonesia," said Marquis, "can be quite piquant. I was educated there, in matters of taste and reason."

"So," said Jeremy. "That's the way it's going to be."

The ancient man didn't respond.

"Mr. Marquis, I don't imagine you'd tell me when Arthur's due back."

"Arthur makes his own schedule."

"I'm sure he does. Good-bye, sir."

"Doctor? With regard to the origins of our little group, suffice it to say that your participation would be considered . . . harmonious in more ways than one."

"Would it?"

"Oh, yes. Consider it a case of the obvious."

"Obvious what?"

"Obvious," Marquis repeated. "Etched in stone."

No caller ID to trace. The bottom-line people said anything beyond basic phone service was a frivolity.

As Jeremy took the stairs down to the rear exit, he digested what Marquis had told him.

Spicy food in Indonesia. *I was educated, there.*

Marquis's baptism of loss had taken place in that island nation. One day, if Jeremy was sufficiently curious, he'd try to find out. At the moment, he had watching to do.

When he got to the rear exit, he found it padlocked. Had someone gotten wise to him? Or was it just a quirk of competence on the part of the security guards?

He made his way back toward the hospital lobby, pausing by the candy machine where he'd spied Bob Doresh and buying himself a chocolate-covered coconut cluster.

He'd never really liked candy; even as a child he'd never been tempted. Now he craved sugar. Chewing happily, he neared the hospital's main entrance. Passed the donor wall.

Etched in stone. And there it was.

Mr. and Mrs. Robert Balleron. Founders Donation, ten years ago. Below that, a more recent contribution, Founders level, four years ago:

Judge Tina F. Balleron, In Loving Memory of Robert Balleron.

The donor list wasn't alphabetized, and that made it a bit more time-consuming, but Jeremy found them all. By the time the last speck of coconut had tumbled down his throat he was flushed with insight.

Professor Norbert Levy, In Loving Memory of
His Family.

Four years ago.

Mr. Harrison Maynard, In Loving Memory of
His Mother, Effie Mae Maynard, and Dr. Martin
Luther King.

Same year.

Ditto: Mr. Edgar Molton Marquis, In Loving
Memory of Kurau Village.

And:

Arthur Chess, M.D., In Memory of Sally Chess,
Susan Chess, and Arthur Chess, Junior.

Arthur had lost his entire family.

Too horrible to contemplate, and Jeremy couldn't
afford that level of empathy, right now. Jamming
the candy wrapper into his pocket, he retraced his
steps through the lobby and headed for the Development Office.

"Development" was institutional jargon for fund-
raising, and Jeremy recalled the place as staffed by
slim, chatty young women in designer suits and
headed by a blowhard named Albert Trope. It was
6:20 P.M.—a window of time remained, Dirgrove
rarely got home before six-thirty, seven. Nonmed-
ical personnel tended to leave well before five, so it
was probably too late to catch the office open, but
he was here already.

The chatty young women *had* left. But the door
was open and a janitor—a morose-looking Slav,
probably one of the recent immigrants the hospital
had taken to hiring because they knew nothing

about labor laws—was vacuuming the plush, blue wall-to-wall.

Jeremy, his professional staff badge in full view, walked right past the man and over to a faux-Regency bookshelf in a corner of the generous reception room.

Good perfume—remnants of the young women—hung in the air. The entire room was done up in high-style pretense; the place looked like a movie set of a French salon. Make the deep-pocket crowd feel right at home . . .

The janitor ignored Jeremy as he pawed through the case. On the shelves were plastic-covered testimonials from satisfied patients, photo albums of cute little kids cured at City Central, gushing accounts of celebrity visits along with the requisite photo ops, and years and years of fund-raising ephemera.

Including journals of the hospital's biggest event, the yearly Gala Ball.

Jeremy had been to one gala, two years ago. Asked to deliver a speech on humanism, then leave before dinner.

He found the four-year-old edition. In front was an explanation of several tiers of contribution. Within each tier, names were listed alphabetically.

Donor, Sponsor, Patron, Founder, Gold Ribbon Circle.

Founder meant a twenty-thousand-dollar pledge. The CCC people had ponied up generously.

He found a picture of all of them, together. Arthur at the center, surrounded by Balleron, Marquis, Maynard, and Levy.

CCC . . . the City Central Club?

So this was where it had started. Five altruists convening for the common good, finding common ground.

No doubt Arthur—charismatic, gregarious, curious Arthur—had played a pivotal role in drawing them together.

He'd lost his family, the man could be excused a bit of enthusiasm for camaraderie. For justice.

"You gutta go," said the janitor. He'd switched off his vacuum cleaner, and the waiting room was quiet.

"Sure, thanks," said Jeremy. "Good night."

The man grumbled and picked at his ear.

Jeremy made it to Hale Boulevard by six-forty, found a terrific observation spot, and sat until nine, when Dirgrove finally showed up.

For three nights running, Dirgrove had stayed at home, and Jeremy kept his expectation low. But when Dirgrove left his Buick in the circular drive and the doorman didn't park it, he knew tonight would be different.

There you go, Ted. Make my life a little bit easier.

At eleven-fifteen, the surgeon emerged, got his keys, tipped the night doorman, and drove off.

South.

Toward Iron Mount.

Straight *into* Iron Mount. The rain had lifted, and the streetwalkers were out in force, bundled in fake furs and padded ski jackets—short garb that allowed a clear view of shapely legs made longer by maliciously heeled shoes.

Young legs, old faces. A high-stepping, prancing parade. Very little auto traffic. No one but working girls willing to brave the cold.

Dirgrove drove past them, unmindful of Jeremy trailing a block back, the Nova's headlights switched off.

A stupid, dangerous way to drive, a couple of times Jeremy narrowly missed hitting dope-blurred women who stepped off the curb.

His reward: curses, uplifted fingers, but what was his choice? Worst-case scenario, some cop would pull him over for a traffic violation. Not likely. No patrol cars in sight. Too cold for the cops.

That made him realize something: There was no police presence at all on these meanest of streets.

For all Doresh's talk about working the killings, these were throwaway women, no one cared. Tyrene Mazursky's name had made the paper, but the following victim, the woman left on the spit, hadn't even merited that. At this rate, the next one wouldn't get a line of ink.

Expediency trumps virtue.

Dirgrove kept going, at a moderate speed, past coveys of hookers. Jeremy waited for him to choose his prey, but the Buick never slowed, cut right through Iron Mount, crossed under a land bridge, passed a grid of shuttered commercial buildings, and entered the neighboring district.

Also low-rent; Jeremy wasn't sure if this area had a name. Not really a neighborhood, just a dark, uninhabited stretch of businesses closed for the night.

Wholesalers and small factories. No streetwalkers, here. No reason for there to be. The nearest bar or strip joint or dope peddler was a good mile away.

Deserted.

Except for the woman who stepped out of the shadows and stood at the curb, in front of a long stretch of chain-link fence. She waited, bobbed up and down on needle heels.

When the anonymous gray-blue Buick came to a halt, she tossed her hair.

43

THE PROSTITUTE GOT INTO DIRGROVE'S CAR, AND
Jeremy sat watching, a hundred feet up, his lights
off. Same for his engine; no exhaust or noise gave
him away.

Between him and the Buick were two parked
cars. He opened his window, stuck his head out a
bit to get a better view. Cold air seared his lungs. He
suffered gladly.

His key remained in the ignition. Ready at any
moment to follow the Buick. Knowing he had to be
there if—*when* things got ugly.

*He'll have to take her somewhere. Keep his car
clean.*

*He needs space to work. Dissection—some make-
shift operatory in the bowels of the slums . . .*

The Buick's lights went off. White smoke curled
from its exhaust pipes, then dissipated. The car just
sat there, five minutes, ten, fifteen. At twenty, Jeremy
began to panic, wondered if he'd been horribly
wrong. What if Dirgrove *did* use the car—maybe
that's why he drove an old one. No, too careless.
You could never get rid of the blood—perhaps he

anesthetized them in the car, strangled them—
should he chance a closer look?

The clap of a car door closing broke into his
thoughts.

The prostitute had gotten out, was tugging at her
clothing. She waved at the Buick, and Dirgrove
drove away.

Decision time: follow the car, or talk to the
woman? Warn her. *Yes, he's a charming guy, this
time you got off easily—*

The prostitute walked up the block, heels clack-
ing, butt swaying, long legs stiltlike.

She got into one of the parked cars.

A streetwalker with her own wheels. That was a
switch.

Nice wheels, a Lexus, one of the smaller models,
a light color, shiny hubcaps.

Maybe this one had no pimp, kept all her earn-
ings.

But working out here, away from the motorcade
of potential customers that cruised Iron Mount,
how lucrative could it be? And why work a freezing
street if you could afford a car like that?

Unless this one went for quality, not quantity.
Men like Dirgrove paying a premium for whatever
it was she offered.

The Lexus pulled away from the curb. Jeremy
waited until she'd made a right at the next corner
before turning the ignition key.

She drove toward downtown. Checking her image
in the rearview mirror, talking on a cell phone once,

but otherwise driving carefully, conventionally, with no eye toward snagging any more business.

One good customer a night? What did she *do* for him?

The Lexus held its course, neared the hospital district. Neared City Central.

The prostitute drove to a quiet street around the corner from City Central. Just yards from the nurses' lot, where Jocelyn had been taken. Parking, she switched off her headlights.

She stayed there for four minutes, during which time Jeremy saw her arms rise and a garment slip over her head. Then another piece of clothing—something with long sleeves—was rolled down in its place.

Changing outfits.

When she was through, she consulted the rearview again, switched on a reading light. Not long enough for Jeremy to get a good look at her, but he could tell what she was doing. Touching up her lipstick. Then, she was cruising again.

One block. To the doctors' lot. Into the lot.

Jeremy followed, okay now out in the open, because this was a place he belonged.

So did she. She slid a card into the slot and the gate opened.

They both parked. The Lexus was pale blue. When she got out of the car he recognized her as a physician he'd seen around but had never met. An internist he was pretty sure had come on staff fairly recently.

Midforties, good figure, pleasant but unremarkable face, blond hair textured in an efficient bob.

She wore a knee-length charcoal wool skirt in place of the mini she'd sported during her tryst with Dirgrove. The garment she'd slipped over her head was a pink cashmere cowl neck sweater that she quickly concealed with a long, gray herringbone coat with a black velvet collar. Spike heels had been replaced by sensible loafers. She wore glasses.

When Jeremy passed her on the way to the covered walkway, she smiled at him, and said, "Brrr, it's chilly."

Jeremy smiled back.

Diamond wedding ring on her finger. What was her name? Gwen something . . .

Should he warn her?

Or did other women need to be warned about *her*?

Every two years, a face book was issued to the medical staff. Jeremy had never found it necessary to consult his, wasn't even sure he'd kept it. But he found it in a bottom drawer of his desk. Hundreds of faces, but only 20 percent were women, so the tale was told soon enough.

Gwynn Alice Hauser, M.D. Internal medicine. An assistant professor.

Dr. Hauser had a secret life.

How far did it go?

Over the next four days, Jeremy observed Gwynn Hauser on the wards and in the doctors' dining room. She made no contact at all with Dirgrove, generally took her meals alone or in the company of other women. A cheerful sort, prone to laughter and flamboyant gestures. When she really got into a conversation, she removed her eyeglasses and leaned forward. Listened actively, as if what the person before her was saying was profound beyond belief.

One time, she lunched with a tall, dark, handsome man in a blue, double-breasted suit and the square, impassive face of a CEO. Wedding band on his hand, too, and he was openly affectionate with her.

The husband she's cheating on.

Not a doctor, some sort of financial type, Jeremy was willing to bet. Taking the time out to share a meal with his busy wife. If he only knew how busy she was.

He encountered an internist he'd worked with, a man named Jerry Sallie, and asked him if he knew Gwynn Hauser.

"Gwynn? Sure. She make a move on you?"

"She's like that?"

"Big tease, I'm not sure she'd come through," said Sallie. "At least not that I've heard. She's married to a bank president, has a sweet deal—he lets her do what she wants. She's a pretty good doc. World's biggest tease, though. Nice legs, huh?"

Friday night, Gwynn Hauser left the hospital at seven-thirty. Jeremy, sitting low in his Nova, behind a pylon in the doctors' lot, waited as she drove away in her sky-colored Lexus. Dirgrove's Buick was still in place.

Twenty minutes later, the surgeon appeared, at a

near run, jumped into the Buick, started the engine up with a roar, and squealed out.

Exact same block in the nameless industrial neighborhood.

Dr. Gwynn Hauser stepped out of the shadows just as she had the first time. This time she had on an enormous white fur coat. Cloud-woman in spike heels; someone's vision of heaven.

When Dirgrove pulled up, she parted the coat, revealed herself naked but for garters and stockings.

How could she stand the cold?

She couldn't. Shivered and drew the fur closed and jumped up and down, pointing to the car.

Let me in, I'm freezing my ass off.

Dirgrove did.

Twenty-two minutes later, they parted ways.

This time, Jeremy followed Dirgrove. The surgeon headed straight for his luxury condo on Hale. He stayed home all night.

Family man.

When would he make his move?

44

DOUG VILARDI LOOKED BAD. SOME OF THE SKIN ON his face and arms had sloughed—an unexpected, allergic reaction to chemo—his white count remained way too high, his spleen was engorged, and his liver function had worsened. In no shape to talk, he remained awake and seemed to react well to Jeremy's presence. Jeremy sat there, talked a bit, found something on TV that caused the young man to smile—recap of a week-old college football game.

Once again, Jeremy took Doug's slumber as his cue to leave, and, once again, he encountered the family on the way out.

Mrs. Vilardi and Marika. Doug, Sr. was at work. They sat down in an empty waiting area. The previous occupants had left behind a stack of interior design magazines, and Jeremy swept them aside.

This time, Marika talked. About everything other than Doug's illness. What he liked to eat, the dishes she'd learned to cook from her mother-in-law. How she was thinking of getting a puppy, and did Jeremy think that would be a good or a bad idea with a new baby coming.

The two women appeared close, literally leaned against each other for support.

When Jeremy asked about Marika's family, Mrs. Vilardi answered for her. "They both passed on. Her poor mama was very young. Rosanna was one of my best friends, a wonderful, wonderful person. When she got sick, I used to take Mari in, to give her a quiet place to play, because Joe—her dad— was working and all she had was this aunt who was . . . you know."

She smiled uneasily.

Marika said, "I had a crazy aunt."

"That's how Doug came to know Mari, from my taking her in all the time. Then Joe passed and it was convent boarding school but she came to visit all the time. Back then Dougie wasn't interested in girls, right, honey?"

She nudged Marika.

The young woman said, "I was a skinny little stick with funny teeth, and Doug was into sports."

Mrs. Vilardi said, "Oh, you were always a cutie." To Jeremy: "I always loved this one, a real good girl. Tell the truth, I thought she'd be perfect for my other boy, Andy. But you never know, right, baby?"

"You sure don't, Mom." Marika's eyes misted up.

"Dr. Carrier, do you come from a big family— excuse my getting personal and all, but you just seem to have that warm heart."

"Pretty large," said Jeremy.

"Nice people, I bet."

"Very nice—I'll come by later to see how he's doing." He squeezed her hand, then Marika's, and stood.

"Thanks as always, Doctor—I didn't offend you, did I? By asking about your family?"

"Not at all." Jeremy patted her shoulder for punctuation.

"Good," she said. "Because just for a second I thought you looked . . . like I offended you. I'm sure it's me, I'm probably seeing everything screwy. Going out of my head with all that's going on, you know."

"You need to rest," said Jeremy.

"You're important to Dougie, Doctor. Back—the other time, he always said you were the only one treated him like a human being."

"He did," agreed Marika. "He told me that, too."

Jeremy smiled. "That's what he is. A human being."

"He's gonna be okay," said Mrs. Vilardi. "I can feel it."

As evening approached, with just over an hour to go before he trailed Ted Dirgrove, Jeremy located Angela through the House Staff office. She'd rotated to Endocrinology. He went there, and the charge nurse pointed to an examining room.

"Diabetic admitted for wound management, she shouldn't be too long."

Angela came out ten minutes later, looking flustered. "Hi. I'm kind of tired."

"Take a break. Let's get some coffee."

"I've already had my caffeine quotient. It didn't help."

"Then have more." He took her arm. "Come on, let's get you on a serious caf jag."

"Then what?"

"Then I study you, write it up, publish a paper."

She tried not to smile. Failed. "Okay, but just for a few minutes."

Instead of heading for the cafeteria, he steered her to some vending machines on the next floor up, the far end of the Rehab Ward, inserted a dollar bill, got both of them coffee.

"That stuff?" she said. "It's putrid."

"Don't think of it as a beverage. It's dope."

He guided her to a couple of hard, orange chairs. Rehab was mostly a daytime thing, and the ward was quiet.

"I really am bushed," she said. "And I'm nowhere near finished with my patients."

Jeremy took her hand. Her skin was cool; she looked away, kept her fingers limp.

"You're important to me," he said. "I miss you, and I know I screwed up. I shouldn't have reacted the way I did. I'm willing to talk about anything."

Angela chewed her lip and stared down at her lap. "None of that's necessary."

"Jocelyn's murder was worse than anything I'd ever imagined. She was a big part of my life, and losing her—thinking about what she went through— ripped chunks out of my heart. I should've dealt with it sooner. Instead I let it fester. Cobblers' kids going barefoot and all that."

Angela raised her head. Tears flowed down her

cheeks. "I should've understood. I shouldn't have made demands."

"No, it's good someone's finally making demands on me. I've been disconnected for a long time."

She drank coffee, made a face. "It really *is* putrid." Her fingers tightened around Jeremy's. "I knew her. Not well, but I knew her. From when I rotated through Neuro. She was a sweet, sweet girl. One time, I was charting, and she was talking to another nurse about her boyfriend. How great he was, considerate, caring. How he always made her feel special. The other nurse tried to make a joke out of it. Something like, you know those shrinks, they learn to be sensitive in school. Jocelyn wouldn't hear it, cut her off, said, 'Don't joke it away, I'm serious. I'm serious about him.' I remember thinking, what kind of guy could inspire that? I didn't know it was you. Even after we started going out, I had no idea. I just liked you because when you lectured to us, you were so intense. About what you did— about bringing out the humanity in everyone. That's the message I wanted to hear when I started my internship but seldom did. It wasn't until *after* we'd gone out a couple of times that someone—one of the other R-IIs—told me you were Jocelyn's boyfriend. I remember thinking, 'Uh-oh, this is going to be complicated.' But I liked you, so . . . oh, Jeremy, I'm not *good* at this."

She put her head on his shoulder.

He said, "Complicated, how?"

"This."

"It won't be a problem. No taboos, nothing off-limits. If you want me to talk about Jocelyn, I will—"

"That's just it," she said. "I'm not sure I want to—you obviously loved her very deeply, she's still a part of you, and that's good. If you could just dismiss her, I'd be repulsed. But the selfish part of me just doesn't know if I can deal with . . . her memory. Hanging over us. It's like having a chaperone—I know that sounds terrible, but—"

"It's hanging over me, not us," said Jeremy. "She's gone. She'll be more gone in a month, even more so in a year, and one day I won't think about her much at all." The backs of his eyes ached. Now his own tears had welled. "Intellectually I know all that, but my damn soul hasn't adjusted."

She dabbed at his eyes with her fingers. "I didn't know psychology believed in the soul."

It doesn't.

Jeremy said, "It'll take time, there's no shortcut." He looked at her.

Angela kissed his forehead.

Jeremy wrapped his arms around her. She felt small. He was about to lift her face for another kiss when a gangly teenage boy, probably someone's grandson, came out of a patient room, loped down toward the coffee machine, saw them, and grinned lewdly.

"Go, dude," the kid muttered, plunking coins down the slot.

Angela laughed in Jeremy's ear.

＊　　＊　　＊

They moved to his office, spent another quarter hour there, sitting quietly, Angela in Jeremy's lap, her head resting on his chest. The portable radio Jeremy rarely played was tuned to insipid stuff that billed itself as smooth jazz. Angela's breathing slowed, and he wondered if she'd fallen asleep. When he lowered his head to look, her eyes fluttered open, and she said, "I really need to get back."

When they returned to Endocrinology, a prune-faced nurse said, "There's a catheter waiting for you, Dr. Rios," and walked away.

Jeremy said, "Nothing like the old Welcome Wagon."

Angela smiled, grew serious. "Time to do some plumbing—Jeremy, thank you. For taking the initiative. I know it wasn't easy."

"Like I said, you're important to me."

She played with her stethoscope, kicked one shoe against the other—a little-kid gesture that pinched Jeremy's chest. "You're important to *me*, I wish we could spend some real time together, but I'll be on for the next two nights."

Me too.

He said, "Let's aim for lunch."

"Let's do that. Dude."

45

HAND-HOLDER BY DAY, SELF-DELUDED VOYEUR BY night?

For two evenings running, Theodore Gerd Dirgrove left the hospital, drove straight home, and stayed there. Both nights, Jeremy watched the cream-colored high-rise until 3 A.M., alternating between sitting in his car and walking around the glossy neighborhood. He no longer felt the cold; some sort of internal oven was raging.

A good place to be spying—the glut of cafés and high-end cocktail lounges ensured a constant sprinkle of pedestrians that made his appearance less conspicuous. The second night, he patronized one of the lounges, a place on Hale called the Pearl Onion, where martinis were the thing. He hazarded one, straight up, mixed with Boodles gin, the eponymous vegetable—a pair—floating in the silky liquid. Arthur's mix.

One drink, only, chased by coffee. He sat at a window booth that afforded him a view, through lace curtains, of Dirgrove's building.

Fitting in. Enjoying the soft music—real jazz—

the clink of glasses, the eager conversation of good-looking, affluent singles at the bar.

He'd made sure to dress well—had taken to dressing better, in general, to meet the needs of the . . . job. Donning his best sport coat and slacks, and a lush, black merino-cashmere overcoat that he'd bought in a deep-discount sale years ago at Llewellyn's department store and had never worn since—*saving it for what?*

He'd even brought a crisp shirt to his office so he could change before he set out on his—

Mission?

Find me a windmill, and I'll tilt away.

That night, Dirgrove's Buick never reappeared. The back of the building was an enclosed courtyard with only one way out of the subterranean parking lot, so even if the surgeon had chosen to retrieve the car himself, he'd have to drive around in front.

Ted was in for the night. Saving his energies?

Jeremy voided the quarts of liquid he'd ingested in the lounge's minty-fresh men's room and drove home. Tomorrow night, Angela would be off-call, and he'd have to find an excuse not to see her. Was feigning illness the tactful choice? No, that would boomerang, she'd want to be with him, dote on him. He'd think of something.

As he crawled into bed, he thought: Martinis; Arthur's drink.

Where was the old man?

What had happened to his family?

*   *   *

Eight o'clock, he was back at his desk, logging on to the *Clarion* archive. He'd tried once before, plugging in "Chess homicide" but finding nothing. Wondering if he should dig deeper.

Now he was better educated; he set his parameters.

The Pathology Department secretary knew Arthur only as a confirmed bachelor, and she'd worked at Central for years. No one Jeremy had spoken to had ever talked of a marriage in the old man's life.

So Arthur had been single for a long time; the tragedy that had shredded his life had taken place decades ago.

Someone besides the CCC people knew the truth—Arthur's neighbor, Ramona Purveyance. She'd known him as a handsome young physician who'd delivered her children.

Before . . .

An open woman, prone to chatter, but when she'd talked about Arthur leaving his home in Queen's Arms, she'd grown evasive.

Knowing the *ordeal* that had transformed Arthur from a liberator of squalling newborns to a surveyor of the dead.

Leading Arthur to a position at the Coroner's. The remainder of his life nurtured by the cessation of life. Still, the old man had hung on to the bricks and the mortar and the baseboards of his memories.

Two children. The doting wife Jeremy had conjured.

That flip assessment seemed so cruel, now.

Arthur, living with ghosts.

And yet, he smiled and drank and enjoyed late-night suppers. Traveled and learned.

And taught.

Suddenly, Jeremy was suffused with admiration for Arthur; but at the same time, the thought of ending up like Arthur scared him out of his wits.

He wrenched himself away from all that, escaped to the cold comfort of calculation: Ramona Purveyance was at least in her midsixties, so her babies would most likely have been born anywhere between thirty and forty-five years ago.

Arthur was what—seventy? Med school and Army service would've made him close to thirty by the time he came to Central to deliver babies.

Jeremy chose forty years ago and plugged in "Chess homicides."

Using the plural because that's what had happened. The computer wasn't smart enough to show discretion; perhaps that's why it had spat back his first search.

Nothing.

How about "Chess family homicides"?

Good call.

Thirty-seven years ago. A strangely dry July.

Three Bodies Found in Wreckage of Summer Cabin

An early-morning arson fire in a cabin near Lake Oswagumi, in the Highland Park resort

area, turned into a murder scene after three
bodies were discovered in the charred ruins.

The remains have been identified as those of
Mrs. Sally Chess, a young matron, and her two
children, Susan, 9, and Arthur Chess, Jr., 7.
Arthur Chess, Sr., 41, a physician at City Central Hospital, was not present at the rental
cabin when the blaze overtook the three-room
structure. Dr. Chess had been called to the hospital to perform an emergency Caesarean section and claims to have stopped at a local
tavern for a beer before driving the sixty miles
back to Highland Park.

Sheriff's investigators have reason to believe
that Mrs. Chess had been murdered and that
the fire was set deliberately to conceal that
crime. Both children likely perished in their
sleep. The investigators further state that while
Dr. Chess is being questioned, he is not considered a suspect at this time.

The last sentence reminded Jeremy of something
else he'd read recently. The account of Robert Balleron's murder. The judge had been questioned,
but police had insisted she'd not been considered a
suspect.

Did that mean just the opposite? Tina and Arthur
knowing what it felt like to have your grief poisoned by suspicion?

Poor Tina. Poor Arthur.

The old man had reached out for him, and
Jeremy had played hard-to-get.

No more. He *belonged*.

*   *   *

Still paying for archive time, he looked up "Kurau Village." That produced only a single, wire-service snippet, dated fifty-one years ago.

Cannibals Rampant!

Kurau, an obscure island in the multithousand Indonesian chain, occupied by the Japanese before the Allied liberation, and now contested territory claimed by several native tribes, fell under the sway of yellow-primitivism as marauding gangs representing various factions rampaged through opposing villages with machetes and confiscated Japanese army sabers, dismembering and disemboweling and parading through the jungle with human heads impaled on stakes. Reports of bonfires suggest that cannibalism, once a fixture in this part of the world, has made an ugly comeback. A smattering of American military and diplomatic personnel remains on the island in an attempt to administer the transition from occupation to local rule. The State Department has issued a travel advisory for all Americans to avoid the region until calm is restored.

The phone rang.

Bill Ramirez said, "Have any time to talk about Doug Vilardi?"

"Sure. How's he doing?"

"How about we talk in person? Pretend I'm a patient or something."

Ramirez was at his office door five minutes later, and out of breath. "Hard to find you—what, your fellow therapists exiled you?"

"Space problem. I volunteered."

"Kind of gloomy," said Ramirez. "Then again, you have your privacy . . . space problem—oh, yeah, the cutters got your suite, didn't they?"

"Expediency trumps virtue."

"Pardon?"

"Have a seat. How's Doug?"

Ramirez pulled up a chair. "Not so great. If his spleen doesn't get smaller, we'll be taking it out. Could happen anytime, we're watching it. The idiopathic reaction to chemo's resolving—whatever it was." The oncologist slid low in the seat and stretched his legs. His shirt was wrinkled. Sweat stains circled his armpits. "That's the thing about cases like this. Keep you humble."

"Always."

"Usually," Ramirez went on, "I'm able to tell myself I'm a hero. Cases like Doug—secondary disease, you start thinking of yourself as the villain."

"If you hadn't treated his Ewing's, he'd be dead. No wife, no baby on the way."

"Spoken like a true therapist . . . yeah, you're right. I appreciate your saying so. Still, it would be nice to not fuck anyone up."

"Become a poet."

Ramirez smiled. "Anyway, that's not why I'm

here. Pathology's still struggling to come up with a fix on the leukemia. Now, they're telling me it could be a mix of lymphatic and myelocytic, or maybe neither—something weird and undifferentiated. Could be acute and chronic at the same time—the kid's bone marrow's a mess. I've got the slides going out to L.A. and Boston because they see more than we do of these weird ones. The key is to see what protocol he fits into, but if he doesn't and we just wing it, we're lowering our chance of initial remission."

He took a deep breath. "Mind if I have some of that coffee?"

"At your own risk," said Jeremy.

"In that case, forget it. Basically, what I came to tell you is that there's a good chance our Mr. Vilardi's going to end up facing a bone marrow transplant. We typed the whole family, the mother was a little antsy but I just figured that for generalized anxiety. Turns out she and one of the brothers are excellent donors."

He frowned.

Jeremy said, "Another good-news, bad-news situation?"

"You *are* a mind reader." Ramirez took a breath. "The bad news is, Doug's not his father's biological son."

"Okay," said Jeremy.

"You're not surprised."

"I am, but not wildly. People are people."

"Gee," said Ramirez. "I wish you were *my* dad. Adolescence would've been a helluva lot easier.

Okay, so that's the big secret. The question is, what do we do about it?"

"Nothing," said Jeremy.

"Plain and simple."

"Plain and simple."

"You're right," said Ramirez. "I just wanted to hear it from you. Get some backup." He got to his feet. "Okay, good, thanks. Onward."

"Anything else, Bill?"

"That's not enough for one day?"

Jeremy smiled.

Ramirez said, "I'm glad you confirmed my initial instincts. Doug's an adult, has a right to his medical records; but I'm going to destroy that part of the report. Just in case someone peeks."

He looked at Jeremy.

Jeremy said, "I back you up on that, too."

"It's the best thing," said Ramirez. "I already did enough damage to the kid."

In the afternoon, after Jeremy had seen all his other patients, he sat by Doug's bedside. No family members were around. Their usual arrival time was two hours later, and Jeremy had timed his visit carefully. He didn't want to look into Mrs. Vilardi's eyes.

Doug was sleeping with the TV on. A sitcom blared—small-town life, corny jokes, Hollywood's take on jovial half-wits playing to the laugh track. Jeremy kept the show on but lowered the volume, concentrated on Doug's swollen, jaundiced face, his big, callused, workingman's hands lying inert. The laugh track began to grate on him, and he switched off the set, listened to the ticking, gurgling, chirping that confirmed the young man's viability.

Doug didn't stir.

Push past this, my friend.

Give me something to be inspired by.

Do *it*.

46

JEREMY CLEARED HIS NEXT THREE EVENINGS BY LY-
ing. Feeding Angela tales of looming deadlines for
the book, grinding pressure from the Head of Oncology, topped by a severe case of writer's block.

He'd need to pull two or three all-nighters,
maybe even four.

She said, "Been there, done it—it'll work out,
honey."

On the first day, he spirited her away for an early
dinner at Sarno's, concentrated on being attentive,
kept the conversation easy and light and flowing.
The ever-present horror track in his head washed
by: filthy, violent images, a mental cesspool that
drained miles from the lover's face he showed
Angela.

By dinner's end, he figured he'd pulled it off. Angela had loosened up, was smiling, laughing, talking about patients and hospital bureaucracy. By the
time he dropped her back at Endocrinology, it was
five-thirty and she was energized.

The next day, she paged him to let him know that
the chief resident had frowned on her cutting out
early.

"How about I write you a note," he said. " 'Angela's tummy was empty, and she needed to eat.' "

"If only," she said. "How'd it go on the book, last night?"

"Painfully."

"Stick with it, I know you'll do great."

"Thanks."

"I don't have time, anyway, Jer. The Endo attendings are mostly high-powered, private practice brutes. They work us like galley slaves so they can be home in time for din-din with the family. So if I get to see you at all, it'll have to be lunch. And tomorrow, lunch is a lecture on growth hormone abuse."

"The schedule."

"I'll let you know if things ease up. Sorry."

"Nothing to apologize for, Ang. This too shall pass."

And I've got my own schedule, now.

"I know," she said. "But right now it seems interminable. Okay, gotta go. Miss you."

"Miss you, too."

Two more nights of Dirgrove playing at family man. Or whatever he did, once he was ensconced in his limestone aerie.

One floor down from the penthouse. Jeremy knew because he'd strolled by when the doorman had gone inside to take a package to a resident. Made his way into the marble-walled lobby and checked out the directory, all those nice, healthy potted palms.

When Dirgrove walked through the door how far did he take the charade? Was din-din with the family part of the routine? Or did he lock himself, straight off, in his study?

Did he pay token attention to Brandon and Sonja? Jeremy's glimpse of the family at dinner said the bastard couldn't care less.

Were he and Patty still sleeping together?

Poor woman, that determined face, the athletic carriage. All the trappings of a fine life, and it would be crashing down sooner or later.

Jeremy was going to do his best to make it sooner.

On the third day, Doug Vilardi was sent to the O.R. for a splenectomy. Jeremy comforted the family but knew the young man wouldn't need him for at least twenty-four hours. None of his other patients were in crisis. Several had been discharged, and he was only called to one acute procedure, a fifteen-year-old burn patient, a girl who'd lost the skin on one thigh and was undergoing painful whirlpool baths to slosh loose dead dermis.

Jeremy found out she liked playing tennis and had her imagine herself playing the French Open.

The girl got through it. Her father, a tough-guy type, some sort of executive, said, "That was amazing."

"Jennifer's amazing."

The guy shook his head. "Man—you're good."

Now, it was 6 P.M., and he was free. He desperately wanted to keep his head clear. To save mental space for Dirgrove, his psychopathology, his tools. The woman who was certain to be his next target.

Dirgrove worked later than usual, not showing up at his car until shortly after 8 P.M. When he left the doctors' lot, he turned south.

Away from his home base on Hale. A first.

Here we go.

A great night for watching. The mercury had dropped even farther, but the air had dried. Gotten thinner, too, as if some deity were sucking out all the unnecessary gases. Jeremy breathed heavily, headily, felt lighthearted. Sound seemed to be traveling faster, and his car windows couldn't shut out the city din. Lights were brighter, people walked faster, every nocturnal detail stood out in relief.

No shortage of cars, tonight. Urban motorists were out in force, enjoying skid-free roads and clarity. Driving too fast, euphorically.

Everyone functioning at peak levels.

Dirgrove headed toward the Asa Brander Bridge—the same route that had led Jeremy to Arthur's rooming house in Ash View. But instead of exiting on the industrial road and connecting to the turnpike, the Buick kept going.

Toward the airport.

Six more blocks, then he turned right on a busy, commercial street. Another two blocks and they were on Airport Boulevard, and Dirgrove had pulled in front of a motel.

Red neon spaghetti spelled out THE HIDEAWAY over a neon cutout of two overlapping hearts. The motel advertised massage beds, total privacy (right out there on the busy boulevard) and adult films on cable. On one side of the building was a filling station, the other hosted an unclaimed-luggage resale store called TravelAid. Farther down the block was an adult book and video store, two liquor emporia, a drive-through hamburger joint.

Mattress dance hall.

The rooms faced a motor court. The entrance was double-wide. Jeremy parked across Airport and crossed the boulevard on foot. He stood at the front of the motel, on the sidewalk, at an angle where he could peer into the court and see the window marked OFFICE. At his back, traffic sped by. Overhead, planes took off and landed. No one walked the sidewalks. The air stank of jet fuel.

The motel office windows weren't draped, and the room was brightly lit. Jeremy's position afforded him a clear view of Ted Dirgrove checking in. The surgeon appeared as relaxed as someone on a wholesome vacation.

Jeremy noticed that he didn't sign in. A regular? Dirgrove got his key, made his way to a room on the east side of the motor court.

Natty in a black coat and gray slacks. Whistling. Room 16.

Jeremy returned to his car and continued to watch The Hideaway from across the street. He'd dropped from sight just in time. Five minutes later, Gwynn Hauser's Lexus swung into a space three over from the Buick.

She got out, didn't bother to look around, walked jauntily toward the motor court, swinging her purse.

She'd capped her blond bob with a long black wig, wore that full, white fur coat Jeremy had seen during her last tryst with Dirgrove. The motel entrance was better lit than the industrial stretch, and, even at this distance, Jeremy could see that the coat was a cheap fake, spiky as magnetized iron filings.

Cheap wig, too, not even close to human hair.

Slumming.

He waited until she'd been gone for ten minutes, made his way over to the office, and purchased a room at the half-day rate of forty-four dollars. The clerk was a reserved young man with oily black hair who barely looked up as he took Jeremy's cash. Nor did he react when Jeremy stated his room preference.

Number 15. Directly across from 16.

He made his way there, sticking close to the building and staying out of the light that washed across the court. Closing the door, he breathed in old sweat and shampoo and raspberry-scented disinfectant. He kept the lights off in the room but switched them on in the pathetic little bathroom— just a fiberglass prefab, really, with a toilet screwed shakily into the floor and a molded shower barely large enough for a child.

The indirect illumination amplified his surroundings: double bed with a mushy mattress and two pillows, a coin-fed vibrator gizmo on the nightstand, a twelve-inch TV bolted to the wall and topped by a Pay-Per-View box. The room's single window was covered by an oilcloth shade. By rolling it up an inch and pulling a chair to the front, Jeremy had a fine view of Number 16.

Lights on, there. For two full hours. Then, off they went.

No one exited the room. Time passed. Nine-thirty, ten, eleven. At midnight Jeremy was nearly out of his mind with boredom and wondering if Dirgrove and Hauser were in for the long haul.

He had his TV switched on. Most of the channels were fuzzy, and he had no desire to call the front office and order a dirty movie. Settling for a tele-vangelist broadcasting from a massive blond cathedral in Nebraska, he sat listening to tales of sin and redemption and knew he was wasting his time. Dirgrove would do no mischief tonight; his girl-friend was keeping him busy.

Unless their relationship had changed and . . . no, no way, too careless. Not with Gwynn's car and his parked right out on the boulevard.

Ted was a man of varied tastes.

They'd fallen asleep, he was sure of it. It was 3:15 A.M. and Jeremy'd had his fill of faith healing and exhortations to qualify as Lambs of God by sending in cookie-jar stashes, spare change, social security checks, whatever led one to a state of grace.

"You will know," promised the graveyard-shift preacher, a skinny, handsome type who looked like a frat boy. "You will *feel* it."

At 3:37, Gwynn Hauser, still bewigged and look-ing shaky, left the room, drawing her fake fur around her.

Five minutes later, Dirgrove exited, stared at the moon, yawned, trudged slowly to his car.

Jeremy followed him. Back home to Patty and the brood.

What would he tell her? An emergency? Saving lives? Or had he gotten past the point where he had to tell her anything?

Would she hear him, smell him as he got between the sheets—would the scent of another woman waft her way in the temperature-controlled atmosphere of their sure-to-be-stylish master suite?

Poor woman.

Jeremy made it to his own house just before four. His block was dead and when he entered his empty bedroom, it felt like the cell of a stranger.

47

DOUG'S SPLEEN WAS OUT, HE LOOKED AS IF HE'D been hit by a train, a catheter drained his urine, his voice was thick, slurred, halting.

He said, "The funny thing is, Doc, I actually feel . . . better. Without that . . . fucking . . . spleen in me."

He had little to say after that. Jeremy had slept three hours and wasn't feeling creative. He sat with the young man for a while, offered smiles, encouraging looks, a couple of uncontroversial jokes.

Doug said, "Gotta get . . . out of . . . here in . . . time for ice fishing."

"You do that a lot?"

"Every year. With . . . my dad."

Mrs. Vilardi came into the room and said, "Oh, my baby!"

". . . fine, Mom."

"Yes, yes, I know you are." Suppressing tears, she smiled at Jeremy. She had on a shapeless brown coat over a polyester sweater and heavy-duty sweatpants. On her feet were shiny brown leather-look boots. The sweater was green and red; reindeer pranced along her ample bustline. Her hair was short, permed, mouse brown with gray peeking through. Her eyes sagged.

Just another middle-aged woman, worn down by the years. When she was young she'd taken a lover and his seed had sprouted Doug. Jeremy had never really looked at her before.

He said, "I'll leave you guys, now."

"Bye, Doc."

"Have a nice day, Dr. Carrier."

Detective Bob Doresh stepped out of nowhere and waylaid him as he headed for the stairwell.

"No elevator for you, Doc?"

"Keeping fit."

"Busy last night, Doc?"

"What do you mean?"

Doresh's heavy face was grim. His jaw muscles swelled. "We need to talk, Doc. At my place."

"I've got patients."

"They can wait."

"No, they can't," said Jeremy. "If you want to talk, we'll do it at my place."

Doresh moved closer. Jeremy's back was to the wall, and for a moment he thought the detective would pin him. The cleft in Doresh's meaty chin quivered. Lord, you *could* hide something in there.

"This is a big deal to you, Doc? *Where* we talk?"

"It's not a pissing contest, Detective. I'm totally willing to cooperate with you—though I can't imagine what the big issue is. Let's just do it here, so I don't lose time."

"The big issue," said Doresh. He inched even

closer. Jeremy smelled his breakfast bacon. "I've got a *real* big issue." He placed a hand on his hip.

The blood left Jeremy's face in a rush. "Another one? That's impossible."

"Impossible, Doc?" Doresh's eyes were on high-beam, now.

Impossible, because the monster played with his girlfriend all night.

How could I be so wrong?

"What I meant to say—my first thought was, not again, so soon. So much death. It's impossible to comprehend."

"Ah." Doresh's smile was sickening. "And you don't like that."

"Of course not."

"Of course not."

"What the hell are you getting at, Detective?"

Movement up the hall caught Jeremy's eyes. Mrs. Vilardi left Doug's room, looked around, spotted Jeremy, and waved. She pantomimed drinking. Letting Jeremy know she was getting herself coffee. As if she needed his permission.

Jeremy waved back.

Doresh said, "A fan of yours?"

"What do you want with me? Let's get it over with."

"Fine," said Doresh. "How about we compromise—not your place or my place—God's place."

The hospital chapel—the *Meditation Room*—was situated off the main lobby, just beyond the development office. Officially nondenominational, not much more than an afterthought, the room was

three rows of blond ash pews over thin red carpeting, plastic windows designed to look like stained
glass, a low, sloping sparkle-plaster ceiling. The
pews faced an aluminum crucifix bolted to the wall.
A Bible sat on a lectern at the back, next to a rack
full of inspirational pamphlets donated by evangeli-
cal societies.

Jeremy supposed the place was utilized, from time
to time, but he'd never seen anyone go in or out.

Doresh entered as if he'd been there before.

What, this is supposed to encourage confession?

The detective strode to the front row, removed
his raincoat, draped it over a pew, sat down, and
tapped a space to his right. Beckoning Jeremy to sit
next to him.

Now we pray together?

Jeremy ignored the invitation and circled in front
of Doresh. He faced the detective, remained on
his feet.

"What can I do for you, Detective?"

"You can start by accounting for your whereabouts last night, Doctor."

"What times?"

"The whole night."

"I was out."

"I know that, Doc. You got home around four in
the morning. Late, for you."

"You've been watching me?"

"Did I say that?"

"No," said Jeremy. "Of course you didn't. Stupid
question. If you'd been watching me, you'd know I
have nothing to do with it."

And neither does Dirgrove, shacked up in the room across the motor court.

Wrong, wrong, wrong!

"Start accounting," said Doresh.

"I left the hospital shortly after eight and checked into a motel near the airport around half an hour later. The Hideaway, on Airport Boulevard. I paid cash, but the clerk may remember me because the place wasn't busy. He's a young guy with dark hair. Greasy, dark hair. Last night he was wearing a green-and-white-striped shirt. I didn't notice his pants. I paid for half a day. Forty-four dollars."

"A motel."

"That's right."

"Who were you with?"

"No one."

Doresh's shrublike eyebrows rose. He shifted his weight, and the pew creaked. "You checked into a motel by yourself."

"Room 15. I stayed there till around three-forty and, as you know, got home shortly before four."

If Doresh or some other cop hadn't seen him, who had? Had to be a neighbor, and the only one who came to mind was Mrs. Bekanescu. A snoop by nature, she'd never liked him, and he'd seen lights on in her house well before sunrise. Sometimes she put food out for stray cats, drew their mewling to the block while the sky was still dark. Whatever the reason, she'd been up, had noticed his headlights, and when Doresh had come asking questions, she'd been more than happy to tell him.

How many neighbors had Doresh spoken to? Did all of them believe him a dangerous man? Was that—not the fact that they were transient renters—why no one spoke to him?

Doresh was staring at him, not saying a word.

"Where and when did it happen?" said Jeremy.

"You're serious."

"About wanting to know? Yes."

"About checking into a hot-bed joint by yourself."

"I did it for the solitude."

"You found solitude at a hot-bed joint?"

"Yes."

"Guy like you, living by yourself, what's wrong with your own house for solitude?" He smiled. "You've got *plenty* of solitude, now."

Doresh's tone challenged Jeremy. *Go ahead, smart-boy, blow your stack.*

Jeremy shrugged. "Sometimes a change of scenery helps."

"Helps what?"

"Achieve peace of mind."

Doresh's face turned the color of raw beef. "You'd do well not to jerk me around."

"Ask the motel clerk. Ask the maid who cleaned Room 15 if the bed was ever slept in."

"You didn't sleep there? What the hell did you do?"

"Sat on a chair. Thought. Watched TV—religious shows, mostly. The one that sticks in my memory is a preacher from Nebraska. Thadd Bromley. Gabby fellow. He wore a blue v-neck sweater—looked like a college boy and talked like a cowboy. From the pledges that came in, he's doing great. I enjoyed hearing him tell me how to live my life." Jeremy's eyes circled the chapel.

"You're a religious guy," said Doresh.

"I wish."

"Wish what?"

"Religion would be a comfort. I'd like to believe."

"What stops you?"

"Too many distractions. Who was she? Where did it happen?"

Doresh ignored him. He turned away, and light through a stained-plastic window rainbowed his face.

"Another Humpty-Dumpty situation," said Jeremy.

Still no response.

"Is there anything else, Detective?"

Doresh crossed his legs. "What you're telling me, is that from eight-thirty to three-forty you were at a cocky-locky dump, all by your lonesome, listening to the gospel. That's some story."

"Why would I make something like that up?"

"Thing is, Doc, maybe the clerk *can* verify your checking in. But I assume you didn't stop to say good-bye to him when you cut out. So how the hell do I know you were there all night? You could've checked out any time."

"Thadd Bromley," said Jeremy. "He was on late. He quoted from Acts. He healed a girl on crutches. And there were others. I can probably remember some of their sermons. I did doze briefly, but for the most part I was up."

"Religious shows."

"The Hideaway doesn't offer a great selection of stations. Most of the reception was fuzzy. I guess the religious channels broadcast with more power."

"You rent any fuck movies?"

"No."

"Those places, they have a great selection of fuck movies, right? That's the whole point of places like that. Except, generally, people bring a partner."

The detective's eyes were cold with contempt.

Jeremy said, "No fuck movies. Check the Pay-Per-View log—"

"Bullshit," snarled Doresh. "What you're giving me is bullshit."

"If I knew I'd need an alibi, I'd have prepared one."

"Sweet. All that nice sweet logic."

"Who got killed?"

"A woman." Doresh uncrossed his legs.

"Vacuum my car if you'd like," said Jeremy. "Confiscate my clothes—come back to my house, spray that Luminol again. Look for fibers, fluids, whatever you want. Do it without a warrant, I couldn't care less."

"How about a polygraph?"

"Sure, no problem."

"No strings attached?"

"Keep your questions limited to my involvement in any murder."

"What?" said Doresh. "We can't ask you about religion?"

"Is there anything else, Detective?"

"A polygraph," said Doresh. "Course a guy like you, master hypnotist and all that, you'd probably know ways to fake out the polygraph."

"There are no tricks," said Jeremy. "Successful faking involves having an abnormally cold personality or practicing on the machine for an extended period. Neither of which applies to me. Oh, yeah, sedation, too. You want to prescreen me for drugs, go ahead."

"Cold personality, huh? I'd say you're a pretty cool fellow, Dr. Carrier. Even right after Ms. Banks got butchered up, when we hauled you into the station, you were damned cool. My partner and I were impressed. Guy's girlfriend gets chopped up like that, and he's gliding through the interview."

Jeremy remembered that time as an endless nightmare. He laughed so as not to hit the bastard.

"Something funny, Doc?"

"How far off base you are is funny. If you're worried about trickery, we can forget about the polygraph."

Doresh gathered his coat and stood and came close. His cleft chin pulsed, and his barrel chest threatened to intrude upon Jeremy's torso. "No, let's do it—maybe tomorrow. Or the day after."

"Call me," said Jeremy. "I'll look at my calendar and fit you in."

"No tricks, huh?" said Doresh.

"I've got none. No surgical skills, either, Detective. And I've never been to England."

Doresh blinked. "Now why would I care about any of that?"

Jeremy shrugged and started to walk around the detective. Doresh blocked him. Feinted with his head—a game-cock maneuver—as if about to strike. Jeremy fell back reflexively, lost his balance, took hold of a pew.

Doresh laughed and left the chapel.

48

JEREMY WAITED UNTIL HE WAS CERTAIN DORESH wasn't coming back before locking the door to the chapel, sinking into a rear pew, and burying his face in his hands.

Not Dirgrove. I've been wasting my time and now another woman . . .

Always wrong, always fucking wrong.

How could it be? Everything fit so elegantly. Tools, lasers, like father like son. Dirgrove a sexual predator, manipulative. Definitely in England when the English girls were slaughtered and the English girls fit, they had to, that's why Langdon and Shreve had perked up their ears, why Shreve had called Doresh, and Doresh had paid Jeremy a visit.

I've never been to England! Why can't Doresh see that, the ass!

The polygraph would clear him, everything they did would clear him, but meanwhile more women . . .

WRONG.

That meant Arthur was wrong, too. The postcards, the envelopes, the entire fucking tutorial the old man had shoved in his . . .

Arthur.

A terrible thought—a horrific atheism—seized him.

Arthur, surveyor of death. Connossieur of the grisly story, game player, par excellence.

Arthur, student of war strategy.

He'd known for some time that the old man had been manipulating him but had endowed the gambit with noble intentions.

Arthur. Enjoyed working with death, used a morgue van for spare wheels—the vehicle that had followed him had been large. An SUV, he'd thought. But why not a van?

The man dissected. Dug with a garden spade . . . no, no way. The pathologist was too old. Old men, stripped of testosterone and dreams just didn't do things like that.

Besides, Arthur had been on the other side of violence, a victim—the ordeal.

His family slaughtered.

An unsolved triple murder.

Arthur with no alibi, driving to the cabin at the time the fire was set.

Arthur taking years to move out of the family home. Living with ghosts.

Ghosts he'd created?

No, impossible, intolerable. The old man was eccentric but not a monster—Arthur being a monster would mean the other CCC people—no, they were victims, all of them. Had endured their own ordeals, nobility through suffering.

Arthur was an odd man but a good man. Jeremy's avatar, guiding him toward inexorable truths.

And yet, the old man had led him straight down the wrong path.

I couldn't have miscalculated that badly.

If I did, I'm finding another line of work. Plumbing, bricklaying, motel clerk at a sleazy hot-bed palace. Better yet, I'll ship out on one of those trawlers that hauls in crabs and bottom feeders and gasping whitefish.

Like father . . .

Why had Arthur *done* this to him?

He sat up, bared his face, caught an eyeful of stained plastic.

Then it hit him—a seizure of bowel-tightening, grandiose insight that made everything . . . right!

He jumped to his feet, ran toward the chapel door. As he lunged for the lock, his pager went off.

"Dr. Carrier, this is Nancy, the charge nurse on Four East. I've got a patient here, a Mrs. Van Alden, one of Dr. Schuster's, she's scheduled for an LP, says you were supposed to be here ten minutes ago to help her through it. We're kind of waiting . . ."

"I got held up by an emergency. I'll be there right away."

"Good. She looks pretty uptight."

He hurried to the elevators, eyes downward, wondering, *How am I going to fake it?*

As he rode up to Four, he checked his appointment book.

Nine more patients, booked consecutively, each one needy. Not counting Doug, and he knew he'd be expected to check in on Doug again; Christ, the poor kid deserved it.

After his clinical duties were over, a Psychiatry case conference. That he could skip, but there was no avoiding the people who depended on him.

Ten patients, no breaks in between because he'd compressed his schedule. Wanting more time for night work, and now he was paying for it.

Windmill work; tilting with a broken lance.

The elevator door opened on ward noise. Mrs. Van Alden needed him, she'd be okay, he'd help her through it.

He'd get through the day, somehow.

A pretty cool fellow.

Right?

49

BACK IN HIS OFFICE, SHORT OF BREATH FROM RUNning, the sounds of the day—pain cries, weeping, sighs of resignation, gushes of gratitude—buried deeply in some dark, little, crumb-littered vest pocket of his brain.

He went straight for the book—there it was, lying atop the *Curiosity* file.

The Blood Runs Cold. Mr. Colin Pugh exploiting very, very bad behavior.

A book sold by Renfrew. Of course, had to be, that made sense, the world remained logical . . .

Flipping feverishly to the final chapter, he turned pages so quickly that the acid-damaged paper flaked, and dust flew off in all directions.

There it was:

Gerd Dergraav enters Brazil using a Syrian passport.

Remarried, with a child.

Another son.

Here?

Arthur leading him . . . that day in the cafeteria. The other man, the dark-haired surgeon with the mustache who'd been sitting with Dirgrove and Mandel as Arthur stared.

The man Jeremy had seen arguing with Dirgrove. The two of them, evenly matched, same height, same build. Teeth bared like fighting dogs . . .

A second son, born in Syria. Part-Mideastern, part-German—the coloring fit.

It was the dark man, not Dirgrove, whom Arthur had focused on.

Had to be, had to be, let me be right . . . Jeremy yanked open the bottom desk drawer, grabbed the Attending Staff face book, and began with the D's, because, like Dirgrove, this one had probably changed his name and hopefully, like his half brother, he'd stayed alphabetically close.

He hadn't.

Jeremy turned back to the A's, scanned every photo in the book. His own image stared back at him blankly—a picture taken shortly after Jocelyn. *Lord, I look shell-shocked.*

The dark, mustachioed doctor was nowhere to be found.

A white-coat, a surgeon, but not on staff at City Central?

Mandel would know. Jeremy phoned the cardiologist's office, was informed Dr. Mandel was on vacation.

"Where?"

"I'm not at liberty to say," said the secretary.

"This is Dr. Carrier."

"Is it a patient emergency?"

"Yes."

"Dr. Rhinegold's taking emergency call for Dr. Mandel."

"I need to speak with Dr. Mandel, personally."

"I'm sorry—"

"Please."

"What I was about to say, Doctor, was that even if I wanted to reach Dr. Mandel, I couldn't. He's backpacking with his family out in Colorado and doesn't have a phone. He made a big point of that. No phone, for three days. He really deserves to get away."

"What hotel is he staying at?"

"Doctor," she said, "maybe I didn't make myself clear. He's *camping*. Out in the middle of *nowhere*."

"Is there a physician in your department, forty or so, dark complexion, dark mustache?"

"No," she said. "Are you all right, Dr. Carrier?"

Not knowing where else to go, he phoned Dirgrove's office.

Hey, Ted, long time, no see. By the way, what's the name of your homicidal sib? And what did he do to irritate you the other day?

Had the argument between Dirgrove and his brother been about something of substance? Did Dirgrove suspect?

The surgeon's phone rang five times before Jeremy was connected to voice mail.

Dr. Theodore Dirgrove is currently unavailable. If this is a patient emergency, please press . . .

Gone for the day. Another meet-up with Dr. Gwynn Hauser?

Hauser. She and Dirgrove had spent six hours together at the motel. That said their relationship was more than kinky role-playing.

Did it involve pillow talk?

He looked up Hauser's extension, and when she picked up the phone, he hung up and put on his white coat.

She shared an office suite with three other internists, two floors below Dirgrove's penthouse spread. Jeremy crossed an empty reception area, knocked on the door with her name on it, and opened it as she said, "Come in."

She was at her desk, writing, and looked up. Smiling, she removed her glasses and put down her pen. "My parking lot friend. I was wondering when you'd show up."

Lashes batted. Her blond bob vibrated as she tilted her face toward Jeremy.

He'd come in smiling, wanting to put her at ease, but this much ease rattled him. She wheeled back in her desk chair, offered him a full view of long legs crossing. She wore a red wool dress and flesh-tone stockings. Great legs. Up close, she looked her age, but it didn't matter. This one poured out hormones.

Jeremy closed the door. "You were expecting me?"

She said, "Is it my imagination, or have you been checking me out? First, that time in the lot, and then various places around the hospital." She winked. "Hey, I'm an observant gal. I've noticed *you* noticing *me*. I even looked you up. Jeremy Carrier, from the shrink department."

Jeremy smiled.

She said, "Chemistry. When it's there, it's there."

"True," he said, sitting down opposite her desk.

"So. *Jeremy.* What service can I provide Psychiatry?"

"I need information."

Her face slackened. Confused.

"About Ted's brother."

"Ted?" Back went the glasses. Her legs uncrossed, and she sat stiffly.

"Ted Dirgrove."

"The surgeon?"

"No need to be coy, Gwynn."

She pointed to the door. "I think you'd better leave. Now."

"I like the coat," said Jeremy. "The big, white fuzzy one. Just the right combination of chic and cheap. What is it, polyester? Like the black wig?"

The color drained from Gwynn Hauser's face. "Fuck you—get the fuck *out* of here."

Jeremy crossed his legs. "Tell you what, I'll send the pictures simultaneously. One set to your husband, the other to Patty Dirgrove."

"You're insane. What pictures?"

"The Hideaway Motel, Room 16. Yesterday, eight-thirty to three-forty. Long date. Must've been fun."

Gwynn Hauser's mouth dropped open. "You're *really* insane."

"Maybe," said Jeremy. "However, the state of my mental health needn't affect the quality of your life."

"What's that, a threat? You think you can march in here and threaten me and bully me? Are you out of your—" She reached for her phone but didn't dial.

"All I want is the information."

"About—why?"

"You don't need to know."

"What has *he* done?"

"You're assuming *he's* done something," said Jeremy. "You're not surprised that *he'd* do something."

Hauser replaced the phone in its cradle. The tendons of her hands were bowstring tight. Jeremy watched as she pushed sheets of paper into a six-inch pile that she interposed between herself and Jeremy.

Pathetic barrier. She knew it. Her eyes were bright with confusion and fear.

"I don't know enough to be surprised. All I know is what Ted tells me."

She tried a little-girl pout. Smiled. When Jeremy remained stoic, she snarled, "Asshole. You don't have any pictures, how could you have pictures?"

"Are you willing to bet on that?" said Jeremy. Sounding cool—the cool fellow surfacing, despite all the noise in his head.

"What do you want?"

"Tell me about him."

"*What* about him?"

"For starters, his name."

"You don't even know his—are you out of your . . . his name is Graves. Augusto Graves, he's part South American. Augie. He's not Ted's full brother. He's a half brother. They're not close. They grew up separately. Ted wants nothing to do with him, they had a big fight years ago, and Ted thought he was free of him, but then Augie showed up."

"He works here?"

"He's here temporarily. One-year research grant in Ob-Gyn. Some corporate grant. Ted's convinced he obtained it just to make trouble for him."

A temporary appointment would account for no photo in the face book.

Jeremy said, "Research in laser surgery."

Her pretty blue eyes widened. "You didn't know his name, but you know that? What the hell's going on?"

"Where's Graves's home base?"

"The West Coast, Seattle, I think. One of the big academic hospitals, there. And England—Cambridge. He travels all over the world lecturing. He's a genius. Full professor by thirty-five. Ted's still an associate. He hates him."

"Jealousy?"

"That's part of it. But I believed Ted when he says Augie's intent on outdoing him at every turn."

"Ted talks about him a lot."

Gwynn Hauser exhaled. "The topic comes up."

"Thorn in the side."

"Big thorn. What did he do, and why do you care?"

"You're assuming he did something bad."

"You're here, aren't you?"

Jeremy remained silent. Therapist's silence, one of the few "tricks" in his puny arsenal. Aimed straight at her resistance.

She said, "Ted says he's got a mean streak. They didn't meet until Ted was in college and Augie was in high school. Ted's father abandoned him and his mother. Married Augie's mother and lived in some Arab country, then South America. Later, Augie and his mother came to America and Augie went to school, there. One day, out of the clear blue, he appeared at Ted's fraternity house, introduced himself, tried to insinuate himself into Ted's life."

"Ted didn't welcome the reunion."

"He'd never known about Augie. No one had ever *mentioned* another family. He didn't know much about his father, period. All his mom said was that he was a doctor and had died doing research in the jungle somewhere."

"Research into what?"

"I have no idea," said Hauser. "No doubt something brilliant. Ted's brilliant, and so is Augie. That's part of the problem. I assume they got it somewhere."

"Like father, like son."

She nodded.

Jeremy prompted her: "Part of what problem?"

"Two oversize brains, two massive egos. Ted's convinced Augie went to med school only because he did. And Augie did outdo him. Got into the number one school, while Ted's was ranked third. Plus, Augie received a full scholarship and enrolled under a double degree program. M.D.-Ph.D., all in five years."

"What's his Ph.D. in?"

"Bioengineering. He's a laser honcho. Plus, he's board certified in general surgery and Ob-Gyn, even did some work in Ophthalmology. We're talking major brainiac." She managed a wry smile. "Poor Ted, he's merely brilliant."

Bioengineering. Jeremy flashed back to the *Curiosity* file. The second article. Laser surgery on women.

An American team, from the West Coast. Physicians and engineers.

Arthur had led him straight. *He'd* missed the cue.

"Have you ever met him?"

"I've seen him around but only talked to him once. Last week as a matter of fact. Ted and I were lunching in the DDR, and he waltzed over, sat down with us." She smiled. "The moment his butt touched the chair he was coming on to me. Nothing you could call him on. Subtly. Looks, smiles. He's a smooth one. Ted was *not* amused. I told him not to worry, the guy's not my type."

"Why not?"

"Too refined. I like 'em a little ragged." She cast a knowing glance at Jeremy.

Trying to take what belonged to his brother. That explained the argument.

He said, "What about the mean streak?"

Gwynn Hauser said, "Ted never got specific. He just said Augie had been known to be cruel—to do cruel things. That Augie made him nervous, he didn't want him near his family. Or me. I didn't press him for details." Another flutter of eyelash. "To be honest, hearing Ted go on about him bores me to tears. Playing nursie to his insecurities wasn't what I'd bargained for."

"Neurotic, not ragged."

"Exactly. Give me raw, misguided energy any day."

Again, her legs crossed. "To be honest, I'm growing a wee bit tired of Ted. When push came to shove, he turned out like all the others."

"Boring."

"Boring and a weenie. He always needs propping up. Thinks he's a player, but down deep he's just a family man who sneaks around."

Jeremy said, "What else can you tell me about Augie Graves?"

"Nothing," she said. Her left hand grazed her right breast. "Boy, you really took over, didn't you? Just burst in here like some Visigoth and got me to do things I never thought I'd do."

Color had returned to her face. Peach tones tinctured by flush.

She smiled, exposed a row of pearly, glistening teeth. "And to look at you, you'd never know it . . . you could show me things, couldn't you?"

"All part of the training," said Jeremy, turning to leave.

"Maybe," she said, "one day you can tell me more about it."

50

EIGHT-FIFTEEN.

Jeremy located Augusto Graves's office number by phoning the hospital operator. She had no listing of any home address; nor did Dr. Graves carry a beeper.

No patients to see, pure research.

Graves's hospital base was the east wing of an auxiliary building across the street from the hospital. A newer building, set apart from the clinical world. Hushed space reserved for the laboratories of promising scientists. A refuge where a brilliant, cruel mind could run wild.

The hospital structure nearest to the nurses' parking lot.

Graves watching, waiting. Seeing Jocelyn walk to her car every day.

Jocelyn happy after a day's work, happier, yet, to be going home to Jeremy. Meeting—*greeted* by a good-looking man in a white coat.

Young nurse, older doctor. Hospital hierarchy dictated respect.

His badge would have firmed it up. M.D., Ph.D.,

full professor. When he spoke, smooth, urbane. Why would she have been suspicious?

Graves's lab was on the ground floor, and the door was open.

Jeremy stood by the doorway and peered in. Large windows on the north wall afforded a clear view of the lot.

He entered. The layout was nothing out of the ordinary, just the usual mix of black-topped tables and glistening glassware and high-tech accoutrements. Jeremy recognized several lasers—stationary and handheld devices, arranged in a compulsive bank, each one labeled and all tagged with DO NOT TOUCH stickers. Computers, scanners, printers, a host of other equipment that meant nothing to him.

One wall had been given over to books. Basic science and surgery. Medical journals collected in open-faced boxes. Everything perfectly organized. No chemical smells; this was clean research.

Graves wasn't there. The only person in view was a woman in a navy blue housekeeping uniform, sweeping the floor, positioning chairs. Probably another Eastern European immigrant, going about her job with a resigned look on her dumpling face.

Graves had created an office space in one corner of the lab. His desk was wide, substantial, covered by a spotless sheet of glass.

Bare, except for a rosewood in-out box. Both compartments contained neatly stacked documents.

Jeremy hurried behind the desk, tried the drawers, all locked.

"Hey," said the sweeper, "you kanna do dat."

Jeremy began rifling through the contents of the

in-box. Nothing he could use. He moved on to the out-box.

"Hey," said the woman.

Before she could protest further, he was out of there. Hot little hand clamped over his find.

Subscription card for a magazine—*The Nation*.

Graves had opted for another year. The card was preprinted with his new home address.

Hale Boulevard.

Four blocks south of the high-rise where his brother played at family man.

51

JEREMY KNEW WHAT HE'D FIND WHEN HE LOCATED the building. An even better address than Dirgrove's cream-colored high-rise.

Graves, the ultimate taker.

Now, Jeremy was certain Dirgrove *had* been interested in Jocelyn. Perhaps it had ended at flirtation. Or Jocelyn had enjoyed a fling with the surgeon before meeting Jeremy.

Nearly everything else he'd imputed to Dirgrove was wrong. The man was an adulterer and an insecure skirt-chaser, but no more than that.

Nothing nefarious about the consult on Merilee Saunders. Either Dirgrove had been genuinely concerned about his patient's reaction to surgery, or he'd been trying to impress Angela with his sensitivity.

Either way, nothing untoward about Merilee's death. Before leaving the hospital, Jeremy had rushed back to the main building, entered the medical library, and located the M and M sheet on the young woman. Cerebral aneurysm. A hidden little blood vessel in her brain had burst.

As Dirgrove had said, one of those things that happens.

But he had taunted Jeremy . . . sins of the father on a subtler level?

But that was of no concern, now. Augusto Graves was an heir of a different sort. Bought into the complete paternal endowment.

Made things happen.

Growing up in Brazil, Graves had been well aware of his father's crimes, the circumstances surrounding his death.

Jailhouse visit. Watching his father treated like a celebrity.

After Dergraav's suicide, Graves's mother had taken the boy to the States.

Where Graves thrived. And twisted further.

A man who lusted and schemed and exulted in the capture of what belonged to others.

Jocelyn had been chosen because Dirgrove wanted her, and Graves had found out.

Graves came on to Gwynn Hauser as well. She'd blown him off. Not her type. Thinking she was in control. How little she understood.

Angela. Dirgrove had concocted a smooth scheme to seduce her.

Did Graves know about that?

If so . . .

Jeremy needed to let Angela know. His warnings about Dirgrove had irritated her.

Sorry, he's not the threat. But . . .

How to do it so she didn't think him mad? It sounded nothing *but* mad.

Jeremy came up with no answer. He paged Angela, anyway. The words would come, they always did.

She didn't answer.

He tried again.

Nothing.

Maybe she was caught up in a procedure. He'd go up to Endocrinology, the ostensible reason letting her know he'd be busy tonight. Then, somehow, he'd work in the terrible truth.

When he got there, an ill-tempered nurse told him, "You tell *me* where she is."

"What do you mean?"

"She flaked on us. Disappeared. Poof. A whole ward of patients, and she just walks off without informing anyone. Talk about unprofessional. I've informed the chief."

She was still griping when Jeremy turned his back and ran back to the elevators.

52

A BEAUTIFUL BUILDING.

White marble facing, copper trim, art deco angles, a circular driveway more commodious than the one fronting Dirgrove's condo. A copper fountain— angels trumpeting—spouted from the center of the drive. Tall spruces hugged the corners of the structure.

Tivoli Arms. Five stories taller than Dirgrove's high-rise.

But only one doorman. And when he finished helping a white-haired couple into their limousine, Jeremy approached him.

He'd changed into the spare shirt he'd brought that morning, had knotted his tie snugly, slicked his hair, washed his face. He put authority into his walk and posture. His black merino-cashmere top-coat was open, and he made sure the doorman caught a glimpse of the hospital badge clipped to his jacket lapel.

He must have looked right because the doorman smiled at him as if he belonged. "May I help you, sir?"

"I'm Dr. Carrier, an associate of Dr. Graves's from City Central Hospital. Is he in?"

"Sure is, got in an hour ago. I'll have someone ring you up. C'mon in out of the cold."

"Thanks."

The two of them entered the lobby, and the doorman handed him off to the man behind the reception desk. Young fellow, pleasant, in a navy blazer with gold buttons, button-down shirt, rep tie. His wheat-colored hair was razor cut. His gold name tag said K. BURNSIDE.

He said, "One moment, Doctor," and picked up the house phone. Held it to his ear, finally put it down. "That's odd. I know he's in."

"How so?"

"I took his car, and he hasn't called for it."

"Maybe he decided to get it himself."

"Hmm. Doubtful. Dr. Graves always has us bring his car around. Hold on, I'll check with the parking steward."

Another phone call. "No, Doctor, the car's still here."

"Nice wheels," said Jeremy, guessing.

"The Porsche or the Navigator?"

"Both." *A Navigator.* A big SUV had followed him. Perfect for transport . . .

The young man grinned. "Dr. Graves likes his cars—I'm sorry, is there some message I can leave for him?"

"No, it's personal." Jeremy leaned across the counter. "Actually, it's a surprise, Mr. Burnside."

"Kelvin. What kind of surprise?"

"Can you be discreet, Kelvin?"

"All part of the job, Doctor."

"Okay, but please keep this under wraps. At least until it hits the papers. Our department was just informed that Dr. Graves has won a prestigious award. The Dergraav. For biomechanical research. We're talking big-time—couple notches below the Nobel."

"Wow, that's amazing." Kelvin Burnside had been transformed into an awestruck teenager.

"I was sent to get him and bring him back to the hospital. The cover story I'm going to give him is some sort of emergency back at his lab. Then, when I get him there, there's a whole surprise party planned." Jeremy looked at his watch. "We timed it perfectly, everyone's waiting . . . could you try his apartment, again?"

"No problem." Kelvin dialed, waited, shook his head.

"Strange," said Jeremy. "He comes home, doesn't answer—maybe we should go up and make sure he's okay."

"Maybe—you know, there's somewhere else he might be. Down in the sub-subbasement. There are storage units there, for the tenants—some of our people hoard tons of stuff. The units are big, more like rooms. Some tenants lease them out, but Dr. Graves uses his a lot."

"For what?"

"I'm not sure, but he's always going in and out of there. I joked with him about it once—said 'what's going on down there, Doc, scientific experiments?' He thought that was funny. Rolled his eyes, and said something like, 'You never know.' I was just kidding, I knew he was a doctor, but I had no idea he was a big-time researcher. Now you're telling me about this award, and I'm feeling a little stupid for that crack."

"Don't worry about it. Augie—Dr. Graves has a great sense of humor. I think I will check out that storage room."

"I'll go look for you."

"No reason for you to leave your post," said Jeremy. "I really want to surprise him. My boss *ordered* me to surprise him."

The young man smiled uneasily.

"I'll be in and out, Kelvin. Dr. Graves will appreciate it—like I said, he's got a great sense of humor."

Jeremy fingered his badge, hoping to draw attention to that symbol of authority.

"Sure," said the young man. "No prob."

A rear service elevator—an unadorned, clanky steel box with an accordion door took him down to Subbasement C.

Two floors beneath the parking garage. He'd expected a dungeon but stepped out into bright space. Two wings of storage units lined rough stone floors. The walls were stone, as well, and bore the marks of hand-hewing. Each unit was numbered. Black iron numerals screwed into stout oak doors fashioned during a previous century. Overhead bulbs in bronze cages provided the light. Electrical conduits and plumbing pipes striped the arched ceiling.

The arches and the stone reminded Jeremy of something—a card Arthur had sent him. The bazaar in old Damascus. Could Arthur have been that prescient?

That scene implied bustle. Down here, all was silent.

No windows, no outside light.

Cool and damp. Jeremy half expected a bat to whoosh out.

No sign of life, not a rat, not an insect. Not a single cobweb, and when his fingers grazed the stone walls they came back free of dust. Even the floor was clean—swept spotless.

Four-star cave, pride of the demimonde.

Augusto Graves's unit was at the end of the left-hand wing. Last door to the right.

Jeremy stopped, put his head to the door. Heard nothing.

The heavy iron key for which he'd bribed Kelvin Burnside twenty dollars ("Oh, you don't have to do that, sir.") rested in his hand.

He inserted it in the bolt, turned slowly, pushed the door open an inch, waited for a creak.

Silence. He touched the bolt, felt grease. The Tivoli Arms was all about perfection. Or, Dr. Graves had taken special precautions.

He pushed some more. Had to put a little muscle into it—the oak was dense, thick, seasoned hard as rock. Six inches open. A foot. Enough space to slip through.

At first, he'd thought he'd made yet another mistake.

No light inside the unit. No one there.

Then he heard the sounds. Humming. The *snick-snick* of metal on metal. A low buzz, like that of a very large bumblebee.

There was light. A trapezoidal patch of light, to the left, hitting the wall at an acute angle.

He stepped closer and saw why. Deflected. An L-shaped drywall partition had been installed facing the door—creating a tiny vestibule.

He inched past the wall.

Was bathed in light. More light than he'd expected, hot and white and piercing. Three halogen bulbs grafted into an overhead power line. Surgical light.

A cell, ten by ten, walls, floor, and ceiling of that same hewn rock. Down in the core of the city.

Augusto Graves stood at the far end of a table, dressed in surgical greens. His head was capped, but he wore no face mask. Earphones from a Walkman transmitted something into his head.

Music, from the looks of it. Graves swayed in time. A syncopated beat.

A jolly beat. Graves was smiling faintly, mustache tilting upward like the wings of a butterfly.

Memories of Brazil?

A pleasant-looking man. Innocuous. Scholarly—reading glasses pushed low on his nose. He didn't see Jeremy. Too busy concentrating on the woman stretched out before him on a table.

Not a surgical table, just a wide, slab door resting on three sawhorses. The platform had been draped in white plastic. At Graves's right hand was a steel tray on a wheeled stand, gleaming with instruments. Next to the tray, a steel box on a similar stand, its contents out of view. An electrical cord trailed over the box's lid and fed into a ceiling socket. In the corner stood several bottles of distilled water. A family-sized container of bleach. A spray can of room deodorizer. "Fresh Evergreen" scent.

Folded neatly in the opposite corner was a pile of clothing. Something dark and cotton. A white bra and matching panties. A flesh-colored wad—panty hose—rested on top. No shoes.

The floor dipped to the left, slanted toward a floor drain. The shiny, stainless drain cover looked new, and the stone in which it set had been bleached a lighter gray.

The woman was slender, naked. Her dark head to Jeremy—he viewed her upside down. No marks on her, but she wasn't moving, and her color was too pale—he knew that kind of pale. Graves had positioned himself at her feet. Was staring at her feet. Her long, dark hair streamed over the edge of the table at the side nearest Jeremy. No movement from her chest. So pale. Around her neck, a faint, pinkish ring.

Wavy hair.

Oh God, Angela—

Graves touched the big toe of her left foot. Put his finger to his mouth and licked it. Reaching into the tray, he extracted a scalpel, and Jeremy got ready to lunge. But after examining the instrument, Graves put it down. Reached into the metal box and extracted what looked like an oversize metal pencil.

Tapered at the point. Electrical cord attached to the butt end.

Graves ran a finger up and down the rod. Pushed a button.

The bumblebee buzz returned.

Graves stood there, still swaying to the music, staring at the laser. He pushed another button, and the rod grew a bright red eye. By the time he turned to aim the laser at the woman, Jeremy was out from behind the partition and on him.

Graves tumbled, landed on his back but didn't make a sound. Instead he stared up at Jeremy. Soft brown eyes.

His earphones had flown off and the portable CD player attached to them landed on the floor. From the phones came a tinny samba.

Graves stared at Jeremy, expressionless.

The man was somewhere else.

Jeremy went for the laser. Graves waved the instrument, managed to push another button. A thin red beam shot out.

The devil's scarlet eye weeping.

Graves swung the beam toward Jeremy.

Jeremy kicked at the buzzing wand, failed to make contact. But his attack caused Graves's hand to waver, and the red beam nicked one of the sawhorses supporting the table.

Sliced clean through it. The table canted, and the naked woman slipped to the floor and landed facedown with a thud.

OhgodAngela—

Jeremy threw himself at Graves. Graves scooted away. The laser wavered, nicked stone, threw off dust. Steadying his laser hand with the other, Graves gave a quizzical look, took aim again as Jeremy ran for cover.

Jeremy tripped on Angela's corpse. Icy flesh. He fell on his face and rolled backward.

Graves stood over him.

"You've interrupted me," he said, without rancor. His eyes were lucid, focused, nothing but intent. He had beautiful skin, the mustache glowed like sable.

Soft, sibilant voice. Gentle. Women would find it comforting.

He licked his lips. "This will hurt a bit." Hefted the laser. A red dot appeared in the center of Graves's forehead.

Someone else with a laser?

No, this was something quite different. A low-tech situation. Thunder followed half a second later and blood trickled, then gushed out of the black-edged hole in Graves's brow. Not dead center, a few millimeters to the right. The frontal lobes.

As he bled, Graves stared blankly. Incredulous. *Where has my personality gone?*

The blood rush was followed by clots of gray-pink brain tissue, pumping out piecemeal, in oatmeal-like chunks. Like swill from a suddenly unclogged drainage pipe.

Graves shut his eyes, fell to his knees, went down.

The laser, still buzzing, had rolled out from between his fingers and landed on the floor. The ruby beam arced toward the clothes in the corner. Set them on fire. Penetrated the clothes and continued into the stone wall where it sizzled, sputtered, died.

No, not on its own. A big hand had yanked out the cord.

The room went silent.

Jeremy rushed to Angela, turned her over.

Saw the face of a stranger.

Detective Bob Doresh lifted him by the arm. "Doctor, Doctor, I never knew following you was going to be this interesting."

53

AT MIDNIGHT, AS HE DROVE TO THE POLICE STATION in an unmarked sedan that smelled of potato chips, Bob Doresh said, "I'm a pretty good shot, huh? Told you military service was useful."

"Where's Angela?" said Jeremy.

"Still," said Doresh, "you never know how you're going to react when it's real. Twenty-three years I've been on the job, and it's the first time I had to fire the damn thing. They say killing someone, even when it's righteous, can be traumatic. I'd have to say I feel pretty good, right now. Think I'll need help later, Doc?"

"Where's Angela?"

Doresh had one hand on the wheel. The other rested on the back of the seat. He drove slowly, with skill. During the onslaught of officers, crime-scene techs and coroner's examiners, he'd kept Jeremy under wraps in the Tivoli Arms rest room. A uniformed cop had stood watch, mute as Renfrew.

No one had talked to him.

"I asked you something, Detective."

Doresh said, "Okay, here's the situation with Dr. Rios. First things first: She's safe, been sitting in her own apartment with my partner Steve Hoker watching over her. Protective custody, if you will."

"*You* called her off the ward?" said Jeremy.

"That's the second thing, Doc. My motivation. Steve's and mine. We pulled her out of the hospital because we wanted to talk to her about you. We thought you were dangerous—okay, we were wrong, but with the way you've been acting—especially yesterday, in the chapel." He shrugged. "Sitting in a motel room by yourself. That's a little . . . different, wouldn't you say? I mean I understand now, you were watching that other guy, but see it from my perspective."

"You told her I was a murderous psychopath."

Doresh touched his temple, kept his foot light on the accelerator. The night was crisp and bright, and the unmarked car's heater was surprisingly efficient. "We were looking out for her best interest."

"Thanks."

Doresh gave him a sidelong glance. "You being sarcastic?"

"No, I mean it. Thanks. You had her safety in mind. Thanks for protecting her."

"Okay . . . you're welcome. And excuse me for wondering about the sarcasm, but let's face it, you can get pretty sarcastic."

"I've had my moments."

"You have," said Doresh. "But no harm, no foul. It was never personal, right? In the end we were both on the same side."

"True."

Doresh smiled, and his big chin jutted. "The difference being that I was doing my job and you were . . . improvising."

"Am I supposed to apologize for that?"

"Here we go again, butting heads. Must be some sort of . . . personality clash. Nah, no apologies necessary. You got a little carried away. In the end it worked out fine. Better than fine—hey, Doc, your hands are shaking pretty bad. When we get there, let me fix you some coffee—mine's a helluva lot better than yours. My partner Steve Hoker's driving Dr. Rios over to meet you. I told him the situation. She won't be scared of you."

"She was scared, huh?"

"The things I told her, you kidding? She was terrified. And I make no apologies for that. I had the game pretty well mapped out, I just didn't know the players."

"Live and learn," said Jeremy.

"You got it, Doc," said Doresh. "Stop learning, you might as well curl up and die."

54

Visiting Doctor Tagged As Serial Killer

Exclusive to the *Clarion*:

Police have identified a Seattle-based surgeon and medical researcher working at City Central Hospital on a one-year fellowship, as a serial murderer believed responsible for the deaths of at least five local women, and a possible suspect in as many as three dozen other unsolved murders around the world.

Augusto Omar Graves, 40, holder of both a medical degree and a Ph.D. in biomedical engineering and an acknowledged expert on laser technology and surgery, was shot dead by police Thursday evening in the subterranean storage locker of his luxurious Hale Boulevard condominium. Graves, believed to have been born in Syria and raised in Brazil and the United States, was found in the company of his fifth victim's corpse. According to the coroner, that woman, Kristina Schnurr, a recent immigrant from Poland who'd worked as a housekeeper at the hospital, had been strangled.

Schnurr, 29, and Graves had been seen talking the day of the murder, and it is believed Graves lured Schnurr on a date, strangled her in his car, and hid her body in the condominium's parking garage. He then drove the car back to the building's entrance so that a doorman would see him enter alone. Graves managed to transport Schnurr's corpse two floors down, to the storage locker, a dank, cellarlike space that he had converted into a dissection chamber.

Graves's other local victims include a nurse from City Central, Jocelyn Lee Banks, 27, murdered six months ago and formerly thought to have been carjacked from a hospital parking lot. Police now believe Graves convinced her to go with him willingly, under false pretenses. In addition, Graves is the prime suspect in the deaths of three recently murdered prostitutes, Tyrene Mazursky, 45, Odelia Tat, 38, and Maisie Donovan, 25. Given the time span between the Banks killing and those of the other victims, as well as Graves's frequent business trips, there is reason to believe that he will be tied into murders in other cities.

Graves has also been implicated in the mutilation slayings of at least two women murdered in Kent, England, during periods when he was conducting research at a London think tank and writing about science for *The Guardian* newspaper. Investigators from Spain, Italy, France, and Norway are reexamining unsolved murders involving surgical dissection that may have links to Graves's methodology.

Police Chief Arlo Simmons cited "numerous man-hours and first-rate detective work" as the factors that led to the discovery of Graves's lair.

"We've been interested in this individual for some time," said Chief Simmons. "I regret that we weren't able to save Kristina Schnurr. However, the death of this man can be truly said to have brought an end to a reign of terror."

55

THREE DAYS AFTER THE DEATH OF AUGUSTO GRAVES, during one of several attempts to steal a moment with Angela, Jeremy's beeper went off.

Seconds later, so did hers.

They were in his office, sitting on the floor, greasy napkins in their laps, takeout burgers in their hands.

A duet of squawks. They cracked up. First time they'd laughed since that night.

"You first," he said.

She called in. Diabetic coma on Four East, and another patient had reacted adversely to prednisone withdrawal. She was needed stat.

She got to her feet, gobbled a pickle slice, wrapped her quarter-eaten lunch in its wax-paper jacket, placed it on his desk.

He said, "Take it with you."

"Not hungry."

"I've noticed. I think you've lost weight."

"You haven't exactly been gorging."

"I'm fine."

"So am I. Dude."

She slung her white coat over her shoulders.

Placed her hands on Jeremy's wrists. "We *will* talk, right?"

"Not up to me," he said, smiling. "The schedule." His beeper went off again.

She laughed and kissed him and was gone.

The call was from Bill Ramirez.

"I'm hearing rumors, my friend."

"About what?"

"Your being involved, somehow, with capturing that lunatic Graves."

"Pretty crazy rumors," said Jeremy. "And he wasn't captured, he was killed."

"True," said Ramirez. "It didn't sound logical. A quiet guy like you being involved in heroics."

"Heroics?"

"That's what's floating around. That somehow you figured things out for the cops, did your shrink thing, helped them profile the bastard. I've even heard a really crazy one saying you were there the night they got him."

"Sure," said Jeremy. "I'm dusting off my cape, as we speak."

"That's what I thought. Maybe it's the administration, floating those rumors. It's been a PR nightmare for them—anyway, I figured you should know—never liked that guy. Arrogant."

"From what I hear, Bill, arrogance was the least of his problems."

"True," said the oncologist. "Speaking of heroics, the reason I'm calling is to give you a little good news, for a change. Our boy Doug has somehow managed to ease himself into a nice little remission."

"That's great!"

"I'd never have predicted it, but that's my line of work—humbling experiences every day. Hard to say if it'll be long-term or not, his presentation's been so weird. But there's no transplant on the horizon, and I'm sending him home, continuing his treatment on an outpatient basis. I thought you should know."

"I appreciate it, Bill. When's he being discharged?"

"Tomorrow A.M., if nothing changes. Talk about a cape. To my mind, *this* kid's Superman."

Marika sat next to Doug on the bed. Both of them in street clothes. Doug wore a Budweiser T-shirt and jeans. His prosthetic leg was attached. Both his hands were hooked up to IVs. His color was better. Not totally right, but better. Some of his hair had fallen out. He beamed.

"Hey, Doc. I kicked major-league medical ass."

"You sure did."

"Yeah, I told you that motherfucker leukemia was going to see who was the boss."

"You're the man, Doug."

The young man nudged his wife. "Hear that? That's coming from an expert."

"You are the man, honey."

"Right on."

"So," said Jeremy, "you're going home tomorrow."

"First thing I'm gonna do is get out to the brickyard, find me some nice used ones, put up that wall in my parents' backyard that I've been promising. Put a little niche for a fountain in, too, and run a water line to it. Surprise Mom."

"Sounds great. Congratulations."

"Thanks—c'mere, Doc. Gimme a shake, I wanna show you my grip."

Doug thrust out his right hand. The IV line looped and thrummed. Jeremy approached. Doug grabbed him, squeezed hard.

"Impressive," said Jeremy.

"Sometimes," said the young man, "I feel like I can *climb* walls."

56

THE DAY ARTHUR CAME TO SEE JEREMY, THE MAIL brought another surprise.

Cheap white envelope. OFFICIAL POLICE CORRE-SPONDENCE stamped on the back.

Inside were two squares of cardboard taped together. Jeremy cut the tape and extricated what was sandwiched within.

The snapshot of Jocelyn and him. Her tiny frame made Jeremy look like a large man. Both of them happy. Her blond hair windblown, all over the place.

He remembered: The strands had tickled him like crazy, and she'd gotten a kick out of that.

Oh, you're ticklish?

She'd gone for his ribs, grabbing with strong little fingers. Giggling like a kid, so pleased with herself.

He stared at the photo for a long time, placed it in an unmarked envelope, set that in a lower drawer of his desk.

Atop the *Curiosity* file.

One of these days, he'd do something with it.

*　　*　　*

Arthur had a tan.

The golden glow merged with his natural ruddiness, turned the old man's skin into something luminous.

Nearly eighty, but the picture of vitality. Traveling—and learning—had served him well.

He found Jeremy just as he had the first time. Sitting alone, in the doctors' dining room. Three P.M., an off-hour for lunch. Jeremy'd filled his days with patients, just as he had since the night underground, had eaten nothing earlier. The room was empty.

Arthur wore a beautiful royal blue pin-striped suit and a pink shirt with a contrasting white collar. His bow tie was gold shantung. A peacock blue handkerchief flowed from his breast pocket. In one hand was a cup of tea, a burnished leather briefcase dangled from the other. A large case, hand-stitched, stamped with Arthur's initials, which Jeremy had never seen before.

"May I sit down?"

"Sure."

Arthur settled, took time to dunk his tea bag. Stared straight into Jeremy's eyes.

"How was your trip, Arthur?"

"Excellent."

"Travel and learn."

"That's what it's all about."

"You taught me plenty," said Jeremy.

The old man didn't answer.

"Why the need to be oblique, Arthur?"

"Fair question, my friend." Arthur sipped tea,

stroked his beard, pushed the cup to the side. "There are multiple answers. First off, at the level of hypothesis, one can never be sure. I truly *was* learning. Second, I felt I needed to pace things so as not to repel you. Admit it, son. If I'd laid everything out, you'd have thought me demented."

He smiled at Jeremy.

Jeremy shrugged.

"Third—and this may offend you, Jeremy, however I think a lot of you and would never dissemble—certain things need to be striven for to be appreciated."

"No gain without pain?"

"A cliché but no less valid for that."

"You guided me with riddles and games for my own good."

"Exactly," said the old man. "Perfectly put."

Jeremy had known this moment would arrive. He'd wondered how he'd react. Weeks had gone by since the subterranean nightmare. He rarely thought about it, and the horror had faded to a macabre cartoon.

Interestingly enough, the late-night supper with Arthur and his friends had surged in his memory—grown clearer, more real.

"After supper," he said, "you seemed to grow distant."

Arthur nodded. "Forgive me. I was . . . torn. I knew what you were about to undergo. I wondered."

Some things need to be striven for.

Now, having asked Arthur the question and receiving the answer, he could only smile.

"Okay," he said.

"That's it?" said the old man. "You're satisfied."

"About that I am. I do have other questions. Since you've pledged not to dissemble."

"Fair enough."

"Was your family's killer ever found? One way or the other?"

Tears sprang to Arthur's eyes, and that was answer enough for Jeremy. But the old man said, "Never."

"Did any suspects arise?"

"One suspect," said Arthur. "A local handyman. A clearly disturbed man. Later I was to find out he'd spent time in an asylum. I'd been concerned about him for some time, was certain I'd seen him leering at my wife." Arthur's voice caught. "She was beautiful, my Sally. Men were always looking at her. I have pictures, in my apartment. One day you'll see them. But this man . . ."

"What happened to him?" said Jeremy.

"Nothing of a police nature, son. Perhaps now, with the technology we have, he might have been arrested. But back then . . ." The old man shook his head.

"You just let it go?"

"At the time, I was too weak to react. Everything I'd worked for, taken, just like that." Arthur sniffed. Blinked. His beard trembled. "My children were sweet, Jeremy. My wife was beautiful, and my children were sweet."

He pulled out the blue pocket silk and patted his eyes.

"I'm sorry," said Jeremy.

"Thank you." Arthur stuffed the silk back in his breast pocket. Perfect casual fold. He said, "Two months after my family was taken from me—sixty-three days to be precise, the handyman was brought to the emergency room, here. Strangled bowel—one of those things that just happens. He was treated but to no avail. His guts turned to gangrene, and he was dead within three days. I never saw him alive. However, I did have the opportunity to assist at the autopsy."

"Rotting from within. Appropriate."

Arthur's hand reached across the table and took hold of Jeremy's sleeves. "It *felt* right. The fact that he'd been taken that way seemed the most fitting thing in the world. It wasn't until years later, when I met others in my situation, that I realized the grand truth."

"Expediency trumps virtue," said Jeremy.

"Virtue is divine, but not limited to God. It's something He shares with us. Something we need to use judiciously."

"The sword of war comes to the world for the delay of justice," said Jeremy. "Disorder."

Arthur withdrew his hand. His glorious tan had been leached of its glow. He looked old.

"May I get you some tea, Arthur?"

"Please."

Jeremy brought him a cup, watched him drink. "Do you have energy for more?"

Arthur nodded.

"I want to know about Edgar, I know about

Kurau, but not Edgar's personal involvement. Was it simply a political matter?"

Arthur closed his eyes, opened them. "Edgar's story is his to tell. What I can tell you is that Edgar invested his personal resources to build a clinic for sick children on the island. Babies and toddlers who might otherwise have perished. Antisepsis and proper medication, well-trained native nurses. Edgar put all that together. The riots destroyed everything."

He reached down for his briefcase.

Jeremy said, "When we share with God, it sometimes gets messy. Michael Srivac, for example. He was a building contractor in Robert Balleron's town. Fierce competitor to Balleron. No one was arrested for Balleron's murder but several months later, Srivac died in a single-car accident. Freakish accident, from what I can gather. The brakes on his car just gave out, and the car had been serviced two days before."

"That is no surprise," said Arthur. "During World War II, more military planes crashed shortly after major maintenance checks than at any other time."

"You're saying that one God did all by Himself?"

"Tina's story is—"

"Hers to tell," said Jeremy. "The same goes for Shadley Renfrew, right? His wife was murdered thirty-two years ago. The evidence pointed to her surprising a burglar. A known criminal was suspected—a cat burglar. But he was never brought to trial due to insufficient evidence. Six months later, his body washed up on the north shore."

"Shadley was a remarkable man," said Arthur. "Voluminous memory, fine eye for detail. Wonderful Irish tenor. He raised his daughter—"

"All by himself. She told me. I walked into the shop just as she was closing it down. I assume the books are being well cared for."

Arthur nodded, reached again for his case, drew out a black velvet box, and placed it in front of Jeremy.

"A gift?"

"A minor token of our appreciation."

" 'Our' being the City Central Club. Renfrew was a member, wasn't he? His passing left an empty chair."

Arthur smiled. Before Jeremy could say more, the old man was up, briefcase in hand, striding away, a bounce in his step.

Jeremy opened the box. The interior was white satin over a compartment formed to cradle its contents.

A repousse silver goblet.

Jeremy removed the cup. Weighty. Inside was a note. Fine blue rag paper, folded once. Familiar writing in black fountain pen ink:

To a young scholar and gentleman,

With gratitude, admiration, and earnest hopes that you'll consider this humble proposition: One soul passes, another enters. Life is fleeting, brutish, ecstatic, mundane.

Let us punctuate our brief sojourn with fine

*food, warming libations, and the sparkling
camaraderie of souls in synchrony.*

> *Fondly,*
> *The Central Conspiracy Club.*

Okay, he'd been close.

57

"**Y**OU'LL LIKE THEM," SAID ANGELA.

"You're sure it's what you want?"

"It's exactly what I want."

Sunday, one in the afternoon. Rampaging blizzards were rumored to be racing down from Canada, but the air, ever perverse, had warmed.

They were lunching at a place near the harbor. Fried seafood and coleslaw and beer. Nice view of the lake. Just far enough to obscure the oily film on the water. From their table, the water was God's own mirror.

The publicity surrounding Augusto Graves's crimes, his relationship to Central City—and to Ted Dirgrove—had thrown the hospital's front office into a tailspin. Dirgrove had taken an extended leave of absence. The charming young women at Development sat idly. The inept security guards contended with reporters.

Jeremy exploited the turmoil by demanding and receiving two months' paid vacation, dates of his choosing. He planned to leave soon. Once all the police business was cleared away. Once his patients were sufficiently taken care of.

He'd also insisted on ten paid days off for Angela, with no downside to her residency rating. He would have tried for more, but she said, "I really do need to be here."

The schedule.

Which was fine. He'd have some time to himself, maybe travel. Learn. The first ten days—the best days—would be spent with Angela, away from emergencies and memories and the pain of others.

In his heart, he felt it would take them to another level.

Angela was thrilled at the prospect. Today, she'd surprised him with a plan: they'd fly out to California, rent a car—a convertible—drive up the coast, just drive. Anywhere the sun was out.

Then the tentative add-on: *Maybe we can spend the last couple of days with my family? I want them to meet you.*

"They'll adore you."

"You're pretty sure of that."

"Hundred and fifty percent sure. Because *I* adore you, and I'm their princess-who-can-do-no-wrong."

"You have that kind of power."

"Oh, yeah."

"Scary," said Jeremy.

"Very." She smiled. Light bounced off the lake and filtered through the waves of her hair.

Beautiful girl. *Here.*

"Can you handle all that power, tough guy?"

"Yeah."

They were sitting across from one another. *Too far.* Jeremy got up, moved his chair next to hers. She bussed his cheek. He stroked the back of her neck, and she said, "This is *so* good."

They sat that way, looking out at the water. Holding hands, thinking separate thoughts.

And some that coincided.

Read on for an exciting sneak preview of
Jonathan Kellerman's new novel

THERAPY

Available in hardcover from
The Random House Publishing Group (May 2004)

A few years ago a psychopath burned down my house.

The night it happened, I was out to dinner with the woman who'd designed the house and lived in it with me. We were driving up Beverly Glen when the sirens cut through the darkness, ululating, like coyote death wails.

The noise died quickly, indicating a nearby disaster, but there was no reason to assume the worst. Unless you're the worst kind of fatalist, you think: "Something lousy happened to the poor devil."

That night, I learned different.

Since then, the Klaxon of an ambulance or a fire truck in my neighborhood sets off something inside me—a crimp of shoulder, a catch of breath, an arrhythmic flutter of the plum-coloered thing in my chest.

Pavlov was right.

I'm trained as a clinical psychologist, could do something about it but have chosen not to. Sometimes anxiety makes me feel alive.

When the sirens shrieked, Milo and I were having dinner at an Italian place at the top of the Glen. It was ten-thirty on a cool June night. The restaurant closes at eleven, but we were the last patrons, and the waiter was looking tired. The woman I was now seeing was teaching a night course in abnormal psychology at the U, and Milo's partner, Rick Silverman, was busy at the Cedars-Sinai ER trying to salvage the five most seriously injured victims of a ten-car pileup on the Santa Monica Freeway.

Milo had just closed the file on a robbery-turned-to-multiple-homicide at a liquor store on Pico Boulevard. The solve had taken more persistence than brainwork. He was in a position to pick his cases, and no new ones had crossed his desk.

I'd finally finished testifying at the seemingly endless child-custody hearings waged by a famous director and his famous actress wife. I'd begun the consult with some optimism. The director had once been an actor, and both he and his ex knew how to perform. Now, three years later, two kids who'd started out in pretty good shape were basket cases living in France.

Milo and I chewed our way through focaccia and baby artichoke salad, orrechiati stuffed with spinach, veal pounded to paper. Neither of us felt like talking. A bottle of decent white wine smoothed the silence. Both of us were strangely content; life wasn't fair, but we'd done our jobs well.

When sirens came, I kept my eyes on my plate. Milo stopped eating. The napkin he'd tucked in his shirt collar was spotted with spinach and olive oil.

"Don't worry," he said. "Not a fire."

"Who's worrying?"

He pushed hair off his forehead, picked up his fork and knife, speared, chewed, swallowed.

I said, "How can you tell?"

"That it's not a big-red? Trust me, Alex. It's a black-and-white. I know the frequency."

A second cruiser wailed by. Then a third.

He pulled his tiny blue cell phone out of his pocket and punched a button. A preset number rang.

I raised my eyebrows.

"Just curious," he said. His connection went through, and he told the phone: "This is Lieutenant Sturgis. What call just went out in the vicinity of upper Beverly Glen? Yeah, near Mulholland." He waited, green eyes dimmed to near brown in the miserly light of the restaurant. Under the spotted napkin was a baby blue polo shirt that really didn't work well with his pallid complexion. His acne pits were flagrant, his jowls gravid as freshly filled wineskins. Long white sideburns frizzled his big face, a pair of skunkish stripes that seemed to sprout artificially from his black hair. He's a gay policeman and my best friend.

"That so," he said. "Any detective assigned, yet? Okay, listen, I happen to be right near there, can make it over in ten—no, make that fifteen—make it twenty minutes. Yeah, yeah, sure."

He snapped the little phone shut. "Double homicide, two bodies in a car. Being this close, I figured I should have a look. The crime scene's still being secured, and the techs haven't gotten there, so we can still have dessert. How are you with cannoli?"

We split the check, and he offered to drive me home, but neither of us took that seriously.

"In that case," he said, "we'll take the Seville."

I drove quickly. The crime scene was on the west side of the intersection between the Glen and Mulholland, up a skinny, decomposed granite road marked PRIVATE that climbed through sycamore-crowned hillside.

A police cruiser was stationed at the mouth of the road. Staked to a tree several feet up was a FOR SALE sign bearing the logo of a Westside Realtor. Milo flashed the badge to the uniform in the car and we drove through.

At the top of the road was a house behind high, night-blackened hedges. Two more black-and-whites kept us ten yards back. We parked and continued on foot. The sky was purplish, the air still bitter with the smolder of two early-summer brushfires, one up near Camarillo, the other past Tujunga. Both had just been vanquished. One had been set by a fireman.

Behind the hedges was stout wooden fencing. Double gates had been left open. The bodies slumped in a red Mustang convertible parked on a semicircular flagstone driveway. The house behind the drive was a vacant mansion, a big neo-Spanish thing that was probably cheerful peach in the daylight. At this hour, it was putty gray.

The driveway bordered a half acre of front yard, shaded by more sycamores—giant ones. The house looked newish and was ruined by too many weird-shaped windows, but someone had been smart enough to spare the trees.

The top was down on the little red car. I stood back and watched as Milo approached, careful to stay behind the tape. He did nothing but stare. Moments later, a pair of crime-scene techs walked onto the property lugging cases on a dolly. They talked to him briefly, then slipped under the tape.

He walked back to the Seville. "Looks like gunshot wounds to both heads, a guy and a girl, young. He's in the driver's seat, she's next to him. His fly's open, and his shirt"s half-unbuttoned. Her shirt's clean off, tossed in the backseat along with her bra. Under the shirt she wore black leggings. They're rolled down to her ankles, and her legs are spread."

"Lover's lane thing?" I said.

"Empty hoouse," he said. "Good neighborhood. Probably a nice view from the backyard. Seize the night and all that? Sure."

"If they knew about the house, they could be locals."

"He looked clean-cut, well dressed. Yeah, I'd say local is also a decent bet."

"I wonder why the gate was left open."

"Or maybe it wasn't, and one of them has some connection to the house and a gate-clicker. For all we know, one of their families built the place. Crime Scene will do their thing, hopefully they'll find their IDs in their pockets. The car's plates are being run right now."

I said, "Any gun in sight?"

"A murder-suicide thing? Not likely."

He rubbed his face. His hand lingered at his mouth, tugged down his lower lip and let it snap back up.

"What?" I said.

"Two head-shots plus, Alex. Someone jammed what looks to be a short spear or a crossbow bolt into the girl's torso. Here." He touched a spot under his breastbone. "From what I could see the damn thing went clear through her and is lodged in the seat. The impact jolted her body, she's lying funny."

"A spear."

"She was skewered, Alex. A bullet to the brain wasn't enough."

"Overkill," I said. "A message. Were they actually making love or were they positioned sexually?"

He flashed a frightening smile. "Now we're veering into your territory."

The techs and the coroner gloved up and did their thing under heartless floodlights. Milo talked to the uniforms who'd arrived first on the scene, and I stood around.

He loped over to one of the big sycamores, said something to no apparent listener, and a nervous-looking Hispanic man in baggy clothes stepped from behind the trunk. The man talked with his hands and looked agitated. Milo did a lot of listening. He took out his notepad and scrawled without breaking eye contact. When he was finished, the man was allowed to leave the scene.

The spear in the girl's chest appeared to be a homemade weapon fashioned from a slat of wrought-iron fencing. The coroner who manipulated it free said so out loud as she carried it beyond the yellow tape perimeter and laid it on an evidence sheet.

The uniforms checked the property for similar fencing, found iron around a pool, but a different diameter.

DMV came through with the car's registration: the Mustang was one year old and registered to Jerome Allan Quick, of South Camden Drive in Beverly Hills. A wallet in the pocket of the male victim's khakis yielded a driver's license that confirmed him as Gavin Ryan Quick, two months past his twentieth birthday. A student ID card put him as a sophomore at the U., but the card was a year old. In another pocket, the techs retrieved a joint wrapped in a baggie and a foil-wrapped condom. Another condom, out of the foil but unrolled, was discovered on the floor of the Mustang.

Neither the girl's leggings nor her gold shirt contained pockets. No purse or handbag was found in the car or anywhere else. Blond, thin, pale, pretty, she remained unidentified. Even after the spear was removed, she lay contorted, chest thrust at the night sky, neck twisted, eyes wide-open. A spidery position no living creature would have entertained.

The coroner wouldn't commit but guessed from the arterial blood spatter that she'd been alive while being impaled.

Milo and I drove to Beverly Hills. Once again, he offered to drop me off, but again, I laughed. Allison would be home by now but we weren't living together, so there was no reason to let her know where I was. Back when Robin and I did live together, I checked in most of the time. Sometimes I was derelict. The least of my sins.

I said, "Who was the guy you interviewed?"

"Night watchman employed by the real estate company. His job is to drive around at the end of the day, check out the high-priced listings, make sure everything's secure. The brokerage gives the key out to their agents, and agents from other outfits can come by and borrow copies. Supposedly a foolproof system, but doors don't get locked, windows and gates are left open. That's probably what happened here. The house was shown today by three brokers. It was the watchman's last stop; he covers everything from San Gabriel to the beach. He's the one who found the bodies and phoned it in."

"But you'll paraffin him, anyway."

"Done. No gunshot residue. I'll also be checking the three brokers and their clients."

I crossed Santa Monica Boulevard, drove east, headed south on Rodeo Drive. Shops were closed, but storefronts were bright. A homeless man steered a shopping cart past Gucci.

"So you're taking the case," I said.

He rode half a block before answering. "Been a while since I had me a nice little whodunit, good to stay in shape."

He claimed to hate whodunits, but I said nothing. The last one had closed a while back, a cold-hearted killer executing people with artistic talent. The day after Milo filed his final report, he said, "Ready for some low-IQ bar shootings, bad guys holding the smoking gun."

Now he said, "Yeah, yeah, I'm a glutton for punishment. Let's get this over with."